THE ZION
COVENANT
BOOK 2

Prague Counterpoint

THE ZION COVENANT
BOOK 2

BODIE & BROCK
THOENE

Tyndale House Publishers
Carol Stream, Illinois

Visit Tyndale online at tyndale.com.

Prague Counterpoint

Published in 1989 as *Prague Counterpoint* by Bethany House Publishers under ISBN 1-55661-078-5.

First printing by Tyndale House Publishers in 2005.

Designed by Julie Chen

Edited by Ramona Cramer Tucker

Library of Congress Cataloging-in-Publication Data

Thoene, Bodie, date.
Prague counterpoint / Bodie and Brock Thoene.
p. cm. — (The zion covenant ; bk. 2)
ISBN 978-1-4143-0108-2 (sc)
1. Lindheim, Elisa (Fictitious character)—Fiction. 2. World War, 1939-1945—Underground movements—Fiction. 3. World War, 1939-1945—Czech Republic—Fiction. 4. Prague (Czech Republic)—Fiction. 5. Jews—Czech Republic—Fiction. I. Thoene, Brock, date. II. Title.
PS3570.H46P73 2005
813'.54—dc22 2004015730

Printed in the United States of America

25 24 23 22 21
14 13 12 11 10 9

This story is dedicated
to our brothers, our sisters,
and our children and grandchildren.
Together we remember the well-worn
Bible open to Psalm 91 and the prayers
of our grandmother for us all.

Acknowledgments

When we think of children and cellos and the Bach Suites, we think of Margaret Tait *first*! What a wonderful dimension her friendship and talent have added to our lives and our craft as writers. We love you, Margaret!

The roster of all those who help in so many ways continues to grow. Our special thanks also to Joseph and Naomi Samuels, who assisted in our research of the city of Prague.

THE EUROPE THEATRE

Prologue

OLD CITY JERUSALEM
MAY 20, 1948

It was over. Only thirty of the Jewish defenders of the Old City survived. Not one bullet remained among them when at last they laid down their weapons before Major Abdullah Tell, commander of the Arab forces.

"If we had known what was left of you," Tell said with respect, "we would have come to fight you with sticks instead of guns!"

All the other Jewish defenders lay dead amid the rubble of the Jewish Quarter. They had held back the thousands of Arab soldiers long enough for the rest of the Jewish Yishuv to arm themselves and prepare to survive the wave after wave of attacks from Jordan, Syria, Egypt, and those who had come from Iraq and Iran to fight the Jewish Zionists.

The great Hurva Synagogue, Nissan Bek, and the rest of the places of Jewish worship were being destroyed. Explosions shook the ancient earth, and two thousand years of Jewish residence near the Wailing Wall came to an end.

Shaken and stricken by starvation and grief, the twelve hundred noncombatant residents of the Jewish Quarter emerged from the cellars where they had taken refuge from Arab bullets weeks before. The old ones, the rabbis who had spent their lives in study and worship, wept as they lifted their eyes to watch. Smoke billowed from the Hurva and flames leaped from the windows, enveloping the dome. *"In blood and fire Judea had fallen; by blood and fire it would be reborn."* Who among them had not heard the ancient prophecy? And yet, for them this day was the end of all hope.

Prodded by guns, women and children joined the old rabbis in the square. Faces were streaked with soot and tears. Most had lost their husbands in the fighting. Now sons over the age of thirteen were being herded away from them. A few were lucky enough to take with them some cherished object from their homes. The rabbis carried the ancient Torah scrolls, while weeping women clutched photographs to their breasts and cried out the names of men who were now buried beneath the rubble of the Jewish Quarter.

"Where are you taking us?" cried one as they were marched past the victorious Arab moquades.

"Taking you, old man?" The soldier jeered. "Your people have lived two thousand years as prisoners to these walls! We are liberating you Jews from Jerusalem; that is all!"

The old ones were to be given safe passage into the Jewish district of New York. The remaining defenders, along with a few others who looked capable of fighting, were to be taken east to a prisoner-of-war camp in Jordan.

Yacov Lubetkin supported his grandfather with one arm and held very tightly to the violoncello that had belonged to Leah Feldstein. Tears ran freely from the old man's eyes and traced the lines of his face like streams on an ancient hillside.

"I will not walk these stones again, Yacov," the old man said.

"It cannot be forever, Grandfather." Yacov tried to comfort him, but the old man's shoulders shook with his sobs. In the course of his lifetime he had lost his family to the Nazis, yet the strength of his soul had been comforted by Holy Jerusalem. Now that, too, was being wrenched from him.

"Not forever, perhaps, Yacov, but not ever again for me." His eyes caressed the stones of the ancient corridors, then lifted to the black smoke rising above them like the smoke of millions that had risen over Poland and Germany.

"We will come back, Grandfather!" The boy wept aloud. "We *must* come back!"

A broad-faced Arab clad in the red-checked keffiyeh of the Arab Legion turned his face toward Yacov's defiant cry. He smiled a gap-toothed smile and narrowed his eyes as he spotted the unwieldy case that contained the cello.

"You! Boy!" he barked and strode toward Yacov. "What do you carry out there?" It was unlike any luggage he had ever seen. He cocked his rifle, and it was evident that he suspected the lad of carrying weapons out of the Old City to be used by the Jews still fighting in the New City.

Yacov stopped. His jaw was set with anger and bitterness against the desecration of the Jewish houses of prayer and study.

Grandfather put a hand on the boy's arm. "Do not speak harshly," he warned. "He would kill us for one arrogant look."

Yacov lowered his eyes as the barrel of the Arab rifle pointed to his forehead. "It is a musical instrument," he said in a quiet voice. He still was uncertain why he had taken Leah's cello. Her records had been smashed. The phonograph had been shot to pieces, and the cello seemed to be the only thing left in the room that was still undamaged. He had almost forgotten he had carried it down the stairs as the cry had risen that the city had fallen.

"Open it, dog!" the soldier demanded, poking Yacov with the ominous weapon. "Open the box, or I will shoot it and you and the old man as well."

Yacov did not question the angry man. He laid the case down on a heap of rubble and, with fumbling fingers, unlatched the locks. He threw back the lid of the case and stepped aside quickly.

The soldier circled the cello as if it were a bomb. He squinted at the instrument, then looked curiously at Yacov. "Take it out of its box!" he demanded. "Play it!" He wanted some proof that it was what Yacov had said it was.

"I cannot play it." Yacov lifted Leah's cello with all the care he had seen her use a thousand times as she had played for the children and old people in Tipat Chalev. "It is not mine." He held it out for the man to see.

"You can't play it? It isn't yours?" the soldier mocked. "Then why do you carry this out from the destruction of the city?"

"I don't know." Yacov was crying now. "I don't know!" He hated the tears that came in spite of his attempt to hold them back. "It brought us happiness!" he cried, remembering the splendid nights when Leah had played for them. Vitorio. She had called her violoncello Vitorio. "It came through so much." He thought of the stories Leah had recited about their escape from Vienna ten years before. "It lived on when she died. Could I let you kill it?" He wasn't making any sense at all now; the soldier looked at him with amused disgust, shrugged, and then passed on down the line to order an old rabbi to unwrap a Torah scroll for examination.

Lovingly Yacov returned the violoncello to the case and closed it, but not before the ash of the Old City Jerusalem had settled on the richly varnished wood of the instrument.

1

Vienna: Final Sunrise

MARCH 1938

He had lived for thirty-four years and had never noticed how many shades of color streaked the early morning sky. But this would be his last sunrise, and the horizon seemed incredibly detailed and bright.

Walter Kronenberger stood at the window of the shabby hotel room and watched the colors change in the eastern sky. Deep purple blended into a thousand hues of blue and crimson and a lighter shade of pink where the sun would soon appear.

Below him German tanks, emblazoned with the emblem of Hitler's Reich, rumbled past on the streets of Vienna. Walter did not look at them. He had seen them before. He had left Germany because of such sights and sounds. Like every fool still in Austria, he had stayed because he thought the tanks could never come here.

Behind him he could hear the deep, even breathing of his sons. Lifting the edge of the shade slightly, he let the faint shaft of light fall on the tousled blond heads of the boys.

Suddenly the sunrise lost interest for him. He turned and gazed instead at the two five-year-olds. They were all that remained of his shattered life, all that was left of the love he had shared with Maria. And they were the only things left that made him regret leaving the world.

The pistol he had purchased was loaded and lay beside two plain white envelopes on the table. When the Nazis came for him, as they surely would today, he would not die without a fight. But he was certain he would die today.

He reached out as if to touch little Charles on the forehead, but he held his hand above the child's head, and in that moment of his greatest agony, he prayed for him instead. Who would love this broken little one now? Who would rock him when he cried in the night from the pain of the earaches that struck him so often? Charles had grown wise through his pain—wise and tender. But who would see this child's heart past the deformity that marked him as an object of scorn and ridicule?

Walter looked at the gun and then back to Charles. *Would it not be kinder?* Walter drew back his hand in horror at the thought. He closed his eyes and prayed still more fervently. Tomorrow the sun would rise, Walter knew, and his sons would be fatherless. But they *must* live!

As if sensing his agony, Charles opened his eyes and blinked drowsily up at his father. *Blue eyes, more beautiful than the sunrise,* Walter thought. *Full of kindness and love. Let someone see his heart, dear God.* Walter stroked the boy's forehead. *These must be Your children now.*

"Are you hungry, Charles?"

The boy nodded slowly.

"Then come along quietly. We will watch the sunrise together and have some strudel while Louis sleeps, *ja*?"

On such a day it would have been more fitting if the sun had not risen over Austria at all. The woods beyond Vienna should have remained silent and dark. The towering spires of St. Stephan's Cathedral should have snagged the passing night and held the blackness over the city like a shroud. Flocks of pigeons sleeping among the hideous carved gargoyles of the building should have slept on until they too turned to stone.

But the sun did rise, and with its coming the hearts of men turned to stone in the light. The traitorous bells of St. Stephan's rang out a greeting to the hordes of Hitler's army. The gargoyles above the cathedral entrance sprang to life. No longer content simply to watch the folly of men below them, they leaped from the parapets and shouted a victory cry for their master: "Heil Hitler! Heil Deutschland! *Deutschland über alles!*"

Austria was no more. It had fallen without a single drop of blood being shed in resistance. The Führer had fulfilled his promise. Germany and Austria were one nation, one people, with one Führer.

Red-and-black swastika flags were unfurled from every window, covering the face of the city in such abundance they seemed to have sprouted from the stones like fungi.

In one day the face of the nation had been stripped away and discarded as though it had never been. The voice of Austria joined the clamor of St. Stephan's bells. The birds swirled upward as though held aloft by the resounding cries: "Heil Hitler! Heil Hitler! Heil . . ." The sun should have hid its face and wept behind the clouds at the sight of such treachery. But it did not.

Leah Feldstein lay beside her husband and stared out the high window at the patch of blue sky. Shimon still breathed deeply and held her close to him as he slept. She did not move, even though she had been awake since before dawn. As long as they lay peacefully together, she could pretend that things were as they had always been. The events of yesterday and last night were only a dream. They would get up this morning and have breakfast and go together to the Musikverein, just like always.

Two small suitcases were packed and placed beside the door. Leah did not look at them. They were a reminder of everything she wanted to forget. She stared hard at the patch of blue and found some comfort that the color of the sky was bright and unchanged. She would not think about what was below the sky. She would not let her mind wander to the barricades manned by Austrian Nazis who blocked off the Judenplatz. She would not let herself remember the way pink-cheeked boys had proudly worn their Nazi armbands and shouted obscenities at her and Shimon when they tried to get to their friend Elisa's house last night.

Leah frowned when she looked at the bruise beneath Shimon's eye. Someone, one of the boys at the barricade, had thrown a bottle at Shimon and hit him in the face. "Stinking Jewish scum!" the boy had shouted. "You'll see what kind of law Germany will bring for the likes of you!"

There had been a hundred of them—maybe more. Throughout the night they had burned their fires and sung their songs. Leah and Shimon had returned to their home in the Judenplatz to wait and watch in terrified exhaustion until at last a merciful sleep enveloped them.

Somewhere in the distance Leah heard the rumble of a truck engine. The Nazi shouts and threats were silent now. No doubt the young Nazis had fallen asleep at the barricades. Evil needed its rest as well, it seemed, to regain strength for the attacks that would surely come today. Down in the square, the mutilated statue of the Jewish playwright Franz Lessing served as a reminder that the Nazi youth would destroy a living, breathing Jew with as much enthusiasm as they had destroyed the bronze of a Jewish statue.

Leah closed her eyes and held tightly to Shimon's big hand. She remembered Elisa's description of the mutilated hands of Rudy Dorbransky. Dear Rudy! How the Nazis had made him suffer! How long until they turned their fury once again to the Judenplatz? There would be no Austrian Schupos now to stop the rampage. The government of Austria was smashed. The Austrian chancellor was under arrest. The laws of Nazi Germany were now in effect in Vienna.

The thought made Leah shudder. She was afraid—for herself, for Shimon, for Elisa. For anyone who would not raise a hand to salute the crooked cross of the Reich's bloody flag. What would become of them now? The Nazis would be checking the identification papers of every man, woman, and child in the Judenplatz. Arrests had already begun. The Nazis would not want to waste any time in bringing Austria into line with the laws and policies of the Third Reich. What had taken Germany many years to accomplish in the campaign against the Jews would now be accomplished in Austria within days.

Shimon breathed deeply and let his breath out slowly. He cleared his throat and then squeezed Leah's hand gently. "Awake?" he asked in a hoarse whisper.

"Too awake," she replied, pressing herself closer against his warmth. He still had his shoes on. They had not dared undress.

Shimon pulled her closer and buried his face in the nape of her neck. "Did you sleep at all?"

She answered with a question. "Did you hear them? Singing those songs down there?" The words of the song had cut into her like sharp knives as the Nazis had paraded beneath their window by torchlight, singing, "Break the skulls of the Jewish rats." Their hatred seemed to remain in the air like the stench of an open sewer.

"Did I hear them?" Shimon gave her a quick hug meant to reassure her. "Of course. They were off-key. Such lyrics will not sell well here in Vienna. Not against competition like Mozart and Strauss." He waited for her to reply, but she did not. He squeezed her again, then sat up. "Then again, Nazi music might do well if all the musicians leave Vienna, eh?"

"Shimon?" Her voice trembled. "What will we do?"

"We have our visas for Palestine."

"You know how much that will mean if *they* decide—"

"Decide what? To throw us into a concentration camp? A cellist and a percussionist? We are of no significance. They have no reason to keep us here, Leah. We will simply tell them that we shipped the china plates to Jerusalem last month. We have nothing left for them to smash." His words contained a false cheerfulness, and Leah knew that he also was frightened.

"What now?" She turned and looked beseechingly up at him.

"Now?" He stared toward the patch of blue sky. "Make coffee. Wash. Comb your hair. It is Sunday, and there will no doubt be a concert for us to play at the Musikverein."

"Stop!" she almost shouted. "It is not just any day! Shimon, quit pretending or I will lose my mind!"

He would not allow her the luxury of self-pity at such a time. "If you lose your mind, then I will have to unpack the dishes myself in Jerusalem. No doubt I will break a few." A near smile turned the corner of his mouth.

Leah blinked back at him angrily. "How can you talk as though nothing has happened?"

"Because at this moment nothing has happened to us." He stretched and stood up, avoiding her eyes as he made his way toward the door. "Not yet, anyway. And before it does, I want a cup of coffee. I want to brush my teeth and go to the bathroom. And I'm going to take my shoes off for a while, too."

He disappeared into the other room as Leah glared after him. She was angry at him now, and somehow it helped her. She sat up slowly and looked down at her rumpled clothes. She would change. Shimon had a point. Nothing had happened to them yet, and she might as well be clean and pressed if something did happen. She heard the clatter of pots and pans in the kitchen as she rummaged through her drawers for a blue sweater and skirt. Shimon was hopeless when it came to making coffee. "I'll make it!" she called, suddenly no longer angry or afraid. Shimon had made it easy to pretend. She glanced again at the sky. They would pretend until reality demanded that they pay attention.

Shimon stood grinning in the doorway. His feet were bare now, his shirt unbuttoned, and the hair on his head stood up on one side. "I was hoping you would." He thrust the coffeepot into her hands.

At that moment a sharp cry sounded from outside in the Judenplatz. The roar of smashing glass filled the little flat.

"This is what we think of Jews!" One stone was followed by another, and then another. Splinters of glass flew across the room and fell to the floor as Shimon pulled Leah behind the door of the closet. What sounded like a thousand voices chimed in with taunting insults.

"We will paint the walls with your blood!"

"Now you Communist Jews will taste justice!"

"Come out, Jews! Come out from your nests! Out into the bright light of Greater Deutschland!"

Shimon closed the closet door behind them, and they stood trembling together in total darkness amid the heavy smell of mothballs and wool. Leah rested her head against Shimon's broad chest. She gripped the coffeepot tightly as still another rock smashed through the high window above the bed.

Leah tried to speak but could not find her voice. The thought ran through her mind that they had waited too long to have coffee. It was a strange thought to have as the clatter of boots sounded outside on the stairs, but at that moment there was nothing she wanted as much as a cup of strong Viennese coffee.

2
Elisa's Question

The tiny bathroom in the ancient house in Prague was something like Elisa imagined the boiler room of a ship to be. Steam from her hot bath curled up around pipes that snaked in and out of the walls and ceiling from every direction. Each time she turned on the water, the pipes wailed and vibrated threateningly. It was obvious from the low, slanted ceiling that the cubicle had once been a closet. There was no window or ventilation, and moisture from the steam condensed on the pipes and dripped down the walls onto the chipped tile floor. Plumbing was a crude afterthought in Prague, and yet, this very minute, no place on earth seemed quite so near to perfection.

Elisa slid down in the tub and let the water wash over her aching shoulders. She laid her head back until strands of thick golden hair floated in the warmth. For the first time in a year her father was home, sleeping safely between clean sheets while Anna kept watch beside the bed in the room upstairs.

"You have been a very sick man, Theo Linder," the doctor had said in a heavy Czech accent. "Very sick indeed." He had clucked his tongue and checked Theo's pulse once again.

"Typhus," Theo had rasped. He did not need a doctor to tell him how ill he had been.

The doctor's eyebrows had shot up, then slammed down in a frown. He repeated the word *typhus* in a respectful tone. "But not here in Prague, surely!" He turned to Anna. "I have not seen typhus in Prague for some time! Who has told him he had typhus?"

"Not here. No one here. No one here," Anna replied, reaching out to smooth back Theo's thin gray hair. "He has been . . . away for a very long time, you see."

"Where has he been, madame?" The doctor looked first at Anna and then back to Theo. "Where . . . that he would return in such condition?"

"Germany, Herr Doktor," Theo spoke softly.

"Germany? We hear of no such epidemics in Germany." The doctor appeared puzzled and concerned.

"I was . . . a place near Munich. Dachau."

Recognition flooded the doctor's face. "Yes," he said slowly, shaking his head. "Such places in Germany we *have* heard of. Here in Czechoslovakia we have indeed heard the rumors."

Theo lay before him as proof of the reality of Nazi justice. Elisa had watched the round little doctor as his imagination colored in all the details. A shadow of fear slid over his features and he stood over Theo for a long time without speaking. Finally he turned to Anna. "Theo is a lucky man, madame, to survive such a place. Here in Prague we are a people who believe in the miraculous." He shrugged as if to say there was no other explanation.

Anna had taken Theo's hand and held it in hers. Tears filled her eyes. Elisa had turned away, as if the moment were too private for anyone to see. Her father had come home. He would get well. There was, indeed, a miracle in that.

As Elisa soaked in the tub, her worries about her father rose and drifted away like the steam. It was only when she thought about those she had left behind in Vienna that another concern surfaced, dripping into her consciousness like the drops on the rusty pipes.

John Murphy had left the house only seconds after the doctor arrived. He would be back as soon as he got a call through to the International News Service office in London. Elisa still held some vague hope that he would come back with news that the British had joined with the French to stop what Murphy called "the rape of Austria." Surely the world could not stand by and watch as Nazi Germany's epidemic of lawlessness spread!

She shuddered in spite of the warmth of the water. Leah and Shimon Feldstein would be among the first destroyed if such an event happened. She closed her eyes and rested her head against the cool iron tub. How naïve she was to hope that Germany's control over Austria was not already a fact! Hadn't Thomas von Kleistmann told her that the German High Command would never let Hitler march if the great powers would only stand firm against him? The celebration of Nazi youth in the streets of Vienna last night could mean only one thing. The resignation of Austrian chancellor Schuschnigg under force could only mean that the British and the French had denied their help in stopping Hitler. Austria was lost. A plague much worse than typhus was finally let loose in Europe.

Thomas had warned her about all of this. But then, Thomas had also told her that there was no hope for Theo. Hadn't he said that Theo was dead? With his words, her hope had died for her father. And yet . . .

A soft knock sounded on the door. "Elisa, dear," Anna called to her, "may I come in for a moment?"

Elisa drew the flimsy curtain around the tub and flipped the lock on the door. "Sure, Mama."

Cold blasted the bathroom as Anna slipped in, then pulled down the toilet lid and sat down at the foot of the tub. "Feeling better?"

"Uh-huh." Elisa sounded drowsy, but she was wide awake and wishing that Anna would come straight to the point. Her mother's tone of voice asked much more than how Elisa was feeling. Elisa suspected this visit had something to do with John Murphy.

"The doctor is gone. He says your father will get well with food—*good* food and lots of rest. It may be some months until he is really himself again, though." There was a long, awkward pause. "Your papa tells me you are married."

Elisa looked down at the lapis wedding band. She wished now it was off her finger. How could she explain her marriage to John Murphy? Anna would not understand the fact that it was merely a business arrangement—something she had done for the sake of an American passport and the protection it brought her.

"Uh-huh."

"To this nice American fellow, John Murphy." Anna sounded hurt. "But you didn't tell me."

"It all happened so fast, Mother." The ache in Elisa's shoulders was returning. She could never explain about her trips into Germany or the refugee children. Or the smuggled passports. Anna had enough to concern herself with.

"So fast? Too fast for a telegram?"

"Yes. I . . . it was . . . very sudden."

Anna cleared her throat in a motherly way. "I don't mean to pry into your business, Elisa, but such impulsiveness is not like you. Not at all."

Anna was right about that. Elisa had been anything but impulsive her entire life. Even her relationship with Thomas had been a matter of years of longing. Elisa had not been impulsive in her marriage to Murphy. The entire matter had been thought out in every detail. But how could she explain to her mother that she was involved in smuggling Jewish children out of Germany? Now she would almost certainly do the same in Austria. Could she really say, *"Mother, he is handsome and wonderful and I think I am really in love with him, but I paid him six thousand dollars to marry me. This is simply a business deal"*?

"You're right." Elisa was grateful for the curtain. She could not see Anna's disapproving face. "I'm not usually impulsive."

Now Anna cleared her throat again. Her voice became gentle and full of understanding. "Elisa, I know this has been a difficult year for all of us. I understand that you must not have wanted to bother me. But if you became involved in something you should not have . . ."

How could Anna know? Elisa had not told anyone outside her small circle about the trips to Munich. Nor about the violin case or the passports or . . . "Involved? What do you mean, Mother?"

"I know how it is when you meet a man. A handsome man. And . . . I know how Thomas von Kleistmann hurt you. And I'm not at all surprised that you might become involved with some handsome young American like this Murphy fellow, and . . ."

"And what?"

"Your father says he remembers you met him at the train station in Berlin over a year ago. That night . . . the night your father was arrested."

"Murphy helped me."

Elisa's head was beginning to throb. She thought about the night she stood overlooking Dachau. She remembered the open stares of the German soldiers on those long train rides into the heart of the Reich. She remembered the look on the Nazi Sporer's face as he had stripped the Jewish woman at the border check last night. And Otto Wattenbarger as he flipped open her passport. "How did Papa know I was married?" she asked.

"He heard the fellow at the border check last night. He said the man seemed to know you. That he commented that you were married now, and—"

"It was Otto Wattenbarger, Mother." Elisa hoped that Otto's involvement with the Nazis would pull Anna from the topic of marriage.

"Not surprising," Anna said after a moment's consideration. "His poor mother. Poor, dear Marta." Then without missing a beat she blurted out, "Are you pregnant, Elisa? Is that why you married this man?"

Elisa laughed out loud at the question. She laughed like she had when she was a child watching a Charlie Chaplin film and the little hobo got a pie in his face. "Mother!" The question seemed unthinkable! Hilarious and outrageous! "Mother!" she said again through her laughter.

Anna was embarrassed but defensive. "You said yourself that you are not impetuous!" she sniffed. "I simply could not think of any other reason why you would marry an American journalist without at least telling me first." The hurt returned to her voice.

"For money, Mother!" Elisa laughed again. It was true; Murphy had married *her* for money, but Anna was certain Elisa was making fun of her.

"All right, then!" Anna stood up. "You can't blame me for asking, for being curious about a new husband my own daughter did not bother to tell me about."

Elisa became instantly subdued and contrite. "I'm sorry, Mama. I was going to tell you when the time was right. I would have. But there were so many things, and I . . . " She held her left hand out through the curtain and extended her ring finger. "He got me this."

"Beautiful, Elisa! Blue lapis overlaid with tiny gold leaves! It is exquisite!" Anna held her daughter's hand. "I am so happy for you, dear." Her voice sounded teary. "So happy for *all* of us!"

Elisa squeezed her fingers and let her hand remain cradled in her mother's gentle grip. "You and Papa were impulsive, weren't you? I mean, when you married him?"

"Ummm. There was a war on. It seemed like the thing to do. Grab every moment of life. I have not regretted it. Not even a moment." Anna sounded wistful and more contented than Elisa had heard her since before that terrible Christmas in Kitzbühel. Anna sighed and let go of Elisa's hand. "I should go to your father now. He is sleeping, but I can hardly believe that he is here. I'll go sit with him for a while and leave you to your bath."

For a long time Elisa sat in the water. She hardly noticed when it began to cool. She stared at the blue band and could not help but wonder why Murphy had bought something so beautiful for their phony marriage. *Probably guilt,* she concluded. *He felt guilty for . . . for what?* Europe was absolutely rotten with marriages of convenience. People got married every day for less reason than a passport and for less money than six thousand dollars! Maybe Murphy had not meant for her to keep the ring. Not forever. She would tell her mother she had lost the blue lapis ring down the drain. She would say it had slipped off in the tub.

The thought of the band sliding off her finger and disappearing down the maze of pipes made her close her hand into a fist. She did not want to lose the ring. It was ridiculous, she knew, but she did not want to lose Murphy either.

She dried off and dressed quickly, hoping that Murphy would be back by the time she put on her makeup and fixed her hair. Maybe he would stay with her. Or take her with him. Maybe they could go back to Vienna together and find Leah and Shimon. And maybe, if they spent some time together, he might look at her and see that there was more than just an American passport for Elisa in this thing.

She rubbed a clear circle on the foggy mirror. "Murphy," she whispered, "do you want me?" That was a silly question. Of course Murphy *wanted* her. It had been obvious he wanted her every time he was with her. She frowned and reconsidered what she would ask him. "But, Murphy, do you *love* me?" She closed her eyes and imagined a dozen ways he could say, *"Yes! We have been through so much together; how could I ever be apart from you again, Elisa? My life would be such emptiness without you. Do I love you? Why not ask me if I want to go on breathing?"*

He might say all those things. But then again, he might also look at her with amusement and say, "Are you kidding? Me? John Murphy in love with one dame? Sorry, Elisa. I've got to catch a plane. See you around maybe. By the way, I've got this girl in London. Would you mail me the ring?"

She shook her head as if to knock loose her own foolishness. Murphy had made up his mind about her a long time ago. She didn't blame him. And she didn't need to ask him either.

3

Murphy's Story

Murphy! John Murphy? Is that you?" The startled voice of Larry Strickland crackled over the telephone from the London offices of the International News Service.

"Right. Last time I looked." Murphy caught his own exhausted reflection in the glass pane of the telephone booth. Even in this imperfect mirror he could see the dark circles under his eyes. After the events of the night before, he was not certain that the grim shadow in the glass was his own face.

"Where . . . " Strickland's voice faded out. "Are you in Vienna?"

"Prague!" Murphy shouted over the static. "Nobody in the INS in Vienna will be calling London for a while."

Strickland sounded angry. "Murphy! What are you *doing* in Prague?" There was an accusation in the question. How dare a reporter desert the front lines in Vienna as Hitler marched in at the head of Hess and his troops?

"You want news, don't you?" Murphy yelled back. "You won't get it from Vienna!"

"Did you see it? Let me get a pencil." Strickland was suddenly attentive. Of course the only accurate reports would have to be sent from outside Austria. The Nazis had closed down every means of communication with the outside world. Even before the German troops had arrived in Vienna, Austrian Nazis had invaded the INS building and closed down the dispatch offices and broadcasting services. The only news from Austria had come in the shrieking banners of German newspaper headlines.

Murphy stared sullenly at the front page of Hitler's propaganda papers, the *Völkischer Beobachter.* "German-Austria Saved from Chaos!" Murphy read aloud. "Is that what you're hearing over there?"

"Herr Goebbels has announced that there were violent disorders by the Reds in Vienna. Fighting, looting, murder. What about it?"

"A lie. Complete. Any lie will do. The only violence I saw in the streets of Vienna last night was after the Austrian Nazis crawled out from under their rocks. They closed off the Jewish districts of the city. Who knows what's happening there this morning? They closed down the newsrooms. Started arresting anybody who looked in the least anti-Anschluss. Most of the Austrian cabinet ran for their lives. I heard they kept a plane waiting at Alpern Airport for Chancellor Schuschnigg until the Luftwaffe started landing. Schuschnigg refused to go. The guy has guts; I'll give him that."

"Where is he now?"

"Under arrest, where else? And there were suicides all over the city last night."

"Suicides?"

"Mostly Jews. Some Socialists. That was the only blood spilled in the whole messy business, Larry. The only blood."

"No defense of Austrian territory?" Strickland's voice seemed preoccupied. He was taking notes, and Murphy paused, then began to remove wads of crumpled paper from every pocket. He held the phone awkwardly between his shoulder and ear as he smoothed out the papers and tried to make sense out of the scrawled lines and paragraphs that he had written as he witnessed the horror of Austria's capitulation.

"Hold it a minute, Larry!" He squinted at the back of an envelope. "I've got it all here. I wrote it all down. Sorry, I didn't mean to ramble. Just hold it and I'll give it to you ready to print."

Strickland cleared his throat. He seemed relieved that he would not have to decipher the torrent of thoughts and emotions Murphy had sent over the wire. "That's our boy. Okay, Murphy. You got a story for me?"

The story was written in the margin of a menu, continued on the back of a torn magazine cover, and concluded on Murphy's bill from the Sacher Hotel. Murphy noticed for the first time that the boys in the press corps had charged a magnum of champagne to his room-service account. He would settle up with them later when he got back to Vienna. That is, if they weren't all in some concentration camp by now. And if anyone went back to Vienna.

"Yeah, Larry. A story. It reads like an obituary." The crackle of long distance consumed the remainder of his words.

"What?"

"I said it reads like an obit! Like a train wreck! The sinking of the *Titanic*! About that terrible, too." He held up the first scrap of paper. "Ready for copy?"

"We got a deadline—"

"Let's give 'em a *real* headline." Murphy tossed the German newspaper to the floor. "Try this: 'Nazis Seize Power after Hitler Ultimatum.' "

"It beats what we've heard from Germany so far." Strickland gave a short, bitter laugh. He was angry, and his anger fed Murphy's own sense of indignation, which had been almost lost in his weariness.

"If you think that will go, how about a box at the head of the column?" He repeated the words that he had written last night after he had left the INS office by the back door when the Nazis came in through the front.

> *"Vienna, March 11. Censorship has started. An order posted in the Central Telegraph Office said all telephone conversations from the room must be in German. Correspondents for the International News Service, an American organization, were detained at their office against their will, without charges."*

"Great! Great stuff, Murphy!" Strickland's admiration seemed to chase away the static, and suddenly his voice came in like a call from next door. "Finish this, and then tell me how you got out."

"I'm saving that story for after-dinner conversation at the Press Club." Murphy did not want to mention Elisa or her father. Theo Lindheim slept peacefully now in the little house near Old Town Prague, but the terror of last night's escape was still too fresh for Murphy to want to talk about it.

"Everybody's going to have a story out of this one," Strickland said. "That will be some conversation!" He laughed, but Murphy did not laugh with him. He was too full of fears for his friends who remained in Nazi-dominated Vienna. He did not want to imagine that such a meal at the Press Club might have a lot of faces absent from around the table.

Murphy shuddered involuntarily. "Well, let's give Americans something to talk about over their pot roasts, huh? Ready?" He began reading from the margin of the menu:

> *"Under threat of force from Berlin, Chancellor Kurt von Schuschnigg of Austria yielded last evening and resigned in dramatic circumstances. The Nazis, with Dr. Arthur Seyss-Inquart as chancellor, are in power. . . . "*

"Slow down!" Strickland sounded panicked.

Murphy could not slow down. He wanted to read the terrible words quickly. He wanted to be done, to tear up the notes and pretend that such news could not really happen.

> *"To an unprepared public, listening to a typical radio program of pleasant Viennese music . . ."*

Images of Shimon and Leah Feldstein filled his thoughts. Why hadn't they stayed at Elisa's apartment? No doubt they had heard the announcement of Schuschnigg's resignation as they listened in the Judenplatz. By then it had been too late for them to get out to safety. No one in the Judenplatz would be safe this morning. No Jew in Austria would be safe now. He paused again to give Strickland time to catch up.

"Okay. I got it. Go ahead."

> *"The voice of the man who may have been the last chancellor of an independent Austria announced at 7:45 PM that, in his own words, he had 'yielded only to force.' "*

"Yielded to force? In quotes?"

"That's what the man said."

"He said that on the radio? With the Nazis coming into Austria? He's a dead man."

Murphy did not reply. Strickland was only too right in his assessment. The Austrian chancellor should have taken that plane from Alpern Airport. Murphy was sorry the man had not done so.

> *"To avoid bloodshed under threat of a German invasion that began even as he spoke, Chancellor Schuschnigg then resigned his office."*

"Got it."

> *"When Schuschnigg had finished, thousands of Nazis began swarming into Vienna's streets to take control unopposed."*

"Thousands?"

The image of the apple-cheeked peasant boys swilling schnapps at the barricades became vivid to Murphy once again. "Kids," he muttered. "Students, mostly. Too young to remember the last war. Too stupid to see where Herr Hitler is leading them."

"You want me to copy that, Murphy?" Strickland was perplexed.

"No. But it's the truth."

"Tell me when you're just talking, will ya?" The sound of the pencil scratching out Murphy's last words came through clearly.

"Sure. Sorry. Deadline, right?" Over the next ten minutes Murphy composed the story of the death of a nation over the phone. The facts were reported clearly, like an obituary. His tired reflection stared back at him in the window. He wanted to be done, to go back to Elisa and put his arms around her and sleep for a week or so. But it was not to be.

Strickland read the complete news story back to Murphy. "This is one for the history books, Murph." He was clearly impressed. "While the rest of the guys are still under wraps, you scooped them all. They'll be boiling mad!"

The thought gave Murphy no pleasure. "That's it, then. I'm going to find a soft bed, and—" Murphy was instantly sorry he had opened his mouth.

"Sorry, Murphy. You can't sleep yet. Not in Prague. Word from the top says we need you here in London. News bureau is putting together a live broadcast. First time we're going to brave a live broadcast to New York. With a story like this we're going to need you here." Strickland announced the plan as though Murphy should be elated.

Normally Murphy would have given anything for such an opportunity, but not this morning. Leaving Prague meant being away from Elisa. How could he leave her now? After last night? After everything? "You're going to have to find somebody else."

Strickland lapsed into a momentary silence, then exploded. "There is nobody else, you idiot! Get a plane! Swim the Channel if you have to, but you've got to be here by midnight tonight." Strickland would not be argued with.

"Tonight? But—" Murphy's reflection appeared as though it might weep.

"Tonight. No *buts*. You miss this one, and you'll find yourself back in the States writing about the soup kitchens and the ladies' charity league! Got it?" The static returned as though Strickland's roaring was damaging the telephone.

Murphy muttered his reply, hoping that he would leave Strickland in doubt about his agreement. But there was no doubt. Not really. Even the tired face in the glass understood that the world needed to hear about Austria. Those too young to remember Germany in war needed to be reminded. Those too blind to see the future needed to see it through Murphy's eyes.

He hung up the telephone with the realization that the story was far from over. Indeed, it was only beginning, and it might be a long time before anyone slept peacefully again.

Anna Linder opened the door before Murphy could knock a second time. "You don't need to knock, John!" She gave her new son-in-law a quick hug. "Elisa told me all about it! You must be really something for our Elisa to marry you without so much as . . . " She snapped her fingers to finish the sentence.

Murphy swallowed hard. He did not know what Elisa had told her mother, but obviously it was not the whole truth. "Well, I . . . I have to get used to this." He smiled awkwardly as Anna took his coat and hat.

"Theo and I got married the same way. Didn't tell my parents. They wouldn't have approved. Although I am sure we would have approved of you. I mean, we *do* approve of you!" Her enthusiasm made Anna look years younger than she had when Murphy had first seen her before dawn that morning. He was amazed at how very much like her daughter Anna Linder looked. An older version of Elisa, but still beautiful.

"How is Theo?" Murphy changed the subject, but he was sure that Theo must be doing well.

"A little care, food, lots of love, and the doctor says he will recover. I . . . don't know how to thank you."

Her gratitude embarrassed Murphy, so he changed the subject again. "Where is Elisa?"

"In your room. Come on. You must be exhausted. I shooed the boys out of their room."

"There was no need, really." Murphy tried to explain that he would be leaving, but Anna was too full of plans to hear him.

"They are down at the bakery right now. Prague has breakfast pastry like you have never tasted. Food in Germany is so dull, don't you think? They'll be back in a while. I'll fix eggs and sausage." She flung open the door to a small bedroom where Elisa sat brushing her hair in front of the fire. In her cobalt blue sweater and skirt, she was like a picture by one of those French painters whose name Murphy could never remember. Her hair shone like corn silk, and the fire glowed behind her.

"Hello, Murphy." Her eyes met his.

"Hi," Murphy said. He couldn't think of anything else to say.

"This is your room." Anna gestured toward the double bed. "I changed the sheets. What a day this is! A terrible day for the world. For Vienna. But God will forgive me if I am happy. My husband has come home, and my daughter has a husband—"

Elisa looked embarrassed by her mother's words. "Mama," she said, interrupting Anna's reverie, "should I help you with breakfast?"

"You two want to talk. Certainly you need to talk alone," Anna hinted. "Anyway this is your room. For the newlyweds."

Murphy squirmed under the attention. "Thank you, Mrs. Linder."

"Not Mrs. Linder!" Anna protested. "Anna. Or Mama, maybe. You are part of our family now." She patted him on the back and hurried off toward the kitchen.

Murphy and Elisa were silent. Both felt the strain of the deception. At last Murphy spoke. "This—" he gestured toward the bed—"isn't going to work, you know."

Elisa nodded. Her face was deep red. "Impossible." She got up suddenly and turned away from him. "I'm sorry. I couldn't find a way to explain to her what this is all about."

"You want to walk a bit?" Murphy felt helpless, foolish, standing beside the bed. He did not want to talk about it. *Clean sheets. The down quilt turned back. Two pillows.*

Elisa nodded and swept past him into the hall. The fresh smell of her skin made him dizzy for an instant. "I could use some fresh air," Elisa said, not looking back at him as she slipped on her coat.

Dumb suggestion, Murphy thought, wishing he had shut the door behind them and taken Elisa in his arms and pulled her onto the cool, clean sheets. He didn't want to walk or talk or think about anything but her. *Blast Austria and the INS and Adolf Hitler and his Nazi lunatics and England and France and . . .*

"You look a lot like your mother," Murphy said, following her out the front door. "She seems really happy."

4

The Bridge

Four tiny pairs of trousers were neatly folded beside the battered suitcase on the bed. Shirts, sweaters, and newly darned socks were already packed.

Walter Kronenberger sat on the edge of the sagging bed and quietly embraced his sons with his eyes. The two small boys stood with their backs to him and stared wide-eyed through the grimy windowpane at the spectacle unfolding in the street below their shabby hotel.

Walter did not seem to hear the roar of the crowd. Men and women crammed together on this narrow side street just off the Ringstrasse. Fathers held children high to catch a glimpse of tanks and field guns and uniformed columns of German soldiers who marched before the cheering masses on the broad thoroughfare beyond.

"We can see everything, Father!" cried Louis, his blond head bobbing enthusiastically.

Charles, his eyes bright to match his twin brother's expression, nodded. His mouth was covered by a dark blue scarf, and in the soft glow of the morning light, it was remarkable how much alike the eyes and expressions of the boys were. How much they looked like their mother. The thought tore through Walter like the hot blade of a knife. He wanted to look away, but he could not. He wanted to call his sons away from the window, to wrap his arms around them and weep softly between them. But he did not want to steal this one last moment of delight from them. They were only five years old. How could they understand that what they watched from the high vantage point of the hotel window was a flood of terror that would soon engulf them all?

Tall buildings framed their view of the parade like partly open curtains on a stage. The boys could see only fragments of the event. First the muzzle of a tank gun appeared, then the barrel slid slowly past like the trunk of an enormous elephant. Finally the body of the tank followed, bearing helmeted soldiers who waved to the crowds in the midst of a cloud of flowers and scraps of paper fluttering in the air. Soldiers with arms stretched upward in the Nazi salute seemed to be reaching toward them.

Charles reached out to take the hand of Louis. Louis, beautiful and unmarred, never seemed to notice the ugly hole that split the palate and lip of his brother. He was the mirror of his brother's soul, the expression of emotions and thoughts and needs that Charles could only convey through inarticulate groans. Although the words and phrases were clear and bright in the mind of Charles, he had not been born with lips to form them.

"Ah-er!" Charles cried, pointing out the window.

"Father!" Louis echoed. "Come quickly!"

Walter stood behind them as the shiny black Mercedes limousine slowly moved by. There, clutching the windshield and standing with his arm raised in rigid salute, was Adolf Hitler. His eyes were hidden by the visor of his military cap. His mouth was turned slightly downward in a stern, proud expression as those he passed raised their voices in adulation. His plain brown uniform was unadorned, yet eloquent in its statement: Here was a simple man who served as the voice of the German people!

Just as Louis spoke for Charles, so Hitler claimed that he raised his voice on behalf of the groaning German race! As a journalist in Hamburg, Walter had declared that Hitler was not a voice but an upraised fist that smashed down on all Germans who dared to disagree. For this "scurrilous lie," as the Gestapo had called it, Walter had been imprisoned for two years at Dachau. When he had come home, he found his wife was dead and his sons were in the care of a neighbor. He had left Germany with his sons in the dark of night. Today he realized too late that he had not run far enough. This glimpse of the upraised arm bearing Germany's fist convinced Walter that, indeed, there was no place on earth that was far enough.

Protectively he wrapped his arms around the shoulders of his sons. He knelt beside them and turned them away from the spectacle to face him. Beautiful blue eyes gazed back at him, matching the seriousness of his expression. "I must go away again," he said quietly.

Both boys frowned at once. "Can we go with you, Father?" Louis asked. Charles reached up to touch his father's cheek in a soundless entreaty.

"No, my sons—" he shook his head slowly—"not this time. But someday we will all be together again."

"But why can't we go?" Tears welled up—angry tears, hurt, confused.

"Where I am going is not a place for little boys." He pulled them closer.

"But where will we go?" Louis asked, and Charles moaned softly, placing his soft cheek against Walter's.

Walter fought to control the emotion that tore at his heart. He wanted to open his mouth and groan in agony with Charles. There were no words to express the gaping wound within him. "Very bad men—" he swallowed hard—"have come to Vienna. You must not stay here. It is not safe for you."

The scarf slipped down slightly from Charles' mouth. In that moment Walter heard again the words of the doctor as he had held the tiny disfigured child in his arms for the first time. . . .

"He will die if we simply leave him alone. Such a deformity is terrible in any time of history. But now, today, in the great Third Reich, beauty and physical perfection are paramount, Walter. Perhaps it would be kinder to the child if we simply let him go."

"You mean let him starve?" Walter clutched the baby closer. Tears fell on the blanket as a little hand with perfectly formed fingers emerged from its folds and brushed Walter on the face.

"He cannot eat without great difficulty. He will never be able to speak. It is becoming quite common, Walter, to let such monstrosities fade away. Someday soon it will be law," the doctor said coolly. "Then we will have no choice in the matter. What place can the mentally deficient and those who are barely recognizable as human have in the Reich? It would be kinder to let this life end before it begins. . . ."

Walter shivered at the memory. He lovingly adjusted the scarf, then lifted Charles' perfect fingers and gently kissed them.

"Ahhhhhh!" Charles wailed in anguish. He hugged his father tightly, not willing to let go.

"Where will we go, Father?" Louis was crying now too.

"Don't cry, my darlings." Walter's tears streamed freely. "There are kind people here in Vienna. I have heard of them. They will take care of you until we can be together once again. Someday . . . all of us. Your mommy. You and me. Together again, my sons! God will let it be so!"

Frightened men, women, and children stood together in the Judenplatz. They were silent, not resisting the uniformed German soldiers and the strutting Austrian Nazis who surrounded them. Harshly shouted questions were answered in quiet monotones. Those being held had learned within the first moments of their captivity that they must not question their captors. Any defiance was answered by a blow to the face with a rifle butt.

Leah stood in Shimon's shadow. She could not see over the heads of the crowd around them. A dozen times in the last thirty minutes Shimon had whispered to her, "They are bringing more now." Then the mass of people would shift slightly and crowd in closer together.

It seemed to Leah that the German soldiers were more polite than the Austrians. Even though she could not see them, the German and Austrian voices were easy to distinguish.

"Let me see your papers, Jewish swine!" the words of a Nazi from Vienna roared. Such rage did not seem to fit with the soft Viennese accent. "So you did not think we would win, eh? You are surprised, Bolshevik Jew? It is not the picture of Lenin that will hang in the Ballhausplatz; it is the picture of Hitler! And you Jews will simply hang!"

Then the words were answered by a sharp cry of pain as the prisoner was struck in the groin with a riding crop. Men winced at the sight of the young Jew falling to the ground and receiving yet another kick to the stomach. Leah wanted to shout out, *"Why?"* But she did not. Shimon silenced her with a look, then drew a deep breath to control his own anger as he looked sullenly away from the scene. Here and there sobs were heard. Occasionally there was an anguished cry from a wife whose husband was torn away and shoved into one of the smaller groups that were herded out of the square. But mostly the Jews of Vienna were silent.

The spires of St. Stephan's were clearly visible. At nine o'clock the bells rang out their final betrayal as they welcomed Adolf Hitler into the city. In the distance Leah could hear the cheering thousands who had gathered to watch the triumphal entry of the Führer followed by the arrogant, goose-stepping soldiers of the Reich. How many Austrians had swarmed to witness this opening act in the destruction of their nation? A hundred thousand? Half a million? The Ringstrasse trembled beneath the press of human flesh. The great concert halls reverberated with the resounding shouts: "Heil Hitler! Heil Hitler!" Over and over the cry was repeated. Leah could hear the words distinctly. There was no doubt what such a shout would mean to those who waited silently in the Judenplatz. Their world had ended. Judgment had come. The bells of St. Stephan's now seemed to be tolling the end of the Jewish life and culture in Vienna.

Leah shuddered. She remembered how the bells had tolled for Irmgard Schüler as the smoke of Rudy Dorbransky's body had risen from the crematorium. The same men who had murdered Irmgard and Rudy were now in control of the city and the nation. Leah looked at her hands and then at the hacked fingers of the statue of Lessing. The law of destruction had now come to consume them all.

In Prague this morning, the hundred spires of the Gothic city were enveloped by a damp, cold mist that rose from the Moldau River. Together Murphy and Elisa walked slowly across Mala Strana Square toward the Charles Bridge. Stone saints stared down at them and the scant handful of other pedestrians who hurried through the early morning fog on their way to some emergency meeting in the government offices near Hradcany Castle. No one spoke. Only the silence of the stone saints seemed fitting after the news that had come from Austria.

Murphy wanted to take Elisa's hand in his, but she plunged her hands into the pockets of her overcoat. She walked with her gaze fixed on the cobbles of the square. Her face was grim, and her eyes reflected the sorrow of a thousand years. It was cold. The mist penetrated the fabric of Murphy's coat, reaching out icy fingers and chilling him to the bone. He pulled his collar closer around his chin; then, certain that Elisa's hand was hopelessly out of reach, he also groped for his pockets.

Everything was gray and lifeless except Elisa. Her skin was pale and smooth like fine porcelain. *Right now she seems as fragile as porcelain too,* Murphy thought. He cleared his throat as if to speak, but the sound seemed an unnatural intrusion, so he let his thoughts drift away in the mist.

Then Elisa smiled sadly up at him. "You were going to say something, Murphy?"

Her question surprised him. "No. I mean . . . do you feel like talking? I thought . . . " He glanced at her. She was staring at him curiously. "I didn't think you felt like talking—"

"Murphy—" she did not wait for him to finish—"I want to thank you. For . . . my father's life. For bringing us here."

He shrugged and peered up at the statue of a saint. "Anybody would have—"

"No." She looked back thoughtfully at the cobbles. "Not just anyone." She held out her left hand. The gold and blue lapis wedding band was the only fragment of color in the grayness. She started to take off the ring. "I suppose you will want this."

Murphy reached out and took her hand. "No, Elisa." She did not pull her hand away, and he intertwined his fingers with hers. A slight blush colored her pale skin. He was relieved that he could touch her, even if it was only this much. Hands clasped together, palm to palm.

After several minutes of silence she spoke again. "Are you sure you don't want it back? You might meet a woman, and . . . "

He frowned. "If that happens, I'll let you know." He was sorry she had said that. She couldn't care much about him if the thought of him with another woman didn't matter. "You might need it. No telling what's coming. You might need a wedding ring."

She shuddered at his words. "You don't think *they* can come here, do you? Not to Czechoslovakia!" Fear was thick in her voice. She looked down at the cobbles again as though she could not bear to imagine Nazi flags fluttering from the buildings of Mala Strana.

"Not if the Czechs have anything to say about it."

"Prague isn't like Austria!" She sounded almost pleading, as though a promise from Murphy would make them safe here in Prague.

A thousand thoughts raced through Murphy's mind. The Czechs had one of the best-equipped armies in Europe. Four million men and reassure her with those words. He would not tell her about the racial Germans who also lived in the Czech Sudetenland or about the Nazis among them who clamored for unification with the Reich.

This morning he would be careful what he said, for Elisa needed hope that Hitler would be stopped somewhere, by some strong hand. "Yes," Murphy said quietly in a confident tone, "the Czechs are a strong government. Their constitution is almost identical to the American constitution. Four million soldiers stand between us and Hitler."

At his words, Elisa raised her head and sighed with relief. She squeezed his hand and smiled as though a great weight had been lifted from her. "Britain and France will stand with them. Czechoslovakia is too important. My father has always said so. That this place will be like Switzerland. Neutral. Czechoslovakia is too important for the great powers to desert her."

Personally Murphy did not trust the great powers any further than he could throw them. Britain and France, with men like Chamberlain and Daladier at the helms, were nearly paralyzed with fear of Hitler's war machine. Murphy would not have believed that German troops could have marched into Austria as easily as they had. But he would not express his worry to Elisa. "Your family is all together now," he answered, caressing her with his eyes. "Safe. That's what matters. You will all be safe here until I can arrange to get you to the States."

Her face clouded again. She looked up toward the bridge tower and the silent stone saints. "There are so many saints in Prague. You could get so used to them that you wouldn't see them anymore." She stopped and gazed across Charles Bridge. The water of the river rushed against the pilings. Closing her eyes for a moment, she appeared to be praying . . . or perhaps remembering something.

"What is it?" Murphy asked at last.

"Leah."

"Leah?"

"We had a picnic here on the bridge." She started to walk again, this time more slowly as they moved onto the bridge from beneath the ancient stone arch.

Murphy did not want to think about Leah Feldstein. He did not want Elisa to think about her or talk about her. Leah was bait on the end of a German hook to pull Elisa away from safety. "She'll be all right."

"You don't know that." Elisa looked at him sharply. "How can you even say that when they didn't make it to the apartment last night?"

"They have their visas to Palestine." He was feeble in his defense, and he knew it. The visas were probably worthless now.

"And you know how much that means." There was an edge of bitterness in her voice . . . and something else. Murphy knew that Elisa would still be in Vienna if he had not found Theo Lindheim when he did. Elisa left for the sake of her father. She would have stayed for the sake of Shimon and Leah; Murphy was certain of that now.

"I'll be back in Vienna in a few days." Murphy had not meant to tell her that he was leaving so soon.

"You're leaving Prague?" She seemed surprised. "When?"

"This afternoon." He looked out toward the gray waters and Kampa Island below the bridge.

"Then I will go with you." The tone of her voice dared him to argue.

He still held her hand, but the gentleness of her grip vanished. "You can't go," he answered simply, and at that she pulled her hand away and plunged it into her pocket beyond his reach. The gesture made him angry. "I'm going to London to broadcast a report on this whole mess first. A news report live over the radio all the way to the States."

The importance of the event evidently escaped her. "And will you tell them about all the people we left behind in Vienna?" Her tone was accusing. She leaned against the stone railing of the bridge and stared down into the current. "What will you tell them, Murphy?"

"What I saw. Then I'll go back to Vienna and—"

"Report whatever is news," she finished for him. "I saw it all in Germany, Herr Murphy. I know what the news will be. I know about the concentrations camps for those who disagree, for those of non-Aryan blood. Shall I write your story for you? You need not go back to Vienna just to watch, Murphy. I can tell you what is coming. This morning. Now. Here beneath the statue of Saint Nepomuk I can see it all. Safe and warm in a house with my parents in Prague, I can see Leah. I remember standing here on the bridge with her, laughing about how silly men are." She turned suddenly to Murphy. Her eyes were frightened and sad and full of the terrible *knowing*. "Leah is my friend. My sister, really. Yes. That is not too strong a word. You go to London and another reason."

"No!" He took her by the shoulders. "I'll get you and your family out of this European mess for good if you'll sit tight awhile!"

"I have hopes that my family will go to your country, but as for me, I have other things to do."

"Just give me a little time!" Murphy was pleading with her. "Just a couple of weeks to take a look at the situation. I'll find them. Stay here, and I'll go back and find them. The Nazis have nothing on me." He shrugged. "I'm an American reporter. So, I'll report. And I'll find your friends. I stand a better chance than you of getting them out of there."

The determination in Elisa's eyes wavered. She looked at him as if weighing the possibilities of what he said. She touched the stone rail of the bridge as though she remembered Leah's hand there. The gesture was an unspoken promise to her friend. "Yes," she said in a barely audible voice. "And will you take a letter for her from me?"

Murphy breathed a sigh of relief. "Sure! And a tin of cookies if you want!" He laughed.

She did not laugh with him. She twisted the wedding band on her finger. "And when will you come back, Murphy?" There was something in the question that Murphy liked. He took her hand again.

"A couple of weeks." He lifted her chin as if to kiss her, but she pulled away and stepped back from him.

"I am grateful for what you have done . . . and what you are doing . . . for my family. For Leah . . ."

"Grateful." He was somehow disappointed by the word. "Sure. That's what you paid me for, right?" He bowed curtly. "Comes with the price of the wedding and the American passport."

His sarcasm stung her. She frowned and looked back toward the Hradcany Castle, where a small patch of sunlight was trying to open up the sky. "Still, I am grateful."

Murphy saluted, but she did not see his gesture. "At your service." He laughed as though it did not matter, as though he really had done everything for the sake of money. "I'm hungry. Breakfast should be ready by now. When will you tell your mother I am just an imitation husband?"

She had already turned back toward the house. "It's not important for her to know. Not now that you're leaving. Let her think of me as the protected wife of an American. She deserves some time without worry for me. And if I have to go back to Vienna—"

Murphy spun her around. "If you say that one more time, I'll tear up that passport and personally throw your ring over the bridge!"

"Then I'll get another." Her eyes flashed the warning that she would not wait obediently here in Prague for very long. Murphy had a promise to fulfill, a letter to deliver to Leah in Vienna. And if he failed, Elisa would simply complete the task herself. Then, as though she realized such an argument with him was useless, she dropped it and acted as if Leah's name had never been mentioned. "Come on, Murphy." Her tone was apologetic. "There's something I want to show you before you go."

5

Departure

It seemed strange to Murphy now, as he followed Elisa back across the Old Town Square of Prague, that Theo Lindheim had purchased a house so close to the Jewish sector of the city, so near to the very identity that he had fled from in Germany.

As though she read his mind, Elisa gestured toward the tower of the town hall. Below it, twenty-seven crosses were set into the cobblestones. "My father has always loved this place," she explained. "His family is buried in the Jewish cemetery not far from here. There is no place in Prague that has more history than here."

"But Theo isn't Czech." Murphy was surprised.

Elisa smiled at him as though he were unbelievably dense. "No. He is Jewish, Herr Murphy. Or have you forgotten? If so, you are the only one who has forgotten such a significant fact." She laughed at him and pointed at the crosses in the cobbles. "Papa used to bring me here when I was a little girl." She stopped. "I brought Leah here. These crosses mark the place where twenty-seven Czech nobles were executed in 1621. I never can remember why they were killed. When Papa is well again, I will ask him all about it. He knows about everything in Prague. He knows it better than I know German history. Better than I know my way around Berlin."

She looks like a little girl, Murphy thought as he watched her eyes drink in the ancient sights and legends as if they were fresh and new. "Prague is a strange place to me." Murphy stepped around one of the crosses in the square. "Maybe when I come back you can show me around."

"There are a thousand stories." His interest pleased her.

"Ah, well, you know me. Always interested in a story."

"Papa always says the old stories are not so very different than the new. Good men fighting against evil. Sometimes it is difficult to tell the difference between the two."

"Sometimes. Not now," Murphy said with certainty.

"Our house is not so far from the house where Kafka was born. He wrote the novel about a man named Joseph who was arrested and tried and executed without ever knowing why." When she turned to face Murphy, her eyes were angry. "This whole year I hated Prague and this house and every thought of Kafka because it made me think of Papa. One night I went to a hill outside Dachau. I stood for a long time and thought of the stories Papa had told me about this place. Men killed for no reason other than the fact that they thought differently than someone else. Maybe that's why Papa chose to buy a house so near . . . so near to where the old stories all happened."

The mist drifted like a veil through the square until Murphy could almost believe that he and Elisa were the only people left in the city. He felt the heavy burden of history here. There was much about Prague that he did not want to know. He wanted to take Elisa by the hand and lead her far from this place. The windows of the buildings looked down on them like so many eyes, and Murphy could not shake the feeling that these silent eyes had seen much and they would see more before the year was out.

"Should we get back, you think?" he asked, not wanting to admit that the place suddenly gave him the creeps. He remembered being a kid at home alone and looking at the piano until the keys seemed to be teeth that would devour him. He had run outside and waited until his folks had come home before he went back into the house. Today he had the same feeling as he stood with Elisa in the square.

"Just a minute more." She jerked her head toward the face of the Orloj, a huge clock set in the tower. "Mother would expect that we would wait here until the hour strikes." Moments later the clock struck 8 AM. Little windows opened before them and tiny statues of Christ and the apostles filed out. "Look at them, Murphy!" Elisa cried, and again it was easy for him to imagine her as a little girl holding on to her father's hand.

He reached out to her, and she laughed and clutched his arm tightly as the figure of Death tolled a tiny bell and an old man shook his head as if to say he did not want to die yet. Death turned the hourglass as a miser rolled past and then a young dandy, adjusting his costume. "Papa always says those last two fellows are to show that you can't take it with you." Elisa laughed with delight again. And then the windows shut tight until up in the gable a rooster appeared and crowed the passing of yet another hour.

"It beats anything I've seen in Times Square," Murphy said, enjoying the closeness of Elisa clutching his arm.

"Times Square?" Her cheeks were flushed as she turned to him at last.

He wanted to kiss her. She was so close, so fresh, and finally free from the worry of the last few weeks. "In New York. Maybe I can show you sometime."

A slight smile curved her mouth. She looked at his lips, then back into his eyes. "Times Square. I would like to see it sometime." She brushed her lips lightly against his. Then, before he could move, she stepped away and hurried back across the square toward the narrow street where the writer Kafka had grown up, to the house where Anna was cooking a huge breakfast for them.

Anna greeted them at the door and immediately took Murphy past the parlor and the dining room to the bedroom, where Theo lay propped up on a dozen small pillows.

"He has been asking for you, John." Anna opened the door slightly and peered in. Theo was awake. "Theo, darling," she softly crooned, "your son-in-law is here. Elisa has decided to share him with us after all."

Murphy wished that Elisa had told her mother the truth about their arrangement. It would have made things a whole lot easier. Anna hurried back down the narrow hall, leaving him alone with Theo in the dimly lit room.

Theo held out his hand to Murphy. The hand was unchanged, though attached to a spindly, bony arm. The hand was still large and remarkably familiar to Murphy after a year. And as Murphy took that hand in his own, he could easily remember Theo Lindheim as he had been a year before in Berlin. How the winds had buffeted the little plane; yet Theo had been determined, unafraid. Now every part of the man seemed to have withered and grown old—all but the hands.

"They have me tucked in so tightly, John Murphy, that I can hardly move." Theo's voice was shrunken and hollow as well. "I think they are afraid I will disappear."

Murphy inhaled as the delicious aroma of Czech sausages filled the old house. His stomach rumbled hungrily. "With food like that, you'll be back on your feet in no time." Murphy sat down across from him.

"Imagine—" Theo touched his fingers to his thin face—"I used to scold Anna for stuffing me with such good food." For an instant his eyes reflected the faraway faces of ten thousand hungry men. Loaves of bread heaped upon a truck, and something else . . .

"Anna said you want to talk to me?" Murphy's voice called Theo back from the memory.

Theo nodded and glanced down to where the metal identification bracelet was still attached to his wrist. He held the crudely stamped plate out for Murphy to see. *J. Stern,* the plate read, followed by a number.

"They called me Stern," Theo explained. "They said that Theo Lindheim had died in a plane wreck. I was Jacob Stern. Too many of my friends might have objected, you see, if Theo Lindheim was in Dachau. Too many friends who have important things yet to do for the true heart of Germany." There was pain in his eyes. "That is why I could not ask them for help. I know they have things that they must do, or there will be no more Germany." He faltered and looked toward the ceiling. "One man could not matter compared to that."

Murphy felt somehow uncomfortable. This old, broken man had deluded himself into thinking that he had friends left within the borders of the Reich. But there were no sane men left in power in Germany. Murphy had witnessed the eerie torchlight processions down Wilhelmstrasse, the book burnings, the ritual bonfires beneath the banners of the broken cross. "They have all gone mad I'm afraid, Theo," Murphy said gently.

Theo turned his gaze on Murphy and smiled as though he knew a secret that he would not tell. "Not all. Not everyone has gone mad. Some have gone to Switzerland. Some to Paris. Some to Prague. And some to Dachau." He waved his arm back and forth until the metal bracelet spun around his wrist. Then the smile faded, and he searched Murphy's face. "And some truly courageous men remain behind. They live and breathe and hope and pray in the valley of this terrible shadow of death. You must believe that those men exist, Murphy. Somehow the English and the French and . . . those outside must believe those men exist. That they will act if only . . . "

Murphy bit his lip. "Theo," he asked, "you know what has happened in Austria? You know what happened last night? The Germans crossed the frontiers. Took the country. There was no one within to protest. And hardly a word of protest from the rest of the world. Where are these men you are talking about? these courageous Germans who will stand up to Hitler? Who are they? What are they waiting for?"

Theo did not answer. He looked even older and more tired, as if Murphy's questions smashed a hope that he had clung to through a year of hell. He simply shook his head from side to side in reply.

"Can it be? Is everyone gone from my country? Have they all run away or been murdered or . . . have they come to believe the words of the madman?" Tears brimmed in his eyes as he grasped Murphy's hand tightly. "I heard the thousands of voices over the radio when he spoke at the Sportpalast. Sometimes the guards put the broadcast through the speakers. And the people cheered Hitler. How they cheered when he said it! I could not believe my ears! Julius and I wept when we heard him say it!" Tears ran down Theo's cheeks now.

"When he said what?" Murphy wished they had not spoken of such things. He grimaced at the sight of Theo's agony and looked down at his hands.

"The voice of Hitler," Theo continued in a faraway voice. "From the loudspeakers on the high walls and guard towers. It filled the camp. We stood shivering in the yard. From the cold. From the guns. The dogs. The electric wire. And then he said it: 'We want no God but Germany itself! No God but Germany! No God!' And the voices of thousands cheered his words. How they cheered! And beyond the walls of our prison the night was so dark. So very dark." He began to shake his head again more slowly as he quietly relived that night. "No God? Germany? The German race before God? That night we heard the voice of Judas a million times over calling for the crucifixion. And it was dark. *Judas,* his back framed in the doorway as he left the table. I saw it there before my eyes, Murphy! I saw Judas walk out into the darkness."

A chill coursed through Murphy at Theo's words. He could not think of anything to say. He sat, blinking back at a man who had watched as Evil entered the heart of his country. Finally Murphy shrugged. "I . . . didn't hear . . . that speech. Must've been in Spain." He shuddered. Spain was bad enough.

From the doorway behind them Elisa's voice called gently to her father. "Papa?" Murphy knew at once that she had heard Theo. She stepped into the room. "Papa—" She swallowed hard and groped for words. She leaned heavily on the chest of drawers, and even in the dim light, Murphy could see that her hands were shaking. Theo's memory was now her own. "There are still men left . . . *good* men!" Her voice was trembling.

"Elisa," Theo began hoarsely. "Child—"

"You can't stop believing, Papa! I know they are there! Thomas told me!" The words came in a rush now. It didn't matter that Murphy was in the room. She seemed not to notice.

"Thomas?" Theo's voice was filled with amazement. "You have seen him?"

"Yes. In the Tyrol. And at my flat in Vienna!" She knelt beside the bed. "He is a good man, Papa, just like we always knew he was!"

Suddenly Murphy was no longer thinking about Germany. The memory of Elisa in the arms of Thomas von Kleistmann was fresh and painful. She had written about this Thomas guy in her note to Murphy. It was plain now that she still loved him. Murphy watched her face as she talked about him to Theo.

"He loved you like his own father," she said. "And he is still your son and the son of Germany."

Murphy stood and walked out of the room unnoticed. He had heard enough. Always it seemed, Thomas von Kleistmann stood between them. *And why not?* Murphy thought. Von Kleistmann had more claim on Elisa than he did.

Wilhelm and Dieter, Elisa's brothers, milled around the parlor. They eyed Murphy with curiosity. Or maybe it was suspicion. At any rate, Murphy concluded, they were probably hungry. Fresh sesame kolaches were heaped on a plate in the center of the dining room table. A platter of eggs and one of sausages flanked it. Anna carried a pot of steaming coffee from the kitchen.

"He is doing well." She beamed. "Don't you think, Murphy? Elisa said you prefer to be called Murphy instead of John. Very American-sounding, if you ask me. Are you hungry?"

Murphy was not hungry any longer. "This looks great. Like something my mother would fix." He noticed two envelopes addressed to Leah and to the maestro at the Musikverein. They were beside his plate. "But the truth is—" he pocketed the notes—"I have to get to London. I . . . " He tried not to look at the disappointment in Anna's eyes. "I can't stay. We're going to broadcast live . . . about the Anschluss, and I . . . can't stay."

"But . . . but, John . . . Murphy!"

"I am sorry. I'll make it up to you another time, but I can't stay. Mind if I take a few of these rolls along with me, though?" He tried to sound casual. The truth was, he simply wanted to leave before Elisa walked into the room. There was the front door. There was nothing to stop him from bolting out right now.

"Rolls? Why, yes. As many as you like. But can't you . . . ?"

Murphy stuffed four kolaches in his pockets, then turned toward Wilhelm, who was eyeing him with open hostility. "Wilhelm? Do you drive?" Murphy tossed him the keys to the car. "Can you take me to the airport? I hate good-byes. Hate to see your sister cry." Murphy gave Anna a quick hug. Wilhelm was beaming now. "Tell Elisa to take good care of the car until I get back, will you?"

6

Call to Vienna

Members of the German consulate in Paris were still dressed in the clothes they had put on the day before—neckties askew, coats and trousers rumpled, and faces unshaved. Throughout the long night of the Austrian Anschluss, they had been harangued with frantic phone calls from Berlin.

"What is the French response to our action? Have they given indication that they will mobilize? What word do you hear from them? Do they intend to carry out their pledge to protect Austria?"

Now, in the cold light of morning, it seemed that the only men in Paris who had gone without sleep were the Germans within these walls. From the beginning of the crisis, the French government had remained silent. No doubt Premier Daladier had gone to bed at his usual time with the thought that he would read all about the fall of Austria in the morning newspapers and later in the briefs on his desk.

The top three buttons of Thomas von Kleistmann's tunic were unbuttoned. He had dozed in his chair occasionally through the night, and now his neck was stiff. He ran a hand over his swarthy, unshaven cheek. His beard felt like sandpaper. His eyes were gritty and burning from the chain-smoking of anxious men who had little else to do.

Ashtrays on the polished tables were overflowing. A blue haze swirled in the air as the first light of morning streamed through the windows. Half-consumed glasses of schnapps and cups of cold coffee were scattered everywhere, leaving rings on the tabletops and spots on the carpets around the sofa and overstuffed chairs in the staff room. Now everyone but Thomas von Kleistmann and Ernst vom Rath had drifted off to their quarters.

Thomas looked out at the wet, shining cobbles on the street outside the embassy. No French troops had clattered by to save the Austrians. No angry Frenchmen stood outside the gates to protest the German action. Nothing had changed. No one cared at all except possibly the Austrians themselves.

With a sigh, he turned away from the window. Across the room, Ernst vom Rath sat slumped in a large easy chair. His naturally pale skin seemed almost transparent with exhaustion. He was watching Thomas with obvious despair. No doubt their thoughts were drifting along the same dark channels. They had both risked much to warn the English and the French of the approaching takeover in Austria. Living in the midst of ardent Nazis, they had chosen to follow their loyalties to a higher morality.

And this is where their conscience had brought them. What good had their efforts been? Hitler had proven himself to be an absolute genius. Had he not fulfilled his promise to unite Austria with Germany? And not one drop of German blood had been shed! Just as he had told his fearful generals: "Britain and France are spineless! They will not raise a finger to stop us!" Now the Little Corporal would be raised publicly to the level of deity!

Thomas held Ernst's gaze. *What use has it been, these risks of ours? What use for the generals to tell Hitler he will plunge us into a war? He has proved them wrong. Maybe we are wrong also. We are so small. So insignificant! What use was it, Ernst?* Although the words were unspoken, they passed clearly between the two men.

Ernst shrugged helplessly. "A quite night in Paris all the same." He glanced at his watch. "There will be a parade in Vienna today, I suppose." He seemed to have no energy to move from the chair. "That girl you are in love with. She is in Vienna, isn't she?"

Thomas looked away toward the staircase and the foyer beyond. "Yes. Yes," he replied in a dispirited voice. He had thought of little else but Elisa throughout the long hours of waiting. It was for her sake alone that he was relieved that the Anschluss had taken place without a battle. But what would surely come to Vienna now with the Nazi government would be more violent than any resistance the Austrians might have shown. He had seen the plans drawn up for Plan Otto. No doubt the waves of anti-Semitic violence had already begun there.

"Bring her here," Ernst said, reading the fears of Thomas.

"I tried. She would not come." He stared hard at the drops of water that dripped from the eaves of the building. "Perhaps now she will." His tone held no hope. If she were seen with Thomas, the Gestapo would certainly recognize her as Elisa Lindheim, half Jewess. It had been noted by them in Berlin that Thomas was seen with her often. Paris was not the answer for their safety. He had realized that months before. Had it not been for his small part in the plan of the General Staff to stop Hitler, he would have taken her away from Europe, but . . . "She would not come with me," he said again. He did not say that she was no longer in love with him. He could scarcely make himself believe that, anyway. He still had hope that he could, with time, heal the hurt that had separated them.

"You had better make her come, Thomas." Ernst seemed grateful for the diversion onto the subject of women. "You'd better go get her. If she is as beautiful as you say, you know who will want her. Vienna will be filled with officers of the Wehrmacht. And those arrogant Schutzstaffel fellows—" he lowered his voice—"some women are actually attracted to those SS types, you know."

"Not her." Thomas imagined the hordes of German soldiers who even now swarmed the city of Vienna. "She is a musician. Sensitive and delicate."

Ernst laughed for the first time in two days as he looked at Thomas—the heavy shadow of his beard, the broad, muscular shoulders. His thick black hair hung down over his forehead. "You can't tell me she likes sensitive types. You are more a prizefighter than a poet, Thomas. How did she ever fall in love with the likes of you?"

Ernst was joking, but Thomas did not laugh or reply. The crisp *click* of the ambassador's shoes sounded on the stairs. He had showered and changed and now looked as though he alone in the embassy had enjoyed a night of restful sleep. He simply nodded at Thomas as he passed the broad double doors of the room on his way to his office.

The telephone on Ernst's desk rang, and he was forced to get up and walk unsteadily into the foyer to answer it.

The noise of the awakening world was jarring to Thomas. He leaned his head against the windowpane and tried to make out Ernst's words as they drifted in from his station.

"One moment, Admiral. Yes, he is right here." Ernst walked back into the staff room. "Thomas! It is Admiral Canaris! He has just arrived in Vienna and wants a word with you!"

It was natural that the chief of military intelligence would arrive in Vienna with the rest of the German bureaucracy, yet still, a phone call from Canaris in Vienna was somehow upsetting to Thomas. He wished that every German officer had simply stood up to the Little Corporal and refused to enter Austria. The presence of Canaris in Vienna was the final confirmation that the Anschluss had been accomplished. It seemed to Thomas like a personal defeat.

"Yes, Herr Admiral." He attempted to sound alert.

"You are needed here, von Kleistmann." Canaris did not attempt to conceal his weariness. "Himmler and his Gestapo are already hard at work on the civilian population. The least we in military intelligence can do is take over the Austrian military files before they do it for us."

His frankness stunned Thomas. He looked over his shoulder to see if there was anyone near enough to overhear such a conversation. Of course, it was no secret that Canaris, as head of the Abwehr, hated Himmler and his Gestapo goons. "Yes, Herr Admiral," Thomas responded.

"Tomorrow morning, the first plane to Vienna!" Canaris snapped impatiently. "Be on it." He slammed down the receiver without waiting for a reply.

Thomas hurried to his quarters to shower and change; strangely, his depression and exhaustion had vanished. It seemed a miracle to him that he was called to Vienna. He did not think about the conquered nation any longer, or the chaos of the city. His only thoughts were directed toward Elisa, toward the little flat around the corner from the Musikverein!

Murphy had already been gone an hour before Elisa emerged from her father's room. A true mercenary, he had played his part and then vanished, leaving Elisa to act out the charade alone before her parents.

"Wilhelm drove him to the airfield." Anna shrugged uneasily. "He said he did not want to see you cry." It was Anna who looked as though she might weep at the obvious disappointment in Elisa's eyes.

Elisa's bright smile faltered, only to be instantly replaced by artificial unconcern. "That Murphy!" She did not look her mother in the eye. She did not want Anna to see the hurt that cut through her like a knife. "He is always running off to cover some story, and I have never cried yet," she lied. She turned away and began to rummage through the cupboard. "Papa said—" she spoke haltingly in a preoccupied tone—"he said he would like a cup of tea." She stood staring at the cups.

Anna put a hand on her daughter's shoulder, then reached around her and plucked a cup and saucer from the shelf. "Those Americans," she said angrily. "Just like they seem to be in the moving pictures! No idea of family or—"

Elisa turned defensively. "But he's *not,* Mother! He is . . . from the first he has been . . . " Tears welled up in her eyes. Why was she defending John Murphy, of all people? She bit her lip. So here it was, in spite of herself, in spite of his obvious disdain for her, she loved him and now Anna would know!

Anna looked stricken. Their first perfect morning of reunion was marred. She put out her arms to Elisa. "Of course he is wonderful, darling." Anna hugged Elisa tightly. "He brought you safely out of Austria. And he brought your father safely home to us!" Her sympathetic voice made Elisa cry even harder. "He must be very wonderful for you to love him so much, Elisa. You have not cried like this since Thomas—" Anna stroked Elisa's hair gently.

"Oh, Mama!" Elisa said softly through her tears. There was so much she ached to say, but she could not. She could not bear the thought of disappointment in Anna's eyes. *I gave myself to Thomas and he left me anyway. I don't know if I ever really loved him. But I let him use me. In the end I lost him. And now I have lost Murphy. Lost his respect. The adoration that was in his eyes. I told him about it, Mama, and now he's gone too.*

Anna took her by the shoulders. "Wilhelm brought his car back!" she said excitedly. "You know how men are—"

No, Elisa wanted to say, *I don't!*

Anna wiped the tears from Elisa's face with the hem of her apron. "Hurry, Elisa! You can drive to the airfield and buy a ticket to London, and . . . maybe his plane isn't even gone yet!" Anna was writing the scene as if she and Theo were the players. "If it were your father, that is exactly what I would do."

But it isn't Papa. And I'm not you. Murphy would roll his eyes and tell me to go home. "He said I couldn't go with him," she answered quietly, looking at the clock. *When did he say his plane was leaving?*

"Of course he said that." Anna guided Elisa out of the kitchen. "He realizes that you might want to be with your father, and—"

Oh, Mother, how can you know? It's all so crazy. So terrible and confusing. He is simply a paid escort.

The violin and a small scuffed leather suitcase sat together beside the bed. Anna retrieved them. A romantic to the end, she was vicariously living the romance of her daughter—even though no romance existed.

"You have time if you hurry, darling. He said he would be back in two weeks. We'll all be together then." Anna was grinning broadly.

Elisa was blindly going through the motions of accepting this unthinkable suggestion. She would spend an hour or so away and then come back with the sad news that Murphy's plane had taken off and there simply were no more seats available on any flight to London. A flurry of quick hugs followed. Then, feeling foolish but relieved to have a little time alone to think, Elisa drove away in Murphy's green Packard sedan.

"The plane to London?" asked the clerk behind the ticket counter distractedly. "It left a half hour ago, Fräulein."

Elisa put a hand to her forehead. Her disappointment was unreasonable, she told herself. She was not even sure why she had come to the airport. She had expected Murphy to be gone. She certainly had not taken her mother's suggestion seriously. And yet, here she was, near tears because John Murphy was already well on his way to London.

"Is there something else I can help you with?" The clerk squinted past her to the men and women in line.

She jerked her head up as the thought of Leah and Shimon hurled through her mind. "Yes! Vienna! Is there a plane to Vienna today?"

The clerk looked at her incredulously. "Vienna?" he snorted. "Look over there, Fräulein!" He pointed to a large group of people who sat disconsolately on the hard benches of the lobby. "They have just arrived *from* Vienna. The very last flight. No planes are going *to* Vienna! And no more are coming out for a while." Then he consulted a clipboard. "As a matter of fact, all flights to Germany have been canceled!"

Elisa blushed. Everyone within earshot was staring at her. Who in their right mind would want to go into Vienna today unless they were somehow associated with the Nazis? "I am a musician," she said in attempted explanation. "With the Vienna Philharmonic."

The clerk stared at her over the tops of his glasses. "Well, if you go back there, you'll be playing a new tune, I can tell you."

She turned away, feeling the scornful looks of the others who had overheard her.

"Himmel!" laughed the man in line behind her. "A million trying to get out of Austria, and this one wants to get in! To play a concert!"

Elisa sat behind the wheel of the Packard for what seemed like a long time. She cradled her violin in her arms and stared blankly at the dashboard. No doubt the trains would not be crossing the frontier in Austria either. She and Murphy had driven to Prague. Could she not simply drive back to Vienna? Now that her father was safe, why shouldn't she simply recross the border of Austria as she had done in Germany a dozen times in the last few weeks? Could there possibly be any more danger in the act of returning to her apartment than she had already experienced smuggling passports and children out of Germany?

The answer seemed suddenly simple. Anna had given her the excuse she had needed. They would believe that she had gone to London with Murphy. Vienna was only a few hours' drive from Prague.

She started the car and headed back the way she and Murphy had come only the night before.

7

Captivity

Already hundreds had been arrested and taken away from the Judenplatz. Why they were taken and not others was a complete mystery. Papers were checked, names compared against a list, and those whose names were on the list were loaded onto the troop lorries and driven away. No one had been allowed out of the area unless he or she could somehow prove to be of Aryan racial heritage, rather than Jewish.

Leah's legs ached from hours of standing. Those detained in the square had not been provided with drinking water. Younger children began to cry from thirst or hunger. But there was no worse torture than being denied access to toilets for so long. The Nazis had gleefully made themselves tormentors in this small way. They seemed delighted when someone asked to use a restroom. Permission was always denied, and the target of their amusement was made to stand apart from the group until at last, after hours of agony, he soiled himself. Then the mocking began. "Dirty Jew! Filthy, stinking animal!"

Again and again this was repeated. *But,* Leah thought, *it is the Nazis themselves who are the animals.* There was something inhuman about the way they denied such a basic need. The men and women they humiliated in this way were then taken under guard to the public restrooms where they were made to scrub the toilets with prayer shawls and holy objects taken from the synagogue.

A tall German SS colonel was in charge of all this. His black tunic was meticulous, his trousers pressed with a razor crease, his boots polished until they glistened in the morning sun. Mostly he was silent. His junior officers asked questions as the colonel listened; then with a jerk of his head he separated those who could stay in the Judenplatz for now from those who would be taken to the new Gestapo headquarters for further questioning.

Leah instantly recognized the colonel's second in command. Dressed in civilian clothes, he wore his swastika armband on the sleeve of a rough tweed coat. His hair was combed down over his forehead in the style that Hitler himself wore. Round, wire-rimmed glasses glinted in the sun.

"That couple there, Sporer—" The colonel pointed his baton at Shimon and Leah. He glanced at their clasped hands.

Sporer nodded and strode briskly toward them. The clipboard was tucked under his arm. His face was thin, and his mouth curved slightly up at the corner as though he enjoyed his work. He looked as he had in his photo in the paper after he had been arrested by Schuschnigg for the riots. This was the man who had pulled Elisa to the ground and had cheered as others had gathered in hopes of raping her. A chill coursed through Leah as Sporer ran his eyes over her, sizing her up like an animal for butchering.

Leah looked away from him and forced herself to stare directly into the face of the SS colonel. Blue eyes. Blond hair. The perfect picture of Hitler's handsome young Aryan god.

"Your names?" Sporer asked in a bored voice.

"Shimon and Leah Feldstein." Shimon held out their identity cards.

Shimon's voice was strained, and Leah wondered if he, too, remembered the photograph of Sporer in the newspaper. Sporer had been one of the first Nazi terrorists released after Schuschnigg and Hitler had met in Berchtesgaden. *Men of such viciousness must be important to Hitler's Reich,* Leah thought. And now this man held their lives in his hands.

Sporer's cheek muscle twitched as he read over their documents. "Jewish musicians," he muttered to no one in particular. "There will be no purpose for you now that Austria is one with Germany, certainly. In the Reich it has been decreed that German music will be played by racially pure Germans." He continued to stare at the identity papers and then searched through the list of names attached to his clipboard.

"Musicians?" asked the colonel. There was a flicker of something human in the face of the officer. He almost smiled at Leah.

"Your politics?" demanded Sporer, letting the pages of the list fall back.

"We are simply musicians," Leah answered. "Must everyone in Vienna be political?"

Sporer raised his chin as if to challenge her. "You are a liar," he said triumphantly. "Both of you are Zionists."

"We plan to move to Palestine," Shimon began. "But we are not political activists."

"Again you lie! Your names are here!" Sporer's voice was loud enough that several in the group turned to see what was happening. "We have your names! Everyone knows that Zionists are Communists!" His eyes gleamed as though he had captured criminals. He turned to the colonel. "Their names have been mentioned by two others whom we have interrogated."

"We have visas to Palestine," Shimon argued.

"And so have ten thousand others!" Sporer snapped. "Along with illegal passports."

"Our papers are in order." Shimon's face showed a hint of fear for the first time.

"There is a new government in Austria that will decide if your papers are indeed in order." Sporer obviously took pleasure in the power he held over the Jews of the Judenplatz.

The colonel listened to the conversation with curiosity. Leah did not turn her eyes away from him. "So you are Zionists," the colonel said at last. "With papers to Palestine." He seemed amused. "Are you aware that the Arabs who riot in Jerusalem daily are more rabid anti-Semites than you will find anywhere?" He tapped his riding crop against his leg. "You are musicians. For whom will you play in Palestine? I hear of no great orchestras being formed in the desert."

He seemed to speak with genuine interest, and Leah answered him politely. "Yes, there is an orchestra there. Just begun in 1936."

"No doubt formed by outcast Jews from Germany," Sporer replied haughtily.

The colonel addressed him. "No doubt that is so." He smiled slightly. "I have always regretted that we have banished such talent from the German concert halls. We have banned Jews from performing while we flock to see performing bears and monkeys."

"At least bears and monkeys do not pretend to be human as the Jews do, Herr Standartenführer. And if there were bears who could play instruments, they would not be allowed to sit with the Aryan musicians on the stage."

"Perhaps, Sporer," the colonel replied, amused by the discussion. "Unless the bears were needed to fill a vacant place." He nodded toward Leah; then he addressed them. "I have always had the highest regard for talent. Even that found in performing bears." He enjoyed his own joke. "Even talented Jews must have some place in the world." He spoke to Leah. "I recognized you at once, Frau Feldstein. Twice last year I heard you perform here in Vienna, and once before in Salzburg."

Leah felt a wave of relief. This was a man who appreciated good music and musicians. Perhaps there was hope. "My performance was satisfactory?" She tried not to think of the fact that they had just been compared to performing animals.

"Quite so." The colonel tugged on his gloves. "Dvorák 104 in B Minor, I believe. Quite nice. And then Bloch's *Hebraic Rhapsody.* Of course, such music will not be played any longer in Vienna since it is written by a Jew."

"A tragedy," Shimon said softly.

The eyes of the colonel flashed resentment at Shimon's remark. "Perhaps the orchestra in Palestine will play it? We really have no need of it here, do we? With so many fine German composers. A pity, yes. The pieces are amusing examples of the cleverness of Jews. But not a tragedy."

Shimon was sorry now that he had spoken. The humanness of the colonel seemed to evaporate in his defense of German policy. "Yes. German composers are . . . of course . . . " He fell silent under the withering glare of the colonel. He wanted to shout his argument that good music was unaware of the heritage of the musician, but he dared not attempt to reason with this racial madness.

"You are a musician also?" the colonel asked Shimon. "I do not remember you in the orchestra."

"I am a percussionist," Shimon explained.

"No real talent in beating drums." The colonel rose slightly on his toes as he pronounced his judgment. "Even bears and monkeys could do as much, *ja,* Sporer?"

Sporer laughed loudly in reply. "This one is more the size of a bear, I think." He sneered at Shimon. Then, in an unexpected movement, the colonel swung back his riding crop and whipped it forward hard between Shimon's legs. With a cry of agony, Shimon dropped to the ground. Leah screamed and flung herself between Shimon and the brutal men who threatened to strike him again.

"You see, Sporer—" the colonel grinned—"even a bear may be controlled and brought to his knees with a well-placed blow."

Shimon was doubled over in pain. He gasped, unable to speak.

"*You* are animals!" Leah shouted. "Go away! Leave us alone!"

"The mate of the bear is upset." Sporer moved as if he might strike Leah.

The colonel put out his hand to stop him. "Wait," he said, still smiling. "The Führer has expressed that the culture of Vienna continue as it has been. For the time being, even Jews will remain in the orchestras. At least until artists of Aryan blood may be found to replace them."

Leah stroked Shimon's head gently, trying to comfort him. She did not hear the words of the colonel. "My darling," she said softly. "Poor darling."

The colonel nudged her with his boot. "Get up," he demanded.

Leah's face was streaked with tears of rage. She had seen enough this morning of the arrogant superiority of the Aryan race. She would not answer to it again.

"He says, 'Get up!' " Sporer grabbed her by the arm and pulled her away from Shimon.

"Why have you done this?" She glared at their tormentors. "Why?"

Cool and totally oblivious to her emotion, the colonel raised an eyebrow slightly. The scene entertained him. "You have a concert this afternoon at the Musikverein, do you not?" he asked.

"There is no music left in Vienna on this black day!"

He slapped her hard across the mouth. "You will be silent, Jewish bitch! And then you will hear the will of the Greater Reich for Vienna!" There was nothing human left in the colonel's expression now. He believed all that he had been told. He was the master race. He was of pure blood, and Leah was subhuman, who was worth nothing beyond the amusement she might provide for the German officers who had arrived by the thousands in Vienna.

Leah did not look at him anymore. Her eyes remained on Shimon and the cobblestones of the Judenplatz. She remembered Rudy. The severed fingers of poor Rudy. She was silent.

The colonel continued, satisfied that he had won the insane and pointless argument. "There is a concert today at the Musikverein, Frau Feldstein. Good German music for the men and officers of the Wehrmacht. It is a chamber piece, if I remember correctly. There is no need for this *bear* to beat his drums." He nudged Shimon, who still fought for breath. "But *you*—" he narrowed his eyes at Leah—"you are the principal cellist, are you not? Most certainly until a comparable German cellist is brought in to take your place, you will be needed at the Musikverein to perform."

Leah shuddered. They intended to make her perform while Shimon was left here as a hostage! Like an animal she must entertain the master race on command. "Shimon must come with me." She raised her chin defiantly.

"If he goes with you, how do we know you will return?" The colonel's voice was patronizing, as if he were speaking to a five-year-old child. "No, I think not. The music you play today does not call for tympani."

"Please let us go." Tears filled her eyes again. Surely there must be some fragment of mercy in this man. "We have papers for Palestine."

"We have not seen these papers," the colonel said sympathetically. "How are we to know?"

"They are in our apartment!" Leah replied. "Please—"

"*Where* in your apartment?" The colonel cocked his head slightly.

"In my husband's desk. You will see. We have sent our personal things to Palestine already."

The colonel snapped his fingers at Sporer. "Go get the documents," he commanded gruffly. "These Jews have violated Reich law. They have sent belongings out of the country without permission of the office of—"

"But—" Leah could hardly find her voice at the horror of this accusation. "But we sent out things weeks ago . . . from Austria, not from Germany!"

"Austria *is* Germany!" the colonel shouted. "And now, it is the will of Germany that bears and monkeys and even Jews perform on command! Your husband remains here in our expert care until your illegal activities are investigated! And of course, you must play today. You must play joyfully to welcome the union of Germany and Austria!"

Bill Skies, Timmons, Johnson, and a half dozen more correspondents were being held as virtual prisoners in the International News Service offices not far from the Rothschild Palace. They were Americans, French, and British, and not in any real danger, but they had watched as four of the Austrian journalists were taken away at gunpoint by the Gestapo for "questioning about ideological irregularities" in their support of an independent Austria.

Bill Skies would lodge a formal protest when the heat was off a little, but for now, the heat was on everywhere. A game of hearts was started over an empty desk. Three members of the SS and two Storm Troopers watched with interest. Timmons shared cigarettes with their jailers, and the atmosphere became almost friendly.

"Why is it you Amerikanischers are so hostile toward the National Socialist Movement?" a young, hard-muscled SS soldier asked as he leaned in to study Johnson's cards.

Johnson pressed his cards against his chest and snapped, "Because you are all a bunch of snoops!"

The SS man blinked in confusion of the term. His comrades rattled off several German attempts to explain Johnson's comment. They all fell flat. "What is *schnoops*?" asked the SS man.

"You tell this cracker what a snoop is, Timmons," Johnson was angry at Timmons now. "After all, you gave them half a pack of the Lucky Strikes."

"Just tryin' to relieve a little tension." Timmons spread his hands in innocence.

Johnson yelled back, "You wanna relieve yourself, go to the toilet! Don't invite the SS to play cards with us!" Then he turned to the young soldier. His eyes were popping with rage and the veins in his neck stood out. "Snoops! I'll get you *snoops*! You're a bunch of Peeping Toms."

"Peeping?" The soldier stood and stepped back. He had the power to arrest this American as well, and he would—if he could figure out what he was talking about. Another soldier shrugged.

"Yeah! Looking into people's private lives! Over their shoulders at their cards!" He threw his cards into the air and they fluttered down onto the floor. "You arrest people for *thinking!* You're crackers! You and that boss of yours!"

The soldier drew himself up very straight, and arrogant superiority descended on his boyishly handsome features. "Herr Johnson!" He screamed his reply. "I must ask you to cease such madness and ravings! If you one word utter about the Reich which is not favorable, I will arrest you for subversion as well!"

Johnson didn't care at this point. He glared at Timmons. "You see what kind of scum you gave your Lucky Strikes to? They won't even let me say what a whimpering fairy that maniac they call the Führer is!"

Bill Skies coughed loudly, as if he were choking on his cigar. "You're drunk, Johnson. Shut up! He's drunk." Skies grimaced in horror at the SS men, who were pulling out their pistols.

"I ain't drunk enough!" Johnson was still shouting. Then, an angelic smile passed across his face. "Just listen to this, you pig-faced Aryan albino! You want to hear what I think about you and your Hitler in German? *Ja*? In Deutsch, *ja*!" Johnson then let loose with a stream of scathing epithets that needed no translation in any language.

Jaws dropped. Eyes turned to steely rage. The Amerikanischer Journalistin had explained without a shadow of a doubt what he thought of Adolf Hitler, the SS, the Storm Troopers, the Gestapo, and by the way, the meaning of the word *schnoop.*

It would take more now than a few packs of Lucky Strike cigarettes to get Johnson out of the Gestapo clinker, but for the moment he felt a whole lot better.

Walter slipped what little money he had left into the envelope along with photographs of the boys for the passports. As a German citizen, Walter had been forced to register with the Austrian Immigration Office. He had been a refugee from Nazi Germany then. Now Austria was Nazi

Germany. It was only a matter of time until the name and address of Walter Kronenberger appeared on a list.

He tucked the envelope into the pocket of Charles' jacket, then changed his mind and slipped it down into the boy's knee-high stocking. "You must guard this very carefully, Charles." He took him by the shoulders. "It is very important that you do not lose the envelope. Inside is a little money. Do you understand?"

Charles nodded, his towhead bobbing in the scarf that covered his mouth.

Walter turned to Louis with the same serious expression. "And do you remember where you are going?"

"But, Father," Louis protested, "you are taking us. Must I remember?"

"In case we are separated, Louis," he explained gently for the third time, "you must know. Tell me the name, Louis. What place will you ask for if we are separated in the crowd?"

Louis stuck his lower lip out slightly. He did not like the thought of losing his father in a crowd. "But—"

Walter gave him a little shake as if to jar the word loose. "Say it!" Even this slight show of sternness brought tears to the eyes of Louis. Walter could not bear it. He hugged the boy close and stroked his hair. "You must be very brave, Louis. Both of you, Charles. Today you must be little men for me, or my heart will break!" He squeezed his eyes shut.

"Musikverein," Louis mumbled.

"There's a good fellow!" Walter patted him on the back. "And who have you come to see?"

"My aunt. *Our* aunt. Only she is not our aunt really."

"But you mustn't say that. You cannot say that she is not your aunt, Louis. Do you understand?"

The boy nodded. "Yes."

"What is the name of your aunt?"

The boy thought for a long moment. "Leah."

"And how will you remember her name?"

"Because it sounds like Louis. Like my name."

Charles clapped his hands in approval. He had memorized it all along with Louis, even though he could not express it. There was no last name to remember. The name *Leah* had been whispered to Walter months before, the night they escaped from Germany. He had hoped that he would never be required to use the information.

Walter stood up and surveyed his sons. They were dressed as he was, in leather shorts and green wool Jäger's jackets that matched down to the stag-horn buttons. They looked the part of Tyrolean peasants who had come to see the great show of the German war machine. Walter could only hope and pray that they would not be stopped for a document check. His papers clearly bore the name of Walter Kronenberger, and that name was known as the enemy of the Reich.

"There is a concert today at the Musikverein." He looked to Charles now, who seemed somehow better able to grasp the situation. "There is always a concert on Sunday. If we are . . . separated, you must be certain that you get there. Go to the back door. There is an old man who guards the door. Louis must tell him who you wish to see."

"But what if she is not there?" Louis was trembling at the thought of being lost.

"The man who stands at the door will know where to find her." He handed each boy a bundle tied in a scarf. "Cheese and bread to eat while you wait." He tried to smile. "Like a picnic."

"Will you eat with us?" Louis eyed the bundle. He could not smile. His father was leaving. Maybe forever, like their mother had left them.

Walter did not reply. He tucked the small suitcase under his arm and opened the door and walked out into the dark hallway. Charles looked back at the bed, then up at the water-stained ceiling high above his little head. He was memorizing, Walter knew. He noticed everything. If Louis forgot this moment, Charles would remember for both of them. His young eyes were filled with the sorrow of understanding that was far beyond his years. He followed his father into the hall, then motioned to Louis that it was time to leave the safety of the room that had been their home.

8

The Refugees

The walls of the Tower of London glistened in the bright afternoon sunlight. Like a tour guide, the cockney taxi driver rattled off the list of hapless Englishmen and women who had been executed there over the years. Somehow Murphy found the grim recitation a pleasant distraction.

"Look at 'enry the Eighth—" The cabbie shoved his cap back on his balding pate and gestured toward the tower. "Why, I says to meself when poor King Edward resigned the throne for Mrs. Simpson, why not leave the poor bloke alone! Didn't 'enry the Eighth marry six times? An' most of 'is wives ended up right there in that tower gettin' their 'eads looped off! An' then ol' 'enry's daughters! The Tudor sisters—"

"Queen Mary and Queen Elizabeth?" Murphy was enjoying this strange application of history to current politics.

"Right, gov! Bloody Mary, we call 'er now! Just like 'er father, she was. Bumped off the Protestant clergy that support 'er father. Even 'ad little Elizabeth tossed into that very tower there! Then when Elizabeth's turn came to rule, quite a bit of blood was shed as well! Rulers are always going t' bump off the opposition, I say. 'Istory is proof of that! So what's all the grief over this 'itler chap, anyway, I ask? An' why should an Englishman give a rip what 'appens in Austria? Never been there meself, an' I never intend t' go either!"

Murphy did not reply. He turned his head to stare back at the tower. Indeed, England had come a long way since Henry the Eighth and Bloody Mary. Now, rather than executing the loyal opposition, the government made them political outcasts. No doubt, Winston Churchill would have been axed if he had lived a few centuries earlier. Now, he was simply shoved onto a back burner. At the present, most of England held the same opinion as this cabdriver: "What's all the grief over this Hitler chap?"

"You know the song, gov?" The cabbie grinned over his shoulder, then burst into song. "There'll always be an England. . . ."

Murphy smiled politely. He was too tired to argue. His head was throbbing by the time the cab pulled to the curb in front of the INS offices on Fleet Street. He counted out the fare from Heathrow Airfield, then held it for a moment when the driver extended his hand expectantly. Maybe it was worth a word to explain to this self-styled philosopher just what was happening in Europe. Maybe he would pass the information along.

"I just came from Austria." Murphy held the money just out of reach. He had a captive audience. "Believe me, Hitler and the Nazis make Bloody Mary look like Snow White."

"An' what's that to do with us?" The cabbie was indignant. "Even Napoleon didn't cross the Channel, gov! An' remember the Armada of Spain? Wrecked on the coast, they did!"

"Napoleon and Spain didn't have airplanes. Something to think about." Murphy laid the cash in the man's palm and stepped out. "Just now I crossed the Channel in less time than it took this cab to drive me here. The Nazis have planes. England has pacifists." Murphy smiled at the stunned face of the cabdriver. The man had no further comment.

Murphy stepped onto the curb and wearily ran a hand across his forehead. Tonight he would simply report what he had seen to the whole world, and then maybe men like the cabdriver would understand what all the grief was about.

Horns blared, and buses and automobiles rumbled past him. So many people, most of whom believed that England was beyond the threat of Austria's tragedy!

Murphy shook his head as if to clear his mind. He looked up at the towering buildings that housed the finest newspaper in the world. What would it take to convince them? A German bomb smashing into the editorial offices of the London *Times*?

"Murphy!" The impatient voice of Larry Strickland called to him from the door of the office. Strickland looked harried, as though he had not slept at all. His sleeves were rolled up, and his sparse crop of gray hair stood up in wisps on his head. He followed Murphy's upward gaze with curiosity. "What are you looking at up there? The sky is clear. No rain. Get in here, you idiot! We got work to do!"

Walter held tightly to the hands of his sons as he guided them through the teeming throngs who had gathered on the Heldenplatz to welcome the Führer. He guessed that there were at least two hundred thousand people jammed into the square. The huge equestrian statues now carried extra riders on their backs as dozens of men and boys clambered upward to get a better view of the scene. This crowd was not only friendly toward the Reich invaders, they were ecstatic. But then, Walter had seen such receptions in Germany. He was well aware that Goebbels, as minister of propaganda, was in charge of providing enthusiastic crowds to shriek their approval of Hitler.

But the photographers who snapped pictures of this final desecration could not record the strong German accents of the cheering crowds. Nor could they capture the frightened faces of the millions of Austrians who stayed indoors today. It was Walter's understanding of these Nazi charades that made him doubly dangerous to the new regime.

His understanding of other, more sinister policies had cost him his homeland; now he was certain it would ultimately cost him his life. His editorials had shouted indignantly against the increasing practice of forced sterilization. Those who were judged by Reich standards as less than perfect, either mentally or physically, were eliminated. Certain members of the church had joined in his outcry, and they too had been imprisoned.

Walter glanced up at the church steeples, where welcoming bells now clanged the arrival of Hitler. Swastika flags were unfurled from the uppermost windows. Cardinal Innitzer, the Catholic primate of Austria, had gone out with a message of greeting to meet the approaching Führer, and now the church bells chimed again and again as the procession moved from Schönbrunn Palace toward the Imperial Hotel!

Walter would find no refuge within the church for himself or his sons. A pattern of moral betrayal had already been established by the cardinal, and those among the clergy who resisted would certainly find themselves behind barbed wire before the month was out. Walter wanted to shake his fist at the clanging bells. They were the tolling of death—not just for Jews but also for little ones like Charles who could not meet the insane racial standard.

This morning Walter had listened to the text of the cardinal's message:

> *"German thoughts and German feelings have never lacked in Austria. Austria's Catholics will become the truest sons of the great Reich, into*

whose arms they have been brought back on this momentous day! Provided that the liberties of the church are guaranteed."

It was a pact with Satan. Hitler was delighted with such patriotic words. He shook the cardinal's hand warmly and promised.

Among the sea of hats, Wehrmacht uniforms, and black SS tunics, the prying eyes of the Gestapo were everywhere. Walter's own eyes were never still as the trio inched their way through the crush. He was searching for the presence he had felt over the last few weeks in Vienna. He had sensed that he was being watched—not that he had ever seen more than a shadow following him back to the hotel. Most of the time he had been able to dismiss the experience as his own paranoia after his arrest in Germany. Now he was certain that the shadows had been more than his imagination. All his fragile illusions of safety had evaporated. He had gone to sleep as a refugee in Austria and when he had awakened, he was once again a fugitive from the Nazis.

The suitcase beneath his arm began to slip. As he stopped to adjust it and glanced upward to the base of a statue, he noticed that a Brownshirt—a man in a brown Storm Trooper's uniform—was looking directly at him. Perhaps the sudden, terrifying chill of *knowing* showed itself in Walter's face. Like a hunted animal, Walter had raised his nose to sniff the air and had caught sight of his pursuer. At the same second the hunter had smelled fear, and now he held Walter Kronenberger in his sights!

Walter looked wildly around for the quickest way of escape. He scanned back toward the man on the statue. The excitement of the hunt was on his face. He was climbing down carefully, so as not to lose his view of Walter.

"Father?" Louis tugged his sleeve. "Where are we?"

Walter bent down and handed the case to Charles. Then he said urgently to Louis, "Where are we going, Louis?"

"Don't you know, Father?" The child was puzzled.

"Yes. I know. But you *must* say it! Tell me, Son! Where are we going?"

The bells clanged insanely. Walter glanced up to see the Storm Trooper fighting his way toward them.

"To the Musikverein," Louis repeated, and Charles nodded in agreement.

"Good!" He embraced his sons. A last embrace. Too quick. Over too soon. The hunter had not seen the boys. "Remember, I love you!" he cried. "Now *go*!" With that, he turned his back on their startled, terrified expressions and began his own desperate struggle to escape through the mass of human flesh that held him back.

The little suitcase clattered to the ground. The crowd swallowed Walter and held back the Nazi who pursued him. "Father!" Louis cried loudly. "Father!"

Charles clasped Louis by the arm and placed a hand firmly over his brother's mouth. His eyes were full of grim understanding. They could not follow. They must not!

The two young boys stood only waist high to those around them. The world had become boots and dresses and crushed flowers on the cobbles beneath their feet.

"Halt!" shouted the soldier in pursuit of Walter. "Stop him! Stop that man!"

Louis stood paralyzed with fright. The color had left his cheeks. He could not remember the name he had spoken only a moment before. Only the word *Father!* shrieked in his consciousness now.

Charles stared at his brother in concern and then very deliberately picked up the suitcase and shoved it toward Louis. He needed help, the gesture seemed to say. He could not carry it alone.

"But where are we going?" Louis asked, tears streaming down his face. "Charles, where are we? Where is Father, *Charles*?"

Charles answered with an angry frown and a jerk of his head. Obediently, Louis grasped the handle of the case and helped Charles lug it toward an empty patch of grass beside a foundation. Then, with a nod, Charles indicated that they would pause here for a moment. He cupped his hand and scooped out some cool water. Hadn't Father told them to wash their faces after a good cry? Charles wiped the cool liquid on Louis' face and then splashed a handful across his own, careful not to dampen the scarf that concealed his mouth.

He stood on tiptoe and tried to see some glimpse of his father, but there was only a sea of adults. Civilians. Soldiers. Most with the armbands bearing the crooked cross that his father hated so fiercely.

The Czech farmland stretched out in a verdant carpet before Elisa. Cattle grazed peacefully, and the scent of newly turned earth and budding orchards was sweet in the air. On any other Sunday this would have been a day for a picnic and an afternoon of dozing in the gentle sunlight.

A long line of Czech army troop lorries lumbered slowly on the road ahead of Elisa. They, too, were headed toward the frontier separating Austria from Czechoslovakia. On the opposite side of the road, the land was crammed with the thousands of miserable refugees who somehow had made it through the Nazi blockades to cross the border. Men and women clung to their meager possessions as they staggered wearily toward the interior. Those who were more fortunate rode the running boards of automobiles that were already jammed to capacity with people and luggage. Horns blared, shattering the bucolic silence of the farmland. Faces were locked in grim expressions of dazed disbelief.

Elisa desperately attempted to search those thousands of faces for Leah. For Shimon. Perhaps they were among these lucky few who escaped the first wave of Nazi terror. *Please, God.*

She did not resent the slowness of the army vehicles. Time and again they stalled on the road before the oncoming flood of human misery. Dozens trekked past her. Then hundreds. Their haunted expressions became one familiar face to her, but Leah was not among them. Dear Leah. Sister. Friend. Why had she not come to the apartment last night? Then they would have all been together in Prague today, safe and free. *Please, God.*

Still some miles from the border, transport trucks and lorries began to peel off from the main highway onto twisting dirt roads. A dozen remained ahead of Elisa. The stream of refugees became thinner now. Just as there would be no more planes, no more trains, so there would be no more hapless refugees crossing the frontier on foot.

Frank, curious stares greeted Elisa at the checkpoint. The few border guards of last night had been reinforced by dozens of Czech soldiers, each of whom carried a rifle or a submachine gun. The wooden crossbar was now surrounded by a barricade of grisly barbed wire, and sharp metal tank traps protruded from the road beyond at hundred-yard intervals.

"Where did she come from?" demanded a officer in charge. "How did she get this far forward?"

"Just followed the convoy in, I suppose," sniffed a soldier uneasily.

The truckload of soldiers who had smiled and waved at her throughout the long journey now disembarked with cheerful cries of "Good luck!" and "Look me up after we beat the German army!" Winks and grins and friendly waves were countered by the stern disapproval of the officer who approached Elisa's window.

"What do you think you are doing here?" he asked indignantly.

"I . . . am trying to get back to Vienna." Elisa bluffed bravely. She acted oblivious to the turmoil around them.

"Impossible!" He jerked his head to where yet another roll of wire was being uncoiled across the pavement.

Elisa haughtily displayed her American passport. "My husband is in Vienna. I am to join him there."

The officer glanced at the seal on the passport. "Maybe yesterday you could have joined him. But you are too late!" he barked. "We are expecting an invasion of the German Wehrmacht. Haven't you heard? They have taken Austria. France and Britain may yet declare war." He sounded hopeful. "War! And beyond that barricade is the front line!"

Elisa followed his outstretched arm as he pointed toward rolling farmland and a few farmhouses. A tiny village glistened in the sunlight. The onion dome of a church was clearly visible on the Austrian side of the border.

She smiled, attempting to humor him. "Certainly Germany and Czechoslovakia can wait ten minutes until I cross the frontier."

He was not amused. "You will have to go back." He straightened up. His jaw was set, his eyes were angry at her foolishness. "You should not have gotten this far in the first place."

"What about all those people you let through?" She pointed toward a few stragglers that trailed by.

In answer, he handed her a pair of field glasses. "See for yourself." He shrugged and stepped aside for her to peer toward the Austrian checkpoints.

A lump rose in Elisa's throat. Her stomach churned at the sight of thousands of civilians milling on the far side of the barricade. Leah and Shimon might be among them. Bayonets gleamed on German rifles. The scene of last night's horror returned to her.

The officer took the glasses. "You see," he said. "Many thousands did not make it. These are a handful. And now you must turn around and go back. If your husband is American, he can leave Austria when he likes, no doubt. But you will not cross the frontier today!"

Did the officer see the weight of disappointment settle on Elisa's features? His voice softened with sympathy. "I am sorry. Perhaps it will not be long before everything is straightened out. We can hope, *ja*? But here are the facts before your own eyes."

The rumble of yet another troop lorry pressed in behind the Packard. Elisa could see the grill of the truck grinning hideously in her rearview mirror. The horn blared at her civilian vehicle. She nodded and eased her car out of the line and onto the side of the road. She was unable to help anyone, and the knowledge of that helplessness made her lower her head and weep for fear of what must be happening in her beloved Vienna. Once again she stood overlooking the white walls and barbed wire of a giant Dachau. "God!" she cried aloud. "Why are You silent?"

There was no answer. She had not expected one. A soft tapping sounded on her window, and she looked up to see the eager face of a young man peering in at her. She unrolled her window and wiped her tears.

"Are you all right, Fräulein?" the young man asked. His hat was pushed back on his head. His wife and three children stood in a small chorus behind him, peering at Elisa. They all looked haggard, exhausted, and hungry. "Have you come out of Austria?"

Elisa nodded, resenting the intrusion.

"So have we." He breathed a sigh of relief. "You have an automobile, Fräulein." He examined the length of the Packard. "Not much luggage." His wife was clutching her children hopefully. "Are you going somewhere?"

It did not seem to matter where. The little family wanted a ride. Any place was better than this place. The very sight of Austria terrorized them. Would she take them away? Prague? Yes, Prague was quite far away from the Nazis, far away from the shouted slogans and the upraised fists that had pursued them from their home. Prague would be safe.

9
Radio News

Like the clatter of a thousand sets of giant false teeth, the newsroom typewriters chewed up the Austrian story and spit it out onto the paper with a triumphant *clang* at the end of each line. The noise was deafening. Telephones and teletypes competed with shouting reporters in the racket. Correspondents from numerous countries sat hunched over their machines as they translated the British reaction to the Nazi takeover for their own newspapers.

No one even looked up as Murphy followed Strickland past the paper-littered desks and overflowing wastebaskets. Any other day Murphy would have been greeted by his bullpen cronies, but not today. The world had gone nuts and, as always, the lunacy seemed to be channeled onto the fifty desks of the INS newsroom. Not even the most dedicated chain-smoker dared to light a cigarette in the midst of such chaos. One tiny spark, and all of Fleet Street would go up in flames.

Strickland shouted over the din, "A couple guys made it out! Bill Jordan and his wife got out of Vienna on the last plane to Paris. He says you stole his Packard from him!"

"I bought it. It's in Prague!" Murphy laughed, relieved that the couple had made it out safely.

"Amanda Taylor flew in from Berlin a couple of hours ago! London *Times* is loaning her to us for the broadcast! What a broad!" Strickland meant the remark as a compliment to Amanda. She was, indeed, "one of the guys," which was quite an accomplishment for a woman.

Murphy was pleased at the thought of seeing the leggy brunette again. He had not been in touch with her since he had left Berlin the year before to cover the Spanish Civil War.

Amanda was, as the guys in the newsroom called her, "a gutsy dame, if ever there was one." She had quite a head on her shoulders, and everything from there down was arranged in a pretty terrific package as well. Amanda Taylor had never been timid about using her feminine attributes to get a story. Big brown eyes and an hourglass figure often accomplished the toughest assignment in thirty minutes, while the most skilled male foreign correspondent failed miserably. Her gender and good looks gave her an enormous advantage over the rest of the newsmen, but no one seemed to resent her. Amanda had always been generous. After she scooped them all, she never failed to share her information.

Murphy could see her now through the glass partition of Strickland's office. She was the center of attention among a half dozen newsmen in the tiny cubicle. At almost the same moment Murphy spotted her, she looked up and noticed him as well. Her lips parted in a broad smile of genuine relief. "Johnny Murphy!" she mouthed through the glass. The heads of the other reporters swiveled to look. Hands raised in greeting as Amanda flung open the glass door and shouted his name. "Johnny! You made it!" She gave him a quick hug, then wrinkled her nose. "Darling, you look simply dreadful!"

"Hi, Amanda." He smiled sheepishly. "You look great as usual. What I wouldn't give for a hot shower and a full night's sleep!" The only consolation was that, with the exception of Amanda, everyone else looked and smelled as bad as he did.

"Hi, Murph." Scat Freeman lifted his chin in acknowledgment.

"How ya doin', Murph?" Tom Phelps nodded grimly. "What's the word on Johnson and Timmons?"

Phelps had been a regular poker player in Murphy's room at the Adlon Hotel in Berlin. He had beaten young Timmons at the game so often that Timmons was usually broke. "Last I saw—" Murphy took an empty seat next to the window—"they were teaching a couple of Wehrmacht guys how to play five-card draw."

"The kid's okay, then?" Phelps was genuinely concerned.

"Timmons? I don't think they'll arrest him for winning."

"Good." Phelps cleared his throat. "He owes me money. Hope he beats the pants of those little . . . " He glanced toward Amanda and checked his flow of language.

"Nazis," Amanda finished for him.

"Yeah," added Scat. "Somebody's gonna have to beat them at their own game, or we're all in trouble."

Murphy glanced around the small room at the familiar faces of his comrades. There was not a man among them who had not spent time in Vienna with the news service. Their sense of outrage matched his own. "Now we can tell the world 'I told you so,' " Murphy said.

Amanda raised an eyebrow skeptically. "And they will say, 'So?' "

Strickland closed the door behind them, shutting out the clatter of typewriters. "Not if we play this right." He sat down behind his scarred desk and studied his notepad. "Bill Morrow is going to interview you clowns. CBS and the BBC are teaming up for this one. Provided the atmosphere and the sun spots don't foul up the transmission, we ought to crackle over the American airwaves about suppertime."

Strickland tapped his pencil on the notepad. "The idea is to make every man, woman, and child drop the fork and let the beans get cold when we start talking." He paused and let that goal sink in. "They're going to hear your experience firsthand. Out of your mouth to their ears. This has never been done before, and it's gotta be good." He looked over his glasses at Murphy. "Okay, Murph, what have you got to make America lose its appetite?"

Murphy closed his eyes and pressed his fingers on the bridge of his nose as he tried to capture the strongest impressions of yesterday's horrors. The vision that came to him was not that of Schuschnigg giving his final farewell to the Austrian people. It was not the Nazi flags unfurling from every public building or the armbands on the young students who manned the barricades. He sighed heavily and did not reply.

"Well?" Strickland asked impatiently.

The tragic melody of Elisa's farewell to Vienna played through Murphy's thoughts. Theo, broken and half frozen on the street, then jammed into the trunk of a car as he was forced to flee from yet another country. But he could not mention that in a broadcast that was to be heard on both sides of the Atlantic.

"All right, Johnny?" Amanda put a sympathetic hand on his arm.

He opened his eyes. "Sorry." He shrugged. "There's so much. How much time are we going to have?"

"Two minutes each."

"Two—" How could he tell the story in two minutes?

"This is radio, Murphy." Strickland sat back. "Just give us enough copy to read in two minutes. A couple paragraphs. An Austrian obituary." Strickland flipped a page of his notes and scanned the sheet. "For instance," he continued, "Bill Jordan is going to link up with us from Paris. He's going to tell about people fighting to get on the last plane out. Clawing to get a place on the plane. It was so full it barely got off the runway. One woman made it, but her husband was left behind. You know, that sort of thing. A real grabber."

"Sure," Murphy agreed quietly. It was more than just a story to him. "In Germany, the death of reason came gradually." He looked out the window as he spoke. "Like throwing a frog into cool water and then heating it up a little at a time. You know?" He was speaking to himself. "The frog will just get used to the heat until the water finally boils. That's what happened in Germany. Everyone sort of got used to it. A law here, a law there. A neighbor disappears, and you hope it isn't you."

Strickland cleared his throat. "Amanda is doing the German side of the story."

Murphy looked back at the group. They were staring at him. Maybe wondering if he was losing his mind. *Just talk, Murphy,* he told himself. *Tell them what you saw!* "The Nazis were already thick at the border by the time we got there. Men and women were being searched and arrested. Hardly anyone was allowed through. I saw a family—" He swallowed hard. "Husband. Wife. Young child. Jewish, I guess. Everybody Jewish wanted out of Austria." He shrugged. "They beat up the man, and right there, in front of him and the kid, they strip-searched the woman."

"You mean right at the checkpoint?" a voice echoed hollowly. "Stripped her?"

Murphy looked at Amanda. Her warm brown eyes were filled with emotion. She knew it was true—and that this one violent act marked the death of all that was decent and civilized in Austria. An entire nation had been thrown alive into a boiling cauldron of hatred. There was no time to become accustomed to brutality. It had simply come upon them—an inferno whose heat would suck the pure oxygen of freedom from their lungs until Austria lay in the dust, morally seared and scarred like Germany.

"You know, of course"—Amanda's crisp British accent was tinged with anger—"that the ministry of propaganda in Germany is saying that there were riots in Vienna. That the Germans were asked to come in and restore order. That Goebbels . . . !" She swore and then glanced at Phelps, who added a few choice words to her comments.

Strickland almost smiled. "Can't say that on the airwaves. Censors would pull the plug after ten seconds. But we ought to make every husband in America look at his wife as though she were the woman stripped in public at the border. Right, Murph?"

Murphy rubbed his hand across the sandpaper stubble on his chin. He just wanted to be done. Just wanted to sleep and dream about tall green grass in the fields of Pennsylvania. He wanted to think about his own mother and younger sister safe in the kitchen, making Sunday supper for the pastor and his brood of kids. Pump organ. Singing in the parlor. Laughter and talk about crops and livestock as the sun slips away. Somewhere in the world things were peaceful and *right*! Now he was about to bring the image of the unthinkable into the homes of America.

"It's still Sunday, isn't it?" he asked. "Is it still Sunday back home?" He could picture the big Philco radio across from his mother's plump blue sofa. His family would hear his voice. He would tell them the story of the young woman's humiliation as she was stripped beneath the glaring lights of the Nazi checkpoint. He would make them hear the anguish of the husband's helpless cries. He would tell it all as though the wife had been his own . . . *Elisa*?

"Yes," Strickland said patiently, "it's Sunday at home."

"Sunday!" Amanda said brightly. "We can teach everyone a new hymn? Have you heard the little tune Noel Coward came out with?" She hummed a few bars, then launched into the lyrics:

> "Let's be sweet to them
> And day by day repeat to them
> That sterilization simply isn't done.
> Let's help the dirty swine again
> To occupy the Rhine again,
> But don't let's be beastly to the Hun."

Whistles and cheers erupted from the group and Amanda bowed slightly, pretending to doff an imaginary hat.

"A little music with the news, huh?" Strickland grimaced. "I'm afraid the folks back home don't want to hear about the sterilization aspect of the Nazi policy. Nor abortions. Nor the *mercy* killings of the aged. You and Murphy tried that story line, remember? Let's stick to the events in Austria."

Amanda pretended to be insulted. "But, Larry, darling, those *are* the events in Austria! Today the Nazis march in; tomorrow they begin their little programs! I'm giving you tomorrow's news today!"

Murphy frowned, certain that what she said was true. All that had come upon the church in Germany would now smash into the churches of Austria. The changes that had broken down the sanctity of the family within the Reich would certainly begin their erosion there as well!

Hours later Elisa once again entered the suburbs of Prague. The running boards of the little Packard were nearly scraping the pavement with the weight it carried. The make of the automobile was concealed by the luggage and bodies of a dozen more intrepid passengers who clung to their baggage and to one another during the tedious journey. Haggard men and women sat on the roof of the car. Elisa had only enough room to see the road past the six refugees who perched precariously on the hood.

With each passing mile, their dazed expressions softened with relief. They were the lucky ones. They were out of harm's way. It was better not to think of those who had not been so lucky. None of these refugees would go beyond Prague into the Sudetenland, the area of Czechoslovakia populated by those of German racial descent. Like a stubborn weed, the roots of Nazi doctrine had gone deep into the hearts of many in that territory, blossoming into sporadic displays of violence under the firm guidance of men like Hans Frank and Albert Sporer. No one doubted that their support came directly from Adolf Hitler himself.

Outside the borders of the Sudeten territory, the country was a haven for refugees from Germany. It was, as Theo had told Elisa, "another Switzerland. Democratic and free." The city of Prague was not cursed with the disease of anti-Semitism that now erupted in Austria and had already begun to spread through Poland. For a thousand years the Jews of Prague had lived in relative harmony with the Czechs. Theo had often said he believed that another thousand years would still find both races living and working side by side beneath the hundred spires.

Elisa pulled to the side of the street that emptied into Wenceslas Square. Beyond she could see the huge bronze of good King Wenceslas overlooking the city. Her passengers slid off the car and thanked her. Piles of baggage were heaped on the sidewalk beside them. No one seemed to know where they should go now. Elisa did not offer to take them farther. She could not even think for herself what she should do next.

Across the square she caught sight of the telegraph office. Unlike the other storefronts that were closed tight for Sunday, the telegraph office was open and crowded with people. Was it possible that telegrams were still being sent to Austria? There was no other explanation.

Elisa joined the long line waiting at the polished marble counter. Extra clerks had been brought in to take messages from worried friends and relatives. The wires could not be sent directly to Austria, but were relayed first to Italy and then sent into the new occupied German territory.

All the while a radio blared from the shelf behind the counter. The roar of the exultant mob in Vienna filled the packed room:

> *"The wonderful scene you hear is taking place in front of the Imperial Hotel on the famous Ringstrasse in Vienna. . . ."*

Elisa froze, rooted where she stood as she listened to the broadcast. The Imperial Hotel was just a short walk from the Musikverein. She passed it every day. As the telegraph key tapped out the fears of the men and women in the cramped room, she closed her eyes and pictured herself beneath the third-floor balcony where Hitler stood before the cheering mob.

> *"The chancellor, Adolf Hitler, just appeared on the balcony of the Imperial Hotel a few seconds ago and was acclaimed again and again by the multitude. . . ."*

"Fräulein, please," a small, bookish-looking man nudged her slightly. She had not moved forward with the line.

She nodded distractedly and stared down at the message she had scrawled. She must be careful what words she sent to Vienna now. The Gestapo would most certainly be in charge of the telegraph offices. The thought made her shudder. As much as she wanted to, she could not send a wire to Leah. A brief explanation of her absence to the orchestra manager was all that would be safe.

> VIENNA PHILHARMONIC: STUCK IN PRAGUE TILL THINGS QUIET STOP TRIED CROSSING TO GET BACK TO VIENNA BUT WAS TURNED AWAY STOP WILL RETURN TO WORK AS SOON AS POSSIBLE STOP ELISA

This much would have to do. Her job with the orchestra was secure as long as she was not branded a fugitive by the Gestapo. The Nazi authorities must not be allowed to assume that she had fled Vienna. At least such a message would verify that she had attempted to get back, that she had no reason to fear the new regime.

As the growling voice of the Führer filled the Ringstrasse and laid to rest any final illusions about his purpose, Elisa paid for her telegram and pocketed a copy of it to show members of the Gestapo in Vienna who might question her absence from the joyous event. *"I would have loved to play,"* she would tell them. *"It was impossible, you see."* Then she would pass the carbon, dated and signed, to them. *"Tried crossing to get back to Vienna. Turned away."* And then she could add, *"But I did get to hear the Führer's speech over the radio."*

The angry and scornful speech crackled like fire:

> *"A Legitimist leader once described the task of Austria's so-called independence as that of hindering the construction of a really great German Reich. I now proclaim for this land its new mission!"*

New cheering erupted from the Führer's audience.

> *"The oldest eastern province of the German people shall be from now on the youngest bulwark of the German nation!"*

Still more cheering interrupted the speech. Elisa knew that such words could not be uttered in the Ringstrasse unless everyone in leadership who opposed them was now muzzled. She realized she had to control her emotion. Even here in Prague there might be observers of Himmler's Gestapo. She must not allow her own sickening sense of dread to show.

Hitler continued:

> *"I can in this hour report before history the conclusion of the greatest aim in my life: the entry of my homeland into the German Reich!"*

Now the tumult grew so loud that even the voice of the commentator was drowned out. *Surely if Leah and Shimon are still in Vienna, they can hear the roar,* thought Elisa. Like the clanging bells of St. Stephan's, no one in the city could hide from such a sound. Elisa stood in the center of the crowded room and listened in silence. She pressed her hand to her forehead with the unshakable conviction that she *must* get back immediately when the frontier opened for travel. Until that was a possibility, she would try to make contact with the men and women here in Prague who were also links in the long chain of smuggled passports for German-Jewish children.

Elisa had no names and no real clues as to where she might find her comrades. Leah had told her that no one in the ring had more than the most superficial information about the others. It was better that way. The sort of persuasion used by the Gestapo could crack even the strongest person, after all. Elisa herself was only a tiny fragment of a network that stretched from Germany across Europe and on to faraway Palestine. She was simply a courier, expendable by the network if she was caught and arrested in Germany. She knew no one but Leah and Shimon and the old instrument repairman in Munich. She knew none of her Prague connections by name or by sight. Now she felt totally cut off. The Gestapo could torture her as they had tortured Rudy Dorbransky, and she still could not tell them anything of importance. This fact was no doubt a comfort to the refugee network, but it was also the most frustrating sort of agony for Elisa.

"Fräulein?" A gentle hand touched her shoulder. "Are you ill?"

Elisa opened her eyes and smiled weakly. "No," she replied, her reverie broken by curious glances around her. "Just picturing the scene." She looked toward the rumbling radio, then hurried out of the telegraph office as though she were being pursued by the events in Vienna.

10

Sanctuary

A powerful wave of movement engulfed Louis and Charles. The suitcase, so carefully and lovingly packed this morning, was dropped and lost to them as they clung desperately to each other. Charles thrust his arm through the leather suspenders of his brother's lederhosen. The adults who towered around them did not seem to notice the two small boys as they fought to breathe and struggled to stay on their feet lest they fall and be trampled.

"Charles!" Louis cried as he was propelled away from his brother. Only a tenuous hold on the suspenders linked the boys. "Charles!" he screamed again and tried to reach out to him. An elbow slammed into his face and he would have fallen except that the crush around him was so tight. He could see the white-knuckled hand of Charles, gripping the strap, but nothing else. A hand poked out between two men who separated the brothers.

Louis could hear the muffled cry of Charles as the grip slipped from three fingers to two.

"I'm here, Charles!" he screamed. "Don't let go of me! Charles! Hold on or we will be lost!" Then he called out for Walter. "Father! *Father!*"

At that moment a great cheer erupted from the mob as Hitler emerged onto a balcony high above them.

"There he is!"

"Heil Hitler!"

"*Sieg Heil!*"

At that terrible instant the crowd thrust forward, and the grip of little fingers was broken. Louis fell to the cobbles on one knee, scraping away the skin. He yelped with the pain and cried out with fear. Where was Charles? Why had he let go?

Someone stepped on his hand. He tried to claw his way to his feet. The press of human bodies pushed the oxygen from his lungs. He could not call out for Charles or Father any longer. He could only gasp for breath as if he were drowning, fighting to surface for air, now fighting for his life!

Shoes, jackboots, trousers slammed against him. His nose was bleeding. His knee was bleeding. None of that mattered. A breath of air! Visions of his mother swirled before him. He tried to call to her but found no voice. He lashed out, slamming his fists against the leather of a soldier's boots. He tore at a man's trouser leg and, in a final act of desperation, opened his mouth and buried his teeth into the man's leg.

Above him he heard a curse. Then a hand reached down and grabbed him by the seat of his lederhosen, lifting him up, up, up into the light and the air.

"What are you doing?" A red, glaring face shouted at him.

Louis was panting, filling his lungs with pure, sweet air. "I fell!" he wailed.

"You bit me!"

"Where is my brother?" Louis frantically looked around from the high vantage point of the man's tight hold. "Charles! *Charles!* Where is my brother?"

"Where are your parents?" the man demanded, not letting him go.

Louis now repeated the name his father had told him, "Musikverein! Musikverein!" He struggled to be freed.

"You'll be killed!" The man shook him. "Be still!" Now he was also searching for Charles. "Two small boys loose in this!" He swung Louis onto his shoulder, oblivious to the bloody knee.

Louis peered into the tightly packed crowd. "Charles! Where are you?"

All around the chants of "Heil Hitler" drowned out his voice. Then, miraculously, he caught sight of a small hand reaching upward. It was Charles! He knew it was Charles! Their fingers were exactly alike. "There!" Louis cried triumphantly. "My brother is *there*!" He pointed toward the hole where Charles was lodged.

The man struggled against the tide, fighting his way to within reach of the child. He elbowed between a wall of chanting men and stretched his hand out to grasp Charles by the collar of his shirt and hoist him up onto the other shoulder.

Sweaty and disheveled, Charles pulled down the scarf that covered his cleft lip and gasped for breath. Then, out of obedient habit, he tucked his chin and covered the deformity once again. He seemed more angry than frightened by their ordeal. He had let go of Louis' suspenders. Such carelessness had almost cost their lives. With a determined look, he threaded the leather of his brother's suspenders through his fingers. They would not be separated again!

"Heil!" the crowd roared as Hitler waved to them.

Charles studied the smiling, waving man with the funny mustache and wondered if the man could see their father from where he stood.

Maps of the "new" Austria were already on display in the windows of shops along the Ringstrasse. Their existence was proof to any doubters that the Führer had this day in mind many months before. Other shops were now marked with fresh red paint that spelled out the word *JUDE!*

Leah averted her eyes and pressed on through the milling crowds that blocked the sidewalks. The grim determination on her face and the heavy instrument made her appear somehow official. People stepped aside for her. Vienna was music, and she must be connected with the great celebration of the Anschluss.

She had forgotten her music, but she did not dare go back. Ahead was the familiar brick facade of the Musikverein. Tears stung her eyes as the multitude roared before the Imperial Hotel and Hitler stepped out to the balcony for his fifth curtain call. At the sight of the steps to the stage door, Leah began to run. She wanted only to be inside, to close the door and shut out this insanity that had so suddenly enveloped her home! *How many members of the orchestra will be here today?* she wondered. No one else was in sight. She clambered up the steps alone and flung the door open as though she were being pursued.

Leah stood in the dim light for a moment. The great hall was silent. There were no musicians tuning their instruments before the Sunday program. The stage was dark beyond the wings. Music stands were empty.

A vague rumble seeped into the building from outside.

"Bitte?" Leah called hesitantly as though she had entered a vast empty crypt. Her own voice answered her. The roar of the Nazi revelers outside replied in distinct counterpoint, "Heil Hitler! Heil Hitler!"

She shuddered and blinked at the music stands and the places where her friends and colleagues should have been. A thousand ghosts—faces of musicians who had become her family—filled the stage as she watched. Where were they now? Had this face of evil frightened them all away? Where was Elisa? Where was Rudy—?

She jerked her head upward at the memory of Rudy. It was as though she could once again hear the gunshots and the horrible words shouted from the balcony by the enraged young Nazi trying to kill him. If she had known then what was to come, she could have warned him to leave this place, to hide somewhere far from Vienna. But she could not see the future then, and Rudy had died. She could not see the future now, and the vast blackness of her uncertainty was terrifying.

Had the Nazi colonel in the Judenplatz sent her here, knowing that there would not be a concert today? Was this some sort of trap? She peered over her shoulder as if an evil presence had entered the building. She held the violoncello as if she found some comfort in its nearness.

Again the roar outside invaded the silence of the hall. Leah wanted to run away, but everywhere there were beatings of Jews in the streets. The bloodred word *JUDE* was now splattered throughout the city. She swallowed hard and forced herself to walk out onto the stage to her place. She touched the stand, picked up the pencil she used to make notes on the score. She gazed at the nicked wood of her chair, then closed her eyes and imagined the utter stillness of orchestra and audience as the conductor raised his baton.

It is that moment, she told herself. *No one coughs or rattles a program. They are waiting. Waiting for the music. It is that moment now,* she imagined. *And I will not be afraid.* For an instant, the thought seemed to settle her. Shimon stood over the kettledrums. Elisa was across from her. The maestro stood poised, and—

From the wings behind her, she heard the sound of a door. And then the nervous cough of a man floated out from the wings.

"Hello?" A man's voice called loudly, shattering the peace of Leah's reverie. "Is anyone here?"

She did not answer. Footsteps clacked loudly against the boards. She was pale in the light. Perhaps she herself was a ghost. If she stayed very still, this human with the loud shoes and harsh, whiskey-rough voice would go away. Maybe he would not see the frightened spirit standing with her cello among the empty chairs and stands.

"You there!" The voice found her. "Hey! Isn't there supposed to be a concert today?" He stood in the wings, not willing to violate the sacredness of the stage.

Leah felt she would be safe if she did not leave her music stand. No one would touch her if she did not leave this spot and enter again into the bright light of the real world.

She stared at the man who was a shadow between the tall canyons and ropes of the stage curtains. "No concert," she replied, startled at the sound of her own voice. No. She could not be a ghost. Ghosts could not speak.

The man let out a sharp burst of laughter. "Ah yes. The *Führer*!" he said, as if that one name explained everything. "Interrupted Chancellor Schuschnigg's plans a bit, didn't he? Today was supposed to be the day of the Austrian plebiscite, wasn't it? No concert. No plebiscite."

Leah regarded him without speaking. She had almost forgotten about the plebiscite. Today's concert was to have been a celebration of Austrian independence. No wonder no one had come to play.

"Are you alone here?" the man asked, and his question brought a surge of fear to Leah.

"No," she lied.

He laughed again. "I don't see anyone else." He inclined his head. The light was behind him and she could not make out his face, but there was movement in the wings where he watched her.

"This is a big place." She lifted her chin defiantly as he took a step nearer.

"Well, I have come on an errand." He sniffed.

"Then maybe you should go to the box office." She still did not budge. If he came for her, she would simply run out the opposite side of the stage and pull the power lever to shut down the light panel. The plan gave her a feeling of superiority. She could find her way into the depths of the building while any pursuers would be left groping in the blackness. Her voice became sharp. "Only performers are allowed backstage."

The stranger sounded suddenly apologetic. "That's what I told them, Fräulein. But they insisted that I come to the stage door and ask for someone named Leah."

Leah hoped that the wave of dread did not show on her face. Her hands became suddenly clammy. "Leah who?" she asked. She was thankful that her voice did not crack.

"I don't know Leah *who,* Fräulein." The man seemed genuinely perplexed.

Leah was certain that the visitor must be a member of the Gestapo who had come in search of her under the colonel's instructions. Had someone already let the secrets of their operation slip? Had her name been added to the long list so soon? Visions of the power lever became clear in her mind. She had in an instant plotted her route of escape. "Leah is a common name," she said.

"That's what I told them, Fräulein. But they insisted. The name of their aunt is Leah. The one boy is certain of it because it sounds like Louis." He stepped aside and two golden-haired children moved forward slightly. They were obviously frightened. One had blood on the front of his shirt. The other, his mouth concealed by a scarf, stared upward into the rigging of the stage and then back at Leah. "They were somehow separated from their father in the crowd." The man shrugged. "This one fell and was nearly trampled. I picked him up. I found the other one, too. Please, Fräulein. I have comrades to join, and certainly their father will come for them here. Or their aunt. The one they call Leah. They were told to come here, and . . ."

Leah did not budge. She looked first at the boys who were identical in every visible aspect; then she looked at the man. If this was a Gestapo trick to trap her into taking the boys, she would not yield to it.

"Why don't you wait outside with them? If they are lost, their father or aunt will certainly come for them."

"Fräulein—" the man cleared his throat nervously—"I simply picked them off the pavement before they were killed. I have brought them here like a good citizen, and now I bid them *Auf Wiedersehen*." He tipped his hat. "And I bid you *adieu*!" He wheeled around and patted one of the boys on the head as he hurried out of the building.

The outside door crashed to a resounding close as the man exited. Leah remained beside her stand. The two young boys stared at her for a moment, then curious hands reached out to stroke the soft red velvet of the curtains. Heads craned back to gape upward at the catwalks and lights and rigging. Eyes glistened with wonder at the sight.

Leah hesitated before speaking. She would have to choose her questions carefully. If these boys were brought here to entrap her, she must not give any hint that she had been instrumental in the escape of dozens of children from the Reich.

"Have you ever seen a stage before?" she asked gently. They were, after all, only children, she reasoned. If they were being used by evil men, it was not their choice.

"Once Mother took us to see *Nutcracker*," one of the boys said eagerly while his brother answered with a nod.

"You are brothers?" Leah asked, even though the answer was obvious.

"Yes," the verbal boy said proudly. "I am Louis, and this is Charles. Who are you?"

Leah ignored his question, feeling as though there were other ears listening in the upper reaches of the balcony. "You must have been very frightened, getting lost from your father."

"Charles held on to my suspenders, but then I fell and skinned my knee." He held up his bloodied knee to show Leah. "But I didn't cry. Not too much, anyway. Then that man picked me up because I bit his leg when he stepped on my fingers, and I told him to bring us here where Father said Aunt Leah would be."

"What does your Aunt Leah look like?" Leah asked, taking a step toward the duo.

Both boys shrugged and looked upward again into the mass of stage rigging. "Father packed us lunch but I lost mine. And we lost the suitcase. But Charles has his lunch." Charles nodded again, touching his hand to his stomach. "Do you have lunch, Fräulein?" Louis asked. He was still stroking the velvet curtain.

Leah smiled thoughtfully. Skinned knee, lost suitcase, only one lunch between them. A five- or six-year-old child could not lie so convincingly about such things. Still she would not continue to talk to them here on the stage.

"Would you like to see the stage?" She gripped the violoncello case and walked toward them. "Top and bottom. It is quite a wonderful thing to see. Then you can tell your father about it when you see him." She reached the wings and touched the quiet child on his shoulder. His eyes smiled. Leah wondered why he wore the scarf around his mouth. "Perhaps you can show your Aunt Leah also when she comes for you."

She guided them through the backstage maze, pointing upward to explain the purpose of different ropes and lights as they went. "Only one lunch for two such big boys! Perhaps I can find something more to share between us." She had lowered her voice to a whisper now. If there were others watching her in the building, she did not want to be followed. "But now we must be very quiet." She put a finger to her lips as they reached a staircase leading downward. The area beneath the stage was a rabbit warren of little practice rooms. Corridors twisted and turned among closets and lockers. Trap doors opened onto the stage above them.

The boys followed her down into the maze. It was as if they knew what it meant to have to remain silent. They held tightly to each other's hands. Charles clutched his lunch as Leah maneuvered the awkward cello case around piles of dusty scenery and props and heaps of extra chairs.

Ahead of them was an inky corridor with steps that led downward into yet another level. At that moment the crashing of a door sounded from somewhere in the building. Leah put her hand out to halt the boys. Above them the loud *click* of boot heels and rough male voices could be distinctly heard on the boards

Words echoed down. "My apologies, mein Führer. All of Vienna has come to see you. No doubt the entire orchestra was among the crowd. A holiday. Even the music of Vienna must be silent when you raise your voice to the Volksdeutsche!"

"I am surrounded by fools and incompetents!" The Führer now raised his voice in anger to a small audience. "Our tanks and lorries litter the roads of Austria! Our arrival here was delayed by hours! We looked like unprepared idiots to the French and the English! Surely they will not overlook the fact that half our equipment has broken down! And then I arrive in Vienna and everything is equally unprepared!"

The whining voice was unmistakable. Leah shuddered and nudged the boys back into the darkness of the corridor. She did not want to hear any more. Hitler was angry at his reluctant generals, and now there would be no concert to greet him. Somehow this glimpse of his fury was satisfying. The great triumph was marred by faulty equipment and the lack of musicians to play for Hitler. It had never occurred to Leah before that a man of such monumental evil could also be so peevish and banal.

Leah could not manage the cello, the boys, and the darkness all at once. "Put your hands in my pockets," she said in a hushed voice as the rage of Hitler echoed from the stage and filled the auditorium beyond. The gloom of the hallway was profound, but Leah knew exactly where she was going. Taking the cello in one hand, she slid the other along the wall as they shuffled blindly forward. Hitler's voice sounded distant now, as though someone had turned down the volume of a radio.

Leah spoke reassuringly to the brothers. "I have counted eleven doorknobs. Now twelve. Thirteen is the furnace room. And now we make a turn." She patted a corner and pulled the brothers along with her. The corridor narrowed here, and she slid her fingers along the cold stone blocks until she found one last doorknob. By now the raging of Adolf Hitler had dimmed to an inaudible rumble behind them. Leah turned the knob and quickly opened the door. Then she flipped on a light switch to reveal a tiny practice cubicle with soundproof walls and an upright piano that took up the entire length of the back wall.

"The light hurts my eyes." Louis said.

Charles merely blinked uncomfortably.

Indeed, after their dark journey into the bowels of the Musikverein, the light seemed unnatural. Leah shut the door and propped her violoncello in the corner. She fumbled a moment with the lock, and then considered the piano. She wished that Shimon were here, but he wasn't, so she would simply move it herself. Unlocking the casters, she leaned into the upright. Charles and Louis helped, and she was amazed at how easily it rolled across the floor. Once in front of the door, she locked the casters again and sat down breathlessly on the bench.

"This is my secret place," she said conspiratorially. "I practice here quite often because no one else seems to want to come this far back. Listen." She inclined her head slightly. The brothers did the same. "Tell me what you hear?" she asked with a smile.

The boys looked puzzled. The air seemed dead. "I don't hear anything," Louis said. Charles shrugged.

"That's right. This is a very quiet place. No ugly shouting can come into this room. It is a magic, peaceful place. Music lives here in the walls. Beautiful music."

"Why can't we hear it?" Louis frowned.

"It won't come out until those very bad men we heard just now are gone. While they are here, we must wait very quietly also." She put a finger to her lips. "We will play the quiet game. Whoever can be the quietest will get a penny."

Louis stuck out his lower lip. "But that's not fair. Charles never speaks."

Leah ignored the remark. "The game begins now. And if you are both quiet, I have a penny for each."

This seemed to satisfy Louis. The boys sat back on their heels and waited, studying the magic walls that surrounded them. Minutes passed. Leah was satisfied that neither light nor sound would escape from the tiny cubicle. If the barest hint of cello music seeped out to someone's ears, they could not trace it to this room behind the furnace. The place was little known even to members of the orchestra. Leah had retreated here a hundred times since she had discovered it two years before. No one had ever found her here.

At last she cleared her throat. The sound seemed foreign in the stillness of the air. "You have both been such good boys." There was no need to speak louder than the softest whisper. "A penny for each of you." She looked deliberately toward the paper bag that Charles clutched in his hand. "Now we may have to share your lunch, Charles. We did not have opportunity to get my box of pastry from my locker, but later I promise."

Charles extended his offering to her, and only then did it strike her that the child had not uttered one sound since she had first seen him. The scarf was securely tied over his mouth and covered even the lower part of his nose. "Do you have a cold, Charles?" she asked.

The boy shook his head and nodded to Louis, who would explain for him. Leah looked from one to the other. "What is it?"

"He can't talk," Louis said simply, hungrily eyeing the lunch bag that Leah held on her lap.

"Are you unwell?" She directed the question at Charles, who touched his fingers self-consciously to his mouth beneath the wrapping.

"No," Louis continued. The explanation was bright and untroubled. Charles began to unwrap the scarf. "Mama says that God left Charles' lips in heaven where they sing night and day to the angels." First one layer was unwound and then a second. "Now Mama is in heaven with God too, and Father says that Charles is singing to her right now, even though Charles and I are—"

Leah tried not to allow her face to show the pity she felt at the first sight of the gaping split where the child's upper lip should have been. A jagged opening ran through the palate into his nose. Her smile became frozen and she wanted to stare, but she did not. Her eyes faltered and Charles noticed that moment of Leah's grief at the glimpse of his deformity.

She lowered her chin slightly when Charles looked away. Then she reached out and lifted his chin until their eyes met in understanding. "How wonderful it is of God to let you sing to your mother. I am sure she would be very lonely for you otherwise."

Tears filled the child's eyes as he nodded slowly. There was an unspoken question there. Leah heard it clearly: *But who will sing for us now?*

His sorrow seemed too much for a small boy to bear. It tore at Leah's heart and made her want to gather him in her arms. But she did not. She had to think. If, in fact, these boys had been chosen by the Gestapo to snare her, they were an excellent choice. She looked away from Charles at that thought.

He frowned and sat back in obvious disappointment. His hand moved instinctively to cover his mouth. The spell was broken.

Just as the tiny killdeer bird draws the predator away from the chicks in its nest, so Walter Kronenberger had run far away from his sons.

Twice he thought he had escaped the snare of the Brownshirt who followed him doggedly. Then members of the Gestapo had joined the hunt.

Through the press of the crowd, Walter pushed as though he fought a riptide. Ahead he could see the Rothschild Palace. German soldiers stood at attention guarding all entrances of the home of this famed Jewish baron. Just for an instant, Walter found himself hoping that the baron and his family had gotten out of Vienna in time. Just beyond the palace was the office of the INS. Walter Kronenberger had no other goal left in his life except to reach the doors of the International News Service offices.

There were at least six men fighting their way toward him now. Their arms were raised as they, too, swam against the crowds. They had long since stopped shouting. Voices and commands to stop Walter went unheeded in the tumult.

Walter was a mere twenty feet from the back of the crowd. Faces were still turned toward the balcony. The sidewalk in front of the INS office was empty. He prayed that someone, *anyone,* from the free world would be inside to witness what was to be his last will and testament. Images of

Louis and Charles swirled in his mind. As he ran the final yards to the door of the office, he prayed for them, not for himself.

Shouts in harsh German accents answered from behind. "Halt! Halt! *Schweinhund!*"

A single shot rang out and whistled past Walter's right ear, then ricocheted off the stone of the INS office. Walter cried out, not from fear but with exertion as he lunged for the door, jerked it open, and fell into the front office.

Startled faces gawked at him as he lay panting on the floor. Men in German uniforms mingled with disgruntled-looking fellows in civilian clothes. Jackets off. Sleeves rolled up. Ink stains on fingers. These civilians were journalists!

Walter wept with relief. He could not find his voice. He struggled to his feet and stumbled through the low-swinging door into the newsroom. SS soldiers pulled out their guns in front of him, and the first of his Gestapo pursuers crashed into the office. Two more followed closely behind him. All of them were as breathless as Walter from the chase.

"What the—" One of the journalists snatched his cigar from his mouth and leaped to his feet.

Already the net was tightening. Walter fought to speak. "I am Kronenberger! Journalistin from Hamburg! They will silence everyone! Silence . . . *kill!*"

A Gestapo agent dashed toward him. Walter struggled to reach into his coat pocket. The startled onlookers stood frozen in horror. As bullets from a dozen Nazi-issue pistols tore through his body, Kronenberger shouted, "Tell them! *Warn—*" A final bullet slammed into his mouth and silenced him forever.

The envelope he had drawn from his jacket pocket fluttered to the floor beneath a desk and lay there, unnoticed.

11

Night Music

Leah would have paced if there had been room in the tiny practice cubicle. Louis spread his meal out in front of him on the floor and nibbled each morsel. Charles turned away to face the wall so Leah could not watch him struggle to eat. If Leah moved one inch she would have stepped on cheese or bread or one of the boys. She was not hungry, so she sat on the piano bench and tried to decide what she must do now.

Only this morning she had rejoiced that all the refugee children had been dispersed from their apartment and were now staying outside the Judenplatz. How then could she bring two boys back into the Judenplatz? The fires of Nazi hatred burned hottest there. She dared not think about what was happening in the neat little square in front of her home. The image of Shimon falling to the cobblestones made her physically ill. She wanted to cry out loud with the worry she felt, but circumstances made it impossible for her to act out her own emotions. Against her will, she now had the feelings of these two children to consider. She was forced to remain strong when it would have been the height of self-indulgence to cry and rage against what was happening. *A good scream would feel luxurious, like a hot bath on a cold night,* she mused.

An hour had passed without any stirring in the corridor outside.

Louis looked up from his lunch. "It's really suppertime, isn't it?" he asked, sensing the lateness of the hour.

Leah checked her watch. It was four in the afternoon. "Teatime," she answered.

"This was a long time to wait for lunch," Louis said. "When will we eat supper, since we ate lunch so late? And will the bad men go away so the music will come out?"

There was little doubt in Leah's mind that they were alone in the vast building now. She cleared her throat and studied the cello case. There was nothing that cleared her mind like practice. "I think it is time for us to hear the music."

Charles scooted around and faced her as he replaced his scarf. *He has handsome eyes,* Leah thought as she maneuvered the case. His sad eyes seemed to notice much more than little Louis could ever see. The eyes now glowed with pleasure as Leah opened the case to reveal the warm, rich varnish of the instrument.

"What is that?"

"He is called—" she removed the instrument and tried not to think of the last night she had played—"a violoncello." She pretended a cheerfulness she did not feel. "His name is Vitorio, and he sings."

She had a captive audience now, and the look on their faces was a comfort to her. She could talk for hours about Vitorio! She could easily pass the time as they waited for darkness to descend outside. When it was dark they could sneak out and go . . . *where?* That was the question. She must get back to Shimon tonight. The German officer as much as said they held Shimon hostage to guarantee her return to the Judenplatz. So what would she do with these two?

"How does Vitorio sing?" Louis chirped.

"We can make him sing." She crooked her finger to beckon Charles closer. "Give me your hand, Charles." She took his fingers and pulled them toward the strings. "Go ahead. Pluck one." The child obeyed and chuckled hoarsely as the cello replied with a clear, precise note. This was the first time Leah had heard Charles make even a slight sound. His laughter pleased her.

Forgetting his scrapes, Louis had already inched forward on his knees. His index finger was ready. "Me?"

Leah nodded, and Louis reached out to pluck one string; Charles roared with delight and plucked another. As they giggled and squirmed, all trauma forgotten for the moment, Leah unsheathed her bow and held it before them.

"And this is called a bow." Little fingers reached out to pluck that as well. "No." She drew it back. "We can't touch the horsehair because it will get dirty, and we can't wash it."

Quickly the hands went behind their backs as if to put them out of reach of temptation.

"And this is what we do with the bow," she said as she slowly drew the horsehair across the strings in one long, sustained note. The sound was soothing, calming. The wonder of it shone in the eyes of the two young captives, and when Leah began to play the clear, lively music of the Bach Suites, they bobbed and swayed with the melody.

Leah closed her eyes and played from memory as she had done when she was a child. There were six suites with five or six cheerful movements in each; she went from one to another without opening her eyes. An hour and a half later, she had considered all danger and possible plans. She knew what she must do. Finishing with a flourish, she opened her eyes to find herself back in the little practice room. She was convinced now that the boys had not been brought to her as some sort of a trap. Their need was genuine.

Somewhere in all of it, Leah had lost her audience. Charles and Louis were fast asleep on the floor in the corner.

Quietly Leah put away the violoncello and pulled the cover off the upright piano. She spread it over the boys, then turned off the light and lay down to wait until dark.

Elisa sat outside the little house in Prague while the last sunlight faded away. The sound of piano music drifted through the windows until the stone structure seemed like a giant music box.

Inside, Anna was playing the piano Theo had purchased for her in 1936 when he first began to believe that they could not remain in Germany any longer. It was a beautiful baby grand, shining walnut inlaid with tiny bouquets of delicate flowers. Of course it was not so magnificent as the massive concert grand in the music room of their home in Berlin, but Theo had hoped that it would be some consolation for his dear Anna. Prague, too, could be a happy place for them.

Yet, in all the time Theo had been in prison, Anna could not bring herself to play it. There had been no music in the house until tonight. Tonight for the Lindheim family, formerly of Wilhelmstrasse, Berlin, there was reason for joy and celebration. Why, then, was it so difficult for Elisa to join her family at this moment? She remained behind the wheel of the Packard and stared up at the lighted windows. She was an observer of the joy, but her own heart could not sing with the happiness of her family when there was so much grief only a few hours from this place.

She dared not tell her mother about her attempt to cross back into Austria, Elisa decided. She would simply explain that the flights to London had been booked for days ahead of time. She was forced to remain in Prague until things quieted down. In her own happiness, Anna would accept any explanation for Elisa's long absence today. Tonight, within the four stone walls of this ancient house, the world was perfect and everything was true and good.

Elisa stared through the smeared windshield toward the halo of a streetlamp. Somewhere within this city, others grieved for Vienna as she did. Somehow she must find those people. In the shadows of a house across the street, Elisa caught sight of the orange glow of a cigarette. For an instant she could make out the dim features of a man's face. Heavy brow. High cheekbones. Thick, drooping mustache. Was he looking at her? She blinked at the darkness where the image burned like the afterflash when a camera bulb goes off. A surge of fear rushed through her. Her hands grew clammy on the steering wheel, and she quickly gathered her purse and small suitcase and the violin and climbed from the car. How long had the man been standing there? And *why* was he there at all?

She hurried up the steps and knocked hard on the door. The music stopped, and she could hear the laughing voice of her brother Wilhelm as he rushed to answer the door.

"It's Elisa!" she called. Even the sound of her own voice startled her. She wished she had not said her name. She glanced over her shoulder into the blackness across the street. There was no sign of the watcher, but still she felt eyes looking down at her.

"Elisa?" Anna's startled expression appeared as she threw open the door. "Why aren't you in London, darling?" She gathered Elisa into the safety and light of the house.

"I tried, Mama," she said with a weak smile. She did not say more; no one was very interested in any explanation, anyway. They were simply glad she was back.

"Theo!" Anna called into the parlor where Theo lay on a sofa beside the piano. "Look who's back!"

"We're having a recital," Theo said in a hoarse but happy voice. "Your mother is playing all my favorites at once, and we are catching up."

Theo's face, smiles, light from the lamps—all reflected in the raised top of the glistening baby grand like a mirror. Anna directed her into the parlor while Wilhelm took her luggage from her. Elisa caught sight of her own reflection in the sheen of the wood. *I must smile, too, tonight,* she thought. *I cannot mar such an event.*

"Well, the piano is a bit out of tune," Anna babbled excitedly. "It has been locked up so long. So much music and happiness all locked up inside!" *Is she speaking of the instrument or herself?* Elisa wondered.

"Even so it is the most beautiful sound I have heard in quite a while." Theo put out his hand and grasped Elisa's fingers. "And now the evening is made more perfect yet."

Anna was singing softly in the bathroom. Theo was reading the Bible by the light of the bed lamp when Elisa poked her head in to wish them good night.

He glanced up and smiled. "Come in for a minute, Elisa," he said quietly.

Elisa obeyed and sat on the edge of his bed. An expectant silence followed. "I am glad I missed my plane," she said, trying to imagine what she would be doing now if she had caught a flight to London to be with Murphy or if she had been allowed across the border. The evening with her family truly had been wonderful, and there had been moments when at last she had put thoughts of everything else out of her mind.

But now there was a question in Theo's eyes. "I see you still have the Guarnerius violin," he stated simply. A flash of understanding passed between father and daughter.

"Rudy's violin." She nodded once. "Yes, Papa. *I* carry it now."

He frowned. "How long have you known?"

She did not answer his question. "I should have known sooner, Papa. You could have told me."

"And risked involving you and your brothers and your mother?"

"Weren't we involved already? You know that Nazi law says if one member of a family is guilty of resistance, the entire family will be punished equally. We were involved, Papa; we just didn't know it."

"That was why I had to get all of you out. Out of Germany. I was not certain that I was being watched until Pastor Jacobi was tipped off."

"How long had you been helping, Papa?" Elisa studied him thoughtfully, as if she were meeting a true hero for the first time.

He closed the Bible and set it on the bed beside him. "You children barely noticed when Hitler first came to power in 1933. Law declared that we of Jewish heritage had to turn in our papers and have them reissued with the Jewish identification stamp. Along with everyone else, we complied. We were Germans. Germans who happened to be racially Jewish, but Germans nonetheless. The papers were returned, marked with the letter *J*, which you carried each time you returned to Germany. The penalty for falsifying your papers was prison, as you know, so we complied. But I sent you away to school, Elisa, so you did not have to experience the rest. You were luckier than most. I don't think you were aware of how serious it had become until Thomas rejected you."

She averted her eyes. Her father seemed to looking into her soul, and she could not bear for him to see her secrets. "I was working too hard to notice," she mumbled.

Theo continued. "There were issues that touched non-Jewish Germans also. As early as 1933, the Nazis drafted laws that forced the sterilization of those considered 'racially unworthy' to produce offspring. Of course, the church was furious. Catholics and Protestants protested and were imprisoned. Jewish groups protested and were jailed immediately. The erosion of German rights began with the abolition of rights for those not yet born. Then children with even a slight deformity were considered 'unworthy of life.' Adults with some defect were sterilized. Next, religious schools were closed down. Jewish, Catholic, Protestant schools were shut, and all education passed into the hands of the state."

"I was so involved in my own life in Austria. Study and . . . " Elisa was ashamed at the recitation of events that had led to this night. She had hardly noticed. Her father was right. Until the one man she thought she loved had turned his back on her, she had thought of no one but herself.

"That was my intention, Elisa. I wanted you to have as normal and happy a life as possible. Your mother agreed with me. We would have sent Wilhelm and Dieter away to school as well." He was trying very hard to make sense out of what was, in fact, incomprehensible.

"But, Papa," she asked, "how long were you involved in the resistance?"

"I provided money. That is all. I did nothing brave or wonderful, Elisa. Others arranged bribes to the Gestapo. Those who were most in danger, they smuggled out of the country. Almost all the leadership in the church with the courage to resist were arrested. They were replaced by those wiling to bend to the Nazi doctrine. Slowly all organized effort to resist was eroded. I was among the least important. I provided money, not courage. I tried to play it safe for the sake of my family. I thought this madness would pass away. It has not."

He took her hand and gazed steadily into her eyes. "And now somehow you have gotten involved." He glanced out toward the parlor and the violin case near the piano bench. "You still have the Guarnerius," he repeated.

She nodded. "Papa . . . , " she began and then paused, unsure of her feelings. "I must play this terrible performance through until it is over. Or until I am stopped."

Theo regarded her silently. "I thought as much," he said sadly. "And today? Did you try to go to London?"

"And Vienna," she replied truthfully. The admission was a relief.

He frowned and pressed his lips together. "Yes. You were worried about someone in Vienna last night. I remember." Then he looked at her sharply. "Elisa, you must not think of going back there now."

"I must."

"Not right away, child."

"I am not a child. Or if I am, I am *your* child! You would do the same!"

"Listen to me!" His voice was urgent but not reprimanding. "All that has happened in Germany slowly over the last six years will now come to pass in Austria overnight! *Overnight!* Do you hear me? What the Gestapo did in Berlin in darkness will be done in Vienna in broad daylight! Elisa, God has spared you the fate of your friends! Whatever organized resistance there might be in Vienna will be shattered! You must stay with us here for a few days. Maybe weeks or months. You *must*! And when the time is right—if there is a right time—you will be an instrument in the hands of God!"

His words drained the last energy from her. If he was right, then she was helpless in Prague—worse than that, she was *useless*! "My friends?"

"Tonight you must pray for them, Elisa." Theo lifted her chin. "There are times when there is no light in the darkness, and then we must pray for even a tiny candle that will guide us." He patted the worn leather cover of his Bible. "That small lesson I learned in a corner in Dachau. Pray, and I will pray with you, child."

She nodded reluctantly. How hard it seemed to wait and do nothing! "Yes. Yes, Papa. But when Murphy comes—*if* he comes back and if he *can* go to Vienna—I must go with him then."

The questioning look remained in Theo's eyes. "Murphy. A fine fellow. Of course you will go with him. He is your husband, isn't he?" He gestured toward her ring.

She flushed deeply. Her father indeed seemed to see right through her tonight. Could he also somehow sense that her marriage to Murphy was simply a business arrangement? "Yes. My husband," she said, but the words stuck in her throat.

"And you love him, don't you?" Now there was a half smile on Theo's face.

She sniffed and sat up rigidly. "We are married," she defended, wanting to shout that she could never love a man who left her so callously, who took money for a marriage certificate. And yet her feelings were raw at the mention of his name.

Theo appraised her with a look that appeared to comprehend every unspoken detail. "An American passport will no doubt be of great benefit. I am happy that you do not need to pretend to be Elisa Linder from Czechoslovakia any longer."

Outside in the hall they heard Anna emerge from the bathroom. The air smelled instantly of tooth powder and perfume. "Mother is . . . so happy tonight," Elisa said, trying not to sound unhappy. "I am glad you have each other."

"Let's keep our little secrets to ourselves, Elisa. No need for Anna to worry, I think." He patted her hand.

She was glad for the chance to be honest with him. He understood the need for her to do what she could. Somehow he understood even about Murphy. He could read her eyes as if he were looking into a mirror. "Thank you, Papa." She kissed his forehead, and he hugged her tightly.

"Yes, you are my child," he answered quietly as Anna came into the bedroom humming the melody of a Bach suite.

12
Curfew

Leah remained with the two boys in the shadows outside the Musikverein. A caravan of troop lorries rumbled beneath a streetlamp. This time they did not carry German Wehrmacht troops, however. Crammed into the back like cattle were the hundreds of Austrians who had been arrested during the day of celebration. Leah could see their pale, grim expressions clearly as they moved into the halo of the light. On the cobbles, like bouquets strewn on a mass grave, lay flowers crushed by the wheels of the lorries. So this was the end of Vienna's first day as a part of the Thousand-Year Reich!

Leah's breath quickened with fear; one of the prisoners might be Shimon! She stood rooted as the melancholy parade continued on and on. This could not be mere hundreds, Leah realized; *thousands* were under arrest! Where were they being taken? The prisons of Germany were already crowded and overflowing into new camps!

There seemed to be no civilians left free on the streets. The cheering masses were gone. The thoroughfares beneath the huge red Reich banners were devoid of life. Only the trucks remained and the sad faces that stared out through the slats at the passing city. Somehow this desolation was more terrifying to Leah than the roaring mob had been. At least in the crowd she had not been noticed. But how could a woman alone with two boys and a cello not be noticed when there was not another civilian to be seen?

She pressed her fingers against her forehead and tried to think what she must do. It had all seemed so clear as she had played her violoncello and thought through a dozen different plans. Elisa's flat was only a five-minute walk from the Musikverein. She would take the boys there, and then go on alone to the Judenplatz to be with Shimon. Even the thought of his name made her search the faces in the slow-moving troop lorries. She *had* to know if he was among those who had been taken!

In her crushing fear for Shimon's safety, she found the courage to act. "Come on, boys." Drawing a deep breath, she stepped out into the light of the sidewalk. Prisoners' eyes continued to gaze bleakly down at her—*through* her—as if she were not there. She raised her chin slightly and tried to keep her eyes straight ahead as the brothers trailed behind her. The smell of reeking diesel exhaust and the drone of engines were not easy to ignore. Her head throbbed with the noise and the smell. Ahead, in the shadowed doorways of the shops, she could see the dim shapes of German soldiers on guard. The trio walked quickly beyond the Musikverein. Still the lorries continued to roll on, under the glow of a streetlamp into the darkness and then once again into the light, until every truck and each ashen face looked the same.

Heads of the soldiers on guard turned toward her in unison. What was she doing out on the street at this time of night? Two soldiers stepped out to block her path twenty yards ahead. And in that terrible instant the face of one captive became clear in the eerie light. Leah gasped and clutched at her heart as large familiar hands reached out to her from behind the slats of a prisoner transport.

"Leah! Leah!" Shimon shouted. His face was contorted with grief. His cry was no hallucination; they had arrested him! Her own Shimon!

The world spun around as the voice hung on the roar of engines; then Shimon's face passed irretrievably into the darkness. The cello case fell from her limp hand as her knees gave way. Even the darkness seemed yellow, and as if from a great distance, Leah heard an echoed slap of hobnailed boots running toward her. She tried to speak the name of Shimon, but no sound came from her lips as darkness closed over her.

That night Elisa lay alone beneath the warm, soft quilts on the bed. Never before had she realized how vast and lonely a bed could be. She reached out to touch the empty pillow beside her. It was as cold and undisturbed as her life had once been. Things were always so much neater when life was solitary. No one to worry about. Nobody else to consult on schedules or plans for meals. One set of dishes to wash. Everything in its place. She had told herself all these things after Thomas had smashed her dreams. She had almost believed that life alone was really better.

Then something had happened. John Murphy had entered her life like a new and unforgettable melody. The music of his laughter, his clear gray eyes searching hers, the gait of his long, lean, muscular body as he walked away from her—all of this played back to her against her will. To love this man was even more hopeless than her love for Thomas von Kleistmann had been.

Murphy was American. Someday he would go back to America. Right now he was here only because he had a job to do. He helped her because she had paid him. She was certain that he would not have resisted now if she had offered to repay him by sharing the warmth of this bed and her body tonight. At the thought of his kiss she put her fingers to her lips and closed her eyes. "Murphy." She whispered his name.

She stiffened in resistance to the desire that rushed through her. No! She would not sell herself to any man out of gratitude. Her marriage to Murphy was a marriage in name only. She would remember that. She would steel herself against the chance that they would ever meet again. If indeed he came back in two weeks as he promised, she would smile politely and ask him how his work had gone. But for tonight she would not let herself give in to the longing. Love for her was nothing but a wish, a whisper in the night that could never be spoken out loud in the cold light of reality.

She turned her head and stared at the coals that glowed on the grate of the fireplace. The fire had blazed within her. She had known the pain of that fire when she had given her heart to Thomas. Her love had been a sweet song he had played along the banks of the soft-flowing Spree. Life had been young then and beautiful. She had allowed herself to dream and to believe. When he had left her, she had walked alone beside the waters and wondered why they seemed so beautiful still. The fire had consumed her, nearly destroyed her. Then the coals had dimmed and finally died. She knew she must not make the same mistake again with this American journalist. Like Thomas, John Murphy would leave. He would leave Europe. He would leave Elisa and never look back.

Through the ancient walls of the house, Elisa could hear the sweet murmur of Anna's voice. Then Theo's soft, familiar chuckle followed. They were together again at last. Their first night together in over a year. In all that time they had never stopped loving, never stopped hoping. He was home now, and their love was stronger than ever.

Someday . . . Elisa dreamed. Maybe someday there would be someone who loved her with such a love. Theo and Anna were friends as well as lovers even after all these years. That was as it should be. Somehow their friendship was a stark contrast to her own loneliness tonight. Thomas had never been her friend. And Murphy? There had been moments when she had *hoped,* a fleeting instant when she had turned and found that he was watching her with such tenderness. But that had been before she had told him about Thomas. After that he had only looked at her with an impatient disdain. And now that he knew she had given herself to another man, his glance held the thought that perhaps she might also be as willing with him.

"Forget it, Murphy," Elisa said aloud in the darkness. She felt the blush of shame color her cheeks. Somehow those words were a script she had written for some future moment when Murphy would look at her and asked for payment. Then the fire that burned within her in hopes of love would grow dimmer with each passing day. Someday John Murphy would be the ashes of a memory in her life, a well-worn American passport, and a name only.

Elisa touched the ring he had given her. She took it off and held it up to the glow of the firelight. The gold of the tiny leaves gleamed softly. She turned it and read again the inscription inside the band: *Elisa—Song of Songs 5:16—Murphy.* She remembered the words without looking at the verse: *"This is my beloved, and this is my friend." Beloved? Friend? How dare he!*

A surge of anger replaced her sorrow, and she flung the ring across the room. With a clatter, it hit the wall, and almost as quickly Elisa was out of bed. She flicked on the lamp and fell to her knees in search of the ring.

It lay in the center of a rosebud on the floral carpet at the foot of her bed. She grasped it and held it to her heart for a moment before she slipped it back onto her finger. "Murphy!" she cried softly. "Oh, Murphy! Why does it have to be such a terrible game?"

There on her knees, the magnitude of her helplessness again returned with a crushing weight. What could she do about John Murphy? Nothing. And what about Leah and Shimon and the others in Vienna? There was nothing she could do. No way to help. Her personal life was out of her control. The events of the world were beyond her comprehension. "What use am I here?" she cried softly. "God, I am so *useless*!"

Images of those she loved came clearly to her mind: Murphy in his rented suit. Row ten, aisle seat. And Leah, laughing at her from across the stage. Shimon, on duty at the kettledrums. And those children. Nameless faces who seemed to be looking at her expectantly for help.

"An instrument in the hands of God," her father had called Elisa. But tonight, like the Guarnerius, she was locked silently away. Waiting. Waiting to be played. As quickly as the thought came to her, it was followed by another. *Even locked away and unused, the Guarnerius had been used. A messenger. A courier in my hands. Across the enemy borders and checkpoints, it had carried messages and passports to safety.*

She bowed her head, and with her fingers working the lapis ring around and around, she obeyed the lesson her father learned in Dachau. One by one she held those she loved before God in prayer, and one by one, she laid them in the hands of one who loved them far more than even she could imagine.

Someone had propped Leah's head on a jacket. "Fräulein?" the worried voice of a young soldier called as he gently patted her hand. "Fräulein, are you all right?"

Her eyelids fluttered open. Something had happened. Now the unhappy face of a German soldier peered worriedly down at her. Suddenly she remembered the face, the hands, the voice of Shimon as he had been carried beyond her reach in a matter of seconds. She moaned softly and closed her eyes. She must not show her grief to this soldier!

Small hands grasped hers then, and she opened her eyes again to see little Charles hovering over her. He lifted her fingers to his cheek. He had seen it all! He had seen Shimon reach out to her from the truck and he understood! He had seen such things before. Now he knelt beside her and stroked her face as someone lovingly had stroked his when he was ill. And in a moment of childish wisdom he put his fingertip to the scarf of his mouth and then touched her lips as if to offer her his silence.

"Fräulein, you have fainted!" The young soldier was joined by two more. Black spit-shined boots formed a ring around them. "You would like us to call a doctor?"

Leah grasped Charles' hand and struggled to sit up. She must be strong! She must not let them see! "I . . . am sorry," she muttered.

The soldier sighed with relief. "It is *hours* after curfew, Fräulein!" He sat back on his heels. "What are you doing out tonight, anyway?"

"Curfew?" she asked. "I didn't know. I . . . I . . . ," she stammered, hoping to find some explanation.

"Are you ill? What are you doing out after curfew? We have orders to shoot looters and any who would . . ."

Leah felt nausea well up in her. "We are not . . . we . . . today in the crowd we . . . I was trying to get home when suddenly I felt . . . faint." She stopped and looked toward the Musikverein. "I took my nephews there to wait and we . . . fell asleep."

"Then you should have stayed until morning. There is a curfew. Everyone is arrested for curfew violation."

At that, Leah began to cry. The tears were not for their predicament, but for Shimon. The last of the troop lorries lumbered by and disappeared around the corner, leaving them alone on the quiet street. "I didn't know," she said softly. "How could I have known?"

"Do you need a doctor, Fräulein?" A tall soldier in a captain's uniform squatted down beside the young corporal who now chastised her for breaking the curfew.

"I just want to go home," she cried, and Charles slipped his arm protectively around her shoulders.

"Can't we go home?" Louis wailed unhappily.

"Fräulein, you have just fainted in the street," the captain insisted. "Are you able?" The concern was genuine.

Leah prayed they would not ask to see her identification papers. "I am not ill," she said in a rush. "Only . . . I am *expecting*, you see, and . . ."

"Ah yes!" The captain seemed suddenly relieved. "Of course, the excitement today would cause you to—" He was interrupted by a tall, slim man who stepped up behind him and put a hand on his shoulder.

"I am Otto Wattenbarger, Captain. Perhaps you have heard my name?"

Leah knew the man was from the Tyrol before he had uttered half a dozen words since his accent was Austrian. She recognized him as one of the men who had been in the Judenplatz with Sporer this morning.

The startled captain clicked his heels respectfully. "She has fainted, Herr Wattenbarger."

"She is out after curfew." The tone of the Austrian was as arrogant as it had been in the Judenplatz.

Leah dared not speak. She silently prayed that he would not recognize her from the ordeal this morning.

"She and the children—" the captain stammered—"she is with child, Herr Oberst Wattenbarger." The captain was obviously intimidated by the arrival of this important Austrian Nazi official.

"You have orders, do you not? Curfew violation means arrests."

"Please—" Leah tried to explain. "We did not know. We fell asleep in the Musikverein, and when we woke up—"

"Silence!" Otto ordered, seeming to enjoy his power to intimidate.

"But, Herr Wattenbarger—" The captain tried to defend the fact that they had not immediately clapped this woman and the children into irons.

The Nazi officer shut him up with a withering glance.

The soldiers stepped back and waited for Herr Wattenbarger to render a decision in this case. "Before yesterday, Fräulein," he said curtly to Leah, "such excuses were a way of life in Austria. Now we must show members of the new order that we from Austria can be as disciplined and hard as they are." The eyes of Otto Wattenbarger glinted steel, just as they had in the Judenplatz that morning.

Is this the man who arrested Shimon? Leah wondered.

"You are with child?" he asked.

Leah nodded. "I could not take all the excitement of today." Her voice trembled in spite of her attempt to control it.

He continued to stare down at her as she sat on the sidewalk. "Yes," he replied thoughtfully. "I can well imagine. Today everyone was a little light-headed." He gave a short laugh, and the soldiers joined him and mopped their brows with relief. Perhaps they would not be reported for not arresting the woman.

"Please—" Leah extended her hand—"help me up. I am better now. I feel much stronger."

The German captain reached out and gallantly helped her to her feet. Louis and Charles immediately clutched her hands and leaned against her skirt. They sensed that the civilian was more of a threat than the German soldiers, and they eyed him fearfully.

"Mothers of the Reich must be treated gently," said Wattenbarger grudgingly. "They are the future of the Reich." He still had not asked to see her papers. "How far do you live from here?" he asked, eyeing the boys.

"Around the corner. Not more than a block or two." Leah still felt dizzy.

"Then I will see that you arrive safely home," said Wattenbarger.

The men around them seemed ready to cheer. She was not going to be arrested! The Nazi would personally escort her home. No one would be reported for being too lenient to this curfew violator.

"We have other duties, Fräulein," the captain said, clicking his heels. "You are in capable hands. On behalf of our Führer, we welcome you and the children to the Reich, and bid you *Guten Abend*! Heil Hitler!"

"Herr Oberst Wattenbarger!" The captain nodded. "A pleasant evening and Heil Hitler!"

Wattenbarger responded with the same salute. Leah did not raise her arm and the captain's smile wavered a bit. Then Louis, after a nudge from Charles, tugged on the captain's tunic for attention and raised his small arm in imitation of the salute. "Heil Hitler!" he cried.

The captain roared with delight and winked at Leah. "Sons of Germany already, you see! Take care of your little one as well, *ja*?" He strode off with the other soldiers. Leah could hear him still chuckling as Otto Wattenbarger picked up the cello case.

"We will have no more unpleasantness, Fräulein." His voice softened. "Tell me if you are dizzy, and we will stop a bit."

"I will be fine once I am home in my own bed." Leah inhaled deeply. She resented this Austrian traitor who now somehow had power over her life. She did not want an escort, especially not one of this kind.

Otto glanced at her, then averted his eyes. "A woman alone on such a night—," he mumbled.

She managed a weak smile. "Believe me, there are other places I would rather be."

"No more of this or I can guarantee that you will find yourself in a Gestapo cell." There was no threat in the words. The statement was a fact, and Leah believed him. She fought to control her anger that such a fact now existed in her beloved Vienna.

13
Small Miracle

It was 8 PM when the European broadcast crackled over the airwaves of New York:

> *"The program of St. Louis Blues, originally scheduled for this time, has been cancelled."*

Groans of disappointment echoed from the youngsters as fathers all over America raised their hands for silence. There was something urgent and frightening in the words of the broadcaster.

> *"Columbia now presents a special broadcast that will include pickups direct from London, from Paris, and other such European capitals as, at this late hour abroad, have communication channels available. Tonight the world trembles as German troops swarm across frontiers in their first offensives since 1914. . . ."*

Historic. That's what they said about the Anschluss broadcast on both sides of the Atlantic. There was a magic moment of silence after Bill Morrow closed out the program, and then a delirious whoop of delight and relief from the technicians and reporters. They had actually pulled it off!

Somebody whacked Murphy hard on the back. "You did great. Had me believing it!"

Suddenly the Nazi takeover of Austria had become old news. The never-before-attempted production was behind the boisterous little group, and they could get on with life. Phelps pulled out a bottle of gin. Strickland produced a bottle of Glenlivet. It was well past midnight, and the English pubs had been closed for hours, but Strickland's little flat in Chelsea was always open.

Murphy somehow forgot his exhaustion as his twenty-some buddies crammed into the tiny parlor and the phonograph blared the latest from Benny Goodman. Women seemed to appear from nowhere. Earlier only Amanda and a secretary at the BBC studio had been here. *The secretary must have called her entire neighborhood,* Murphy reasoned as a bevy of girls flooded through the door, chattering as though it were early evening instead of nearly 1 AM.

Scat Freeman grabbed a homely girl with a big bosom and began to dance as her companion sidled up to Murphy and put an arm through his. She smiled broadly, showing too much of her gums with her teeth. Her hair was piled up on her head, and her neck was too long.

"You're a good-lookin' Yank," she said, sizing him up. "Some party!" Her voice was high. Eleanor Roosevelt with a cockney accent.

"Yeah." Murphy laughed nervously, looking past her. "Wake the neighbors."

"We *are* the neighbors!" She pinched his cheek, then giggled.

"Convenient." Murphy spotted Amanda talking to a group of three broadcast technicians from the studio. They hovered over her attentively and, to Murphy's amusement, she was looking for a way out of the corner. Her eyes caught Murphy's; she smiled with relief, raised her glass to him, and excused herself, walking through the noisy bunch toward Murphy.

"My place is right next door." The neighbor girl batted her eyelashes suggestively. "You look like you could use a little—"

"Sleep," Amanda interrupted, wrapping her arm around Murphy's shoulder protectively.

"Is he yours, dearie?" the woman asked in mock innocence.

"You're propositioning a married man." Amanda leveled her gaze at the woman. "Or didn't he tell you?"

"Cheeky." The woman sniffed and moved quickly on.

Murphy laughed and kissed Amanda. "Right! You *are* cheeky! She had just gotten started on me. I didn't have time to tell her anything."

"Well, now we know why Strickland lives in Chelsea, don't we?" She scanned the room disapprovingly as a woman's high, shrill laughter nearly drowned out the music of Benny Goodman's clarinet.

"Gotta keep the troops entertained!" Strickland shouted over the din. Phelps gave Amanda a broad wink.

"I think one of the troops just killed a camp follower," Amanda replied dryly.

"What kind of news reporter are you, Amanda?" Phelps teased. "You don't like the press party?"

Amanda cleared her throat. "Really, I think I'll catch a cab and read all about it in the morning news." She smiled too sweetly.

"What?" Strickland feigned injury. "Nothing here of the opposite sex that interests you, Amanda?" He waved his hand drunkenly around his head.

For an instant she studied at Murphy. She had been looking at him with interest the entire night and he liked it. She reached up and stroked the stubble on his cheek. "And you, Johnny! You should go back to your hotel and lie down before you fall down. You look absolutely appalling!"

Since Murphy had gone straight to the news office from the airport, there hadn't been time to get a hotel room. He had mentioned that to Amanda before the broadcast. "That bad, huh?" Murphy replied as she pressed herself against his arm to let a couple past.

"That's what marriage will do to you," Phelps laughed.

"Bad as the Nazis!" Strickland added.

"Don't listen to them, Johnny." Amanda did not step back. "Marriage suits you. I always said you were the one decent man among these louts!"

"That's not saying much," Murphy laughed, feeling anything but decent. He couldn't remember if he had noticed in Berlin that Amanda was more than just another news reporter. Tonight she was a little drunk and he liked her better that way. She seemed less formidable with that crisp British accent slurring a bit.

Phelps was leering slightly. He had noticed the way Amanda leaned against Murphy. "So, Murph, where's your little woman?" He checked around comically as though he expected Murphy's wife to enter the room and bash Amanda over the head.

Amanda batted her eyelashes at Phelps. "Where are *all* the little women?" she smirked. "Back home, minding the children!"

"Children?" Strickland was following a little more slowly. "Moving a little fast aren't you, Murphy?"

"No children." Murphy was determined not to let the banter affect him. Elisa was linked to him in name only. He wouldn't let the thought of her interfere with the delicious feeling of Amanda Taylor against his arm. "No wife! We're separated!" he shouted over another roar of laughter behind them.

"But you just got hitched!" Strickland protested.

"Her mother didn't like me! We're getting *unhitched*!"

"You should have married another news reporter." Phelps looked from Amanda to Murphy, then back again. "Like maybe Amanda. Ink in her veins."

"Ink, yes—" She smiled and slipped her arm through Murphy's. "But warm ink."

"Ink and whiskey." Phelps gave Murphy a knowing look.

"Well, congratulations on your first marriage, anyway."

"And on your divorce." Amanda looked pleased. She leaned more heavily against him.

Phelps raised an eyebrow. "There you have it, Murphy." He grinned. "Warm ink. Hot off the press." He laughed and cupped his hand to Murphy's ear. "We gonna read about this one in the morning paper, Murphy?"

They had time for two more drinks before the taxi arrived. The gin and tonic hit bottom a minute after Amanda and Murphy walked out of the party.

"We'll go to my ex-husband's place," Amanda said confidentially. "I still have a few things there. You can shower and borrow a suit of his clothes."

"Is your ex-husband in them?" Murphy leveled his gaze on her lips.

The corner of her mouth turned up in an intoxicated half smile. She shook her head conspiratorially. "He's off in Italy somewhere. Buying wine. That's his business. Wine."

"What would he say if he found you in his house, and me there in his . . . clothes?" Murphy kissed her as the headlights of the taxi turned the corner.

"We have an arrangement." Amanda touched her fingertip to the cleft in Murphy's chin.

Murphy took a deep breath. "I'd better find a hotel," he said seriously.

"I told you—" she pulled him to the waiting taxi—"he's away buying Italian wines. French wines. German wines. All for England. He'll make a killing if war breaks out." She slipped into the backseat, giving Murphy only enough room to squeeze in beside her.

The long ride to the house was a vague echo in Murphy's mind. He thought of Elisa only once; then he kissed Amanda more fiercely. He wished that Elisa could see the two of them together, wished that she could ache for him the way he had longed for her.

The taxi deposited them on a street lined with tall, stately, Georgian-style houses. Amanda paid the driver, then tugged Murphy up the steps of the house and into the foyer. He swayed slightly and looked around, bewildered. Amanda laughed softly, waving a pound note under his nose. "I'm worth more than half a crown, wouldn't you say, Murphy?"

He could see the glint of Amanda's smile from the dim light of a streetlamp that came in through the window. "Half a crown?" he asked, genuinely puzzled.

She laid her head against his chest as she loosened his tie. "Remember that night in your room at the Adlon Hotel in Berlin? King Edward's speech?" she prompted. "When he gave up his crown for the woman he loved?" She giggled and kissed his throat. "You said you could buy all the love you needed down at the cabarets for half a crown."

Yes. He remembered. In one instant he saw himself as he had been that evening. Drunk and cynical, he had somehow equated love with lust. Love had been something he could buy, until . . . "Elisa!" He spoke her name aloud, and the impact of it crashed through their passion like a bomb.

Amanda stiffened in his arms. "Who?" Her voice was harsh.

He stood silently and unresponsive to her touch. Suddenly he was drained and exhausted. Closing his eyes, he could visualize Elisa as he had seen her that first night climbing into the taxi on Unter den Linden. Even then he hadn't noticed anything but the shape of her legs. Then she had brushed his life again, and he had come to see so *much more*! Her love had become more precious to him than his own life.

"Who is Elisa?" Amanda asked, trying to recapture the fire of a moment before. "No. Never mind, Johnny." She kissed his chin.

"Amanda—," he started to explain.

"I don't *care* who she is."

"The woman I love." He moved her hands away from his shoulders.

"A dangerous thing, love." She pressed herself closer to him, not willing to give up. "Men throw away all sorts of things for love. Kingdoms. Crowns." She laughed a brittle laugh. "Me?"

It would be so much easier just to let her help him forget Elisa. His whole body ached to find some relief, but—

"Amanda." He pushed her back gently.

"Kiss me again, Johnny!" She was begging now. "I can make you forget her. You don't have to suffer." She threw her arms around him, and he pushed her forcefully away.

He could smell her perfume and the whiskey on her breath. "No! You can't!" His words were slurred, but his mind was clear. "*I* can't!"

She stood before him, a shadow in the dark foyer. She drew herself up and raised her hand.

For a moment Murphy thought she would strike him, and he didn't blame her.

She lowered her fist and said coldly, "I suppose you haven't suffered enough, then."

Her words were meant to sting him, but instead he felt a wave of pity for her. "I'm sorry," he said simply. He wanted to hold her for a moment to calm her, to comfort her, but he didn't dare. "This isn't personal," he added lamely.

"Sex rarely is," she spat. "What has this got to do with *her,* anyway? Just a little diversion, Johnny."

How could he explain? A few months before he would have accepted her offer without conscience. "I'm sorry." He let his breath out slowly. "It is more than that to me now, Amanda."

"What's happened to you? You used to be amusing, at least."

"I just . . . " He groped for words. He was grateful she hadn't switched on the light. They stood on opposite sides of the dark foyer and spoke through the echoing darkness. "I guess I found out, Amanda, that love is worth more than half a crown tossed to some dame down at a bar. And—" he took a step toward her, then stopped—"and I'm worth more. And, Amanda, so are you."

She began to weep softly and turned away from him. He knew that he could not allow himself to comfort her or they might end up in bed in spite of everything.

The light from the streetlamp gleamed through the leaded glass door panels like a beacon of safety. Without another word, he opened the door and slipped out into the misty streets of London.

If it had not been for the two young boys at her side, Leah would have cursed the Austrian Nazi who now led them down the narrow lanes toward Elisa's flat. She would have spit on the swastika emblem Otto Wattenbarger wore so proudly on his armband. It would have been simpler if he had arrested her along with Shimon and the others who would now vanish into the yawning blackness of this horrifying night.

She held her chin high as Charles and Louis clung tightly to her hands. She had to protect them, and this one duty somehow protected Leah from herself and the madness of a grief so profound that her own life suddenly had no meaning.

Her teeth were clenched, and her pale face reflected eerily in the glass of shopwindows as they passed.

"There is something going on up ahead." Otto turned to Leah.

In front of Elisa's apartment building a long, black, official-looking car was parked. From the light of the open foyer door, Leah could clearly make out the frightened face of the little concierge as he stood between two members of the SS. He was obviously under arrest.

"The *concierge*!" Leah blurted. "Why?"

"They have their reasons. We must not doubt that." He made no attempt to move on toward the apartment. "Seyss-Inquart is a Nazi, you know. Hitler made Schuschnigg appoint the man as Austrian minister of interior." He glanced toward the shivering little man who was being led out to the Gestapo car. "A smart move on behalf of the Führer, I think. Today everyone who was in support of Austrian independence is being taken for questioning."

"Arrested? The concierge? He is harmless."

"Simply detained until they know if he is harmless, indeed. When the Austrian chancellor stepped down, Seyss-Inquart turned all the security office files over to the Nazi Gestapo, you see. It makes the cleanup so simple. Those like me, who yesterday were enemies of Schuschnigg, are now free men. And those who were enemies of the union of Austria and the Reich are now prisoners." He sounded matter-of-fact. He glanced down at the boys. "A lot of Austrian loyalists are going to learn the Nazi salute overnight, I imagine. But it may not do them any good. Not since the Austrian security files are now in Himmler's hands."

Leah did not reply. She watched in horror as the apartment concierge was shoved into the backseat. The car roared off moments later. "Why?" she whispered. "*Why?*"

Otto stared through the shadows at her. His answer was not harsh but firm. "*Why* is not a question we dare to ask in Germany. Tonight—*now*—you must erase such a dangerous word from your mind and your lips forever." He laughed a short, bitter laugh. "Or at least until the end of the Thousand-Year Reich. Whichever comes first, *ja*?"

As the Gestapo car disappeared around the far corner, Otto stepped off the curb and marched toward the still-open door of the apartment building. At the step, he turned about-face and clicked his heels together. "Heil Hitler!" He saluted; then, without another word or glance back at them, he left them gaping blankly after him.

"Go upstairs," Leah told the boys, turning away from the strange Austrian Nazi who had not waited for her to reply with the Nazi salute.

The door of the concierge's apartment was closed. Leah remembered how angry Elisa had been when the man had allowed Austrian police officers into her apartment without her permission. But the Austrian Schupos had been as gentle as nuns compared to what Herr Haupt now must face at Gestapo headquarters.

Leah grasped the handle of the violoncello case. The stairs seemed to rear back as she stared up toward Elisa's apartment where the boys waited for her on the landing. She seemed to have no strength left to climb the steps. "Elisa?" she called weakly. Then, "Louis, that is the door, there. Knock. Tell Elisa that Leah has come."

Louis smiled down at her but did not move. "Are you our Aunt Leah?" he asked. "You did not tell us your name."

Leah exhaled loudly. It did not seem to matter anymore what happened. *Let the Gestapo arrest me for being the Aunt Leah of a thousand children orphaned by the Reich,* she thought wearily.

At the admission of her identity, Charles reached into his gray woolen kneesock and pulled out a thick envelope.

"Father said we should give this to you, Aunt Leah!" Louis chirped too loudly.

Suddenly Leah realized that it really *did* still matter after all. With a newfound strength, she lugged the violoncello up the stairs and took the envelope from Charles. Then she put her finger to her lips to silence any further words. Someone might overhear them. Every move could be reported as suspicious.

Leah was filled with a sense of apprehension. She did not bother to knock, but ran her fingers along the edge of the worn carpet until she found the extra key Elisa always left for her. Her hands were trembling as she opened the door.

Louis and Charles crowded into the dark apartment behind her. The room was cold. The blinds were drawn. Leah did not need to call Elisa's name. She knew that her friend was not there.

The thought struck her with stunning force: *Perhaps Elisa had also been arrested.* "Everyone!" Leah turned and gazed around the familiar room in bewilderment. "Everyone!" she said again with a choked voice.

She felt a persistent tug at her sleeve and glanced down to meet the concerned gaze of Charles. He shook his head solemnly to contradict his newly acquired aunt. *"Not everyone had been arrested,"* he seemed to say. *"No."* He was still free. And Louis. And Leah was free tonight. At the end of Austria's blackest day, the three of them together made up one small miracle at least. And was there any corner on earth more in need of miracles than this place?

14

One Sad Little Boy

Those men who met with Adolf Hitler in his suite at the Imperial Hotel were among the privileged few who had led the long and desperate struggle of the Nazis in Austria. The Führer had also included in his private audience the Nazis of Czechoslovakia who still had much to do before the prophecies of *Mein Kampf* could be fulfilled.

Otto Wattenbarger, though a latecomer in the struggle of Austria, now stood beside Sporer in the line of a dozen men as Hitler grasped each hand and offered his thanks and congratulations. Sporer received a hearty clap on the back as well.

"And now, Sporer, after such an excellent performance here in Austria, you will return to your homeland in Czechoslovakia and inspire others to follow the lesson we have taught here!"

"I have no homeland but the Fatherland, mein Führer," Sporer protested. "My goal only is that Germany be one great homeland in the very heart of Europe." He clicked his heels. "And that is your goal."

This was the first utterance of modesty that Otto had ever heard from Sporer. Indeed, the personality of Adolf Hitler had a way of making even cruel and ruthless men seem mild.

The words of Sporer pleased Hitler. He gazed intently at his loyal follower. Mesmerizing blue eyes sparkled with emotion. "Indeed that is my goal. The Reich will not forget the men who pledge their lives to such glory!" There was promise of promotion for Sporer in those words.

Now the Führer reached out and clasped Otto's hand. "And you worked for the Anschluss in your native Tyrol, Sporer tells me. When there were but a handful, you were among them. The Fatherland thanks you." He expected no reply from Otto. Enough time had been wasted on such trivialities.

Otto simply nodded in response; he was speechless, as men often were when faced with Adolf Hitler.

The Führer clapped his hands together loudly. "Now to business!" He turned abruptly toward the leaders of the Sudeten Czech Nazis. The party was illegal in Czechoslovakia, Hitler began, as it had been in Austria until he forced Schuschnigg to back down in February. He would do the same with the Slavic pygmies who headed the government of the wretched democracy. What he had done in Austria would now be fulfilled in Czechoslovakia—and the process would not take years, but less than a month, he promised.

No man in the room dared to contradict the great leader's lesson in the management of foreign policy. There were no members of the German military here today to protest what he vowed to accomplish.

"From the beginning the Nazi Party has been a party of the people's will!" As Hitler spoke, his words gained momentum and volume until he was almost shouting, pacing back and forth in front of his small awestruck assembly. "You must rouse the will of the masses! Until you tell them what they must believe, they are too ignorant and docile to know! As Führer of the great German peoples, I myself thus become their will." He paused, his eyes sweeping over each man. "And the will of the Volksdeutsche is that we are one German Reich!" He strode the length of the elegant hotel suite to the window that overlooked the place where thousands of Austrians had cheered him. The memory seemed to please him.

His voice was calmer as once again he began his instruction. "On my bed table—" he gestured toward the double doors that led to his sleeping quarters—"you will see even now a copy of the writings of Machiavelli." He clasped his hands behind his back and rose slightly on his toes. "Next to Wagner, perhaps his writings have most influenced my course."

He was enjoying his erudite display and now began to quote from Machiavelli:

> " 'A prince must not mind incurring the charge of cruelty for the purpose of keeping his subjects united and faithful. For this is more merciful than those who allow disorders to arise, for disorder injures the whole community, while executions carried out by the prince injure only individuals.' "

He raised his hand as if to silence any objections or comments, though no one in the room dared to speak. " 'It is much safer,' says Machiavelli, 'to be feared than loved.' "

Drawing a deep breath of satisfaction, Hitler turned to the men of his classroom. "Those of you who remain in Austria to rule must remember this rule and one other." His eyes blazed with the conviction of his words. "He only injures those whose lands and houses are taken to give to the new inhabitants. In this case we speak of the Jews. Those others who are not injured will be easily pacified, fearful of offending lest they also lose everything. You see? It is written in the book, men must be either caressed or annihilated! They will avenge themselves for small injuries but cannot avenge themselves for great ones. What we do to our enemies must be so severe that we need not fear their vengeance!"

The meaning was clear. The rule of Austria was to be without mercy. Now he leveled his gaze upon those who would return to Czech soil. Again he used the ideas of Machiavelli. "You who return to the Sudetenland must remember how to imitate both the fox and the lion. A lion cannot defend himself from traps." He spoke as though his words were for children. "A fox cannot defend himself against wolves. You must be a fox to recognize traps and a lion to frighten the wolves. Those who wish only to be lions do not understand this. " He smiled benignly, almost gently, as he spoke. "Therefore, a ruler should not keep the faith if it is against his interest and when the reason that made him bind himself no longer exists. We can always find legitimate grounds for breaking our word when the time is right. As it will be soon in the Czech territories."

He gazed off toward a corner of the room as though the words of his prophecies were written there in blood. "As our work continues in Czechoslovakia, it is important that we disguise this method. Learn well to be a great feigner and dissembler. Men are so simple and stupid and ready to avoid conflict that the one who deceives will always find those who are ready to be deceived."

The pause here was long and expectant. Finally Sporer cleared his throat, and the eyes of the Führer leaped to him. "Do you speak of negotiating with the British and the French over the issue of Czechoslovakia? or with the President Benes himself in Prague?" Sporer asked.

The question pleased the Führer. Once again Sporer had found favor with him. "In the end, the Czech government will have nothing to say about what we do there. We must find a way to keep the French and the British from interfering with our goals. The plan is simple. You are to rouse up unrest among the racially German population in the Sudetenland. We will provide the funds, of course, and if agitators are needed we will send the required number as we did here in Austria. You must make *demands*!" The word was shouted with a raised fist. "Demands that are impossible for the government of Prague to fulfill! Again and again you must make impossible demands as the unrest continues.

Some Germans will be killed. It must be. This will provide more fuel to our fire! We will shout to the world about the oppression of the racially German population by the vile Czechs! Then when the government of Benes in Prague refuses to meet the demands of the oppressed people, you must walk away from the bargaining table and we will *march* across the border! Their refusal will be our justification to the world. If I march to save my German kindred, can England and France condemn me?"

The pattern had been set, Otto thought as he listened to the exchange. The blueprint of deceit had been written by Niccolo Machiavelli in 1498. Men were waiting to be deceived then, and now a greater deceiver had entered the world. The simple-minded statesmen who believed in truth and honor would be the first to fall; they would lead their nations into the power of this twisted wisdom.

"The night we marched into Austria we made one demand." Hitler was raging now. "When the office of Schuschnigg met our demand, we made yet another and *another* and *another*! They met them all, but *still* we marched, and the world sipped tea and watched without a word! We have proven the theory! And now we have only to follow it, and the world is Germany's own garden!"

The raging voice dropped to a pleased and quiet whisper as the Führer turned to gaze out the window onto the streets of Vienna. His mouth turned slightly upward as he remembered the cheers of the multitudes. "You see, this garden of ours is made up of many small details. Many intricate flowers together make up the beauty of our Reich. Already the great hand of fate tends to these small details for us." He rose on his toes and clasped his hands behind his back in pleasure at his metaphor. "Here in Austria, the criminals who sought to undermine our plans for the purity of the Aryan race are already being delivered into our hands and brought to justice." He turned now to face the awestruck little band who hung on every word. "Well you may remember the first days of our war against the church. Those men fought against our plan of eugenics and opposed the destruction of the weak, the simpletons, those half-human monsters, and those who gave them birth!"

Otto remembered well the plan of the Nazi Party to separate the weak from the strong among the German people. Those with a deformity were registered and sterilized. Mothers and fathers who had given birth to a child with a defect were registered and sterilized. Some shadow of freedom had remained then, and news of protests by church leaders had filled the newspapers. The fierce debate between those who would eliminate the weak and those who would protect them had finally ended in thousands of arrests. Yes. That issue had once been as strong in Hitler's Reich as the hatred against the Jews. Now that those who were judged as deficient had been put in their place, the Reich had turned to the problem of the Jews.

Hitler's eyes seemed to radiate with the news he was about to give his faithful believers. "I am pleased to tell you today that yesterday as I stood on this very balcony and spoke to the masses, fate delivered into our hands one of the most violent of our former enemies! Surely you must remember the journalist Kronenberger of Hamburg! Ah yes! The case was quite interesting. *Twins.* His wife delivered twins. One was perfect and the other a monstrosity with only half a face! He refused to let the monster die a natural death at the advice of his doctor, even though this . . . thing . . . barely had a mind and was unable even to speak! Then, on the grounds that he and his wife were Catholic, he refused sterilization of the child. He fought it publicly in the courts, and even after his arrest and release, after the death of this woman, he fled the country, taking the monster and the normal child with him." He paused dramatically.

Otto could see on the faces of every man in the room that they remembered the case well, as did Otto.

"So!" the Führer continued, "yesterday as I spoke, the criminal was captured. He fought, and after threatening the lives of civilians, he was killed by our brave Gestapo! A voice against our plan for the master race has been silenced! I take it as a sign that as I raised my voice for the unity of the Greater Reich, such vileness was destroyed at that instant!"

There was a question on the face of one of the men. Hitler saw it instantly. "Well?" he said impatiently.

"Where are the children of this Kronenberger fellow, mein Führer?" the young man asked.

"We assume still in Vienna. It is of little importance. They will be found. They are on the list with other fugitives and criminals. They cannot hide! Two small boys, and one with only half a face! One a half-human monstrosity! We control the city of Vienna now! Every building will be searched. Every concierge has been charged with a duty to report not only this case but others like it. They will not escape to whine about their misfortune to the other nations of the world. I can guarantee this!"

He dismissed the notion of their survival with a wave of his hand. "The same force that brought Walter Kronenberger to his bloody end will also bring his two offspring to us." Now he stared upward as though trying to remember something more urgent. "I use this only as an example of those small details that Providence is sure to complete for us! Today it is the larger plan that we consider! This I promise you who are faithful: What was done in Austria will soon be accomplished in Czechoslovakia as well! Indeed, it is our destiny to crush out the weakness from among us and to rule the world, with the perfection of the German race!"

Like a prisoner playing a hand of solitaire, Leah once again laid out the contents of the envelope on the table. Two passport photos for Charles and Louis. Expired German identity papers. A father's note of hope and farewell to his sons. The few shillings that had tumbled out onto the pile were not enough to purchase even one child's ticket to the Tyrol. It was all they had, however, since Leah had not brought even pocket change out of the Judenplatz.

Wearily, Leah rested her head in her hands and studied the note Elisa had left for her. Delicate letters on the page still trembled with the fear and excitement that had flowed from Elisa's pen.

> *Dear ones,*
>
> *What joy that you have found your way here! We waited until we could wait no longer. My father has come out and we must take him home. I leave you food enough for a week. Stay here and I will be back. My prayers and love are yours. E.*

At least here was some hope. Hold out for a week until Elisa comes back. Stay off the streets, out of sight, far from the raging brutality that must surely consume itself as a fire consumes dry wood and then dies!

Leah sighed and glanced toward the sleeping children. The sons of Walter Kronenberger were kindling for the Nazi inferno. She herself was dry wood. As long as they remained in the German Reich, the flames would seek them out. Did she dare wait even a week for Elisa? Or would it be better to take the boys to the Tyrol now and then return to Vienna until she could gather some ransom to buy Shimon's freedom? And what if Elisa did not come back?

Three times this morning, Leah had tried to telephone some colleague from the orchestra, only to be cut off by an official-sounding voice stating that the telephone system was being reorganized and phone calls for private use were *verboten*! Not only was Leah totally isolated, she was also entirely responsible for the safety of these two small boys.

She stared at little Charles, who slept a sound and untroubled sleep. Probably this was the only time the little boy was unaware of his deformity. *Merciful sleep,* Leah thought, caressing him with her eyes. *May his dreams be sweet.*

Hours ago, when she had first examined the contents of the envelope that had been in the boy's sock, the name Kronenberger had sounded in her memory like an alarm. How could anyone forget the haunting eyes of the child in the newspaper, the child judged by the Nazis to be "unworthy of life" and marked for sterilization? The father had carried on a courageous battle with the help of a priest and their Catholic congregation. Doctors had been brought to testify that in the case of twins, such problems could and did arise, but that did not mean the child was a monster as the propaganda of the Nazi paper proclaimed. In the end, Leah recalled, the child's father had been arrested. The priest had also disappeared. The parochial school of the parish had been closed after charges of immorality had been leveled against priest and nuns and anyone else who had dared stand for the rights of this one child.

The child's mother, pregnant again and guilty of having produced a racially unfit child, was forced to have an abortion, from which she died. A curtain of silence had fallen over the case as it faded from the minds and memories of the public. Such events were commonplace now. Most believed that Walter Kronenberger should not have rocked the boat. He should have submitted without protest. After all, hadn't his resistance led to the destruction of his priest? the parish school? And how many lives were destroyed in the bargain?

Leah put her fingers to her lip and tried to imagine what it must be like to be only five years old and despised for something you had no control over. How she ached for this child! She had seen this pain in his eyes. And she knew that these children would not have been sent to her—a Jew and therefore also "unworthy of life"—unless they were in grave danger.

She quietly made herself a cup of tea as she thought through to an inevitable conclusion. Little Charles had indeed been a symbol of resistance against tyranny. There had been many such symbols, all of whom had quietly disappeared into the Nazi abyss. It was a certainty that if the Nazis realized that this child still lived, they would also ordain that he disappear forever. They would not want to risk that he might escape to freedom and somehow stir people's memories once again. It would not do to have the people beyond the borders of the Reich ask, "How could such a thing be? And could this happen to me?"

Leah leaned against the counter and cradled the cup in her hands. "He is just a child," she whispered. "Not a symbol. He is only one sad little boy."

15

Duty

Uniformed SS men stood at attention on either side of the entrance into the new Nazi headquarters in the Vienna Ballhausplatz. Only a few weeks before, the Nazi swastika had been forbidden in Austria. Now it was everywhere.

Thomas presented the papers identifying himself as a member of the army intelligence unit under the command of Admiral Canaris.

"Second door to your right, sir," the SS guard said in a brisk, official monotone. He raised his hand and clicked his heels. "Heil Hitler!"

Thomas returned the salute, then strode past the row of black-shirted soldiers who lined the foyer to the staircase. The murmur of conversation filled the room. Records of the former Austrian regime had fallen into the hands of the Gestapo, and now newly appointed administrators swarmed into their offices in the same building where Dollfuss had been assassinated four years earlier. The Nazi takeover of Austria had failed then, but now the same men who had gone to prison for their involvement in the plot were firmly in control of Austria.

Thomas wondered if his own grim emotions were evident as he walked by the excited members of Austria's Nazi Party.

The offices of the Austrian Military Intelligence Department were much larger than Canaris' Berlin office. The anteroom was decorated sparsely. The painting of the slain Chancellor Dollfuss was propped against the wall, and Hitler's picture had been put in its place.

A plump, pleasant-looking woman of about fifty was already hard at work typing memos for Admiral Canaris. It was a minute before she looked up to acknowledge Thomas. She smiled and spoke with a

German accent rather than Viennese. It was obvious that the admiral had brought her in from Berlin to fill the position.

"Major von Kleistmann." Thomas clicked his heels together in correct military fashion.

"Ah! He is expecting you! And Colonel Oster is with him now, Major von Kleistmann."

So, Canaris was not alone. Colonel Oster was second in command to Canaris, but Thomas was uncertain of the man's sympathies. Oster was probably a man Thomas could trust, but he felt uneasy now just the same. "Will they be long?" Thomas glanced at his watch. He was desperate to go to Elisa's apartment. "I came here immediately from the airfield as I was instructed."

"I think they both wanted a word with you." She opened the door and stepped in. Seconds later she held it wide and smiled brightly at Thomas.

"Shut the door behind you, Frau Porte," Canaris called to her.

Thomas snapped to attention before his two superiors and gave the Nazi salute.

Oster, a tall, slender man about the age of Canaris, smiled coolly, then reached out and pushed down the outstretched arm. "Please, none of that," he said dryly.

Thomas looked at him in wonder, then back to Admiral Canaris. "Colonel Oster is one of us, Thomas," Canaris explained. "Salutes are not necessary."

Oster laughed. "Haven't you noticed that every arm in Austria is suddenly spring-loaded? Let an SS officer walk by and up pops the arm. Heil Emil!"

"Emil?" asked Thomas, feeling a wave of relief.

"Emil is the colonel's nickname for Hitler," Canaris explained.

"I am the son of a pastor, you see," Oster said with a wry smile. "There are other names one might use for our darling leader, but *Emil* keeps me from using profanity. A little trick my father taught me when I banged my thumb with a hammer once."

Thomas liked Oster, but such outspoken resistance to Hitler made him nervous. Always before, such things were talked about in more obscure terms. When men mentioned duty and loyalty and justice, the absence of those qualities in Adolf Hitler were an unspoken condemnation of his laws and politics. No one had ever created a nickname for the beast.

"Emil." Thomas grinned in spite of himself.

"Of course each of the letters stands for *something*," Oster continued brightly. "I will leave that to your imagination."

In spite of the seriousness of the moment, Thomas found himself working out the meaning of each letter. The combination of profane words was endless. The colonel was a brave and defiant man, not to mention witty. But now that Hitler had taken Austria without so much as a peep out of the Western powers, the best that could be done was to mock him privately among those one trusted totally. Apparently, Oster trusted Thomas, even though the two men had known each other only casually.

Admiral Canaris had filled Oster in on the details of Thomas' useless trip to Cannes to see Anthony Eden and Churchill. That was why he had been called to come to Vienna now. The mission Thomas had undertaken had been a total failure. The spring-loaded arms popping up all over the city, with frightened cries of "Heil Hitler," were evidence of that failure.

"Sit down, Thomas." Canaris motioned toward a chair. Oster sat casually on the edge of Canaris' desk. He looked amused, even though there was nothing left to be amused about. "There is a reason we called you here."

"I came on the first plane as you instructed," Thomas began.

"Good!" Oster replied. "Now there are more German officers in Austria than in Germany. There are more Germans in Austria than Austrians. All the Austrians are under arrest anyway, so it doesn't matter." The amusement in Oster's voice vanished. Suddenly he was angry.

"It is the Austrians' own fault!" Canaris replied in a surly tone. "Seventy percent of our army vehicles broke down on the way into the country. If these fellows had shown the courage of their grandfathers, we would still be on our own side of the border!" His icy blue eyes flashed beneath the heavy brows. "So, now instead of Hitler coming as the maniac he is, they have hailed him as a hero! And this, Thomas, after you have risked your life to warn the British that Hitler planned to take Austria by force. 'No bloodshed,' the Germans are saying now! 'Not one drop of blood in the takeover!' But this week alone there have been seventy-seven thousand arrests in Austria by Himmler and the Gestapo! Jews are still being rounded up by the thousands, and . . . what can those fellows on the other side of the Channel be thinking? We would have arrested Hitler for endangering the peace of Germany if only someone had stood up to him." Canaris was red-faced now. Fury flashed in his eyes, even though his words were spoken in a near whisper.

Oster's bemused expression returned. "They brought Emil flowers when he rode into Vienna, Austrian flowers. No doubt plucked from Austrian graves. It was really a funeral march, you know. A funeral!"

"The whole world has gone mad." Canaris tapped his fingers on his desk. "They've given the madman just what he wanted. Every senior officer in the German High Command warned Hitler that the army was not ready to march. Told him such a move would start a war. And now he crows and struts and shakes his fist at us." Canaris paused as though he could see some scene reenacted before his eyes. "But we are not finished, von Kleistmann."

Thomas felt helpless as he listened. "Admiral?"

"I speak of the older generation of officers. Men the age that your own father would have been had he lived. He was a good and decent man. A loyal German. As you are. I know that there are others among their generation who feel as we do. Hitler has proclaimed that his is a movement of the young generation of Germany. If brutality and lawlessness are a trait of the young, then perhaps he is right. But there must be men among you, Thomas, who remember their fathers and the ways of their fathers. The ways of justice and morality."

Thomas knew a dozen among his closest friends who spoke in quiet disapproving tones about Hitler. "Yes. There are many."

"Then there is some hope for us. Some hope for Germany and perhaps for the world. We have much to do, and you must be a part of it."

Thomas knew that his involvement in the previous attempt to warn the British already entangled him in a web of conspiracy that would cost him his life if Himmler's Gestapo caught wind of it. "I already am a part of it, Admiral," he replied softly. "But what else is there to do now? This is—" he gestured out the window toward the swastika flag that waved over Vienna—"already accomplished."

Canaris grunted distastefully. Colonel Oster picked lint from his trousers, then added wryly, "A wise man, our darling Führer is. He chose to invade Austria on a weekend when all the English gentlemen have left London for their country estates. If you think back, von Kleistmann, the Führer always makes his most audacious political moves on the weekend when the English Parliament is not in session."

Canaris smiled and shook his head. "The difference between Hitler and Prime Minister Chamberlain?" He winked at Oster.

"Exactly," Oster replied.

Puzzled, Thomas looked from Canaris to Oster. He was missing the joke.

"The difference between Hitler and Chamberlain," Oster explained, "is that Chamberlain takes a weekend in the country, while Hitler takes a country in the weekend."

Thomas shook his head incredulously at the nerve displayed by this officer of the Reich. No one he knew would dare display such open disrespect for the Führer. But in spite of himself, he laughed. Then he sobered, suddenly aware of the serious truth behind Oster's wordplay.

The joke was not only funny; it was entirely correct. Every open treaty violation had occurred on a weekend. By the time Parliament returned to London on Monday morning, the act had already been accomplished. There was some genius in Hitler's diabolical methods. In 1936, German troops marched into the demilitarized Rhineland on a Saturday. Everyone believed that the mighty French army would have routed the Germans immediately if only the British government had showed their support. But the British government had been dispersed throughout England's countryside at the time, and when Parliament returned to session on Monday morning, forty-eight hours had passed since the violation of the treaty. German military occupation of the Rhineland was a fact. No one lifted a finger, and now the only thing that separated the French territory from German forces was the Maginot Line.

What had happened in 1936 had now been repeated in 1938. Yes, there truly was a method to Hitler's madness. Now that the buffer state of Austria had been absorbed into the Reich, only the defenses that the Czech government had built in the mountainous countryside of the Sudeten territory stood between Hitler and Czechoslovakia. The progression seemed remarkably clear to Thomas as he sat in the office of Admiral Canaris. Could the British and the French not see where Hitler's next target would be? Were they blind? Or were they as insanely naïve as Hitler was evil?

Thomas thought all this within a matter of seconds. He exhaled slowly, then raised his eyes to meet the piercing gaze of Canaris. "You already know what is next, don't you?" Thomas asked him.

Canaris lowered his chin once in solemn reply. "The Sudeten territory of Czechoslovakia. Ultimately Hitler intends to march into Prague." He glanced toward Oster. "Hitler will lead Germany to war. And if war, then destruction. He must be stopped."

Oster laid out the details of the Nazi plan to take over the Sudeten territory from the nation of Czechoslovakia. "We have an Austrian working for us who has penetrated the Nazi Party here in Vienna. He has been one of us for quite some time. From him we learned of Hitler's plot to assassinate his own ambassador in Austria and then blame a Jew so that he would have an excuse to march into Vienna. We warned von Papen through connections in the Western powers, and that particular plot did not go through."

All Oster's wit seemed to disappear now. "As it turns out, Hitler did not have to have his Austrian ambassador assassinated. He accomplished his purpose another way. But Czechoslovakia is another matter." Oster lit another cigarette and inhaled the smoke thoughtfully before continuing. "Already we have made contact with our Austrian, who has worked shoulder to shoulder with the worst of the Nazi terrorists here. Secret orders have already come from the top that those 'clandestine heros of the Reich,' as Hitler and Himmler call their thugs, must now begin their work in Sudetenland in earnest. They are to create *incidents*—" Oster waved his hand as if to say that these men had been given freedom to use their imagination in the creation of terror in the Sudetenland. "I am sure that it will follow a familiar pattern. Those who are racially German will be murdered and the Czechs will be accused. Riots will occur. Hitler will rage that he is marching to rescue his Volksdeutsche from the evil Untermenchen."

Untermenchen, literally meaning "subhuman," had become a common term used by Hitler and his master race for those who were not Aryan. Hitler hated the Slavic peoples almost as much as he hated the Jews, Thomas knew. In his tirades he called them a pygmy race and vowed to put them in their place.

"And what do we do to stop it?" Thomas spread his hands in helplessness.

Oster and Canaris exchanged looks. "Even I am being watched by Himmler's Gestapo," Canaris said. "Our two intelligence organizations are rivals, as you know. Himmler would seek any way to discredit me with Hitler—"

"If that were to happen," Oster interrupted, "then certainly an admiral's position would be filled by a more *enthusiastic* member of Hitler's following."

The word *enthusiastic* might have been replaced by *brutal* or *fanatical.* Thomas understood what was being said all the same. Canaris must not be implicated in any plot if Himmler somehow discovered that there was a hard core of anti-Nazis among the military.

What neither Oster nor Canaris had explained was clearly understood by Thomas. "Admiral Canaris," Thomas said hoarsely, "you are not expendable. If Hitler is indeed to march Germany into war, there must be some sane men left to fight against him in another way."

Oster smiled slightly at Thomas' understanding of the precarious situation. "I am a major only," Thomas added, his words coming with difficulty. "It is easier to lose a major than an admiral, I think. What is it that duty requires of me, Herr Admiral?"

Canaris studied Thomas intensely. "Treason," he answered quietly. "A violation of your blood oath to Hitler. Perhaps you will earn the hatred of the German people who will blindly follow this madman into hell. If you are discovered, certainly you will lose your life in a most horrible way. And if they extract our names from you by torture, we will deny you, Thomas von Kleistmann! You will die forsaken by your nation and your comrades!"

Thomas looked away from the steely blue eyes of the admiral. Outside in the square, the bloodred banner of the Reich snapped in the wind. The room was filled with a heavy silence. The sounds of trams and taxi horns penetrated the window. There was life outside this office and away from the penetrating gaze of Oster and Canaris. Thomas could stand up and walk away from this moment and live as every other Wehrmacht officer and soldier. If he chose, he could simply close his mind to what was happening until the events carried him away, along with all who looked the other way. So many were helpless against the tyranny, Thomas knew. But if he was willing to deny himself and his honor, perhaps he might be able to do *something*!

"So much for duty," he replied at last. "And what does treason require of me?"

For the next hour, detailed instructions were given to Thomas verbally. Nothing was to be written down. There must be no trace of the treason against Hitler. From this moment on, Thomas would have no contact with either Canaris or Oster until his success was assured. And if there was no success and Czechoslovakia fell to Nazi Germany on the date the Führer had set for his next conquest, then this day and this meeting and all that would follow in the precarious days ahead must be obliterated forever from mind and heart and history. Thomas himself, in that case, would also have to be eliminated.

Thomas left the offices of Admiral Canaris like a man who had heard he was dying of terminal cancer. Every detail of the scene before him stood out in vivid relief. A steady wind was blowing and the Reich flag strained against the ropes on the flagpole. The sky was bright and clear above him, and in the distance high white clouds billowed up on the horizon. He breathed in the scent of newly budding trees and the flowers that had begun to bloom in the public parks and gardens of the city.

There was some relief at least in facing the fact that his failure would require his death. He had nothing left to lose, and somehow this terrible fact was a great release to him. A new spark of determination burned within him.

Arms raised in salute as he passed the black-shirted SS guards. But even as Thomas mouthed the words "Heil Hitler," he smiled in his heart and secretly uttered the name "Emil."

As Canaris and Oster had instructed him, Thomas went from their meeting directly to Fiori's Bookstore on Vienna's Kartnerstrasse. Now he stood outside the obscure little shop and held a book tightly in his hands. Traffic whizzed by, and the thin fragile pages rustled in the wind.

Thomas skimmed the words, as one does after purchasing a new book. He could not find the message that was concealed there. It was just a book. Ordinary in every way. He closed it and slipped it back into the brown paper wrapper, then into the pocket of his tunic.

Fiori's Bookstore was only a few blocks from Elisa's flat, Thomas knew, but he would not go there. Not today. Maybe never again. He would not begin this desperate campaign by involving her. In his pocket he carried duty. Treason. Perhaps his death warrant. No, he would not involve Elisa.

Glancing at his watch, he hailed a taxi. Alpern Airport would be swarming with Gestapo, but they would not search Thomas. He was safe for now, even with treason in his pocket. There was just enough time to catch the afternoon flight to Paris. Just enough time to pass his information to the bookseller on the Seine and then, if all went well, to Winston Churchill before morning.

"Go on, Elisa," Anna urged, turning to search her wardrobe for an appropriate dress for her daughter to wear to the concert at Prague's National Theatre tonight. "Wilhelm and Dieter and I have had the tickets for two months." She smiled over her shoulder and pulled out a blue silk evening dress. "Beethoven's Fifth, and George Schleist conducting! Something nice for a change, Elisa! You will be able to sit in the audience and listen."

Elisa could hardly find the enthusiasm to smile let alone think about attending a concert tonight. Schleist had been a guest conductor with the Vienna Philharmonic only a week before Rudy Dorbransky had been murdered. At the rehearsal, the conductor had interrupted the orchestra again and again, asking that a certain passage be repeated. At last Rudy had bowed slightly and replied, "If you interrupt us once more, we shall play it as you conduct!" The pointed insult had brought a chorus of half-suppressed snickers from the orchestra, and that night throughout the entire performance Elisa had forced herself to frown seriously and avoid Leah's amused gaze from the other side of the stage. Afterward they had dissolved into tears of laughter when Rudy had quipped, "I don't know what he was conducting, but I think we played Beethoven's Fifth quite well!"

That same night Murphy had been there. Row ten, aisle seat—in his rented dinner jacket, totally oblivious to the undercurrent of hysterical laughter that had threatened to break out onstage. Yes, Elisa remembered Murphy's gaze on her. Twice she had glanced up, and he had made her forget everything else.

Somehow the happiness of such a memory seemed far too painful to bring up now. Rudy was dead. Leah was lost somewhere within the iron fist of the Greater Reich. And Murphy had simply vanished without a word of farewell.

Still, Anna had purchased the tickets months ago, and perhaps an evening out would be a diversion. "I know why you want me to go." Elisa touched the blue silk of the gown. "You and Papa want to be alone." She was only partly teasing.

Anna lowered her chin slightly and replied with uncharacteristic coyness, "Something like that."

Anna was young once again and seemed almost oblivious to the harsh reality of what was taking place in Austria. Theo was home. Her children were safe. Was there anything else that mattered? Elisa could see that it still had not entered Anna's mind that soon enough Elisa must return to Vienna. She would never be content simply to attend the Prague concert hall as a spectator. No. A performance awaited her in Austria, and she would return with or without Murphy.

Elisa held the dress up and gazed in the mirror. Her blue eyes were bright with her secret. "If that is the case, Mother," Elisa replied, "then I suppose I should go."

16

Private Battles

The concert at the National Theatre was indeed painful for Elisa. It was not the wobbly horns or the lack of precision in the first violin section that bothered her, but rather the thousand memories that flooded her heart. Notes written on a page and then brought to life in wood and strings and reeds and brass—all that remained the same. Only the faces of the musicians were different. Even the instruments outlived the artist who caressed them so gently, just as the Guarnerius violin had outlived Rudy. And Elisa imagined that the violin would outlive her as well.

The applause faded as the lights of the auditorium came up. Elisa moved slowly through the crush of the crowd in search of fresh air and freedom from the emotions that pressed so heavily on her.

Tall and remarkably handsome, Wilhelm took his sister's arm. "Would you like to go back and have a word with Conductor Schleist?" he asked.

Elisa managed a smile of disapproval. "Was *he* here tonight?"

Wilhelm and Dieter both laughed heartily at her remark. "They say that Schleist is all they have left to conduct in the Reich," Wilhelm said in a low voice as they passed a group of German-speaking concertgoers. "The music has gotten so bad there that this is the *real* reason so many people are trying to get out!"

Elisa giggled in spite of herself and hugged his arm. Wilhelm had grown to look so much like Theo over the last year and had acquired quite a wit as well. Young Dieter seemed more quiet and sensitive, and bore a resemblance to Anna. Elisa was proud of them both for the way they had helped Anna through the last year of uncertainty. They had, it seemed, become men overnight.

"Anyone for coffee?" Dieter asked cheerfully, not willing to let go of the evening.

"Or perhaps something stronger to help us forget the music!" Wilhelm agreed.

"You're not *that* grown-up," Elisa chided. "But coffee? Yes. Where shall we go?"

They stood together on the steps of the theatre as the crowd surged around them. Across the square the lights of Café Slavia beckoned brightly. Here the Czechs would enjoy their after-theatre coffee and drinks. "We can go to the Slavia if you will not speak German, Elisa. They will throw us out if you speak German in there. *Only* Slavs allowed!" Wilhelm held her hand in his protectively.

"We could go to the Café Continental on the Graben," volunteered Dieter.

"There one must *only* speak German," Wilhelm warned. He frowned. "I am afraid I don't want to go there, either." He made a fist. "All I need to hear is one comment about the lovely Führer and the peaceful Anschluss, and I might . . . " He shook his fist playfully.

"My big, strong brothers," Elisa said, pushing the fist down to Wilhelm's side. "And where do we fit? Not with the Czechs and not with the Germans anymore, certainly. Maybe we should just take a walk so nobody bashes any heads, *ja*? We have already heard the murder of Ludwig von Beethoven tonight, and I don't think I am up to any more violence!"

Ignoring the numerous green taxis of Prague, the three walked arm in arm down the dark, narrow streets of the Old City. They spoke but a few words to one another, and yet in unspoken agreement they moved toward the Charles Bridge.

The soft ripple of the Moldau River sounded against the pilings. A thousand votive candles flickered at the feet of the statue of St. Nepomuk. Elisa had been here with Leah, then with Murphy. Now she leaned against the rail between her brothers and gazed into the dark waters below.

Long, peaceful minutes of silence were shared by the three until at last Wilhelm spoke. "I am glad Papa has come home." There was more than just relief in his words; there was *release.* "We have lived in Prague for over a year. I am eighteen now. The same age as Papa when he learned to fly."

The words were a rock thrown into a glassy pond. Elisa looked at him sharply. "What are you saying?" she asked, even though his meaning had been clear enough.

"I am joining the air corps next week."

"But, Wilhelm, your schooling! The university!"

"There are things that seem more urgent. We have made this place our home, Elisa. The Czechs have welcomed us. They do not have the hatred of Jews as the Germans do. And now Austria has fallen. Our new home is surrounded on three sides by the Reich. And on the other side is Poland, and Russia beyond!" He was staring intently into the darkness.

Dieter gazed in wordless surprise at his brother.

Elisa argued gently, somehow realizing her words could not stop him. "There will be no war in Czechoslovakia, Wilhelm. Finish your time at the university, and then—"

"No." He shook his head. "Nazis on one side, Elisa, and Russia on the other. Tell me, please, how we will survive in the middle of Hitler and Stalin?" He leveled his gaze on her. "I spoke with a Russian fellow yesterday who says that during the last year Stalin killed a million, maybe more, in a terrible purge. We are locked between two madmen here, Elisa. No matter which way we turn, we cannot find peace. And all the wishing of Papa will not make it so."

"But the air corps, Wilhelm!"

"Perhaps with the help of France and Britain, we may remain strong here. I want to be a small part of it." He turned away as though he saw his future in the blackness of the night. "This nation welcomed us. It is my home now. Yes. I wish to be a flyer. Like Papa was. I will fight for my new homeland. Against Germany, if I must. Against the Aryan boys who were once my friends. Papa is home now. Mother will have to let me go," he finished.

Elisa took his hand and forced him to look her in the eyes. *"Bis dahin!* I suppose it has come to that," she said sadly. She did not tell him of her own private battle. She would not tell him. He would fight openly, but she must remain silent like the silent stone St. Nepomuk who gazed down upon all three of them with pity.

No doubt the entire shabby neighborhood on the outskirts of Paris had heard the bitter shouting of Herschel Grynspan's uncle. "Life is difficult enough without another mouth to feed! Of course I said you could come! What else was I to do when my brother writes from Germany such a desperate letter? Yes, I said you could come! But if you are to stay here in Paris, you will have to find work!"

"I supposed I could work for you, Uncle," Herschel said in a hurt voice. The wildly gesturing man before him bore no resemblance to Herschel's father. It was difficult to believe that this red-faced little tyrant was any relation at all.

"Work for me? Ha!" It was an accusation. "I barely have enough work for myself. All of Paris is crowded with tailors; Jewish tailors running away from Germany! Now they will come from Austria as well! Prices for my work have gone to nothing. Nothing! And now my own brother sends me the very thing that has nearly driven me to bankruptcy—a refugee! You *can't* work for me. And if you plan on staying here any longer, you will find a job!"

Herschel nodded guiltily and stepped back as though the words of his uncle were blows. The boy had fled Germany and come to Paris expecting to find a reflection of his father's kindness and hospitality with his uncle. From the beginning, his hopes had been broken. Herschel had been greeted with an almost grudging reserve at the station. The first meal with his aunt and uncle had been silent except for a few obligatory questions. Herschel had been given a corner in a windowless and unheated attic. His hoped-for haven had turned out to be a hell of silence and resentment. Now the boy hung his head and listened as the haranguing continued far past any purpose.

"Are you clear on this? I cannot support you! The only redeeming factor is that you are small! Not so much to feed, although certainly too much!"

Herschel nodded, fighting back tears of loneliness and a longing to see his father once again. *Could it be that there are two Israel Grynspans in Paris, and I have gone to the wrong one?* the boy wondered silently. "Of course. Yes. I will try to find work."

"Good! Then tomorrow you will apply for a work permit." The color in Israel's cheeks remained deep red. His voice was still harsh in the reply to Herschel's every comment.

"Where . . . ?"

"Do you *hear*? At the government offices, you fool! Can this truly be the son of my brother?"

Herschel determined that he would ask no further questions of the raving man before him. He swallowed hard, feeling that he might be sick unless the shouting stopped. "Yes. First thing in the morning. You will see. I will have a work permit."

Israel eyed him with silent disdain. He snorted like a bull, then turned on his heel and left the small kitchen, slamming the door behind him.

Herschel blinked at the door. He stood in the center of the room, uncertain where he should go or what he should do next. The path to his attic led right past his uncle's overstuffed chair. Herschel did not want to risk another outburst.

He was suddenly very thirsty, but even a glass of water seemed like an imposition. His aunt had looked at him angrily when he asked for a glass right after she had washed the dishes. Turning slowly around, Herschel scanned the small table and tiny counter. This was not home—not even a slight resemblance either in setting or emotion. There was no thought of making an application to the university now; only the desperate hope that he could indeed acquire a precious work permit and somehow find a small flat of his own. "A prison, Papa," he murmured. "More certainly than if I had stayed at home in Berlin. Paris has become a prison."

The boy could whisper those words now, but he could not write them to his father at home. News from Paris must be only good. Herschel had determined that fact long before he had passed over the border. He would send back words of hope to his parents to tide them over through his father's long convalescence after the Gestapo's midnight attack.

From the top of the stairs, a woman's voice shouted down on him, "Is he still here?"

"I don't know," Israel answered. "I think he left through the kitchen."

"Thank God! A little peace!"

At that, Herschel bolted out the back door and scrambled down the rickety wooden stairs into an alley littered with garbage. He ran wildly between rows of tenement apartments. Tears streamed freely down his cheeks as he searched for some open place, some patch of sun.

Ragged children shrieked and played as he charged past them. No one commented on his flight; it was not unusual to see young men running away in this neighborhood. He tripped and fell, tearing the knee of his trousers, but he did not seem to notice or care. Above him was a crisp blue sky, but he was lost in a dark and lonely maze of the back streets of Paris. He lay panting for a moment beside a pile of garbage; then he looked up at the thin line of cold blue sky and shook his fist in the face of an uncaring heaven. "*Gott!*" he cried. "*Warum? Warum?* Why, why, why?"

Slowly he pulled himself up, wincing now at the scrape on his knee. He stood in the narrow alleyway with his hands hanging limply at his sides. Ahead, the filthy corridor opened onto a larger boulevard. Bright-colored taxis raced by, and Herschel walked wearily toward them.

He had seen nothing of Paris in his short and dreary stay. Without thinking, he stepped onto the sidewalk of the boulevard and glanced up at the street sign. "Rue du Cherche-Midi," he read aloud, testing his French. "Search for Noon." It was a strange name for a street, certainly, and stranger yet was the thick-walled building just across from where he stood. Massive arches and tiny slit windows gave the building the appearance of a massive, airless tomb. Above the main entrance the words *Search for Noon* were repeated; just beneath that was a plaque that identified it as a prison.

As though hypnotized by the sight of the structure, Herschel stepped off the curb and walked toward it. A taxi swerved and honked as he crossed in its path. "I know this place," Herschel murmured. "Yes. I know this place!" He put out his hand to touch the solid stone of the archway. He pressed his fingers to his forehead, trying to recall where he had seen a photograph or woodcutting of the military prison.

"Search for Noon." Herschel frowned and stepped back to stare up at the tiny windows of the forbidding place. He imagined the men still held as prisoners even now. Perhaps they stood at the narrow slits and gasped for air. Perhaps they looked down at him at this very moment and envied him his freedom. Slowly he raised his hand in greeting to his unseen comrades behind the immense stone walls. They could not know that he, too, was a prisoner.

Although Thomas knew that the precious book he carried held some secret message for the British, he had not been able to find it. Curiously he stared at the pages as he sat beside the broad Seine River where the Paris booksellers had set up their stalls. The fact that the message was hidden even to him was a comfort to Thomas. After all, if he could not find the coded words of warning from Hitler's inner circle to the British, then perhaps the Gestapo would not find the secret either.

He inhaled the sweet spring air of Paris. Sunlight warmed his back, and hope warmed his mind. The great bell tower of Notre Dame rang out the hour of noon as Thomas closed the book and tucked it into his pocket. Acres of busy bookstalls stretched out beside the riverbank. As he had been instructed, he browsed slowly from one stall to another, flipping through the pages of books on dozens of tables. He must appear as though he were not in a hurry as he moved steadily closer to the stall of the old man they called Le Morthomme. His name meant "the Dead Man," and when Thomas had eyed Canaris and Oster doubtfully about the genuineness of such a name, they had both smiled and sworn that this was the true name of the old bookseller. One had only to ask for directions for the bookstall of Le Morthomme in Paris, and any ordinary citizen knew where to find him. The Dead Man, it seemed, was very much alive and quite well-known for his vast collection of rare books.

Thomas put his hand into his pocket and touched the book. Le Morthomme would know what to do with it, and by tomorrow morning it would be in the hands of British Intelligence.

"Excuse me, *bitte,*" Thomas asked a busy bookseller as the man unpacked a crate of old magazines and spread them on his table. "I am looking for the stall of Le Morthomme."

The bookseller did not look up. He jerked a thumb toward the opposite aisle. "That way to Le Mort. Third stall down. You look for German books? I have a few. Look here first."

Thomas thanked him and walked toward the stall. He recognized Le Morthomme from Oster's description. Nearly lost behind towers of tottering books, the old bookseller bargained happily with customers, usually winning his price. Thomas watched him, relieved that the little man was exactly as Thomas had been told to expect. His leathery face was wrinkled with pleasure. A shapeless beret perched on the right side of his head. He wore a thin black string tie around his neck, and he gestured broadly and emphatically as he spoke.

"For such a meager price I cannot sell this book, monsieur! Can you not see the quality of the binding? the gold lettering here? Two hundred years old, and still the book is exquisite! You could not have a book re-covered for what I offer this for! Take a shabby book to a bindery, monsieur, and see for yourself! I will not take less than this! And if you will not buy it for that price, I swear that within the hour someone else will!"

Thomas drew in his breath and exhaled nervously as he approached the victorious Le Morthomme. He had won. His customer counted out the cash as the wizened old face smiled and reassured the man that this was the greatest bargain in Paris. Perhaps it was. Thomas was in no position to doubt anything today. He removed the precious cargo from his pocket now and approached the Dead Man.

"You were recommended to me," he said quickly.

The old man's eyes rested on the cover of Thomas' book, then shifted back to his anxious face. "Sooner or later every bibliophile in the continent comes to the table of the Dead Man." He grinned, and Thomas could see that most of the old man's teeth were missing in front. "You come to sell or buy?" The Dead Man already knew the answer. The volume that Thomas displayed held the reply.

"Perhaps a trade. An appraisal, at any rate. They say you are the best judge of the worth of a book." Every word was prearranged as confirmation of Thomas' identity, and yet the expression of the old bookseller betrayed nothing sinister or out of the ordinary. He extended his wrinkled hand and took the book from Thomas.

Flipping through the pages, he seemed to examine the binding and the typeface. "Of course. You are in a hurry, monsieur?"

"No. A day or so . . . "

"A day. Yes. For a franc I can give you an accurate appraisal. What I would pay wholesale, or what you might expect if you consign the book for sale with me. Your name?"

"Von Kleistmann."

"A German! Paris is full of Germans, all looking for good books! You will find every book banned in Germany here on my tables, monsieur!"

"Perhaps I will have time tomorrow to look," Thomas replied, glancing at his watch.

"Come back at noon." The old man knelt and wrapped the book in newspaper, then slipped it into a box under the table. "I will have a reply for you, and perhaps we will do business."

The Dead Man dismissed Thomas with a wave of his hand, and without another word he directed his attention to a customer who flipped through a first-edition volume of *The Count of Monte Cristo.* "Monsieur!" he barked. "Do not handle such a treasure as if it were the Paris telephone directory!"

Thomas suppressed a smile as he walked away from the bookstalls. It had all been so easy, so remarkably easy! His treason had been accomplished without a slight twinge of pain or fear or even guilt.

17

The Summons

At least the members of the House of Commons had the decency on this dreary Monday morning in London to sit somberly in their places. Murphy took his seat in the press gallery among the correspondents from nearly every major newspaper in Europe and America. It seemed as though there were more members of the press gathered than the building could hold. Murphy's bleary-eyed colleagues filed past him. Amanda Taylor was not among them. *How could she miss such an event?* Murphy wondered.

This morning, no one doubted, Winston Churchill would certainly stand up and shake his pudgy finger at the members of Parliament with a firm *I told you so!* To which he might add a further word of warning about Hitler.

No sober newsman in London would dare miss such a show. Murphy looked down the long row of expectant journalists. At the end of the row sat Helmut Andiker, correspondent for the largest daily newspaper in Czechoslovakia. Three rows behind him, looking very smug and self-satisfied, was Georg Bacher, the German correspondent for Hitler's own Berlin-based propaganda sheet. He was the only man in the entire gallery with a tight-lipped smile on his face. The mood among the others in the press corps was so grim and angry that Murphy wondered how Bacher had managed to elbow his way into the assembly without losing a few teeth in the process.

Murphy searched for the face of the usually cheerful and gregarious Isaac Fliker, the Austrian correspondent. He was not with the others. Murphy hoped that he had not returned to Vienna. The man was Jewish, and right now a Jewish journalist in the new Greater Reich would stand less chance of survival than a bug crawling across Trafalgar Square. They had all heard about Hitler's triumphal entry into Vienna yesterday amidst cheering, possibly terrified, crowds of onlookers. Murphy sincerely hoped that Isaac had not gone crazy and decided to write his last article in Vienna. Maybe he had slipped away and gotten quietly drunk. There was little else to do.

Murphy shifted uncomfortably on the hard bench. He ached all over. He could not remember now when he had had his last full night of sleep. Even when he had the opportunity to close his eyes for a few hours, his rest was full of uneasy dreams, memories of German bombs dropping in Madrid in the cause of Franco and Fascist Spain, and visions of the future. Visions of apocalypse here. In London. In all of Europe. And in the midst of it all he saw the upturned face of Elisa as she had laughed at the tiny figure of Death with his hourglass in the clock of Old Town Prague. The sands were running down for everyone. There would soon come a day when Death did not retreat any longer at the passing of the hour.

Winston Churchill knew the face of Death as well as anyone. And when he began to speak, it was obvious that his knowledge was resented.

He began with a slight nod of acknowledgment to Prime Minister Chamberlain, who sat very still and aloof from the stares of every man in the room. At first it seemed that Churchill directed his oratory only at Chamberlain as if there were no one else to hear.

"The gravity of the events of March 12 cannot be exaggerated." He cleared his throat as if to let that thought sink in. "Europe is confronted with a program of aggression, nicely calculated and timed, unfolding stage by stage." He glanced at his notes, then looked away as though mere words could not capture the danger of this moment. Murphy focused on the ashen face of the Czech reporter as Churchill continued. "There are only two choices open, not only to us but to other countries: either to submit like Austria, or else take effective measures while time remains to ward off danger; and if it cannot be warded off, to cope with it!" A grudging murmur of approval rippled through the hall as the speech gained momentum.

Murphy scribbled notes in his own strange shorthand. "If we go on waiting upon events, how much shall we throw away of the resources now available for our security? How many friends will be alienated? How many potential allies shall we see one at a time go down the grisly gulf? How many times will bluff succeed until behind the bluff, continually gathering forces have accumulated reality?"

"Hear, hear!" shouted one young MP enthusiastically, and a few others tapped their feet against the floor in agreement.

The voice of Churchill rose to a resounding crescendo. "Where are we going to be two years hence, for instance, when the German army will certainly be much larger than the French army, and when all the small nations will have fled to Geneva to pay homage to the ever-growing power of the Nazi system, and to make the best terms that they can for themselves?"

The question, like Murphy's vision, was a prophecy of doom and terror for Europe. The audience shifted in their seats and, unable to face such a prophecy, most of them closed their ears to his words. Murphy watched as men looked away to the ceiling and scribbled notes to one another. Churchill cried out his warning for the perilous safety of Czechoslovakia and her giant Skoda munitions industry. Then he spoke of the rich oil fields of Rumania, which also stood in the path of Hitler's plan of conquest. But he had already lost his audience. They simply did not want to hear or believe that more might be lost to Europe than little Austria.

"Czechoslovakia is only a small democratic state, but they have an army two times as large as ours; they have a munitions supply three times as great as Italy's! They are a virile people and have a will to live freely!"

Some Englishmen were even uncertain how to pronounce the outlandish name of Czechoslovakia. How could they be expected to care about the country that must certainly be next on Hitler's agenda of conquest? Murphy wanted to stand up and shout to these men with hooded expressions who yawned politely behind their hands: *"Wake up, you fools! Listen to him and act before it is too late!"* But he sat in silence with the rest of the press corps.

"Czechoslovakia is now isolated! It may now be cut off unless out of our discussions arrangements are made securing the communications of Czechoslovakia."

No one hears you, Winston. Murphy felt sick. *They don't want to hear you. A voice crying in the wilderness* . . .

Murphy mentally checked off a list of the procedures he would have to follow to get Elisa and her family out of Prague. A visa to the United States. He would show her Times Square. It was only a matter of time now until the hour would toll for the Nazis, and Death would ring his little bell.

The arguments of Churchill were inevitably ridiculed by the prime minister and dismissed by the members of Parliament as the sort of nonsense that sold newspapers but served no real purpose. Just as Hitler had received a verbal slap on the wrist when he invaded the Rhineland, the invasion of Austria was "deplored," but no action would be taken.

Disappointed but not surprised, Murphy filed out of the press section with the other correspondents. As it turned out, Amanda had not really missed much by staying away. Several members of the press corps would have been better off if they had nursed their hangovers and listened to Churchill on the radio at home.

Strickland looked undamaged by the previous night. He met Murphy just outside the entrance of Parliament and slapped him hard on the back. "Still dressed like a bum, I see." He eyed Murphy's wrinkled suit. "Thought Amanda was going to dress you last night."

Murphy shrugged. "I got fresh. She let me have it and sent me packing." Murphy hoped he could at least salvage some vestige of dignity for Amanda. No doubt they had been the subject of gossip last night after they left together.

Strickland did not seem surprised. "Figures. So, are you packed?"

Murphy laughed. "Everything I have I'm packing on me. This is it."

Strickland glanced at his watch. "That makes it simple. You've got less than an hour to get to Heathrow."

"You sending me back into the fray so soon?" Murphy was relieved at the thought that he would not have to stay on in England. To return to Vienna now meant that he would be back in Prague with Elisa at least a week before he had thought it possible. He had a lot to tell her.

Something had happened to him along the way. He had fallen in love. He felt a new wind blowing in his life and waking him up. He *had* to tell her the truth. When he had muttered the words of the short version of the wedding ceremony, he hadn't realized that it really had meant a lifetime commitment for him. Maybe she would listen. If only he could have the time to look her in the eye and—

"A different kind of fray I'm sending you into," Strickland answered as he pulled a neatly folded telegram from his pocket. "I don't know what you did, Murphy, but the Chief sent this wire all the way from California this morning."

"The Chief!" Murphy exclaimed. That title was used for none other than Arthur Adam Craine, the undisputed king of American publishing, who owned the *Times* and the INS, and who took a certain pride of ownership in his employees as well. He was the monarch. They were his loyal servants. He ruled his empire from a castle he had purchased in Spain and had dismantled and shipped to California. From his mountaintop lair, the old lion watched over his world, dictating editorial policy, influencing government policy, and intimidating everyone from lowly mayors to the president of the United States himself. A wire from the Chief was ominous. Murphy swallowed hard. "A wire from California? What's he want?"

"He wants you."

"Me?"

"He says he wants to see this young John Murphy fellow. He heard the broadcast. Read some of your copy, I guess." Strickland held out the telegram, and Murphy backed away from it.

"So what's he want me for?"

"If he wanted to fire you, Murphy, he wouldn't want to see you in person. You'd already be on the street. He wants you back in Vienna for a couple days. Pick up impressions. You know nothing is getting out, so he wants you to carry the story out in your mind. See? Like you did for the broadcast."

"Two days in Vienna." Murphy was mentally calculating how long he would need to search for Leah and Shimon Feldstein. And if he found them, what could he do to help them in two days? "Then where?"

"Well, the Chief is in California, and if he says he wants to see you in person, it's a cinch that he's not coming here."

"California! But . . . " Images of Elisa flooded his mind.

"Yeah. California. At the castle. Like Sir Lancelot being called to Camelot. Probably means a promotion. Nobody gets invited to San Sebastian unless they are a movie mogul, a gorgeous dame, or about to get promoted."

"But I can't leave Europe now!"

"You can file your story in Paris at the INS office. You'll have a day before you head for New York." Strickland grinned. "You'd better practice your salute." He clicked his heels and raised his hand. "Heil Craine!"

"What I have to do in Vienna will take more than two days!" Murphy protested.

Strickland shrugged. "The Chief has you on some sort of schedule. Says he wants you for a really big story—*the* story in Europe, he says. But first he wants you to meet some bigwig celebrity in California."

"I can't go. Not now."

"Then you *will* be fired."

"Tell him you couldn't find me."

"Then *I'll* be fired."

"California!" Murphy's heart sank. He had promised Elisa that he would be back. First Vienna, then Prague. He had given his word that he would try to find Leah and Shimon. How could he go all the way back to the States? A trip to California would take weeks!

"You're booked to leave Paris on a dirigible in two days. Sure beats ocean liners, don't it? 'Course, I don't know if I want to fly across the water in one of those things either. Not after the *Hindenburg* crashed and burned. Is that it, Murphy? You scared of flying?" Strickland was talking to him now as if he were a child.

"I just don't see how I can go. The story is here."

"The story is where the Chief says it is." The decision was made. "So, you're booked to New York and then cross-country to California from New York by plane."

Murphy sighed in resignation, even as the thought of resigning from his job flitted through his mind. Travel by air would cut the wasted days by half. If the meeting with Craine didn't last long, maybe Murphy could make it back to Prague before he was missed. "Guess so," he muttered.

Strickland eyed him with fatherly concern. "Look, pal, the last time the Chief noticed you, he screamed an order for you to shut up and lay off the Nazi government. I thought you were going to get canned then. Old man Craine has a little soft spot for Hitler because he thinks the Nazis are fighting the Communists. He's scared to death of Communism. No wonder. The guy is the champion capitalist millionaire. He got along swell with Hitler when he visited in '34, and now Charles Lindbergh has filled his head with all the great stuff Hitler is doing to fight the Communists." He slapped Murphy on the back. "Don't you get it, Murphy? The Chief has forgotten all about that reprimand you got! Not only are you *not* going to get fired, you're going to get promoted! And you're going to get a juicy assignment—whatever it is. At least smile, will you? Snap out of it."

"Strickland, I don't want a promotion. I don't want to be noticed." Murphy knew his protest was futile.

"Well, this is the way not to get promoted. But you'll be noticed all right. Arthur Adam Craine will personally see to it that you don't have a job. He'll make sure you can't get a job, get it? You don't say no to him. As a matter of fact, you'd better agree with everything he says, even if you don't agree. See? Otherwise don't talk politics!" Strickland took Murphy by the arm and was guiding him down the steps toward a waiting taxi.

"How can I not talk politics?"

"Remember, he doesn't want the U.S. to get involved with Europe. He hates the French. Likes the Italians, and thinks Hitler is not far wrong on a few points." The matter was settled. Murphy was going. "He had Winston Churchill at the castle in 1929. If you want to make a point, quote Churchill. Craine likes Churchill."

Murphy jerked his arm from Strickland's grasp and turned, looking him squarely in the eye. "This doesn't make sense!" he snapped. "How can the guy agree with Hitler and like Churchill at the same time?"

"I dunno, Murph," Strickland responded. "But it doesn't matter much. The Chief's in charge of a very big boat. Don't rock it, or you'll end up in the drink."

Murphy got into the taxi, and Strickland jumped in beside him. "This is nuts, Strickland. I'm a small fry. Why'd he have to take an interest in me, anyway? I just want to stick around Vienna." He was really thinking of Elisa in Prague.

Strickland paid no attention. He rattled off a string of orders and emphasized each one with a jab at Murphy's arm as the taxi pulled into traffic. "The Chief loves animals. All kinds. Mice. Birds. He's got a zoo at the castle. Antelope, gnus, lions, and stuff. Tell him you love animals. Tell him you're a dog lover. He loves dogs." Strickland was rattling on like a machine gun, listing the topics that were safe for discussion and those that would arouse the fury of the Chief. "He's dedicated to preventing cruelty to animals. Don't mention hunting, for goodness' sake!"

Murphy blinked at Strickland in disbelief. "Yeah? Hates seeing the little animals get shot, huh? Well, how does he feel about *people* getting shot? Austrians? Jews and the like? Huh, Strickland? Can I talk to him about that?"

Strickland considered the question, not seeming to notice the sarcasm in Murphy's voice. "Gee, I don't know, Murphy. I don't think the Chief is as interested in people as he is in animals. Play it safe. Follow his lead. He doesn't like anybody to disagree with him, you know."

Strickland accompanied Murphy to the Lufthansa passenger plane bound for Vienna. A call from the INS office had kept the plane waiting at the airfield. Strickland stood back and waved broadly as Murphy boarded and the plane finally lifted off.

Murphy sat at the window and sighed deeply as Strickland and London became mere specks below him. The cessation of Strickland's voice was a relief. Then it suddenly occurred to Murphy that he had not had the time to file his story about Churchill's stirring speech to Parliament this morning. As the plane left the coast of England, Murphy decided that maybe nobody on either side of the Atlantic would care much. A.A. Craine, the most powerful publishing mogul in America, was probably more interested in closing down the fur trade than revealing to the world that Europe was about to be devoured in one gulp by men who themselves were more cruel than animals. The thought settled on Murphy with a gloom darker than the clouds that settled over the English Channel.

He did not speak to the other passengers during the entire trip, leaving them to speculate as to why the takeoff had been delayed until he had arrived. "Someone quite famous," they would mutter. "It's a pity we don't know who. . . ."

18
Dead Man

Since the Anschluss and the shooting of Kronenberger, the INS office in Vienna remained mostly deserted. Only a few correspondents were on duty; the covey of reporters who usually hung out there had found other quarters. The place gave everybody the creeps. As a matter of fact, all of Vienna gave everybody the creeps. But there was definitely something morbid about the thought that a man had been shot to death within these walls as Austria cheered the Führer.

Bill Skies gazed around the pressroom at the empty desks. The place had been a sort of press club, even for the independents. The usual hand of poker had folded on Anschluss day. Skies already missed the old gang. *In and out, and in and out. What's new? Nothin'. You wanna play a little gin or drink some?*

Some of the foreign correspondents were Jewish. The smart ones had left a step or two ahead of Hitler. A group of them was now in Prague, where something new was simmering. A few were in Paris, and some of the guys, like Murphy, were in London digging around Whitehall and Parliament.

Then there was Johnson. After twelve hours in a relatively tame Gestapo cell, he had been rousted out at the insistence of the American Embassy and driven to the border, cursing all the way. He was now on the blacklist of Herr Doktor Joseph Goebbels, head of the German Ministry of Propaganda. Johnson was told not to come back to the Reich or else. It was a shame Johnson had gotten himself arrested before the man had been mowed down by the SS in the office. Maybe Johnson could have written something about it when he reached the INS office in Geneva. As it was, Bill Skies and everyone else who was left still had their hands tied by censorship.

Bill hoped that the guys who were still in Vienna would drop in. Maybe in a few days they wouldn't think about the bullets and the blood splattered all over the front desk. The bullet holes had already been patched, and fresh paint covered the bloodstains on the plaster. Bill thought now that he maybe should have repainted the whole office. The fresh paint was almost as obvious as the blood had been. The black-and-white-checkerboard tiles on the floor had been cleaned by two Jewish women the SS had dragged in off the street after Walter Kronenberger's body had been carted off. Still, it was easy to imagine the thick red puddle oozing beneath the desk.

The spectacle had sickened every journalist in the office. The SS and the Gestapo, of course, justified their action loudly when they found the pistol tucked into the dead man's belt. With strict censorship the rule, the incident was barely a footnote to the publicized happenings that week. Walter Kronenberger, they said, had stormed the INS offices, waving a pistol and shouting that he would kill the Nazis. It made a good story.

Was Kronenberger just another crazy pushed over the edge by the sight of the German army in Vienna? Bill Skies wondered.

It was a remarkably common and tragic story. While thousands were being arrested, hundreds were ending their own lives. Poison. Pistol. Gas. A rope over the rafter. When the Gestapo broke down the door to take away another "enemy of the Reich," they often found that their victim had chosen a quicker alternative to a slow Gestapo death. *Maybe that is what Kronenberger decided to do,* Skies mused. *Maybe the guy just didn't want to live anymore. Maybe he spit in a Storm Trooper's eye and ran in here yelling bloody murder. And the SS goons were more than happy to oblige.* Well, whatever it was all about, the poor man sure had managed to empty out the INS office. Until the contrast of the fresh paint toned down a little, the place definitely gave them all the creeps.

As if reading his mind, Timmons mumbled, "Never did like the smell of fresh paint. Makes me sick."

Bill Skies stared at the wall and plugged a cold cigar butt into his mouth. "Yeah," he agreed.

But it wasn't the paint that sickened him. He shivered at the memory of the bullets, tearing flesh and breaking bones. Then he saw, once again, Kronenberger's hand raised in that last desperate instant.

What had been in his hand? Not the gun. The truth was, Skies reflected, the man was shouting that the Nazis would kill *him* . . . which they did promptly. And he *wasn't* waving a pistol.

Bill Skies' reporter instincts kicked in. His mind began churning.

The INS telephones had been tapped. All dispatches had to be cleared by Goebbels himself, who had come to Vienna to make certain that the transition from free press to censorship went smoothly. Austrian newsmen were already rotting in concentration camps. An efficient lot, these Nazis.

A pervasive gloom had settled on the tight fellowship of foreign correspondents. Today, John Murphy was coming back to Vienna, but it was unlike the Vienna they had all loved.

Skies lit the cigar stub. Smoke rose around his big, square head like a cloud. He imagined it smudging the new paint a little, helping it to match the old paint a bit better. He continued to look at the newly painted patch on the wall. No change. Still too bright, whiter than the rest.

Again the picture of Kronenberger flashed through his mind. What had the man reached for? Not the gun. It was something . . .

He sat down heavily and scratched his head as the question persisted. He was supposed to be a newsman. Supposed to notice stuff like that, and remember. He felt old. "Hey, Timmons?" he asked quietly. "The guy who was killed . . . "

"What about him?" Timmons' voice was reluctant. He was only just getting used to the paint smell. Any more talk about what was under the paint and he was going to lose his lunch.

"Right before they got him"—Skies talked around the cigar—"remember?"

"Yeah," Timmons said weakly, wishing he didn't remember. He was a sportswriter, after all.

"He reached into his pocket and pulled something out . . . something." Skies stood up in the place where Walter Kronenberger had drawn his last breath.

Timmons' eyes grew wide. He looked pale. "Knock it off, Bill. I told you, I feel a little queasy."

It was too late. Skies was reenacting the drama—mentally hearing the shouts of the doomed man once again. "Tell them—" he reached into his jacket and then, as he had seen the fatally wounded man do, raised his hand high, and—

"An envelope!" Timmons jumped to his feet. "They shot him just when he got it up. He was yelling at us, not the SS!" Timmons walked quickly to Skies, who stood frozen in his pose.

"That's it!" Skies began searching the floor. "Did they take it? Did the Gestapo get the envelope?" Now both men were on their knees, searching the black-and-white tiles for the envelope.

"It was thick! I don't even think those rats noticed it."

Skies and Timmons ran their hands beneath the adjacent desk, a space too narrow for the scrubwoman's brush to reach. Each at the same moment grasped a corner of the envelope that had fallen unnoticed and camouflaged onto a white tile. With a shout of discovery they held it up to the light.

Printed neatly on the front were the words *The Last Will and Testament of Walter J. Kronenberger.* Two tiny flecks of blood seemed to mark the period at the end of the line.

Churchill had spoken boldly to Parliament about the planned German takeover of Czechoslovakia. In Paris that morning, Thomas had listened to the broadcast with other members of the German Embassy staff.

An exchange of glances told Thomas that Ernst vom Rath had also heard in Churchill's words confirmation that someone in the German High Command had sent the British a message.

Ernst had no way of knowing who had sent the message, or that it had been brought from Vienna to Paris by Thomas himself. Although Thomas trusted Ernst, he would not involve him in this. There was no use endangering Ernst in what was surely a death sentence if Thomas was caught.

Other couriers no doubt ran the same risk, but Canaris and Oster had decided that the less each participant knew about the others, the better their chance of safety if any member was captured and tortured by the Gestapo. Thomas agreed; he did not need to know more than the location of Fiori's Bookstore in Vienna and the bookstall of Le Morthomme on the bank of the Seine in Paris.

It was almost noon when Thomas reached the book market. He walked quickly toward the strange little bookseller's stall. The Dead Man appeared the same as he had yesterday—same shapeless beret, same string tie and frayed yellow shirt beneath a dusty-looking black coat. The bookstalls were not so crowded today, and the Dead Man looked up expectantly for Thomas as the bells of Notre Dame chimed the noon hour.

Thomas was certain he had not been followed and now, in the quiet of the empty stall, he examined the book that the Dead Man pulled from beneath the table. It was not the same book that Thomas had brought here yesterday, but the cover was remarkably similar.

"Our English friend did well," said the Dead Man of Churchill. "But no one cares."

"To whom shall I return this?" Thomas asked in a soft voice.

"Fiori. He will see that it reaches the top."

"What do the British reply?"

The Dead Man opened the book to page 178 and held the page to the light. Pinpricks of light shone through the first letter of each word in the message. Without the light behind the page, the tiny holes could not be seen. *Name, date of planned operations will stand firm.*

So here was the British promise to those within the German command against Hitler. Warned of the coming moves of the Führer, Britain would stand firm against any further violation of territory by Hitler's army.

Thomas closed the book with relief. This was all so very simple. Such encouraging words from the British would certainly strengthen the resolve among the German military to resist further aggression by the Führer! Thomas slipped the book into his pocket and paid Le Morthomme two francs. His book had indeed been valuable! Winston Churchill himself had appraised the information in it and had believed the threat against the Czech nation. Canaris, Oster, and the rest would believe his promise that England would stand firm.

A quick trip back to Fiori's in Vienna would let them know what they must do. Britain must know the date ahead of time! With that information in their pocket, they could deal easily and publicly with the threat.

Thomas smiled. "Tell me how you came by your name, the Dead Man?" he asked the bookseller.

"I have said always that rare old books are like the voices of dead men, crying warning and wisdom and folly to all the future dead men of the world." His ancient leathered face warped into a grin. "You are a dead man. I am a dead man. We are all heading for the same place, *oui*, monsieur?"

Thomas patted the book in his pocket. "Not too soon, I hope."

The smile on the face of the old man faded as he watched a man walk slowly past and cast a furtive glance toward Thomas. The Dead Man lowered his voice. "By Friday noon I look for you," he whispered.

Thomas followed his gaze and watched as the observer strolled on by. Friday noon? Yes. That would be just enough time to get back to Vienna. If there was a date already fixed for the invasion of Czechoslovakia, certainly someone would know of it.

Thomas nodded. "Fine. Yes. Friday will do."

It was early in the morning when Leah was awakened by the sound of men's voices and jolly chortling at the foot of the stairs. She cracked the door slightly and peered down to the foyer.

Three men stood together in the light. The door of the concierge's flat was open. *Have they been searching for something?* Leah wondered.

"Congratulations on your appointment, Herr Hugel!" A uniformed SS officer clapped his civilian companion on the back.

The civilian laughed again and nodded in eager reply. "The reward for loyalty to the Führer all these years!" he said proudly, peering into the concierge's flat. "It has been a hard climb for the Hugels in Austria, but today I reach the summit!"

So this Herr Hugel was to be the new concierge of the apartment building. He looked to Leah like a gross mountain of lard. He was dressed in lederhosen and the woolen jacket of a native Austrian. His enormous belly extended over the waist of the leather knickers, and he seemed to have no neck. Folds of flab were even evident in his drooping eyelids, and his laugh revealed short, yellowed teeth.

It must have been a hard climb for a man of such physical immensity, indeed! thought Leah. She wondered how low a position he had begun from, since his ultimate "summit" was a position as Nazi informer in an apartment building. And now, how many human backs would he climb on for the approval of his superiors? He guffawed again and wiped tears of delight from his watery blue eyes.

"We shall leave you to your task, then, Herr Hugel," said the officer with a *click* of his heels.

Herr Hugel was not ready to give up the importance of his great moment. "Ahhhh . . . the Jew. The Jew, Herr Haupt! A weasely little fellow. Whenever I came to deliver the coal, he spoke badly of our great leader! I did not dare to answer him back then for fear of what the Loyalist government would do if they knew my sentiments."

He wagged his head seriously. "I knew the time would come, though! The little Jew would pay for his remarks. And one day I could speak out!" He peered into his new apartment again. "Quite a nice flat." He chuckled. It seemed to be part of his speech—words and then a burble of laughter. "Too bad my wife did not live to see this day! Always she warned me to keep my mouth shut about National Socialism, but she knew nothing of politics. She knew nothing much, really. A brainless ninny." Again the laughter. "Ah, but I miss my bride. She would have set everything in order, and how proud she would have been of her little Hugel then, *ja*?" Now there were tears of sentiment along with a low snorting chuckle. "Well, I do go on!"

Leah saw the two German soldiers exchange glances. They managed to smile in mock sympathy, but it was obvious that they were not as impressed with the summit of Herr Hugel's success as he was. The new Nazi government in Vienna had need of informers. Men of the basest and most ridiculous natures would suddenly become important. Herr Hugel had not wasted a moment in reporting the anti-Nazi remarks made by

Herr Haupt. Suddenly Herr Haupt was the enemy, and in his place was this greasy coal man who thought so much of himself that he would stop at nothing to elevate himself from his own gutter-rat existence.

So this is an example of those who will hold even small positions of power in Vienna! Leah realized as she shut the door quietly. The thought of a man like Hugel in the same building made her shudder.

Yet somehow his presence also convinced her that she could not wait for Elisa any longer. Days had passed, and her dear friend still had not returned. The news reports, though now slanted to the Nazi perspective, stated that the frontier to Czechoslovakia was closed because of Czech military threats against the Reich. As long as this remained true, Elisa would be unable to get back into Austria. She would not be able to fulfill her promise to return.

Leah stood in confusion in the center of the little kitchen. Perhaps she could take Charles and Louis to the Tyrol herself. But where would she find the money to purchase tickets? That problem alone seemed insurmountable.

There was still plenty of food in the cupboards. What Elisa had figured would feed Leah and big Shimon for a week seemed to stretch on and on. Grief and worry for Shimon had robbed Leah of her appetite, and these two small boys ate little. If they stayed here and hoped for Elisa to come, there was still enough to last them for a considerable time. If it had not been for the installment of Herr Hugel downstairs, that would have seemed the safest course to follow. Why place themselves in danger on the streets when for the moment they had food and shelter, and no one asked any questions?

Outside, she could hear the heavy footstep of Hugel on the landing. The clap of his meaty fist on the door caused her to jump. She did not move to answer his knock until it sounded more insistently once again. Pulling her robe close around her, she tiptoed to the door.

"Who is there?" she asked in a sleepy voice.

"Herr Augustus Hugel!" came the proud reply.

"Who?" She let anger tinge her voice. It was, after all, very early.

"Herr Hugel. New concierge of the apartment! Open the door, please!"

"Go away!" she said angrily. "I don't care who you are! It is only six in the morning, and I am a musician who works late and must sleep!"

There was silence on the other side of the door for a long moment. Herr Hugel was thinking, which was a difficult process for such a mind. The voice that finally answered was less arrogant and somewhat apologetic. Leah knew she must be strong in order to handle this oaf. *"Bitte,"* he stammered, "I am an early riser myself, and I forget. . . ."

In a show of bravery she cracked the door open and faced him. His face was flushed and he was sweating from his walk up the stairs. Leah wished that the flat were on the third floor. He would not often lug his weight up three flights of stairs to bother the occupants above her. Her scowl caused him to back up a step. He looked confused, and once again he chuckled with embarrassment.

"All night last night I performed for the highest members of the Nazi Party," she lied fiercely. "I received many compliments from the Gauleiter! How do you think he will like it if I tell him my performance is ruined by the apartment concierge banging on my door at some ungodly hour because he is an early riser!" Her voice carried, echoing in the hall behind him.

He lowered his chin, causing layers of flab to gather around his neck like a fleshy ascot. His eyebrows arched with shame. "*Bitte,*" he whispered now, "yours was the first flat I came to, and I . . . " He was perspiring heavily. He mopped his brow. "I simply wanted to introduce myself to the tenants."

"You'd better wait until the sun is up!" she snapped angrily. "Or your tenants may throw you down the stairs!" Then, in a burst of inspiration, she raised her hand haughtily and pronounced words of dismissal. "Heil Hitler!" The effect was wonderfully devastating.

The fat man meekly flipped up his wrist and stammered his response. "H-heil, uh, H-h-itler."

With one last withering glance, Leah closed the door on his face in triumph and locked it. She leaned against the doorjamb as total weakness engulfed her. Slowly she slid to the flood and sat trying to catch her breath as Herr Hugel tiptoed away from the apartment.

19

Silent Testament

As Murphy's plane circled above Vienna, he could clearly make out the flag-draped buildings. He remembered not long before when he had viewed Berlin with the same ominous sense of death, and he was relieved that Elisa had remained in Prague.

He fingered the letter she had sent for him to give to Leah. Below him the spire of St. Stephan's rose up like an accusing finger. He knew that Shimon and Leah Feldstein must be still within the shadow of the cathedral; that is, unless they had been dragged off like the thousands who had been caught in the first sweep of the net. If they were down there, Murphy would find them. He had promised Elisa, and he would stick to his promise.

Bill Skies was at Alpern Airport to pick up Murphy. Skies looked ten years older, thin and haggard. "I haven't slept at all." Skies could hardly look at Murphy. His eyes darted all around the building, which was crammed with uniformed soldiers of the German Wehrmacht.

"Even God rested after six days, Bill." Murphy tried to joke, but his words fell flat.

"God left Austria when Hitler marched in." Skies was not joking. He added in a painful voice, "You won't believe it, Murph. You just won't believe . . . "

When they arrived at the Sacher Hotel, they found it swarming with German officers and administrators who had been brought in from across the border. The wheels of Nazi justice were churning as quickly as possible to obtain housing for these new officials. Jews were being driven from their homes through German "legal proceedings," but still such matters took time.

"Every hotel is full of them," Skies muttered as they left the lobby and climbed back into the car. "You can stay with me."

Murphy had already decided that he would stay at Elisa's apartment. He still had some hope that Leah and Shimon had made it there to safety and were managing to escape the net of the Gestapo. "It's okay." Murphy let his mind drink in the masses of German uniforms on the sidewalks. "I'm staying at my wife's apartment."

Skies narrowed his eyes. It was evident he had forgotten that Murphy was married. Skies did not reply or speak until they turned onto the main road from the airfield. His face was grim and pained, and his hands nervously clenched and unclenched the steering wheel.

A thousand questions raced through Murphy's mind, but he sat in silence as if the city were now some vast cemetery. Skies did not seem to want to rehearse the details of the last week, and Murphy did not ask.

When at last they turned onto the broad Ringstrasse, Bill Skies said slowly, "It's been hell around here, Murph. Just hell, that's all."

Murphy could not tear his eyes away from the buildings. Banners and slogans and huge posters of Hitler were evident everywhere—except for the shopwindows smeared with the word *JUDE!*

Now that Bill had opened his mouth, there was no stopping him. "Even the embassy had trouble getting Johnson out of the Gestapo claws. He's in Geneva now. Better not come back, either, they said. But the worst of it—" he swallowed hard—"the worst was the guy they killed in the INS office. It was bad enough when we thought he was just some crackpot, but then—" he frowned at Murphy—"hey, you covered the war against the churches, didn't you?"

"Amanda Taylor and I did as much as we could." Murphy could see the church spires over the roofs of the other buildings and wondered how long it would be until they too faced the ordeal of the churches across the border in Germany. "We had a few contacts among the clergy. One guy used to meet me in the Tiergarten in Berlin with information. After the Gestapo murdered him, I pulled back from the whole thing." His mouth grew dry at the memory. "The Nazis pretty well crushed all the opposition within the church. Amanda still kept up with it. Told me there were eight hundred pastors arrested last year."

"Eight hundred and seven." Skies reached beneath the seat and pulled out the white envelope. He tossed it onto the seat. "Does the name Walter Kronenberger ring any bells?"

Murphy stared down at the name and the words that were neatly printed across the front of the envelope. The name stirred his memory, but so many names had come and gone while he was covering the first gruesome days of the Reich. "Was he—" he fingered the envelope—"pastor? No. Journalist, wasn't he?"

Skies emitted a short, bitter laugh. "You bet. One of the last with the guts to speak out." He glanced at Murphy as they slowed to a stop behind a tram. "The story is all there, Murph. He was on his way to the INS when the SS goons stopped him. Shot him. Blood and brains all over the newspaper office." He laughed again, but there was no humor in the laugh. "Seems a fitting way for a reporter to die, don't you think? He came in to file his last story with us, and they shot him full of holes." Now the gravelly voice caught and Murphy could see dampness around the tough newspaperman's eyes. "But they didn't get the story away from him. Timmons and I found it on the floor. White envelope lying on the white tiles under the desk in the corner. Read it, Murph.What a story! We gotta find a way to get it out of here and publish it in the West."

That would be easier said than done, Murphy knew. At Alpern Airport, the Nazis were literally tearing suitcases apart in search of smuggled foreign currency and any papers that might be considered detrimental to the image of the Reich. Reporters would be searched with special thoroughness. Contraband papers were almost as difficult to smuggle out of the country as human contraband. What had been true in Germany was now doubly true for Austria.

Murphy tucked the envelope into his jacket pocket as Skies pulled up in front of the INS office. Two large, cruel-looking men stood beside the door.

"Gestapo," Skies breathed, turning pale. As head of the INS offices in Vienna for many years, Bill Skies had run the communication service without having to face the Gestapo methods—until this week. The murder of Kronenberger had been a brutal introduction, and the last few days had contained nightmare after nightmare, none of which could be written down or communicated to the outside world.

Murphy, on the other hand, had been in Berlin from the beginning of the terror. He had learned to deal with Himmler's hoodlums with a certain amount of bravado. "Let me do the talking," he warned in a low voice.

The Gestapo agents blocked the door as Murphy and Skies tried to enter. "You will come with us, please," they commanded. "This office is closed for now."

"Routine questioning," the German officer explained as Skies protested. "You will be taken over there—" the man jerked his thumb toward the Rothschild Palace—"along with the other foreign journalists who witnessed the assault of the criminal Kronenberger."

Murphy raised his hands in mock surrender. "Well, if it's witnesses you want, friend, you can let me go. I just flew in from London." The white envelope containing Walter Kronenberger's testament seemed ready to burn a hole in Murphy's jacket.

"That's true," Skies agreed quickly. "Mr. Murphy is an American journalist. Just in from London. He was in no way connected." Skies nudged Murphy. "Show them your plane ticket, Murphy."

It was obvious that Skies had already thought of the Kronenberger document as well. If the story was as hot as Skies believed it was, then the Gestapo and the Ministry of Propaganda would be most anxious to destroy it.

Murphy pulled out his ticket and stood in nonchalant confidence as the officers scrutinized it. "You have only just landed at Alpern." The smaller of the two grim men scratched his head as if deciding what to do with Murphy.

"Right. My luggage is at Sacher Hotel." Murphy was certain that his room had been taken over but still had some hope that the friendly porters had gathered up his belongings and stashed them safely away.

"You are staying at the Sacher?" Now the larger officer doubted him. After all, only officers of the Reich were quartered there now.

Skies interrupted. "He is staying with me. At my apartment. We just left his bags there with a friend in the meantime."

"A friend?" The man's eyes narrowed with suspicion.

"A porter has some of my things in storage," Murphy explained. He was relieved that Skies had given Murphy an address at his flat. If Leah and Shimon had somehow found their way to Elisa's apartment, the last thing Murphy wanted was to draw any attention to that location.

"Regardless," Skies defended, "Herr Murphy has endured a long and exhausting trip. He is no way connected with anything that has happened here the last few days. I fail to see what purpose will be served by questioning a man just in from London about an event that happened in Vienna." He was smiling at the foolishness of detaining Murphy any longer.

"Quite right." The officer nodded curtly and clicked his heels as he presented Murphy the airline ticket. "You are free to go, Herr Murphy. This is only a routine examination of witnesses so that we might have some verification of the state of mental derangement of Kronenberger when he ran into the room."

Skies fished out his car keys and the key to his apartment. "I'll call you at home when we're through. Then come pick me up, huh?"

The signal flashed from Murphy's eyes to Bill Skies'. The Kronenberger document would be safely hidden even as the Gestapo gathered their testimony from the journalists. Beyond the borders of the

Reich, the words of Walter Kronenberger himself would speak louder than the men who merely witnessed his death. The document in Murphy's pocket spoke of life as it had been beneath the iron boot of the Nazis in Hamburg. Relief filled Skies' face as Murphy climbed back into the car and pulled away from the INS office.

Murphy drove slowly through the armed camp that had been Vienna. Nazi flags hung from the spires of St. Stephan's; this seemed like the final blasphemy. The shadows of the spires fell across the roofs of the surrounding buildings and pointed toward the Judenplatz, where Vienna's remaining Jewish population waited for the next outburst of violence.

It was not sandbags that blocked the entrance to the streets of the Jewish district but broken furniture from Jewish homes, long benches from houses of study and prayer, and desecrated Torah scrolls torn from the synagogues.

Murphy could see no sign of life beyond the barricades. The presence of swaggering Hitler Youth members at the barricades kept the tormented Jews indoors. As in Berlin, Murphy thought, it was the youth who seemed most filled with hatred and violence. Hitler had proclaimed that the old ones did not matter to his policies, for he held the pride of the Aryan youth in his hands!

With the Kronenberger document stuffed in his coat pocket, Murphy did not dare to stop at the entrance of the Judenplatz to ask about the Feldsteins. His jaw was set as he rolled past the destruction of the beautiful old district. Leah and Shimon could not have remained unscathed by such violence. Their little flat was at the center of it all, just as their lives had been at the center of Vienna's Zionist movement.

Murphy frowned. If they had not escaped the first onslaught of the Nazi arrival, they could not have escaped this place at all. They had made no secret where their sympathies were. If they were still alive today, their only regret must be that they did not leave sooner for settlement in Palestine.

Now it was too late for multiple thousands of Jews in Austria. Most had never seriously considered immigrating to that desolate, ragged patch of land. One night had made the difference. *How they must long now for the relative safety of that place!* Murphy thought.

Five minutes away was Elisa's flat. Murphy had no intention of stopping, but he drove by all the same. Perhaps he would see some sign of life behind the lacy curtains. What he saw filled him instead with hopelessness for the fate of Leah and Shimon.

In front of the door of every apartment building on the street stood an SS guard. Bayonet fixed. Jackboots spit-shined. Helmet in place. These fierce young men could not have been more than nineteen or twenty years of age, and yet they alone seemed to control the ageless city of Vienna.

The sight of these cocky young guards in front of Elisa's building made Murphy instantly angry. He pulled the car to the curb, set the brake, and forgetting the papers of Kronenberger for a time, he climbed out and walked directly toward the door leading into the building.

Heels clicked, and then the rifle descended, blocking his path. "Halt!" shouted the fair-skinned, rock-jawed young man.

Murphy felt himself tense for confrontation. If the kid had not been carrying a rifle, Murphy was certain he could easily have pushed past him.

"I live here," Murphy said defiantly. He was instantly sorry he had not simply stopped and smiled politely. The young sentry pulled a clipboard off the stone ledge on the building.

"Your name, *bitte*?" He searched the list.

"Bitte," Murphy apologized, realizing that his name would not be on the tenant list. "My German is not so good. I mean to say that I have a friend who lives here."

"And the name of your friend?"

Now Murphy had done just what he had not wanted to do. If he mentioned Elisa's name, then some attention, however small, would be focused on the flat. Murphy stammered, pretending not to clearly understand the question.

Impatient with this ignorant American, the sentry snapped his question again. "And what is the name and apartment of this friend of yours?"

"The name of my friend?"

"Ja, ja, ja!"

"Bill Timmons," Murphy replied. "An American journalist, as I am."

Hard eyes scanned the clipboard. "There is no tenant here by that name."

Now Murphy feigned confusion. "I don't understand. He said the address was 541—"

"This is 145! *Dummkopf!"*

Murphy smiled. They were not only fierce-looking, they had no manners, either. "Well, so it is." He tipped his fedora and thanked the sentry, who simply rolled his eyes in irritation.

Angry at himself now, Murphy climbed back into the car. He would not try to enter the apartment again—not while there were sentries on guard, at any rate. If every apartment in Vienna was being searched—and that was certainly the case in Elisa's building—then Leah and Shimon could not be here either. The tidal wave of Nazi rage was still washing over the city. Murphy could only wait now and plan on searching through the debris after the waters abated.

From the apartment he drove directly to Bill Skies' flat; it was two blocks from the Vienna State Opera House in an elegant little neighborhood where Beethoven had once lived. Small brass plaques marked the historical structures surrounding Skies' apartment building, and a dozen paint-smeared doors now bore the word *JUDE!* The Nazi flag hung from the roof of every house but those with the red paint and the crude Star of David.

No corner of Vienna had escaped it. No street. No building. No life, it seemed to Murphy. There were left in this unhappy city only two marks of identity: the broken cross and the six-pointed star that branded the forsaken people of a long-ago kingdom.

20
Kronenberger's Legacy

From behind the slit in the curtain, Leah had watched John Murphy confront the SS sentry below the apartment. A mixture of hope and dread warred within her. She longed to have the comfort of his presence in the flat; but if he came up these stairs, if he argued with the sentry or pushed his way past the stinking bulk of Herr Hugel, they would follow him up the steps and into the apartment.

Tears of frustration stung her eyes as the lanky American journalist announced that he had certainly come to the wrong place! *"No!"* she wanted to shout. *"We are here! I read Elisa's note! Please, Murphy! Help me! Help us!"*

Instead Leah had silently watched him drive away. He had done the only thing he could do. And now Leah was a prisoner, trapped by Herr Hugel and the Nazi sentries who stood guard at the door day and night. How long could such an arrangement go on? What were they guarding against? And whom were they looking for? She had turned away the fat Nazi concierge by pure bluff. Would she be able to do it again?

As the car disappeared around the corner, Leah stepped back and turned to face the pensive stares of the boys. They were only children, but they had lived through more in their short lives than Leah herself. What had they done when they had been prisoners in their own home in Germany?

Little Charles frowned and clasped his hands together as if in prayer. Louis spoke for him. "Mama always said when we are afraid that we should pray, Aunt Leah."

What did those prayers gain them? Leah thought angrily as she gazed into the mournful eyes of children who had never been able to lead a happy, normal life. Entreaties to the silent heavens had not made Charles whole. It had not saved Walter from prison, or his wife from an abortion and death at the hands of Nazi doctors. What benefit had any prayers been in Germany through these long, bitter years? The leaders of the church who had not been arrested had turned their hearts to stone against the innocent. In the name of Christianity, the Jews were hounded unto death, and the weak among the flocks were sorted out and marked for the slaughter. Hitler now surely prayed for the glory of a perfect human specimen—one with a beautiful physical body but without any soul at all. This was the Nazi ideal! This was the empty cup that had been drawn up from the well of their prayers!

Leah did not answer. The sadness in Charles' eyes deepened as he glimpsed her own emptiness. *"No!"* she wanted to shout. *"I have no faith in miracles!"*

Charles lowered his clasped hands and shook his head as if to tell her that she was wrong not to believe. She replied to his silent accusation. "If such a thing keeps you from being afraid, then certainly you should pray."

Louis glanced at Charles, then said, "But what about you, Aunt Leah?"

"You will pray for me, yes, children? Pray that I will know what I must do. And if you like, pray that I will not be afraid."

That answer seemed to satisfy them. Charles nodded solemnly, and Louis promised that they would indeed pray for their Aunt Leah, who could not pray for herself.

Two dozen German-Czech Nazis sat in the sweltering room with Albert Sporer, Konrad Henlein, Hans Frank, and Otto Wattenbarger. Here, in the Czech Sudetenland city of Eger, the battle lines were being drawn.

"The riots must begin by next week at the latest," Frank instructed his men. "Germans here in Czechoslovakia must rise up as one to declare their wish for union with the Reich. Like Austria, we will be a part of the Greater Reich." He looked around the room for effect. "What will this cost us? Perhaps our very lives. But what is that compared to the glory of the United Fatherland?"

The men did not answer. They had been given their assignment.

They would first attack a Czech police station, and by this act they would begin the rebellion. Those among them who might perish would be proclaimed martyrs for the Fatherland. Their names would be screamed from the Nazi podiums and pulpits! The Sudeten Germans would accept nothing less than death or freedom from the Czech government in Prague!

Determination steeled each face as the plans were outlined. The times of each shift of police had been noted. The attack would begin at 3 AM, just as the early morning officers arrived outside the station on their bicycles. What would be simpler? The Nazis would attack and flee. The Czech government would strike back. The Führer would have his propaganda.

The pattern was exactly the same one Otto had witnessed in Vienna in the months preceding the Anschluss. He had witnessed the murder of the German woman Irmgard Schüler and her Jewish lover, Rudolf Dorbransky. From that small flame, riots had been kindled. A hundred such events over the months had led to the end of Austria, the end of many things.

Spirits were high as German-made weapons and ammunition were issued to the men. Otto lingered behind as the terrorists filed out of the hotel one at a time.

"You look doubtful, Otto," Sporer said to him quietly.

"I am not from the Sudetenland. I am Austrian." Otto shrugged. "There will be killing. Men will certainly die. You know I am not afraid of that, Albert, but—"

"But what?"

"What good would the death of an Austrian do here in this?"

"Are you planning on dying?" Sporer gave a short laugh and clapped him on the back.

"Your leaders must be from the Sudetenland; otherwise the Czechs will say that you have imported troublemakers from Austria."

"They said the same of me when I was arrested in Vienna," Sporer defended, not liking the fact that Otto Wattenbarger was trying to get out of the coming fray.

"Yes, they said that of you. And it hurt the cause. When the end of Czechoslovakia comes, let it be said that the German patriots living here brought it about." Otto frowned. "There is enough for me to do at home in Austria."

Sporer regarded him with some disdain. "Austria is insignificant compared to Czechoslovakia. You have heard the words of the Führer with your own ears. Czechoslovakia is the aircraft carrier of the West. If the Führer should attack France and Britain, this place will forever threaten the rear of the Reich unless it becomes a part of the Reich! The Führer cares little for the two and a half million racial Germans inside the border of Czechoslovakia. He wishes military security. Austria was only a stepping stone." The face of Sporer grew animated as he explained once again what Otto already knew.

Otto had known it all from the beginning. He knew enough, and now he simply wanted to return to Vienna. He nodded. "All this will be done even if I do not take part in the battle. You can surely find some other use for me. I do not wish to prove an embarrassment to the Führer and the Reich. There is no need to use imported agitators here as we did in Austria."

"By the end of May armies of the Reich will take over the Sudetenland. And then they will march to Prague. Otto! *Comrade!*" Sporer patted him on the back again. "Surely you do not wish to give up your place in the glory of the event!"

Otto raised his eyebrows slightly in weariness. "If you cannot see the reasonableness of my request, Albert—" Otto sat down—"we have seen eye to eye on everything."

"And that is the point, is it not? We have been comrades since the first days in Stuttgart. Shoulder to shoulder for the Führer and the Fatherland."

"And so we are still. But my heart is in Austria first. A small request. That I return to serve in Austria."

Albert Sporer was visibly disappointed. He shrugged and slumped down beside Otto. They had seen so much action together, and now Otto was leaving him to face it alone. Had they not been the closest of comrades? Had they not shared the same hatred of the Jews and those who set their faces against the Führer and the Fatherland? Sporer had always admired this would-be priest turned Nazi. He had respected the fact that Otto Wattenbarger abhorred violence and yet had faced it and had accepted his duty to the Fatherland above all else. Otto Wattenbarger had brought something more to the movement than mere enjoyment of brutality. He had somehow bestowed an element of purity to the cause—and hence, to Sporer himself.

"Well," Sporer said at last, "still thinking like a priest, are you?" He sighed then. "You have never liked the sight of blood. Even Jewish blood. I have known that all along." Sporer wiped sweat from his brow. "I, on the other hand, was born for this." Otto did not reply as Sporer reasoned his way through to a conclusion. "If you must leave while we're still in the thick of it, then I'll make certain you're still in the middle of the whirlwind, my friend. Your mind, your reason, give us all a bit of dignity. Himmler himself said as much about you. Why do you expect that I would give up your help here easily?"

Otto looked sharply at him. "Because you will do very well without me. I am an Austrian-German and could be better used in Vienna."

Sporer laughed. "There! You see? A man of reason to the last!" He extended his hand, and Otto knew that he had won. "When will you leave?"

"Tonight. Now."

"Then Heil Hitler!" Sporer saluted him.

"Heil Hitler!" Otto replied solemnly.

His valise tucked beneath his arm, Otto Wattenbarger slipped from the hotel and boarded the train for Vienna, long before the first shots were fired in the opening riots of Czech Sudetenland.

Before Murphy took the Kronenberger document from his pocket, he bolted the doors of Skies' apartment and pulled the draperies. Somehow, even that did not seem like enough, so he went to the lavatory and, perched on the edge of the huge claw-foot bathtub, he pulled the papers from their envelope and began to read.

The lettering was neat German script, in handwriting so beautiful that Murphy had a sense he was holding some ancient, medieval document. That feeling was dispelled the instant he scanned the first paragraph.

Beneath the heading, which was phrased much like any other will, the story began:

> *I, Walter Kronenberger, being of sound mind and body, on this the thirteenth day of March 1938, leave the reader of this document all I have.*
>
> *And what do I have left to give you in these last moments of my life? I have no material possessions left, certainly. I lost those long ago. By the end of this day I expect that even the clothing I wear will be blood-soaked, torn by Nazi bullets. But what I have, friend, I will give you. I offer you my story, with the prayer to Almighty God that my story will not also be your story one day! I offer you my warning, not as a dead man but as a husband and father, as a man who has wanted nothing more than to live in freedom with my loved ones! Like you, I have wanted nothing more than to love my family, to serve my God and my homeland as my heart instructs me. For me it is too late. Perhaps it is not too late for you.*

Murphy shifted his weight on the lip of the tub. He looked up from his reading, sensing that Kronenberger was speaking directly to him. The voice was almost audible, echoing in the tiny blue-tiled room.

"Okay, pal," he said quietly. "I'm listening." He focused back on the page, and the voice became louder and more insistent with each well-chosen word.

> *This morning as I write this, the table beneath my pen is trembling with the roar and vibration of Nazi tanks passing beneath our window. Listen. You will hear them. You will feel their presence in the room where you sit. Close your eyes and sit here with me. Share this moment. It is all I have to give you.*

Look with me at the water-stained ceiling of this shabby hotel. My two sons sleep together in the bed in the corner. Tousled blond heads peep out from beneath the quilt. They are nestled together like spoons, Charles and Louis. Do you see them, friend? They share the same pillow, just as they shared the same warm womb of their loving mother. Louis came into this world whole and unmarred. Little Charles emerged with his lip and palate not perfectly formed. And yet the heart of that child is so deep and so perfect that I think he must remember what heaven is like.

How can I share what I feel with you? For just this moment, I ask that you think of those you love most in the world. Picture them in your mind, or gaze gently on them with your eyes, and then imagine what I feel now. They sleep and dream sweet dreams and yet when they awaken I must find some way to say good-bye to them. Now I look my last on them. How can I embrace them, knowing that when I let them go I will never touch them again? How can I say good-bye with the certainty that they will never hear my voice again? What should my last words be? I love you? I am proud of you? Do not be afraid? They are only five years old. Will they remember this morning of our final farewell? Will they believe that the heart of their father broke at this moment, this moment when everything is ending?

I will long be in my grave before these questions are answered. For this short time they sleep there together, and I cherish the sight of them—the sound of their sighs and the scent of little boys in the room. These things I bequeath to you.

Hear my heart, dear reader and friend. I have brought you here to share this moment in my life when death is certain. Can you hear the clatter of tank tracks against the cobblestones now? Do you sit here with me at the wooden table as I write? Do you see Charles and Louis there beneath their quilt? Can you find in your own heart the love for them that I feel, and the grief at our parting?

Yes, I sense somehow that my words will find a way to you. I reach across the great chasm of time to you. And you reach now for me. Listen, then, to our story; and for the sake of those you love, stand firm for all that you know is true and holy before God. Do not bend a fraction when the winds of evil blow upon you! Do not sway with others, or one day this terrible moment of farewell will come upon you, too.

Murphy looked up from the paper, surprised that Walter Kronenberger was not in the room with him. How strongly he felt the life of this man! The effect was like a shattering blow to Murphy. Once again he remembered the slack jaws of the children who had been crushed by the Nazi bombs that rained on Madrid! Evil had overpowered the most beautiful of days. Death had come unexpectedly to men and women and children who had not thought of it at all when they had risen in the morning. The Nazi planes had smashed an ordinary morning and ordinary lives beyond repair. The victims had no time to cry their warning to other men and women like themselves. But Walter Kronenberger had foreseen the certainty of his end, and now he shouted his warning clearly to any who would listen! *It can happen to you! Fight evil before it finally overtakes you! Stand firm before it is too late!*

Murphy bowed his head and closed his eyes in the sense that he held something almost holy in the papers of Kronenberger. Somehow the man had even envisioned his own death. *Bullet-riddled clothes. Nazi bullets. Blood on the floor of the INS office.* And in all of it, Murphy heard the warning clearly: *It could happen to you as it has happened to me!*

With a sobered sigh, Murphy opened his eyes and continued to read the terrifying story of one ordinary family caught in the whirlwind of evil that had swept Germany.

> *The Nazis closed all schools run by the churches. State doctrine was substituted for the teaching of the Holy Scriptures. Small children were taught to recite this prayer at bedtime: "Adolf Hitler, you are our great Führer. Thy name makes the enemy tremble. Thy Third Reich comes, thy will alone is law upon earth. Let us hear daily thy voice and order us by thy leadership, for we will obey to the end and even with our lives. We praise thee! Heil Hitler!"*

The evil had come gradually, the document explained, at first through legislation. While church leaders who protested were thrown into prison camps, most Protestants and Catholics floated along, hoping that they would not be forced to make a choice. But members of the Nazi Party ridiculed Christians, and everyone knew that one could not remain true to the doctrines of love taught by Christ and also belong to the Nazi Party that proclaimed hatred everywhere.

In Bavaria, church members fought to save their schools. Nuns were dismissed without pensions. Convents were forcibly closed. Priests rebelled against Nazi orders and preached sermons condemning Nazi policy from their pulpits. Those priests spoke out against the forced sterilization of those considered "racially unworthy." They decried abortion as the murder of the unborn and marched against the state-financed institution that performed the procedures. Those who protested were arrested. Children continued to be indoctrinated. The state took absolute control over the education of the young. And, of course, the forced sterilization programs continued.

At this point the tragedy gripped Walter and his family by the throat. The order came that Charles was to be sterilized as racially undesirable. Walter and his wife protested and then were faced with a court order that they, too, must report to the clinic for sterilization. After all, had they not given birth to a defective child?

The family had gone to the church for help. Those who came to their support were ultimately arrested, as was Walter. His wife, carrying their third child, had been taken to the clinic for an abortion. Infection set in, and she died while Walter was in prison. He was also sterilized and returned home, broken in health and spirit. His wife was dead, and Charles had been subjected to sterilization as well.

Hitler was rapidly winning the minds of the nation's youth, even as leaders among the Christians vanished one at a time. The empty pulpits were filled by those who advocated the policies of the state. The Old Testament was taken from the churches first because of the "Jewish influence." Then the New Testament was removed because of the "weakness" embodied in its teachings of love, forgiveness, and compassion. The Bible was replaced with Hitler's book, *Mein Kampf*. The cross was torn down and replaced with the swastika. Racial purity, hatred of the Jews, and the elimination of the weak were preached and practiced.

The will of Hitler had been voted into law in Germany. Praised and worshiped by the young German nation, Hitler became the messiah of evil. Torchlight processions honored him. Hundreds of thousands of schoolchildren prayed the prayer they had learned in state-run schools:

> *"Thou who hast saved Germany from deepest need, I thank thee today for my daily bread. Remain at my side and never leave me, Führer, my Führer. My faith. My light. Heil, mein Führer!"*

Through the long and tragic story, Kronenberger wrote of the gentle love he had shared with his wife and sons. Once it had been perfect. They had not believed that this could happen! *When,* he asked, *had it become too late to turn back? Where, along this long road into darkness, had the ordinary man and woman of Germany finally sold their souls?*

The answer was simple, Walter reasoned:

> *It was already too late when the ordinary man or woman saw the Jewish shopkeeper being beaten but did nothing to help. It was too late when the neighbor was taken to the clinic to be sterilized as a racial undesirable. It was too late when the bishops of the church*

cowered in fear at the sight of the Storm Troopers! When they failed to protest and continue to fight against the evil of abortion and racial selection. When they did not tear down the signs declaring JUDEN VERBOTEN, *it was too late. Too late. And soon the blackness swallowed them alive into the tomb of tyranny.*

Now Austria is also lost, devoured whole in one night. What evil will come upon this place when the morning sun is up? Listen to me; I beg you! Wherever you are. Look to your own world and know that this, too, can come upon you! Look at your children, as I look now upon mine. Stand now for those things that are filled with love and a reflection of the pure heart of Christ. Judge well between that which is the true love of Christ and that which is only illusion masquerading as light. Do not be deceived, or I tell you from the brink of my grave that my end will become yours. Your homeland will be torn and devoured. Your children will vanish with you, or they will also wear the face of evil.

This is the end of my testament. I pray that my warning will reach your heart and awaken your will to stand for the right. If it does not, then close your eyes and listen. Listen to the rumbling of the tanks as they move beneath your window tonight. Your children will drive those tanks. They will become the tools of darkness in the hands of the evil that has existed on this earth since the first. The weak will be sacrificed and the strong will break the bones of those who awaken too late. It is too late for me. I pray it is not too late for you also.

Murphy was perspiring by the time he finished reading the document. Skies was right; this thing was dynamite! The perfect explosive to blow anyone off his apathetic resting place. Kronenberger had written it, but first he had lived it and died for it. There was no middle ground left. It was one side of the fence or the other!

His head was throbbing as he folded the papers and slipped them back into the envelope. Such dynamite could well explode in his face if he were caught with it. Yes, it must be published. But how was he going to get it out of the country?

21
Orchestration

It was a foolish hope, Murphy realized now as he stood in the wings of the stage at the Musikverein. Leah and Shimon Feldstein were not in their usual places as he had prayed they might be. An older man with stooped shoulders and a shock of white hair now stood at the kettledrums. Leah's char was occupied by the sensitive, bespectacled young man who had been second to her in the cello section. As Murphy quietly watched the rehearsal, he gradually became aware of other missing faces among the group. Perhaps a fourth of the first-violin section was now filled with people Murphy did not recognize. Elisa's chair was taken by an older woman who looked worriedly from the score to the conductor, then back again to the score.

Murphy was unfamiliar with the music they rehearsed. He found himself thinking of how quickly Elisa would have recognized the piece, named the composer, and reeled off the occasion and date of its composition. The thought made him angry all over again that she and the others were not here, that they *could not* be here! Most of the musicians now absent from the orchestra had been close friends of Leah and Elisa. It was obvious why they were missing. The German laws against Jewish musicians were now the laws of Vienna.

The conductor appeared especially rumpled this morning. His face was pained, and frustration oozed from his outstretched hands as he directed the newcomers in his orchestra.

Lowering his hands and staring unhappily at the woman who sat in Elisa's chair, he spoke in a controlled but obviously angry voice. "Keep in mind, ladies and gentlemen, that Haydn, who is the composer of this piece . . . for those of you who might have dropped out of the music academy before you got that far—" there was an uneasy stirring among the new musicians as the insult hit its mark—"Haydn had in mind a caricature of a military march!" The voice began to rise to a forte, and the face reddened. "We have been over the second movement a hundred times and—"

Elisa's replacement raised her bow to comment. "That is not how it is played in Berlin. In Berlin we play it with the strength that the Führer enjoys in such a work!"

The conductor glowered at her. "This, Frau . . . " He rolled his hands as if he was trying to remember her name.

"Frau Schönheim," she obliged.

"Frau *Schön*heim, as in *beautiful*?" The words were patronizing, and it was clear that he thought the name was totally inappropriate for the creature who now challenged him. The rage of the conductor escalated to fortissimo. *"This is not Berlinnnnn! This is Viennaaaaa!* The skull of Haydn is right downstairs in a glass case! Last I saw of the dear composer, he was grinning! But *now,* I am quite certain that the smile on his skull has vanished! If I but look—if I *dare* to look at the skull of Franz Joseph Haydn—he will not be grinning unless it is over the hideous, *odious* laws that forced us to replace the finest musicians in the world with imports from Berlin who cannot even *pronounce* the name of Haydn correctly, let alone read his music!"

"Good for him!" Murphy muttered as the matronly violinist rose nose first and exited stage right. She was followed moments later by a bevy of new faces, all of whom, Murphy noticed for the first time, wore Nazi Party badges and armbands.

The conductor glared after them, and when the last member of the invading tribe disappeared through the curtains across the stage from Murphy, the man raised his baton. "Now, children," he said gently to the remaining members of his orchestra, "remember, Haydn was thinking of toy soldiers when he wrote this. Perfect for our departing guests, I think. A *caricature* of a military march! Light!"

Murphy laughed as the music began. It was, indeed, a caricature of the Nazis who stamped around the Imperial City. The old man at the kettledrums had not left with the others. Murphy remembered that he had substituted once for Shimon. A broad smile covered his face as well. Despite the vacant chairs, the unity of the orchestra was easily discernable, even to Murphy's untrained ear.

"Good! *Good!* Yes! Can you *feel* the pulse!" The conductor roared his approval over the music. Only Murphy seemed to notice the angry curses of the expelled musicians as they swept behind the curtain and then out the door of the auditorium. The music seemed to mock their anger. Now Murphy recognized the piece. The orchestra had played it once when he had sat in the audience for no other purpose than to gaze at Elisa. "Yes, children!" The conductor shouted encouragement.

After a moment he put the baton down on his stand. His musicians were still smiling at him. Then, in a show of approval, they began tapping their feet against the stage. Murphy applauded also, though he could not help but wonder what would happen to the brave conductor who had ousted Nazi substitutes from his orchestra. At last the thumping died away. The conductor bowed slightly and said, "Haydn is certainly smiling again!"

In the maestro's small, cluttered office, Murphy gazed mutely at photographs showing the conductor standing with men like the now-arrested Chancellor Schuschnigg, Churchill, King George, and a host of other dignitaries who were definitely not on Hitler's guest list. The kindly conductor now read Elisa's note from Prague.

"Thank God!" He sighed, carefully folding the note. "I was afraid I had lost the best violinist in my first-violin section! Thought perhaps she had been dragged away with the others." His face showed the strain of the last few days.

"When you say *others*—" Murphy felt the dread of Leah's fate even before her name was said.

"Leah Feldstein and Elisa have been inseparable; certainly you know that."

"I have tried to locate Leah."

"She and her husband have been arrested, I am told." He shook his head sadly. "Why is, of course, the question of the hour here in Vienna! I thought that Elisa's closeness might have brought her to the same fate."

Murphy leaned forward in his chair. "You are sure, Maestro?" He could hardly speak.

The tousled head nodded as he looked toward a group photo of the orchestra. "We can come to no other conclusion. Shimon was seen being beaten and then placed onto one of the prisoner lorries. Leah left the Judenplatz carrying her violoncello, but, to our knowledge, she never arrived here at the Musikverein. The Nazis were pulling Jews off the street—men, women. It didn't make any difference. She probably did not make it two blocks before they picked her up. I am afraid, Herr Murphy."

Murphy studied the old gentleman, who now had tears brimming in his eyes. "Elisa will need to stay in Prague until the first waves of violence stop."

"Of course. Although she is the perfect physical specimen of their ideal Aryan woman," the maestro spat angrily, "this connection with the Feldsteins might place her in danger."

Murphy thought of this morning's expulsion of Nazi musicians. "And what about you? Are you concerned at all for yourself, after this morning?"

The maestro dismissed the thought of his own safety with a wave of his hand. "They may search my pedigree. It is perfect. A conductor has the right to dismiss inferior, idiotic imposters who call themselves musicians, and I doubt that the Germans will have much to say about it. After all, the Reich cannot have music played in a shoddy fashion, now can it?"

Murphy grinned with admiration. "Is there anything to be done about Leah and Shimon and the others?"

"I have already lodged my most extreme protest with the new Reich officials, indicating that such arrests will cause the quality of music in the German Reich to diminish. The problem, of course, is that the Feldsteins were planning on leaving Austria anyway. The Gestapo indicated that their visas to Palestine had been confiscated. I don't know how much more I can do for them since they had a fixed date for emigration. The Germans have all records of that sort in their hands now." He bit his lip and continued to gaze at the photo. "I am not sure how far my influence will go. Or even if I still have influence."

He glanced to Murphy. "But, please, when you see my little Elisa, tell her I am doing all I can. Tell her that she may come back when she feels it is opportune to do so. As long as I am maestro of the Vienna Philharmonic, she will always have a chair among my children."

He carefully folded her note and opened his file drawer to slip it in among a mix of musical scores and correspondence. "There! If the Germans should question her whereabouts—and they will—then I shall simply produce this note from her in Prague and tell them that she is on leave for important family matters."

"Thank you. She told me you would be willing—"

"Of course. A violinist like Elisa Linder comes into the life of a conductor only once." He smiled knowingly. "But then, you already know her worth; do you not, Herr Murphy?" He narrowed his eyes and peered up at the ceiling. "Ah yes! She is not Linder anymore! I shall have to have her name changed on the program notes. *Murphy.* Murphy." He repeated the name several times. "Perfectly dreadful sound to it. *Murphy.* It sounds so . . . "

Murphy laughed and stood to go. "American?"

"That's it! It sounds perfectly American. And what we all wouldn't give for an American-sounding name these days."

The conductor was joking, but the thought of Elisa marrying him for an American passport struck Murphy to the core again. "Y-yes," he stammered, suddenly uncomfortable. "I'll tell her . . . tell her you're changing her name on the program. Thanks." Then he shook the conductor's hand and walked out past the darkened stage. Memories of Elisa's laughter as Rudy had clowned and Leah had teased her into accepting a dinner date with Murphy overwhelmed him. How melancholy the stage was without all of them! How dark and empty!

Thomas von Kleistmann left the Vienna bookshop with a thin paper-wrapped volume in his hand. Within the pages was the reply of the German High Command to certain British questions.

Although everything appeared quiet now, the earth beneath Czech-Sudetenland would soon begin to tremble. Already the agents of the Reich moved quietly among the Germans within the borders of Czechoslovakia. The riots would begin soon. By the middle of May the Führer hoped to annex the Sudetenland—by force, by sheer intimidation! The pitiful showing of the German Wehrmacht in the invasion of Austria proved that the Nazi forces were still not ready to fight. A show of strength by Britain and France, therefore, would keep the German divisions on their own side by the border. Of this, the generals of the High Command were certain.

Hitler had taken Austria by a bully's bluff. He planned on the same tactics in Czechoslovakia. "Stand firm!" This was the message of Canaris and the others who opposed Hitler. "Do not believe the illusion of force the madman displays to the world!"

Thomas felt as though he carried the hope of all the world in his pocket as he walked quickly away from Fiori's shop. And with that hope he carried the burden of fear within himself.

Once again he turned the corner of Elisa's street. His eyes swept upward to the lacy curtains of her apartment. *Is she there?* he wondered. He slowed his pace as though some unseen hand held him back. He imagined himself climbing the stairs, knocking on the door of her apartment. He could almost see the surprise on her face as she threw open the door and pulled him into the warmth of the place that was so very much her own.

Then he turned his face away from the building as the roar of a German bomber passed over the city. The shadow of the plane swept toward him, touching him, and he remembered the face of Le Morthomme. "We are all dead men," Thomas whispered under his breath as his eyes fixed on the swastikas painted on the wings of the plane.

22
A Futile Risk

The photograph of Hitler, his arms outstretched over the multitudes in the Heldenplatz, took up nearly the entire front page of *Der Führer*, the official Nazi newspaper. Headlines in forty-eight-point type proclaimed, "TRIUMPHANT WELCOME IN VIENNA!"

This and *Der Stürmer* were the worst of the propaganda sheets put out by Goebbels and his Ministry of Propaganda. Newsboys with swastika armbands were handing copies of each newspaper out freely on every street corner in Vienna.

A half dozen issues were spread out on the floor of Bill Skies' flat this evening. Murphy stared down at the multiple images of the Führer greeting his cheering masses.

"He looks like the pope or something," Murphy said.

"Haven't you noticed?" Timmons drawled. "He thinks he *is* the pope!"

Skies blew his nose thoughtfully, then peered down at the identical front pages. "All the same," he remarked, "Murphy's right. It's perfect! *Perfect!* There's not one of those goons tearing through luggage at Alpern Airport who would dare lay a finger on a victorious front-page photo of their precious Führer."

Murphy grinned. "You can bet anybody who tore up a picture like that would be shot immediately."

"Well, you can hope so, Murphy." Timmons seemed doubtful. "Have you seen the way the Gestapo is going through stuff down there? I'm tellin' you, pal, they're gonna go through your shorts looking for just this kind of thing!" He jerked his thumb toward the Kronenberger documents. "And if they catch you with that, it's gonna take a whole lot more than a word from the American Embassy and a special dispensation from the pope to get you out of a Gestapo dungeon! This is the kind of stuff that gives the SS goons the opportunity to shoot people. I saw it happen, remember? Walter Kronenberger is pushin' up daises over this, Murph!"

Murphy nodded. He had considered all of it, but Skies was right. The Kronenberger letter was something that deserved attention in the free press—just the kind of story that might keep the free press free a while longer. "If I get caught, promise me you'll come visit, will you?" he joked, but Timmons and Skies did not smile.

Skies chewed his lip nervously. "Maybe we'd better wait until things calm down a bit."

Murphy shook his head. "You and I both know that this isn't going to calm down. It's going to get worse. Just like it did in Germany. Just like Kronenberger wrote it." He clapped his hands together to say that the discussion was finished. "Okay, Timmons, you were the pasteup man for your college paper. So get to pasting."

Walter Kronenberger had written his last testament on thin onionskin paper, filling up both sides of each sheet with tiny, neat printing.

Timmons laid the newspaper out with the photo of Hitler facedown. Then, with a worried glance at Murphy, he placed tiny dabs of paste onto the corners of the first sheet of the Kronenberger document. With all the care of a boy with a pasteup scrapbook, Timmons pasted each thin piece of stationery onto the back of the newspaper. There was room enough for six sheets on the section, and when he had finished, he picked up a second identical front page and laid it carefully over the first. Glancing up for approval he said, "It's going to be a little thick."

"Go ahead," Murphy reassured him. "I'll chance it."

With a shrug, Timmons pasted the identical section over the first, concealing the onionskin pages of the document. He and Murphy examined the section carefully for any lumps or traces of glue that might give away the fact that illegal contraband was concealed between the pages of the newspaper. Except for the extra weight of the front page, it looked like any other.

"Some sandwich," Murphy said, pleased with the results.

Twice more Timmons repeated the procedure, each time using pages from the newspaper that had photographs of Hitler prominently displayed. They hoped that such photographs would keep the Gestapo from looking too closely at the double-thickness of the newsprint while the precious document was hidden inside this secret envelope.

Murphy reassembled the newspaper and laid it on the table where they studied it for effect as they shared a pot of strong coffee. The conclusion was unanimous.

"I got a couple of awards for my pasteup," Timmons said proudly.

"Yep," Skies agreed. "Looks like another one of Goebbels' propaganda rags to me!"

Timmons frowned slightly. "We'll just hope the SS goons at Alpern think so too."

At Murphy's request, Bill Skies drove slowly past Elisa's apartment for one last look. Their headlights illuminated the front entrance, where yet another SS sentry stood talking to a fat man just inside the lobby.

"No getting past those guys without a bunch of questions," Timmons said mournfully from the backseat.

Murphy peered up to the window of Elisa's flat. No lights shone through the shade. Like the stage of the Musikverein, the place seemed dark and empty. "It doesn't matter," Murphy mumbled, regretting that he had been able to do so little in the search for Shimon and Leah. "Nobody's there, anyway."

"The German army will be there soon enough, then," Skies said with certainty. "They've got men billeted everywhere now. You might as well forget about it, Murphy," he vainly attempted to console his friend. "There isn't one of us who hasn't seen friends disappear since those goons marched in. And what can we do about it?"

Murphy found some comfort that the maestro had at least lodged his protests with the authorities. He would tell Elisa that much when he saw her. But the plain truth was that Murphy felt his failure to find Leah and Shimon was somehow a failure of his promise to Elisa.

"You can't expect to fix every mess, Murphy," Timmons added. "The best you can do is get this Kronenberger thing into the news."

Skies cleared his throat. "Right. And don't get yourself arrested in the process, will you?"

The newspaper carrying the Kronenberger document lay innocently between them on the seat. Murphy glanced down at his "souvenir of the Anschluss" and silently whispered a prayer as they pulled into the line of official German vehicles and taxis heading for the airfield.

Wehrmacht soldiers directed civilian traffic to the left, and Nazi vehicles to the right, toward the choicest parking places near the terminal building. Planes roared overhead, an uninterrupted line of military aircraft taking off or landing. The peaceful little airport had become the hub of all Nazi activity in Vienna.

There were more soldiers and officers than civilians. The soldiers appeared cocky and self-confident. The civilians, most carrying small bags, wore worried, hunted expressions. They fell into lines outside the building, where their suitcases were torn open for inspection.

Traffic inched forward. Murphy nervously clutched the handle of his small valise and slipped the newspaper under his arm. "Let me out here," he instructed. "If they nab me, there's no use you two getting tangled up in the thing as well."

Skies nodded and stopped the car. "Good luck, Murphy." He licked his lips, and Murphy sensed the apprehension in his final handshake.

"Grüss Gott." Timmons extended his hand with the traditional Austrian blessing.

Murphy left the car and did not look back. He was confident that his American passport and his press identity card would save him from the indignity of the strip-search and the probing fingers of the white-coated Nazi doctors who searched every possible orifice on the bodies of their unfortunate victims.

At the head of the line, a small, matronly woman rebelled as she was herded into the women's line. "I won't!" she shouted in French.

"Then you will not leave the Reich, madame!" a gruff, middle-aged German replied in broken French.

Tears came as she shook herself free from the grip of the large, thick-boned woman in a Nazi uniform. "What are they looking for?" she shouted at the other potential passengers, who averted their eyes and privately vowed that they would endure the ordeal and then find a place on an airplane heading anywhere away from this place.

The only Jews at the airfield now were those who held foreign passports. These people were treated with particular abuse. Murphy clenched his fists angrily and looked away as the Nazi guards shoved one woman to the ground after she proclaimed that she was an American citizen and therefore would not submit to such a search!

"You are a Jew! You think it matters how your passport is stamped? We can smell the stink of Jews! Get up!" The same huge blond Nazi matron took the American by her hair and lifted her to her feet. Rage dissolved into tears of protest. She shouted angry American obscenities as the Nazi woman shoved her into the examination room.

Now a brutal-looking officer with a scar across his cheek stepped out of the office. He crossed his arms and glared at the frightened, angry men and women in the lines.

"You see, such ridiculous protests only make it worse! We search for contraband—foreign currency, jewelry, and such—which some foolish people believe they might sneak past us and out of the Reich! Such thoughts are not only foolish, they are *dangerous*! If you have something that has been forbidden to take from the Reich, then you must report it now. Your jewels will be found—" he smiled—"no matter where you may have hidden them! I assure you, ladies and gentlemen, no one is exempt from examination. If contraband is discovered concealed on your person, you will be arrested and prosecuted."

He clapped his hands together like a schoolmaster. "Therefore, I urge you, if you have anything to declare to the custom authorities, you should excuse yourself from the line and make your way to the public restroom to retrieve your hidden valuables. You will be given a receipt for your items and reimbursed in Reichsmarks."

The man in front of Murphy muttered, "In Reichsmarks? What good are they? No other country in the world will exchange Reich currency for their own."

Another man turned and said wryly, "It is a shame we cannot receive our Reichsmark bills *before* we go to the restroom. That is one good use for German currency."

Several men laughed bitterly at the remark, and after the German officer retreated into his office, those men left one at a time for the restroom. Several women also excused themselves. No one doubted the threat of the Gestapo officer.

Murphy was sweating as he approached the wide table where luggage was being searched. He determined that he would simply close his eyes and endure the indignity of the search, just as he had done when he had his physical for the army. His only concern now was for the precious newspaper and the documents that could cost him years in a Gestapo prison—or worse.

"Next!" shouted a cranky little German behind the table.

Murphy hefted the small valise up and left the newspaper tucked beneath his arm as he displayed his passport and press identity. "American," he said.

"Journalistin!" snapped the man. "And what will you say about our search of departing guests?" He had already begun to paw through Murphy's valise.

"That the Reich is very thorough," Murphy replied as the prickle of fear moved up his spine.

"Ja!" The man dumped the entire contents of the bag out; then with a straight razor he slit the lining of the bag. "An honest American," he pronounced as he finished his meticulous examination. His beady eyes rested on the folded newspaper. "What is that?" he demanded, extending his hand.

"My souvenir of the Anschluss." Murphy obligingly laid the newspaper in the man's hand.

"Ja! Often foolish people fold up currency in such a souvenir!" He

smiled, and Murphy noticed that his teeth were rotten, like his breath and his soul. This was truly the bottom rung of the Nazi ladder. He began to flip through the pages one by one.

"Rather a good picture of the Führer, I think." Murphy heard his own voice as if it were very far away. "And look at the masses of people cheering him in the Heldenplatz. I doubt that anyone outside of the Reich has seen such a photograph. Maybe they won't believe the victorious welcome to Austria unless they see it."

The little man continued to scan the pages, chuckling here and there at particular photographs. The extra thickness of the pages seemed to scream at Murphy. *How could we have thought he wouldn't notice?*

"*Ja.* A very good issue. I have saved a copy myself for history," the man said triumphantly.

"May I put my things back in my bag?" Murphy asked politely.

"*Ja, ja.*" He closed the newspaper but continued to stare at the face of Hitler as Murphy crammed his clothes back into the valise.

"Would you mind if I packed my newspaper in the bag? I would hate to lose it in travel."

The man frowned, looking intently at Murphy. He picked up the paper and tapped it against his hand, then thoughtfully laid it down on top of the disheveled clothing in the valise. "*Ja,*" he said. "It is a good thing for a man to remember such a day, I think." He raised a hand. "Heil Hitler!" Then, with the same hand he pointed toward the men's room. "You will go there and remove all your clothing. The doctor will come in and examine you shortly." With that, he closed the bag and sealed it with the Gestapo seal.

Beneath such a seal, beneath the smile of Hitler and his teeming admirers, the Kronenberger document would be safe for the moment. With that thought in mind, Murphy hardly noticed the rough hands of the Nazi doctor. When he was pronounced free of contraband and allowed to board the plane for Paris, he even managed to say thank you.

Below the plane, the lights of Paris sparkled like diamonds on the black velvet of a Cartier showcase. Beacons atop the Eiffel Tower warned off aircraft, while floodlights illumined the Arc de Triomphe.

Strangely, Murphy had expected sighs of relief from his fellow passengers as the plane banked to the right and circled the city in an approach for landing. But there was only silence among them. Those who were Jewish and had somehow bribed their way to freedom from the Nazis seemed unwilling to believe that they were safe until the wheels of the Lufthansa aircraft touched the field. Murphy understood their apprehension. With the Kronenberger document tucked away, he would not feel at ease until he placed it on the desk of the INS news director in Paris. Until then, he could not shake the feeling that this German pilot might change his mind about landing on French soil and turn the aircraft back to the Reich.

Only after the metal steps had been wheeled into place and the pitiful mix of refugees and foreigners inhaled their first sweet breath of Paris did the facades of control finally crack. Women and men alike wept openly. They were free in France now, mainly because they held passports for nations other than Germany or Austria. But what of those whom they had left behind?

Murphy exhaled loudly and walked around half a dozen men who embraced one another and exclaimed in choked cries, *"Vive la France! Vive Liberte!"* If they had not understood the meaning of the phrase before, tonight they embraced their freedom like drowning men who had been pulled to safety from a riptide.

Walter Kronenberger had not been so lucky. His sons, wherever they were, would probably perish as well. But perhaps, Murphy thought, these words of tragedy and warning might make a difference to others faced with the same brutal choices. The joyous weeping of Murphy's fellow passengers followed him into the terminal building. He could share their relief but not their joy. He, too, had left people behind. He had failed Elisa. Leah and Shimon Feldstein were as much beyond his reach as ever.

Unable to smile, Murphy hailed a cab. The news director would not be in the office at this late hour, but for what Murphy had it was worth dragging him out of bed.

"Number 2, Rue Balny d'Avricourt," Murphy instructed the taxi driver. Even saying the address was difficult for Murphy. Suddenly he realized that he had not spoken at all for hours. The thoughts of what he had seen and what he now carried with him had driven words from him.

Murphy awakened Leonard Duprey, chief of the Paris INS office, from a sound sleep. His welcome was anything but cordial. Still, Murphy hoped Duprey would warm up a bit after reading the Kronenberger document. The newspaper that hid the story beneath Hitler's photograph was carefully opened with Duprey's own straight razor. Now the disgruntled editor sat in his striped robe behind a cluttered desk. He scanned the material without the enthusiasm Murphy, Skies, and Timmons had hoped for.

The downturned mouth of Duprey twitched a little at the corner as he finished reading the last dramatic paragraph. Other than that, there was nothing on his face to show that he considered the story worth his loss of sleep. He quietly let the last page drop to his desk as he sat back and scowled at Murphy.

"This couldn't have waited until morning?" he growled.

"I'm leaving for the States at six," Murphy explained for the second time.

Duprey tapped his finger impatiently on Kronenberger's story. "Well, I can tell you right now that you have wasted your time and my sleep with this."

Hardly able to believe the response, Murphy leaned forward in his chair. *"Wasted?"* After everything they had gone through to smuggle this document out—not to mention the fact that Kronenberger had died trying to reach the Western powers with this story—it seemed impossible that Duprey could be so brutally uninterested!

"Wasted!" Duprey snapped.

"Mr. Craine himself sent a wire that he wanted a good story from Vienna. Here it is!"

"Old news, Mr. Murphy. We covered the war against the churches last year and the year before. What has this got to do with the Anschluss? Old news. Kronenberger was dead long before he hit the floor of the INS office in Vienna. People just don't care anymore about this stuff." He tapped his throat with a forefinger. "Readership has had this sort of persecution story up to here, and you know it. Craine would scream so loud we could hear him from California if I sent this over the wires."

Murphy was stunned and angry. This was not what he had expected, but then, Duprey had not seen the patched office wall at the INS, the holes from bullets that had passed through a man's body. Skies and Timmons and the rest had not been able to tell what it had been like watching Kronenberger riddled with holes before their eyes. "This has everything to do with the takeover of Austria, and you know it!"

"Tell it to Craine!" Duprey said with a disgusted wave.

"What happened in Germany is happening now in Austria! It is happening in Vienna to guys like Kronenberger, who just want their kids to be safe."

Duprey was smiling in a tight-lipped way. "I can walk out on the streets of Paris and gather ten thousand stories like this! The whole city is full of refugees, and every one of them has a sad tale! Have you walked through a sidewalk café in Paris lately, Mr. Murphy? You think this is news? The second language in France now is German, spoken by German Jews and social misfits."

"Misfits?"

"Yes, misfits! Like your Herr Kronenberger and his brood! Is it any of our business if the Germans are weeding out those who are not quite up to standard? We'd all be better off if we thought about it. Hitler wasn't going to *murder* these people, you know! Only stop reproduction of the same kind of weaklings." Duprey leaned so far back in his deep leather chair that Murphy thought the man might fall over. His voice was patronizing; his face seemed to portray the reasonableness of his arguments. "Like culling a litter of puppies, if you will."

Murphy stood now and angrily began to gather up the precious document. "Two kids aren't puppies. They're *kids*!"

"We printed the whole struggle when it happened in Germany." Duprey was becoming defensive. "The issue is dead."

"The issue is *murdered*! Executed! Or in Dachau along with every parish priest and Protestant pastor who spoke out!"

"Old news!" Duprey repeated. "And Mr. Craine himself would be the first to say so. If this is the story you brought the Craine syndicate from Austria, I can tell you right now that the Chief will not be pleased! You'll never publish this in a Craine paper. You're a couple of years too late."

Murphy did not reply. He was already groping blindly for the door. He had not expected such lack of concern from Duprey. Stepping squarely on the photograph of Hitler, Murphy fled the apathy of one of the most influential news editors in Europe.

It was not until he was outside in the quiet street that a thousand sensible replies entered his mind. *If we had covered Hitler's war against the church and thousands of families like the Kronenbergers with more enthusiasm, then Paris would not be full of refugees, and Vienna would not be full of Wehrmacht troops!*

But the argument had come to him too late. He stared up at the window of Duprey's study as the light winked out. The editor, no doubt, had returned to his bed and drifted off to a peaceful sleep once again.

23

Traveling Alone

Since John Murphy had left Prague, there had been no word from him. Elisa had barely spoken of him in that time. She avoided the sympathetic looks of her mother and found ways each day to be alone.

Her thoughts were filled with frightening images of Vienna and the friends she had left behind. Each evening when the radio blared the news of the latest political events in the new Greater Reich, Elisa felt physically ill. It was so much like what had happened in Berlin, only so much more fierce in its suddenness. Like some terrible Day of Judgment, the destruction had come upon them before they knew what was happening. And now she trembled for the fate of Leah. For Shimon. For the others in the orchestra who had been family to her these last few years. Mixed up with all of that was the slow-burning impatience with Murphy. Why hadn't he contacted her? Why had he left without even a word of good-bye? Was he back in Vienna yet?

Elisa was sure that her impatience would soon erupt into an angry determination to do something—*anything*—if she did not hear soon. The news broadcasts were frightening enough, and rumors in the vast Prague marketplace told of long, desperate lines of hopeful refugees trying to cross the Czech border. Those few who were lucky enough to get out of Austria brought horrible stories of thousands being arrested by the Gestapo every day. Were Shimon and Leah among them?

Her dreams had become a reflection of the fear she felt. Each night she climbed into bed alone and still found herself wishing that Murphy were there beside her. *Clean sheets, the quilt turned back.* She wished for strong arms to hold her close and gentle hands to stroke her hair and tell her this was all just a bad dream. But when, at last, she tumbled into an uneasy sleep, the dreams that came were savage reminders of reality. . . .

From row ten, aisle seat, Murphy sat and watched her as she played the golden violin that once belonged to Rudy Dorbransky. Leah sat across from her on a stage so vast that surely she could not hear the music.

Then the men in black shirts entered the hall and bullets sprayed the stage! Rudy lay broken and bleeding at her feet. As he raised his hands toward the violin, his beautiful fingers were consumed in fire and smoke that licked the hem of Elisa's gown.

She called for Murphy, but his seat was vacant now.

As the flames from Rudy's body leaped higher, the Blackshirts dragged Leah away. . . .

Always the nightmare was the same. Elisa woke herself with a soundless scream and then lay for hours in the sweat-drenched bed until morning brought her back again to some pretense of normal life. She walked numbly through trips to the market and the bakery. She helped with the dishes and read quietly to Theo. But when Anna tuned in concerts on the radio, she left the room, left the house. Was there any music that did not now remind her of her friend? They had laughed and joked through every rehearsal and talked about music long into the night over cups of strong coffee. No, she could not listen to music. Not now. Every score became a well-rehearsed script. She could not hear the notes any longer. She was left with visions of Leah and of her dear Vienna.

Somewhere in the vast city of Prague were men and women who, like Elisa, had been involved in the organization that provided passports for refugee children of Germany. But where were they? The past weeks of solitary worry had left Elisa aware of just how well covered the tracks of the clandestine group were. Always before, Leah had told Elisa where she must go and what words she should speak to identify herself as the courier. The time and place had been different on each occasion. Elisa had never even been certain what she carried across the border into Germany in the violin case. Now, without Leah's instructions, Elisa was totally cut off. For six days she had wandered through the city, visiting each of the meeting places in turn. The Charles Bridge. The Orloj clock in Old Town Square. A certain tower at the university. Three times she had gone to the enormous Prague train terminal and walked through the crowded lobby and along the endless platform where trains hissed and fumed while passengers emptied into the safety of Czechoslovakia from Germany.

Did any small children pass from one adult to another? If they did, Elisa did not witness the exchange. Had the entire operation been destroyed with the fall of Austria?

Now, as the voice on the public address system blared out destinations and departure times, Elisa sat disconsolately on a bench and searched for some face she might recognize, as a lost puppy searches for its master in a crowd.

"Cities of Eger! Bratslavia! Budapest! Belgrade!"

The train used to pass through Vienna, then follow the Danube south, Elisa knew. But even after a week, there were no trains into Austria from Czechoslovakia. The thought of what must be happening on the other side of the closed border made her shudder. She had not heard even a word from Murphy since he had gone to London. He had promised that he would return to Vienna and search for Leah and Shimon. Now Elisa wondered if he would be able to get back into the country.

A man in a navy pin-striped suit was staring openly at Elisa from a bench opposite hers. He smiled over the top of his newspaper. She smiled hesitantly back at him as she stared at his face for some recognizable feature. She was certain she had not met him before. He was middle-aged, with thick glasses and gray hair beneath a fedora. Most of her contacts had been young, and—

"Excuse me?" he asked, lowering his paper. "Don't I know you?"

Elisa looked past him, feeling suddenly apprehensive. She did not like the way he was smiling at her. "No, I don't think so," she said.

"Are you waiting for someone?" He inclined his head. "You have been here a long time. I know, because I have been here a long time."

Elisa nodded a reply. She was waiting for someone, she just did not know whom she was waiting for. She twisted Murphy's wedding ring on her finger. "My husband."

"Ah." The man looked disappointed. "I see." He glanced toward the ring. "Which train is he coming in on?" He smiled again, and his gold-capped teeth glinted.

"I'm not sure." Elisa answered in a way that made it clear this was none of his business.

He shrugged. He had gotten the message. "If you are going to wait so long, you should bring a good book to read, at least." He raised the newspaper to cover his face again.

Elisa sighed and watched as the last of the passengers boarded the train that would come so near Vienna and yet would not dare cross into Reich territory. The margin of safety for many of these travelers was only as wide as the line that marked the border of one nation from another. The end of human rights and the beginning of human suffering could be reached in a single step. She had seen the glistening white walls of the buildings in Austria across the border. It had seemed so tranquil and unchanged. But today Elisa knew that she could never go back to what had been. Someone had broken the fence between heaven and hell, and hell had flooded in.

As the train chugged slowly away, Elisa stood and looked one last time around the terminal. Was there no one here who might recognize her as the courier? Was she the only one left of the enormous unseen change she had imagined herself to be part of?

Frustrated in her helplessness, she returned to the little house just off Mala Strana Square.

Far below the gondola of the giant transatlantic airship, freighters and passenger liners bobbed like tiny toy ships on the waters.

Murphy stood silently at the window of his compartment. The space was smaller than the berth of a train and much less comfortable than the suites on an oceanliner, but none of that mattered to Murphy. The football-shaped shadow of the dirigible passed over the waves of the ocean twice as fast as the fastest ship in any fleet. Speed was all that mattered to Murphy now. Travel to the States, do what he had to do, and then come back. Back to Europe. Back to Elisa.

Since the airship had left Paris the day before, Murphy had barely acknowledged any of the other passengers. At the evening meal, a string quartet played the Dvorák piece that Elisa had once explained to him was written in America. Even with the monotonous drone of the engines in the background, Murphy could almost see her sitting across from him as she had done that night in Sacher Café. He closed his eyes and tried not to hear the engines. Tried not to feel the gentle rocking of the airship. How desperately he wished that he were back in Vienna to relive that moment when they had first talked about her coming to America! Her skin had been smooth and creamy, and her blue eyes had dreamed with him for a moment of the faraway place, where Dvorák had written his song about America. Iowa. Yes, Murphy remembered the childlike look on her face and the funny way she had pronounced *Iowa.*

"A place called Spillville, I-Owa."

Murphy smiled now at the memory of her voice.

"Spillville, huh?"

"You have been there?"

"Lots of farms in Iowa."

"Yes. I can hear that in his music. Do you hear it, Herr Murphy?"

"Just Murphy."

Yes. Murphy had heard summer in the music, but only after Elisa had pointed it out. Buggy wheels on dusty roads. Horses' hooves clopping in time to the chirp of crickets! He *had* heard it. And Elisa had not only heard it but somehow envisioned it all through the music.

"America must be a beautiful place if it sounds like this."

Then he had taken her hand in his. He could almost feel her fingers resting quietly in his hand now, and the nearness of her made him ache for her. The thump of the airship engines was nearly lost to him as he remembered.

"Would you like to go to America, Elisa? I'll take you to Iowa."

"But I do not really know you, Murphy. I cannot go with you."

"Then I'll send you."

"I must work."

"You can work there."

"My home . . . family . . . Papa . . . what is left of our heart . . . "

"My parents have a farm in Pennsylvania. Until this blows over . . ."

"There is no storm in Vienna."

"I wrote my parents. You would be most welcome, and . . ."

"Why would they take in total strangers?"

"Not strangers, Elisa. I want you to . . ."

Somehow the memory of his own surprise at the proposal of marriage brought him back to reality. "Marry me," he said aloud to the empty place across the table. Then, with a start, he noticed the waiter standing over him with his pencil poised on the paper. The rocking of the airship had nearly emptied out the small dining area. Murphy was grateful that only the waiter had heard his recitation of what had been a very foolish proposal.

The waiter smiled and bowed slightly. "Traveling alone, sir?" He gestured toward the empty chair where Murphy's imaginary Elisa had been sitting only an instant before. "Or are you expecting someone?"

Murphy shook his head and looked back to the menu card. "Alone," he said brusquely. And even as he said it, the longing welled up in him again! How he wished she were here! What a lunatic he was to be leaving her again! If ever he sat across the table from her again, he would not take *no,* or *maybe,* or *good-bye* for an answer!

"Your order, sir?" The waiter was all dignity. He pretended he had not heard Murphy's conversation to the air.

Murphy was pretending now, too. Pretending that he was all right. Pretending he was really thinking about anything but his stomach. "Veal."

The maitre d' approached behind the waiter. He bent low over the white starched tablecloth and gleaming silver. He whispered to Murphy and motioned toward the door of the dining compartment, where a tall, shapely brunette in a green silk evening dress stood smiling coyly in

Murphy's direction. Green eyes glistened and held a hint of promise. An evening of good conversation. A little wine and laughter. Light against the silk accentuated her curves. There was perhaps more than a hint of promise there, too.

"Mr. Murphy," the headwaiter said, "the young woman is also traveling alone. She would like to join you for dinner tonight?" This was not really a question. Only a lunatic would turn down such a request.

Murphy cleared his throat. "No," he said softly. "Thanks anyway. Tell her . . . thanks . . . anyway. But this is a business trip . . . uh . . . no thanks."

The brunette's nose rose slightly in indignation. She must have been able to read lips. She had certainly misread the lonely expression on the handsome young journalist's face. Murphy was not in need of just any female companion. He was in need of Elisa.

"I beg your pardon," said the maitre d'.

"Don't worry about it," Murphy replied lightly. "I'll take the veal."

The rest of the transatlantic journey Murphy did indeed work. Locked away in his compartment, he pored over the tragic testament of Walter Kronenberger. Duprey was right about one thing: Craine's publications would never touch this story. Craine had already made clear to Murphy that he had heard enough prophecies of doom about the European situation. The subject—like Craine's mind—was closed. But Murphy wasn't licked yet. If the Craine papers wouldn't publish Kronenberger's document, somebody stateside would. He'd see to that.

By the time the airship glided past the Statue of Liberty, the Kronenberger papers had been translated into English, and Murphy had written his own version of events in Austria to go along with it. It was only a matter of finding a publisher before the Craine plane took off with Murphy for the West Coast.

The statue in the harbor seemed almost to shout the answer to Murphy. "*Liberty Magazine*, you dope! This is just the kind of stuff they'll eat up!"

24
The Search for Noon

Days of waiting still had not brought the precious work permit to Herschel. By seven o'clock in the morning, the lines of desperate refugees wound from the doors of the Paris Ministry Building to the door of Madame Dupon's Fine Millinery Shop a block away. There it stopped. Beyond that point there was no use waiting. Experience had told them that it took an entire day from there to reach the counter of the clerks in charge of processing the thousands of requested permits.

Lately, the majority of permits were being rejected.

Inspired by this reality and curses of his uncle, Herschel Grynspan had risen each morning before daybreak to make his way to the line. He reasoned that his persistence might move the heart of some French official, since he had no money with which to bribe those who held the power to decide his future.

From the first day that he made his application, Herschel had known one terrible fact: If his permit was denied, he would not be allowed to remain in France. He was certain that his uncle had known this rule when he had insisted that Herschel appear at the Ministry Building. He must have also known how difficult it would be for a relatively unskilled boy of seventeen to acquire a work permit. The failure would give his uncle the excuse he needed to send the boy back to Berlin and not feel guilty. All of this instilled in Herschel an even stronger desire to prove the man wrong.

It was nearly four o'clock by the time Herschel reached the desk. All day people had left the counter with disappointment on their faces. To the left and the right, he could hear the denial of permits being pronounced.

"You must be patient," urged a clerk to the dark, brooding man who had stood just in front of Herschel all day. "You only applied last week. These things take time."

"How much time?" the man asked in a low voice. "How many francs?" he whispered.

Herschel strained to hear the reply. "A few well placed, perhaps . . . no guarantee. . . ."

"If I had that kind of money, you think I would need a permit to work?" The man stared angrily at the clerk, who shrugged.

"Everyone has to have a permit. It is the law." The clerk was finished with the conversation and peered over the shoulder of the man to where Herschel stood. "Next?" At the sight of Herschel, he scratched his head in wonder. "*You* again!" He smiled. "I could almost set my watch by you! Have you nothing better to do than to stand in this line?"

Herschel stepped forward and leaned against the counter. He looked like a small, pleading schoolboy. "Please, how much? How much for a permit? I have nothing now, that is sure, but if I could acquire a permit, I would share my wages with you."

The clerk stepped back, appalled at the suggestion. Herschel had spoken too loudly . . . and at a time when the department supervisor was walking slowly by.

"What? What did you say? What was that he said, Andre?" the supervisor asked.

"Honestly"—the clerk appeared puzzled at the supervisor's questions—"I know nothing of what this boy speaks!"

The supervisor leveled his gaze at Herschel, who now appeared even smaller. "How old are you, boy?" he demanded.

"Seventeen."

"Name?"

"Herschel Grynspan."

"You cannot have a wife, I presume."

Herschel looked confused. "No. No wife."

"German also, are you?"

The clerk intervened. "They are all Germans. Some Poles. Nearly all Jews, except for the politicals."

The supervisor waved his hand impatiently. "Yes, of course. I know all that." He returned his attention to Herschel. "Look, young man—" he pushed his glasses up on his nose—"there are fellows here much more worthy of a work permit than you. Men with families. Wives and children to feed, you see? And we are forced to deny even them."

"But I was a tailor. In Berlin. At the store of Theo Lindheim. You have heard of Lindheim's?"

"No, I have not," the supervisor said dryly. "Berlin does not interest me. Berlin has only complicated my life and work, you see." He waved a hand broadly at the line that still stretched across the marble foyer and out to the sidewalk. "But the fact remains that you are only seventeen. Much less worthy of a permit."

Herschel heard all his hopes crash down in the logic of the tall, stern man before him. "But I can pay . . . as soon as I have a job."

The clerk, looking embarrassed, put a finger briefly to his lips. The supervisor snorted at the suggestion; then he turned to the flushed clerk. "Application denied, Andre. Stamp his papers *Denied.*" Hardly looking at Herschel, he added, "He will have one week to leave France. Add that to his papers." Then he turned on his heel and strode off toward his office, slamming the door forcefully behind him.

"Please!" Herschel fought back tears as the clerk pulled his application from the file.

"Quiet!" hissed the clerk, who also seemed saddened by the finality of the decision. "Shut up, will you?"

"But if only I could—"

"There is no *if only,*" the clerk whispered, "unless I am to find myself also in some terrible line." He shook his head and inked the rubber stamp, then slammed it loudly across Herschel's papers. Scribbling in the deadline for Herschel to leave France, he shoved the application toward the boy. "Denied."

"Please . . . "

The clerk was finished. He looked beyond Herschel to the next man in line. "Next, please."

Herschel plunged the papers deep into the pocket of his tattered overcoat. The day was bright and warm as he walked through the maze of bookstalls set up along the bank of the Seine, but he felt cold—lost in the darkness of his own thoughts.

Men and women browsed in the stalls, bargaining for used and rare books that were stacked in long rows among the tables. Herschel passed them all, unaware of their words or even the place where he now walked. His hand, still clutching the documents, was wet with sweat, no doubt smearing the ink of the signature. *Denied!* The word pursued him, shouting to the passersby that all his hopes were now at an end. *Leave France in one week . . . back to Berlin!*

He stopped beside a bookstall and stood for a long time staring sightlessly down at a stack of old pamphlets. *Denied!* The papers burned in his hand, erasing all reality of the moment. Once again he heard the muffled moan of his father, the cries of mercy from his mother as the Gestapo agents shouted their accusations.

"He's a Jew! You can't expect him to give Lindheim away!"

"How much did Lindheim pay you? How much?"

All around the bookstalls the questions echoed back. *How much? How much?*

Herschel ran his fingers through his thick, black hair. A voice pulled him from his thoughts. "You wish to know how much, boy?"

Herschel looked into the leathery face of an old bookseller wearing a shapeless beret on his head and a thin black string tie at the frayed collar of his yellowed shirt. "I don't . . . " Herschel frowned back.

"You don't speak French?" the old bookseller asked gently.

"Oh yes, I speak French." Herschel's accent betrayed his Berlin upbringing.

"Good! Good! Then you also read French. We also have German books here." He gestured to another table, more crowded than the others.

Herschel remained rooted, uncertain what to say. "Yes," he said dumbly.

"Herr Hitler has burned the best German works, it seems," the old bookseller said with a shrug. "So Germans come here to purchase what cannot be had there any longer. The best German books *and* their authors are all in France now, I think. As well as those who find *Mein Kampf* dull and ridiculous reading, yes?" He spoke loudly to the boy, no doubt to draw other browsers. "Now, how can I help you?"

Herschel glanced down at the table again, grateful for the words of the old man. Silently he contemplated the pamphlets. His eye finally fell on a yellowed little booklet with a photograph of the military prison of Cherche-Midi that had held such a strong fascination for him when he had come upon it two weeks earlier. He picked up the booklet and studied the picture. Men in uniform guarded a man being led beneath the arch of the prison. "This is Dreyfus!" Herschel said, recognizing the scene. "I knew I had seen it before!"

"So you are interested in the famous Dreyfus, are you?" The bookseller sounded triumphant. "Yes! And this is one of the original pamphlets. You can see the date. 1894. Yes, many people are interested in this story. Certainly. A rare booklet you hold!" A few more browsers stopped at the stall.

"Yes." Herschel had almost forgotten his own misery as he examined the unhappy face of the prisoner. "I saw this prison. I saw where they took Captain Dreyfus! It has a strange name. 'The Search for Noon.' A very strange name, don't you think?"

"Not so strange." The bookseller was proud of his knowledge and ready to display it. A couple paused to listen. "It was a convent, you see.

Louis XIV, the Sun King, helped to build it. The nuns used to provide food for the poor each day at noon. Early in the morning beggars would come and wait for the kettles of soup, and so the street and the building got their name—The Search for Noon."

"But it is a prison now." Herschel could not take his gaze away from the sad face of the man in the photograph.

"Converted, you might say, during the French Revolution when the jails were overcrowded."

Browsers began to come to the bookseller with queries of "How much? How much?" The old man moved away from Herschel to make change and wrap purchases with stiff twine.

Herschel remained rooted before the table, scanning the details of the case of Captain Dreyfus, the French Jew accused of selling military secrets to the Germans. He felt foolish for not recognizing the prison immediately. He knew the history of the case quite well and must have seen the photograph a dozen times in the history books. Dreyfus had been stripped of rank, convicted, and imprisoned. The entire case against him had been manufactured and used as a springboard to arouse anti-Semitic hostilities among the French population. Twelve years after the imprisonment of Dreyfus, he was proven innocent and set free. But his case had divided the nation into two angry camps.

Herschel stared at the pamphlet. When this was printed, of course, the issue would not be decided for many years yet. The boy wondered how long it would take for Germany to decide the final case for those who were falsely imprisoned there now.

The bookseller turned his attention back to Herschel at last. "This case of Captain Dreyfus interests you, yes?" He seemed quite pleased with the business their conversation had brought to him. "And yet I do not hear you ask, 'How much?' "

Herschel replaced the booklet. "I do not have a single franc, sir," he said apologetically.

The bookseller looked thoughtful. He scratched the gray hair beneath the beret. "Then I shall lend it to you," he replied at last.

"I must leave France soon."

"Yes? America? Palestine? You have a visa?"

"No." Herschel frowned. "I could not get a work permit. They say I must go back to Germany."

The bookseller drew back in astonishment. "*Oui?* Back there? Where they burn books and still believe that poor Captain Dreyfus is guilty and should be hanged? And only because he is guilty of being a Jew, at that!" He seemed indignant. "Who says you must return to such a place?"

"The French ministry of—"

"Clerks!" He spat on the ground. "How are they to know if you stay or go?"

"I must have a permit to work—"

"Who says this?"

"Everyone!"

"Not everyone, I think." He glanced at a woman who stood struggling with a particularly high stack of purchases. In an enthusiastic and sympathetic voice the old bookseller said, "Madame! How far must you carry these things?"

"The Rue Royale." She grimaced at the thought.

"No, madame!" he protested. "When you purchase here, we also provide a service. For a few francs more, my boy here will carry your packages for you!"

She seemed relieved. "How much?" she asked as Herschel took the heavy bundle from her.

25

Shattering the Innocent

Bright fields of golden poppies swept upward from the shoreline into the mountains of the California coastal range. Murphy had never been to California, and to see it in spring from the high vantage point of the Craine airplane was almost intoxicating. For the first time since he had left Elisa in Prague, he found himself wishing he could one day bring her here.

He leaned against the glass of the cockpit as the pilot banked the plane slightly to soar over a mountain covered with blue lupines. Earth and sky and the sparkling Pacific Ocean blended together in a thousand hues of blue. The lacy line of surf crashing against the cliffs was the only sign of movement below them. Everything else in the picture seemed content simply to bask in sunlit beauty. And Murphy felt content simply to gaze at it all in silent wonder. He almost forgot about the pilot until the man spoke loudly over the drone of the engine.

"Beautiful, ain't it?" he said. Murphy nodded. "'Course you just come from the Alps," the pilot continued. "Guess that's more beautiful."

Murphy shook his head but did not take his eyes away from the rocky shoreline for an instant. "Different. Pretty, too—" He waved his hand as if to demonstrate. "But different. Not so gentle as these mountains, and there's no ocean. Lots of high rocky points. Like the Rocky Mountains." His breath frosted on the windowpane. "My wife is from there. I mean, close to the Alps. But I'll bet she'd like this. Bet she'd like to see it." Murphy said the words softly, but still they surprised him. Except for his conversation with the conductor at the Musikverein, he had not mentioned Elisa to anyone since the party at Strickland's in London. And then he had talked only of getting "unhitched." Now in the face of such beauty, he could not think of anything but sharing this sight with her.

"You got a wife?" The pilot was also surprised. A couple of days cross-country in a small airplane, usually about everything there was to know about a guy was discovered in the first few hours. "Didn't think you was the type!"

"Neither did I," Murphy mumbled. "Just full of surprises, I guess." He did not want to pursue the subject. A sudden ache coursed through him at the thought of Elisa. There was no guarantee that he would ever again share anything with her. She had shared her music with him, and now he wanted to show her the world. A beautiful world, without swastikas and strutting German soldiers. Someplace like this, where they could just live and forget about all that other stuff.

Hardly anyone in the States really thought about Hitler and the Nazis much. Old man Craine filled the editorial pages of every one of his newspapers with his own comforting prophecy that there would be no war. The leaders of Europe were too smart for a war, and the United States, at any rate, would never become involved no matter what happened. Looking down on Craine's domain, it was easy to see how he could believe all that. From here, even Murphy could almost believe it. If he hadn't seen it with his own eyes, the terrible events of Austria would indeed seem remote and insignificant right now.

The pilot tugged the sleeve of the borrowed Craine coveralls that Murphy wore. "Don't worry about clothes," he said, completely changing the subject. "The Chief knows you left in an awful hurry. Strickland wired him from London that you didn't bring nuthin' with you. The Chief liked that. He liked it that you didn't even pack. Anyways, don't worry about it, Murphy. San Sebastian has a basement as big as Macy's Department Store, and it's full of racks and racks of clothes. You go pick what you need, there's a tailor who alters it right there, and then you get to take the stuff home." He seemed proud of his intimate knowledge of the great man's castle. He leaned a little closer and confided, "I fly them movie-star types up all the time, you know? Clark Gable and Cary Grant always come with empty suitcases." He laughed at Murphy's amazed expression, then banked out to sea and began a slow wide turn back toward the mountains.

"When will we be there?" Murphy yelled over the engine.

With a wide grin and a nod toward the nose of the plane, the pilot tipped his hat. "Take a look!" He laughed.

Straight ahead, on a pinnacle of a mountain overlooking the ocean, loomed an enormous castle. Two turrets flanked a high, steeply pitched roof. Smaller buildings surrounding the castle seemed dwarfed by comparison, but Murphy could tell that these buildings were also enormous. Sparkling aqua waters of a giant swimming pool were surrounded by Roman statues, and a waterfall tumbled down into the pool and then flowed on to a fountain before the main entrance of the castle. Farther down the road was a small zoo. Murphy could clearly make out lions and several different kinds of large jungle cats lounging on rocks in the sun. A small herd of antelope, startled by the sound of the engine, stampeded across the face of a lesser hill. Cattle and buffalo grazed side by side on the grounds. A tall giraffe nibbled at the leaves of a tree at the bottom of a hill not far from the landing strip.

The place was Shangri-La. Camelot. A mythical kingdom that could not exist in reality. Murphy had heard all the stories about the Chief and his eccentric lifestyle. He had heard of the old man's devotion to his young mistress, of the flocks of Hollywood elite who vied for a treasured invitation to the place. Winston Churchill had been here once, Murphy knew. But that had been nearly ten years before, when Churchill believed that all the nations of the world must disarm for the cause of peace. Ten years ago, before Hitler began the massive rearmament of Germany. Murphy doubted if Churchill would be invited back to San Sebastian now. Although Craine professed to like him, one old lion to another, they no longer saw eye to eye on the issues at hand in the real world. San Sebastian was not the real world.

So why, Murphy wondered again as the plane touched down, was he summoned to the court of Arthur Adam Craine? John Murphy was little more than the smallest cog in the giant Craine publishing machine. His own opinions about the future of Europe differed sharply from those of the Chief. He had kept his opinions largely to himself since the sharp reprimand had come from New York, but certainly his anger at the rape of Austria must have been evident in his voice during the broadcast. Murphy didn't like the Nazis; surely the old man must know that. He seemed to know everything about nearly everybody. That's how he always managed to get his way, some said.

Why me? Murphy wondered again as he shook hands with the pilot and then climbed into the sleek black limousine that would carry him up to the castle of San Sebastian. Signs beside the twisting road read: *All Animals Have Right of Way.* Murphy remembered Strickland's advice clearly: *"The Chief loves animals. Talk about animals. Avoid politics!"* But surely A. A. Craine had not brought a small-time correspondent halfway around the world to talk about his private zoo, Murphy reasoned. They would talk politics, undoubtedly. The trick was for Murphy to nod in agreement when he did not, could not, and never would agree with the handing over of Europe piecemeal to the Nazis.

The German sentry in the foyer went away, but John Murphy did not come again to Elisa's apartment. Daily, Leah watched through the slit in the curtains, hoping for some glimpse of the tall, easygoing American. A dozen times a day, she caught sight of the bulky form of Herr Hugel as he lugged out the garbage or stood outside chatting with anyone unfortunate enough to get caught by his garrulous, self-centered conversation. His gurgling laughter punctuated his speech and penetrated the glass of the window where Leah watched. He was an obese, mindless watchdog whom the Gestapo had chained to the post by flattering him into thinking that he was important.

It must be the same all over Vienna, Leah thought wearily as Herr Hugel shouted a greeting to the apartment manager of the next building. That man, too, had an unkempt, greasy appearance and swaggered behind his Nazi Party badge.

Seeing Murphy that time had almost made Leah's isolation worse. The telephone had been disconnected within hours of her arrival here. She was unsure whom she would have called anyway. Had the maestro at the Musikverein even noticed her absence? Had he cared enough to inquire about the disappearance of her and Shimon?

No one had come to Elisa's apartment to check on her—no one but the very cautious John Murphy. *Why did he not return?*

News from the Greater Reich Ministry of Propaganda blared night and day over the radio. Often the music was interrupted by a burst of horns and a military march, and then the voice of Goebbels or Hess or Hitler would spit its venom out over the airwaves.

> *"Today a nest of Jewish Communists was rooted out of their hiding place in the Seventh District. . . ."*
> *"This morning at dawn three female spies were beheaded for their involvement in foreign . . . "*
> *"We will yet see an end to the vile plots of these Jews who seek to rob the German race of our . . . "*
> *"Seventeen smugglers of foreign contraband were captured at the border of the South Tyrol. They will be imprisoned for . . . "*
> *"The efforts of England and France to interfere with the family business of the Reich are laughable. . . ."*
> *"Today in a plebiscite of all Austrians of voting age, our Führer won the overwhelming approval of 99.75 percent of the voters! Heil Hitler!"*

Occasionally, late at night, Leah fiddled with the knob of the radio and managed to draw in stations from Switzerland. Once she heard a broadcast from Prague and imagined Elisa listening to it. That only made the loneliness more acute. The next night she tried again to pick up the Czech station, but instead, the voice of Hitler growled at her, promising to eliminate from the Reich all Jews and those who opposed the elevation of the Germans to their proper sphere. This was the stuff that nightmares were made of. Leah was living a nightmare now.

The pain of not knowing Shimon's fate was almost unbearable. If it had not been for the quiet perception of little Charles, Leah was quite certain she would simply have given up and walked out onto the streets in hopes of being arrested like Shimon had been. What was the purpose of staying alive, after all? If the responsibility for these children had not been forced upon her, she would have gladly let go.

But here was hope. Charles lugged the cello case over to her and laid it on the floor at her feet. He could not speak, but his eyes begged her to play, begged her to teach him how he too might make the glowing wood of Vitorio sing.

For hours each day, Leah lost herself in teaching the child how to play the cello. Louis played with dominos on the floor while Charles absorbed each lesson with hunger that startled even Leah. *"Let me speak and sing and pray with this voice of wood and string!"* he seemed to say. *"Teach me, Aunt Leah, so that I might make this voice of beauty my own!"*

Charles' hunger to learn made them both forget others' hungers and fears. Perhaps Elisa would come to help them. Perhaps she would never come. In the meantime, Leah made sure that little Charles learned to play the notes of the Bach Suites one by one.

Within the offices of the German Ministry of Propaganda, every foreign newspaper and magazine was carefully scrutinized for any item pertaining to the Reich and the Führer. Those matters that were considered important enough were translated and placed on the desk of Dr. Goebbels, minister of propaganda. Then the spidery little man would analyze such items further and make decisions about how the terrible foreign attacks must be countered.

This morning, secretaries raised their heads as a great roaring erupted from the office of Herr Doktor Goebbels. The roaring was expected; a whispered warning had been issued by the young woman who had translated the story about Walter Kronenberger and his defective offspring. *Liberty Magazine* was the guilty publication in this case. That particular magazine often was guilty of printing anti-Nazi stories for the appalled American public to read.

"Send a wire!" Dr. Goebbels shouted. "A wire to Craine in America! The author of this story is John Murphy, the American journalist with INS!"

"But, Herr Doktor, *Liberty Magazine* is not under the control of Herr Craine or his publishing empire!"

"No, but Herr John Murphy *is*!"

"*Jawohl*, Herr Doktor. What would you like this wire to say?"

"Tell him that if he cannot do better to control his journalists from printing such nonsense about the suppression of dissidents and imbeciles in the Reich, we shall shut down the INS operation. Tell him that his Murphy must change his tone or be dismissed! Let us see something *positive* from the American press, for a change."

After the wire had been sent to Craine in America, another wire was sent to the Gestapo headquarters in Vienna:

> IT IS IMPERATIVE IN THE LIGHT OF SUCH ADVERSE AND CONTINUING PUBLICITY IN THE CASE OF THE KRONENBERGER AFFAIR THAT THESE CHILDREN BE ROOTED OUT FROM THEIR HIDING PLACE LEST THEY ESCAPE BEYOND THE BORDERS OF THE REICH AND BE USED AS PROPAGANDA AGAINST US. SUCH MONSTROUS DEFORMITY IS EASILY SPOTTED, AND THE FÜHRER QUESTIONS WHY THE GESTAPO HAS FAILED TO ELIMINATE THESE SUBHUMAN CREATURES FROM AMONG US. HOW LONG WILL THE VOICE OF THIS DISSIDENT CRIMINAL KRONENBERGER CONTINUE TO PROTEST AGAINST THE WILL OF THE FÜHRER FOR THE WELFARE OF THE GERMAN RACE? NOTIFY IMMEDIATELY WHAT ACTIONS ARE TAKEN IN THIS UNPLEASANT MATTER. HEIL HITLER! MINISTER OF PROPAGANDA GOEBBELS

The furious order from Himmler's Gestapo headquarters reached even the lowliest of Nazi servants in Vienna. Early photographs of the monster Charles Kronenberger were pulled from the files and distributed. If this imbecile child with the hideous face was seen, he was to be reported immediately to headquarters. Matters would then be handled quietly and discreetly. It was understood, of course, that anyone found harboring these children would also have to be disposed of. Word must not go beyond the ranks of the most loyal and dedicated party members, but this Kronenberger offspring had been an issue to rally opposition to the Reich, and they must not be allowed to raise questions again. The matter must die. Anyone connected with the matter must also die. A reward of five hundred Reichsmarks was offered for the apprehension of the enemies of the Reich.

The civilian in front of Otto Wattenbarger's desk tapped his hat nervously against his thigh as he recalled the incident.

"Yes. There were two of them, sir. Almost the same size. They fell in the crowd and were almost crushed. If I had known, I would have let them be trampled. If I had known that they were these Untermenschen spawn of the criminal Kronenberger."

Otto raised his hand sharply. "And how do you know they are the same children in the dispatch?"

"How could they be any other? The one boy had a scarf wrapped around the lower half of his face. Like this." He demonstrated the concealment of the child's deformity.

Staring hard at the man, Otto challenged him. "It was a cool day."

"Yes . . . but . . . well, they asked me to take them to their aunt. At the Musikverein. They were both blond. Quite Aryan-looking from the eyes up. I thought on such a day I should do a good deed—"

"And now you undo it."

The informant straightened with resentment at the charge. "On the contrary. I correct my misdeed. If these . . . might be used against the promotion of the race, as our Führer says—"

"Yes, yes. Get on with it."

The man cleared his throat and began again. "So, I took them there. To meet their aunt . . . so they said. What was her name?" He frowned and stared up at the ceiling. "Lena, I think. But she was not there. Not at all. Only one person was there. A musician all alone on the stage."

"How do you know she was a musician?"

"She held her cello in the case. Like a big suitcase. I can tell the case of a cello, I assure you."

"And?"

"It wasn't my job to do more. This woman was not their Aunt Lena, but I left them there all the same." He looked down at the floor, then back at Otto. "If you find this person, you might find the children. You will find this Lena person, at any rate. Easy enough. She works at the Musikverein. How many Lenas can work there?"

Otto ran his hand through his hair wearily. A dozen such stories had passed through his office since the word had been sent from the top. "You have done well to report this," Otto congratulated the informer.

"And will I receive a reward?"

"If they are caught and your story is verified." Otto held up a finger in warning. "I would not tell the details to anyone else, however, lest someone else decide to trace your clues. Then you will not get any payment at all."

At that word, the face of the informer became very pale. He had, no doubt, repeated the tale in several beer halls. Otto could read that much on his face. "But, but . . . I came here first with the information."

Otto smiled patronizingly. "Of course you did. I have it all on file. I'm simply telling you that it is time to remain absolutely silent on this matter from this moment onward. The state police will take care of the matter, and you will be notified."

"I will not speak another word." He raised his hand to salute.

"Sensible. I have no doubt in my mind that you will be repaid for your action in this case. Now leave the rest to us, *bitte*?"

Nodding in awed agreement, the man backed out of the room, leaving Otto to contemplate the story. He thumbed through the thin file, looking at the dim photographs of two small boys. One was whole in countenance and smiling broadly as his broken brother embraced him. These two, left alive, were a threat to Hitler's policy of eugenics: selection of the fittest for breeding of the master race. Their existence was the one remaining testimony to the battle between church and Nazi Reich that had taken place in the early days.

Otto frowned as his eyes reached for the gentle gaze of the child with the torn face. Quietly he quoted the words of Faust's demon: "Shattering those who answer innocently is the tyrant's way of easing his embarrassment."

Otto smiled bitterly. The words of the demon were true. In this case, they were as true as words from heaven. The very existence of these children was an embarrassment to the Reich. There remained no choice but to shatter them utterly.

26

Solitary Confinement

The red leather-bound copy of *Faust* lay on the night table beside Theo's Bible. Within hours of his arrival in Prague, Theo had asked for it. Elisa could clearly remember the night in Berlin when she had watched her father pick the book from his library shelf. She had never asked him why he had chosen such a volume from among the thousand priceless first editions that he owned.

Tonight, as the round-faced Czech doctor finished his examination, he lifted the book and smiled curiously. "You are an admirer of Goethe's *Faust*, Herr Linder?" he asked, absently turning the pages. He seemed fascinated with the edition. Only last night he had pored over it as Theo had slept. Now Elisa stood in the doorway as her father answered.

"More so of Marlowe's," Theo said, his eyes moving from the book to the face of the doctor.

After a long moment, the doctor sighed and closed the cover. "Marlowe. The English writer. Very good, but I have not read his version, I fear."

"Someday you must." Theo took the book from him and thumbed through the pages as well. "My daughter Elisa is married to an American. Perhaps she might pick up a copy for you. A small token for your kindness." Theo was looking at Elisa now. The doctor had not noticed her behind him, and he followed Theo's gaze and sat silently considering her.

Elisa felt uncomfortable when he did not reply but continued to stare expectantly at her. "Of course," she blurted at last. "My husband is in London now."

"There is a possibility she will be joining him soon in Vienna," Theo added grimly.

"Vienna?" The doctor frowned and rubbed his cheek thoughtfully. "A dangerous place indeed, nowadays. Easier to get into than out of, as they say. But if you are married to an American . . ." He again looked at the edition of *Faust* in Theo's hands. He stood abruptly and changed the subject to the issue of Theo's health. "You are a man of great stamina, Theo," he said in a cheerful voice. "And Anna makes a better physician than I do in this case. Soon enough you'll be strolling along Charles Bridge and sightseeing in Old Town again." He pumped Theo's hand vigorously; then with a slight bow at the waist, he turned to Elisa. "And you, Elisa"—his plump cheeks were flushed—"will you still be here in three days when I come back to check on your father?"

"I hope by then to be with my husband," Elisa replied, hoping that her impatience to return to Vienna did not show.

"Ah well," he said in mock disappointment. "All this time I have come here to enjoy your mother's cakes and tea and to catch a glimpse of Theo's lovely daughter." He laughed. "He is practically recovered, you know, and now I shall have less reason than ever for coming."

Elisa felt relieved by his announcement of her father's health, even if he was half joking. All week he had come and spoken in urgent whispers as he examined Theo. His voice and manner had somehow frightened Elisa. Today, his lighthearted attitude lifted any final worries about Theo's recovery from her mind. "Mama will still make you tea and cakes." She smiled as the doctor closed his black bag.

"Then perhaps we shall see each other again before you leave," he said cheerfully, patting his rotund belly. He clicked his heels and took his leave.

Elisa showed him to the door and then watched out the window as he walked briskly toward the square. Just beyond the corner, the doctor was joined by another man, tall and lanky, wearing a coarse wool suit. The doctor uttered a few words, and both of them looked back toward the house. Their faces were anything but cheerful. Elisa felt a chill as she watched them through the slit in the curtains. Some moments of conversation passed before the doctor took the young man's arm and they walked slowly out of her view.

Leah used the last of the stale bread, carefully cutting away the mold on the crusts. Not once had she left the apartment since they had first entered it. She dared not leave Charles and Louis alone, yet the thought of taking them out terrified her.

Their complexions grew more pale each day. Again and again the image of the farm in the Tyrol, where Elisa had taken other children, came to Leah's mind.

Louis toyed listlessly with his food. No eggs. There never had been any milk. And now there was no butter to soften the rock-hard toast.

"You should eat, Louis," Leah said irritably, looking out the window and across the rooftops of Vienna toward the Judenplatz. *Who is left that I can trust?* she wondered. *And what, dear God, has become of Shimon?*

"Will we go shopping soon?" Louis asked. He looked unhappily at his toast. Charles stared hungrily at his own, then dipped a corner in his tea and carefully tasted it.

"We can't go anywhere yet." Leah softened her tone, realizing that she must not let her own frantic worries be obvious to the boys.

"Why not?" Louis was whining now. "You said we would get the pastry from your locker, Aunt Leah, but you forgot."

Leah imagined the box of Demel's sweet rolls, which by now must be a fuzzy green lump in her locker. She wondered if the lock had been changed yet—which blond Aryan musician would take it and take her place in the orchestra. Suddenly she was angry all over again. Did anyone in the orchestra care what had happened to their Jewish colleagues? Had anyone even bothered to check on the fate of Leah and Shimon? Was the management aware that Shimon had been arrested and their visas to Palestine had been taken? "And why doesn't Elisa come back?" she muttered. Just like the sweet rolls in her locker at the Musikverein, the three of them were growing a little fuzzy in their solitude. Herr Hugel prowled around the first floor of the apartment building not daring to bother Leah again after that first morning. But how could she slip the boys past him even if they had someplace else to go?

"You can go shopping without us," Louis said hopefully at the urging of Charles. "Father left us often when we lived in Germany."

Leah still did not reply or turn away from the window. Like a prisoner gazing out beyond bars to freedom, she longed to stretch her legs and carry a basket into the farmers' market. Milk. Eggs. Fresh bread. Cheese and heaps of cabbages. And yet, to spend their precious few shillings on food now would put them just that much more beyond the reach of train fare to the Tyrol and the farm, where such things magically appeared on the table in the Herrgottseck. *Elisa, have you forgotten?*

A gentle tug on her arm finally brought Leah's mind back from beyond the Viennese rooftops. Charles gazed solemnly up at her, worry and sadness in his eyes. He had seen other adults stare out the window. His mother. His father. And now Leah had done the same. She felt suddenly ashamed. She was supposed to be confident and in control. It seemed terribly unfair to let the fears that haunted her at night still remain in the morning. She cupped his sad, broken face in her hand. "What is it, Charles?" she asked gently.

He took her hand and she followed as if he were the adult leading her to some answer. They walked the quick few steps through the tiny front room to where the cello case stood like a silent sentinel in the corner. He touched the scarred case and guided her hand to it as he opened his mouth and tried to sing the first few notes of a Bach suite she had played. *"You need to think,"* he seemed to say, *"and here is where you will best think for us!"*

Leah obeyed meekly, as she had done as a child when her father had bellowed that she *must* practice, or why on earth had they spent a fortune on lessons and the instrument? *"You are not like other children, Leah! Let them play their games; what good will it do them? They might hop and run, but they are still on the ground,* ja? *You must play the cello; then you will fly above the rooftops on your music!"*

This morning, Charles sat beside her on the sofa as she played. His eyes followed every movement of her fingers and the sweep of the bow across the mellow strings of the violoncello.

The guesthouse at San Sebastian where Murphy stayed was furnished in dark medieval splendor. Huge tapestries purchased from the king of Spain hung on the walls. The floors were covered with priceless Oriental rugs. The bed Murphy slept in had once belonged to Cardinal Richelieu, who served Louis XIV of France. The huge armoire, where Murphy's new clothes now hung, once belonged to the Sun King himself. The bungalow was named Casa del Sol, "House of the Sun," the butler had told Murphy on the first day. Windows opened to the beauty of sunsets over the Pacific Ocean, and Murphy had watched the sight with awe the first time. But that first day had given way to a second, and still Murphy had not been taken to meet his host.

The first day's schedule was a blessing; Murphy had been so exhausted that he fell into Richelieu's bed and was conscious of nothing at all for the next eighteen hours. When he awakened the afternoon of the second day, he was told, "Mr. Craine is busy with other guests." Murphy was taken to be fitted with a new wardrobe of business suits and hats, advised that he simply could not meet the Chief until he had the "proper attire." After all, one could not have conversation with America's king of publishing while dressed in coveralls!

Now, as the sun cooled itself in the ocean, Murphy paced the length of the Oriental carpet and back again. He was angry. He had been rushed all the way from Europe at a whim of the Chief, and then shoved off into this glorified prison while Arthur Adam Craine "entertained his guests."

The shrill laughter of a woman drifted up from the swimming pool;

to Murphy the sound was like fingernails on a blackboard. While Craine and his Hollywood celebrities sipped champagne, Murphy and the events of Austria had been locked away, out of sight and out of mind. *Nothing unpleasant must disturb such privileged people, after all,* Murphy thought sarcastically. *The real world must not intrude on San Sebastian.* No thought of Hitler could be allowed to mar conversation or pull attention from the millions of dollars of European art that Mr. Craine had acquired.

Murphy sank down unhappily onto a chair that had once belonged to some king or another. He had already forgotten who. It didn't matter. The fact that Murphy was in the midst of some of the world's greatest art treasures did nothing to cheer him up. While Craine showed off his art collection here, men like Hitler and Göring were robbing Austria of her national art treasures. *Things* had come to mean everything, and human life itself held no value unless it served the Reich.

As Murphy gazed forlornly at the priceless objects that surrounded him, he felt that same current of perverted values here in the palace of America's self-proclaimed king. Craine determined what was important in his domain. Proper wardrobe. Proper conversation. Nothing unpleasant over dinner, thank you. And by all means, one must not mention that Europe was sliding toward the abyss of war. No, leaders like Hitler and Mussolini were too intelligent for that! Keep a lid on it! After all, as long as Craine could still purchase art from European dealers, America was safe!

Such bitter thoughts would cost Murphy his job if he expressed them, he knew. Craine did not want his employees to come into his presence with any ideas of their own. Like Cary Grant and Clark Gable with their empty suitcases, those called to San Sebastian were expected to come with empty minds waiting to be filled by the thoughts and opinions that he demanded they adopt as their own. After three days of simmering quietly in the Casa del Sol, Murphy was no longer certain that he could pretend to agree with anything Craine said. For the first time, it occurred to Murphy that maybe Craine kept people waiting to throw them off balance, to make them fear for their jobs and silently practice speeches of submission. *"Avoid politics; follow his lead; talk about animals,"* Larry Strickland had warned him.

A plane roared over the roof of the bungalow, and Murphy closed his eyes as he thought of other planes in Germany, in Spain, and now over Austria. Suddenly there was only one kind of animal that Murphy wanted to talk about with Craine—the black-shirted goose-stepping kind, the strutting Heil-Hitlering kind of animal!

Murphy almost laughed out loud. If Craine had left him in isolation this long to make him more compliant, he had made a mistake. Murphy felt anything but docile right now. He had promises to keep in Vienna, and if Craine was too busy to see him, Murphy determined that he would simply find his own way back to Europe. If he was not allowed to see Craine by morning, he would leave; he would go back to find Leah and Shimon, and then on to Elisa in Prague.

A soft knock announced the entrance of the butler who served the guests of Casa del Sol. He bowed slightly and said regally, "You must dress for dinner tonight, Mr. Murphy. Your dinner jacket. Mr. Craine wishes you to join him and a few other guests in the refectory tonight at eight."

So here it is at last! The summons to the Presence. Dinner at eight. Of course. Murphy smiled and nodded as the butler proceeded to lay out the elegant dinner jacket and draw the bath. Solitary confinement was about to end.

27

The Barter

Charles had been right in his assessment of what Leah needed to clear her mind. Although she had stopped playing, the music still seemed to fill the room, lifting them up to a soaring freedom over the rooftops and spires of Vienna, and beyond.

Charles touched the rich, glowing wood of the precious instrument; then he looked searchingly at Leah. The peace and confidence had returned to her face.

"Yes, Charles." She spoke for the first time all morning. "It is a magic carpet, isn't it?"

He nodded. His eyes smiled with relief. Aunt Leah was somehow well.

"That is what my father said when he bought me Vitorio. He said, 'Other children are earthbound, but you, little Leah, will soar like a bird with the help of Vitorio! High above the Grunenwald! Float above the Danube, then on and on until you hover between the highest peaks of the Alps!' " She laughed with delight as Charles flapped his arms and rose from his knees to sail around the room with Louis close behind him.

"What? What will we do, Aunt Leah?" Louis asked breathlessly as they finally landed before the cello.

"My father must have been a prophet." Leah stroked the fine instrument gently as if it were a much-loved family member. "Do you know what a prophet is?"

The two heads shook in unison. This was a word they had not heard before.

"Well," Leah said, laying her hand softly on the smooth wood of Vitorio, "it is someone who can see the future."

The boys exchanged wondrous glances. "Could he see us now?" Louis asked.

Leah pondered the question. No, there was no Jewish father in all of Europe who could have seen this terrible darkness for his children. "I think not," Leah answered carefully. "But if he had been able to foretell these circumstances, I know what he would have me do." Now she spoke to herself, not to the little ones who tried to follow her words. She looked from the cello into the faces of the children who needed her so desperately. "Vitorio will indeed carry us far away from here, as my father said." She smiled. "Vitorio is our magic carpet, Charles and Louis!"

Imaginations leaped to life. Would they ride the cello in loops and swirls in the sky like a giant eagle? "We will have to be very careful of the German bombers!" Louis giggled as the drone of German planes rumbled over the apartment. Such roaring had not stopped since the morning the Germans had come to Vienna.

"No," Leah said, allowing her eyes to focus on the vibrating light fixture in the ceiling. "We will fly away another way. And we will have to leave Vitorio behind, I'm afraid." The boys both groaned in loud protest. "He will not mind." Leah put the instrument into its case. Then, before she closed the lid she looked lovingly at what had been her most precious possession. "It does not matter." She spoke to the strings and wood and glowing red varnish that had reflected her soul since childhood. "I will take the music with me." The strings hummed softly as she brushed her fingers across them and closed the lid in a final, irrevocable decision.

Leah had no instructions for Louis and Charles as she prepared to leave the apartment. If she did not return, their fate would no doubt be linked to hers. But she would not think of *not* returning to them. She *must* come back!

"Quiet now, like little mice." She put a finger to her lips. "Remember the big, fat cat, Herr Hugel, prowls around downstairs!"

"Charles is always quiet," Louis reminded her. "I will also be quiet," he promised with his eyes wide at the thought of Herr Hugel, whose laughter often drifted up the stairs.

"Not just quiet," Leah warned, "but also very still. If you must walk, then walk on your tiptoes! He will be listening after I leave!"

They understood perfectly the danger inherent in the fat man who seemed so harmless and brainless. Leah had often warned them of the power that belonged to such petty and evil men now. He was the kind who would seek to better himself by tearing the life out of others. He had sold his humanity for a minuscule kingdom, and if he still had a conscience, it must now be stroked by the approval of his superiors. Approval would be gained by some small bit of information or, more glorious yet, by the discovery of some secret within the walls of the apartment building. Louis and Charles were Leah's secret.

She embraced them and kissed each boy lightly on the cheek. Then bravely, she hefted the violoncello and left the apartment, securely locking the door from the outside. Twice before, Leah had suspected Hugel of sniffing around the hallway. She had intimidated him beautifully on the first morning of his arrival. He was a sneak but lacked courage, Leah knew. At least Leah hoped this was the case.

At the top of the landing she paused, gathering courage. The world outside the walls of the apartment was now terrifying. To walk among the enemy as if she were one of them required a bravado she was unsure that she could find. She softly hummed a few notes of the Bach suite. She would let her music be her courage. It must carry her today!

Carefully she walked down the steps. The violoncello felt awkward and heavy. It seemed like a lifetime since she had been out of the little flat.

As she reached the bottom of the stairs, Herr Hugel opened the door and greeted her with a respectful, giggling exuberance. He rubbed his hands together. He looked at the cello and his eyebrows arched. "Ah yes! The musician of apartment 2-B."

"Heil Hitler," Leah answered crisply, not slowing her pace.

"Heil Hitler!" He stepped in front of her. Smiling with stubby, crooked yellow teeth, he stood fawning and grinning as he blocked her path. He towered over her. Leah had not noticed that he was tall as well as immense. He must have weighed three hundred and fifty pounds, she guessed. There was no room for her to go around him.

"Herr Hugel, I have a rehearsal now. I have no time for talking, *bitte*?" She stepped to one side, hoping that her curtness would remove him from in front of the door.

"Ahhhh. Yes! I can sometimes hear soft music from your flat. Sometimes voices." Subtleness was not characteristic of Herr Hugel.

"My radio, no doubt." Leah quietly determined that for as long as they remained in the apartment, they would whisper from now on. She nearly stamped her foot with impatience. "If you don't mind . . . "

He blinked at her as though trying to understand what he might mind. "The radio? Why, no! I don't mind at all! Good, strong German music! Wagner, they say it is." He tried to sound knowledgeable. "None of that Jewish drivel."

"Yes. Well." Leah let the remark slip by. "I have a bit of good, strong German music to rehearse now, Herr Hugel!" She smiled.

The repetition of his words flattered him. He laughed again, wanting to talk longer with her, as though being seen with a musician somehow bestowed some knowledge or glory or talent on him. "We must talk again!" He gave a silly, ignorant laugh, the laugh of a man who sees only his own circumstance and not the pain of the toppled world around him.

Leah brushed past him. "Yes, we must!"

Again he laughed.

Leah guessed the man was imagining himself being seen in conversation with the musician from 2-B who plays for the highest German officials in Vienna.

Through the slit in the curtain, Charles watched Leah and her cello wind through the crowd of pedestrians on the sidewalk below until she rounded the corner and slipped out of sight. How often had he watched his father do the same? Always he wondered if Father would come back. The last time he had not. Maybe this kind and gentle woman would not come back to them either.

The thought had only just torn through him when he heard the heavy tread of Herr Hugel on the stairs. The fat man's wheezing breath preceded him in asthmatic warning that he was coming here to violate the safety of this apartment.

Louis, who was quietly practicing his letters at the table, froze. His face was a mask of fear. Eyes grew wide and his gaze locked with Charles'. "Charles?" he whispered, his pencil poised above the paper.

Charles stared at the door as Herr Hugel's wheezing turned into a violent and angry cough just outside in the hallway. He cleared his throat, spitting over the rail.

"He's coming here!" Louis mouthed as the jingle of keys rang loudly.

There was not a moment longer to hesitate. Charles ran to the side of his terrified brother and pulled him quickly toward the bedroom. Where could they hide? Leah had not told them what to do in such a circumstance. They had not imagined that Herr Hugel might have a key. Who could foresee that the fat man was simply waiting below for Leah to leave?

"The closet?" Louis started to move toward the door. Charles pulled him back. Herr Hugel would surely search in the closet and if he was to discover them there, he would call the Gestapo!

A key scraped into the lock. The doorknob rattled, and Herr Hugel swore quietly as he pulled the key out and tried another.

Curtains hung down to the floor. Would the fat man look there? Or behind the chair?

There was only a few inches of clearance beneath the bed, but it was enough for Louis and Charles to squeeze their small bodies between the footboard and the floor.

Again the rattle of the doorknob echoed in the apartment. Charles closed his eyes. He could feel his heart pounding fiercely against the floor as the latch caught and the front door crashed open. Now the labored breath of the fat man flooded the room. The floorboards groaned beneath his weight as he stepped forward.

Charles held tightly to the hand of Louis. Charles looked at his brother. Tears brimmed in Louis' eyes. *"It is a game,"* Charles wanted to reassure Louis. *"Pretend we are playing hide-and-seek."* Charles slowly raised a finger to his broken mouth, a signal for silence. Louis simply stared at him as the footsteps of Herr Hugel approached the kitchen. The boys could hear the clatter of cups in the sink, the sound of cupboard doors opening and closing as Herr Hugel searched every inch of the apartment. For what? For them?

Leah did not dare carry the violoncello to a legitimate instrument shop for fear she would be recognized. This obscure little pawnshop had seemed the logical choice with its display of instruments in the window and the little shopkeeper who seemed as dusty as the cluttered shelves in his shop.

Now, as the beautiful old Pedronelli cello lay before him on the counter, Leah regretted that she had come here at all.

"It is quite old," she explained. "And very valuable."

"So they all say, madame," he said as he rubbed his bald head and smiled doubtfully. "I have a dozen like it in the back room. All in better shape than this one, I assure you, madame."

"But the quality of this cello is unsurpassed, and—"

"Every musician trying to leave Vienna has said the same. There is an abundance of such items on the market. No one will buy it for the price you are asking, madame! I cannot make a profit! I sell to students, poor students who come here because they cannot afford to walk through the door of an instrument shop. So they come here. What do you expect? I cannot make a profit! You could take it elsewhere, and you would not get better than what I offer you. I tell you, this is nothing but wood and strings to me, and such wood as this is being unloaded all over Vienna these days."

"But what you offer is not a tiny fraction of what it is worth!" Leah protested. She considered gathering the cello up and trying another shop, but no doubt the vile little man before her was correct. The value of an instrument in Vienna was practically nothing.

"If you need good solid Reichsmarks, madame, I offer you what I can. So how am I to know that it does not squawk and screech like a cat with his tail in the gears?" He widened his eyes and plucked a string. "Wood and strings. I pay you just what I might get if a poor student might happen to wish to buy it in the next year or so. Take it or leave it."

The instrument was like a revered old friend to Leah. Somehow its sale now seemed like a betrayal. It had delighted thousands of concert-goers in Vienna, and now it was to gather dust in some obscure little shop until a penniless student happened upon it. "It is a treasure," she defended desperately.

The pawnbroker plucked another string. "And who can prove such a claim? No doubt the friend you sell this for is a Jew, yes, madame?" He inclined his head and narrowed his eyes in suspicion. "So if this is of such great quality, tell your friend to come in and play it for me himself."

Leah's mouth suddenly became dry. For a moment she imagined Gestapo officers waiting behind the faded green velvet curtain that led to the back room of the shop. Did the little man know who she was in spite of her lie? Was he playing some game with her, daring her to prove herself, tempting her to reveal her own skill and condemn herself through the beauty of her music? She could sit on a street corner in Vienna among a hundred other musicians and stop traffic if she dared to play this "mere woods and strings."

"I . . . I . . . told you," she stammered, "my friend is not a Jew. He is ill. Very ill and in need of a doctor's attention. A hospital. Medicine." The lie sounded unconvincing even to her ears.

The pawnbroker did not attempt to conceal a smirk of disbelief. "Tell your . . . *friend*, whoever he may be . . . whatever his condition, that every shop in Vienna will say the same. This is nothing but wood and strings. It is of no value to me whatsoever unless I can resell it for profit. Which I doubt. And it is of no value to your sick friend unless he can turn it into a boat and float away from the Reich on the Danube. Perhaps he can play the "Blue Danube Waltz" as he paddles? Or perhaps your sick Jewish friend would do better to refuse the money and keep his cello"—the smirk became a grin—"for a coffin."

Leah felt her face flush with anger and humiliation. She slammed the lid on the cello and fumbled with the lock. "I will go elsewhere!"

The pawnbroker continued to smile confidently. "Then I should perhaps call the Gestapo and tell them there is a woman trying to sell a very valuable cello for some Jew in hiding?" He whined the question. "You will not walk a dozen yards from my door before you are arrested, madame."

Leah stared at the cello. What had she done? How foolish she was to imagine she could get a fair price for the priceless instrument! Now the pawnbroker was counting out a pittance of its value. The student bow she owned was worth more than she was being paid for the entire instrument. He shoved the meager stack of bills across the counter to her.

Vitorio had been her friend. Her living. But now there was no life for her here, and other lives were in danger. *The violoncello is only an object,* she told herself as she continued to stare at the case. Here before her was enough cash for two one-way tickets to the Tyrol, and her own round-trip fare to Kitzbühel and back to Vienna. The cello for train fare, safety for the children of Walter Kronenberger.

She looked up at the vile little man who still grinned at her from behind the counter. She had no choice. He knew it, and so did she. She hated him for knowing how vulnerable she was. She hated him for his power over her.

"You are a thief," she said calmly, picking up the money.

He laughed at his victory. Yes, he was a thief, but he was a successful thief, the laughter seemed to say. And he would be a very wealthy thief before all this ended. "A businessman, madame," he said happily, pulling the cello off the counter and out of Leah's reach.

She turned quickly away so he would not see her tears. His laughter followed her out of the dusty little shop and echoed horribly in her mind as she hurried away to the train station.

28

Out of Captivity

The main assembly room of the Craine Castle was so large that Casa del Sol would have fit inside it easily. Two dozen guests were dwarfed in the eighty-by-thirty-foot room. All those assembled could have stood inside the enormous fireplace. Huge tapestries hung from the ceiling above dark oak-paneled choir stalls purchased from a sixteenth-century monastery. At either end of the room ancient Roman busts were perched atop gold-leaf pedestals twenty feet high. A marble statue of Venus gazed shyly down on the guests.

In his starched white shirt and black dinner jacket, Murphy imagined that he must look like one of the servants. He stood apart from the others, most of whom he recognized from movies. They played cards and sipped champagne while they chatted amiably and waited for their host. Clark Gable and Carole Lombard sat together on a long red-and-gray, floral-print sofa at the end of the room. The statue of Venus seemed to eye them in particular, Murphy thought with amusement. He wondered if Gable had also advised Miss Lombard to come to San Sebastian without any clothes in her suitcase.

Marie Dressler, her matronly figure draped in fox fur from head to toe, chatted with western star Joel McCrea as they played bridge with a man and woman Murphy did not recognize.

All the while Murphy hung around the huge grand piano and talked quietly to the piano player. No one seemed to notice either of them, and Murphy was relieved that he blended into the surroundings. The "beautiful people" gathered in this room were the other guests Craine had been entertaining for the past week. Murphy recognized the laughter of a slim blond woman dressed in a blue silk evening gown, but he did not know who she was. As he leaned against the piano and watched his companions, he was left with the sensation that these guests were also mere adornments of Craine's grand castle. They were like the paintings and tapestries, like the sixteenth-century choir stalls that served no other purpose than to decorate the room.

The pianist finished playing Chopin's *Nocturnes,* and no one even looked up or applauded.

"You know any *jazz*?" Murphy grinned. "Scatman Caruthers?"

The pianist, a young man of twenty-five, nodded. "Not here, friend," he said, quietly shuffling through his sheet music. "The Chief doesn't allow it." He chose another piece by Chopin. "There are a couple of dives in Frisco where I play the hot stuff. But not here. The Chief says it would clash with the decor. Guess he's afraid his Venus might wake up and jive! Quite a museum he's got here," the musician added under his breath. "Gotta play stuff to match the decor."

Even the pianist was part of the total image. So how, Murphy wondered, did he fit in? And why was he now being called out of confinement to sup with the Chief and his elegant guests?

His answer came, strangely enough, from the mouth of the musician. "So you're the journalist, huh? The one from Europe?"

Murphy eyed him curiously. "Been in Europe a while, and here too long."

"You going back with Lindy, I hear."

Murphy squinted, trying to catch up with the piano player's thought. "Lindy?"

"Yeah. Lucky Lindy. Charles Lindbergh." The pianist looked amused at Murphy's confusion.

"That's news to me."

The pianist laughed at what he thought was a joke. "A good one! News to you! Did you hear the plane this afternoon?"

"The plane?" Yes, Murphy had heard a plane. But he had not connected it with Lindbergh.

"*His* plane. He buzzed the castle. Boy, you sure know how to play dumb. Everyone knows. You don't have to pretend. They all know why you're here. Going to cover Lindbergh's trip to Germany. Right? Going to fly along with Lucky Lindy while he gets his medal from Hitler."

So this was the "hot story" Murphy had been summoned to cover! He had not heard that the American hero was to be decorated by the Führer. Nor could he quite grasp that he had been chosen to write the story of this ill-timed and inappropriate pilgrimage. Murphy continued to stare hard at the inside of the grand piano. He did not speak as he let the information sink in. "How'd you hear all this?"

The young man inclined his head at the guests. "They've been talking about it all week. Can't keep any secrets from the piano man. They hang around here every night and gossip. Think the servants and the musicians are all deaf, I guess. They think we don't have ears." He laughed. "Stand around the piano and gossip. You wouldn't believe the stuff I know!"

"Like whether Lindbergh is coming to dinner?" Murphy tested.

"Sure! He's upstairs with the Chief in the Gothic study talking it over right now. The Craine papers have bought an exclusive on the whole thing. And you're the man going along for the ride. Everybody knows, from the cook to the hairdresser to the tailor. I sat down in the alterations shop and jawed with the tailor while he finished your suits. What a deal! All I ever get out of this is a new dinner jacket once in a while. I like your suits. Like the brown double-breasted one best. And the brown wing-tip shoes." He was grinning broadly at the expression on Murphy's face.

The man was right. Murphy wouldn't ask him what he thought about the argyle socks. The piano man knew the details about Murphy's life better than Murphy did. "Well, if you know so much, tell me why Mr. Craine hasn't seen me all the time I've been here."

The pianist looked blank. "I don't know. Why?"

Murphy drew himself up and tugged on his bow tie. "My clothes weren't finished. Can't meet the Chief in coveralls."

The pianist shrugged and glanced up at the clock. "Three minutes," he said cryptically.

The guests fell silent and looked toward the tall paneled door beside the great stone fireplace. The clock inched toward eight. Servants stood at rigid attention as the seconds ticked off. Then, as the minute hand touched twelve and the bells in the bell tower chimed, the door opened and the tall, stern figure of Arthur Adam Craine emerged, followed by Charles Lindbergh, who appeared very young and boyish. It had been ten years since Lindy's flight across the Atlantic to Paris. Murphy had still been in high school. He had seen Lindbergh several times since then in Europe, but always among a mob of other newsmen. Until Lindbergh had toured Germany and pronounced the infallibility of Hitler's air force, Murphy had always considered him a hero. Tonight, however, in the glow of the tall silver candlesticks of the Assembly Room, Lindbergh's image seemed a bit tarnished.

"Good evening, ladies and gentlemen." Craine extended his thick arms wide. "You all know Colonel Lindbergh, I assume?" Then he gazed directly at Murphy. "And soon you'll know him better. The Craine newspaper chain has just been granted exclusive coverage of the colonel's upcoming journey to Europe." He smiled a perfunctory smile in Murphy's general direction. "Beginning with tonight's dinner, if you please, Mr. Murphy."

The red flags were everywhere. Leah lowered her eyes and pulled her scarf over her hair. On the crowded sidewalk she brushed past what seemed like a thousand groups of laughing German soldiers. Black, shining jackboots against the pavement was all she could see. The threats of the pawnbroker followed doggedly after her. The man was nothing more than a thief; now that he had stolen Leah's lifeblood, would he also call the Gestapo? Was she being trailed at this moment?

She overheard snatches of conversation as she walked by a group of Blackshirts.

"My right arm, Hans . . . so weary."

"A tough one, was he?"

"Yes, but he cracked in the end. They all do. But still, my arm is quite sore from the beating I gave him." The comment was completed by raucous laughter.

Leah wanted to cover her ears with her hands and run from this nightmare, run from the thought that these evil men might be boasting about the beating they had given Shimon. Her Shimon! Her heart cursed them. *Run, Leah! Run and they will shoot you, and everything will be finished. If they killed Shimon, then you cannot live either! Run! Run from the life that is not life anymore at all!*

But she did not obey her thoughts. Instead she walked steadily onward toward the train depot. No one stopped her along the street. They did not notice the small woman with her eyes averted. She blended into the stone facades of the buildings. Voices echoed. The scuffing of soldiers' boots and laughter pursued her as she focused her mind on the children. On little Charles, symbol of the last fight of many good men in Germany. Now they were dead. But Charles must live! If there was a God, then this helpless little boy must live!

Her legs carried her up the steps of the depot as though she were simply a passenger in her own body. Beneath the familiar arches of the building she at last looked up. Here too, where her beloved orchestra had come and gone a hundred times, the dreaded swastika draped the vast hall.

Thousands of people were crammed into the waiting area; baggage was piled on the platform. Stern Gestapo watchers were evident behind every pillar, at every entrance and exit. Faces of hopeful passengers were strained and fearful. Could there be any moment more frightening than the last moment still within the reach of the Nazi authority? Leah could see it plainly. Those who waited in the long serpentine lines to purchase tickets were also terrified.

"Travel documents!" barked the rock-jawed agent who prowled the length of one line and then back along another. "What? You do not have the proper papers to travel in the Reich! Trying to sneak past us?" he roared at one ashen-faced woman. "You know there is no excuse! To travel without proper documents is to find oneself in Mauthausen!"

"But I did not know!" she protested, clutching his arm. "Please!"

He shook himself free and shoved her to the ground. With a snap of his fingers two men appeared like grim apparitions and dragged her away as she wept loudly.

Travel papers! Leah had none. Nor could she acquire any. She had not known! How *could* she have known? She could not purchase train tickets without them!

A wave of dizziness swept over her. She leaned heavily against the stone wall of the building. She had lost Vitorio for nothing. It was hopeless. Not only was it impossible for her to fly away on the winds of the magic cello, now she could not even take a train from this place.

As all eyes turned toward the unfortunate woman who had attempted to purchase a ticket without Nazi permission, Leah drew a breath, steadied herself, and slipped out of the echoing hall into the sunlight.

Still more soldiers walked past her on the steps. Could they see the terror on her face? The hopelessness?

Run! her mind shouted, but instead, her trembling legs staggered forward. *Back to the apartment. Back to confinement.* And now there would be no music to comfort them as they waited. Leah could not even think any longer what it was they were waiting for.

Charles could hear the rustle of paper in the other room. They had left the sheet on which Louis had been practicing the alphabet in plain sight. The fat man laughed, delighted to have discovered the childish scrawl before him on the table. Louis squeezed Charles' hand tighter.

Where had Leah put their papers? Charles gasped as he remembered their German identity cards and his father's letter had been placed in the drawer of the night table. Yes. Herr Hugel would look there, too.

Heavy footsteps walked toward the bathroom. Herr Hugel did not bother to close the door. There was no other moment for Charles to act. While Hugel was busy obeying nature's call, he tore his hand free from Louis and squirmed out from under the bed. He crawled across the floor to the nightstand.

The toilet flushed as Charles quietly slid the drawer of the nightstand open and pulled out the incriminating papers. Footsteps walked toward the bedroom. Charles closed the drawer quietly even as the doorknob turned. The child lunged for the bed, scrambling under it and out of sight just as the bedroom door crashed open and the worn shoes of Herr Hugel crossed the threshold and stood still. His labored breath smelled plainly of stale beer and sausages, and he reeked of sweat. The boys held their breath as the bursting leather shoes walked toward the bed and stopped. After a while he moved to the dresser. Drawers opened and closed. Herr Hugel chuckled once again and stood motionless; then a pair of lace panties fell to the floor. With a grunt of effort, the fat man bent his bulk to retrieve them. The drawer slammed shut.

Feet splayed outward to support his weight, he walked toward the closet. He threw it open and beat his hands against the dresses as he searched for . . . for what? for whom?

The fat man sniffed loudly in disappointment. No one was hiding in the closet. He turned in a circle. Charles could see his toes pointing toward the bed again. The fat man was thinking, sniffing the room for a clue like a cat sniffing for a mouse. He walked the two paces to the bed. The toes of the ragged shoes poked beneath the footboard. He lifted his foot to measure the inches between floor and footboard. Charles could almost hear him thinking: *Small enough for a mouse. But not for a human.*

Louis squeezed his eyes and gritted his teeth as Herr Hugel circled the bed. He repeated his calculation with the side rails that were a fraction higher from the floor than the footboard. The fat man started to stoop down, but the effort proved too great. He scraped dust from beneath the bed and nudged it with his toe. The dust seemed to satisfy him.

With a grunt of confusion, he turned once again to see if there was any place he might have missed. "Night table," he muttered, pulling open the drawer and pawing through its contents. The drawer slid back, but Herr Hugel did not move for a moment. Then he sat heavily on the bed.

Above the boys, the springs groaned and sagged, pinning them painfully against the hard floor. Louis grimaced as the weight of Herr Hugel pressed against his head and shoulder. Charles almost cried out with agony as his tender face was pushed down against the unyielding floor and his breath was nearly cut off.

For a full two minutes the boys remained pinned beneath the fat man's build. Then, just as the pain became unbearable, Herr Hugel struggled to his feet and stood in the room for a moment longer before he cursed and walked slowly toward the front room. He closed the door behind him, careful to leave the place as he had found it.

Trying to regain their breath, the boys followed the shuffle of the fat man's footsteps through the apartment as Herr Hugel searched the place one last time.

What had he found? Nothing. Nothing but a childish scrawl on a slip of paper. The moment Herr Hugel had envisioned as a great victory for his prestige with the Nazi Party now ended as he lumbered out into the hallway and locked the door of the apartment behind him. But he was not finished. His exit now did not mean defeat. There was something—*something*—he had overlooked, and he would wait and watch until he found it.

29
The Mutiny

Murphy was seated to the left of Lindbergh at the long dining table in the room Craine called The Refectory. The table was at least twenty-five feet long. It, too, was a part of the priceless cache of antiques Craine had purchased in a foundering Europe. Four hundred years before, this had served as a nuns' dining table in a convent in Italy. Murphy could not help but wonder if the good ladies now looked down from heaven and shuddered at the conversation around their table.

Six silver candlesticks, each three feet tall, provided the only illumination in the room. The dim light was lost in the high ceiling above them. Behind Craine hung an ancient French tapestry depicting scenes from the life of Daniel. It was flanked on either side by still more ornately carved choir stalls. *How many cathedrals,* Murphy wondered, *how many convents closed by the European Fascists have been shorn of their treasures?* The glory of dozens of churches and monasteries now adorned this castle built for the glory of Craine. First sold by the government authorities to dealers, the art had been gleefully purchased by Craine's agents. Besides the things on display here, two entire warehouses were crammed full of Craine's possessions.

This knowledge caused Murphy to remember uneasily that Hitler and Göring had also accumulated a mass of treasure from the collections of those condemned by the Reich as "vile Jews." Murphy had seen the Rembrandt and da Vinci paintings that hung so prominently at Göring's Karinhall mansion. He had not dared to ask where they had come from. He already knew the frightful answer.

"Europe is awash with art treasures," Craine was saying. "I picked up these candlesticks for a song in Munich last year. They are from a synagogue there. Quite lovely. I thought it appropriate to light the room with them. Candlesticks from a Jewish synagogue, a table from a nunnery. You see, at least I unite two hostile religions in my dining room!"

Polite laughter answered him. *Polite but reserved,* Murphy thought. Maybe Murphy wasn't the only one feeling uneasy about this. Charles Lindbergh grinned with genuine approval, however, and he ate heartily. Lindy was convinced that Hitler had done great things for Germany. He did not seem to notice that those who objected in Germany simply vanished, and their possessions turned up in the house of some Reich official of high or low rank, depending on the value of the item. Lindbergh had made no secret of his admiration for "things German." And now Adolf Hitler was about to reciprocate with the highest medal the Nazi Reich could award to a noncitizen.

The thought made Murphy's food stick in his throat. He had seen what had happened, first in Germany and now in Austria. Sitting here tonight and trying to eat by the light of confiscated candlesticks from a synagogue made him feel like a traitor. The thought of traveling with Lindbergh to visit the Führer made him feel ill, not to mention angry. The order not to talk politics grew more dim with every passing moment.

"Winston Churchill believes that Hitler has his eye on Prague," Murphy blurted out. "That ought to bring in quite a haul of art."

The murmur of conversation grew still. Craine, whom Murphy had interrupted in the midst of a story about serving dishes, glared at Murphy. "And so what if the Germans annex the Czech Sudetenland? Everyone there speaks German."

"Except for those who speak Czech," Murphy countered. Even in the soft glow of the candlelight, he watched his host's craggy face redden.

"How does that affect us in America?" The taboo was smashed. Politics, the most dreaded of all violations at the dinner table, loomed like a horrible specter in the hall.

"It may make the value of art drop," Murphy replied. "There is already a glut on the market. But then I suppose there will be lots of folks over here who will just buy, buy, buy. I had my eye on the statues on Charles Bridge. Ever seen the statues on Charles Bridge, Mr. Craine?"

Craine was smiling now. His eyes had narrowed like a cat watching the tiny mouse hole at feeding time. "As a matter of fact, young man, I have walked the Charles Bridge many times. There is a statue there of St. Nepomuk. His motto is *Tacui.* Silence."

The message was unmistakable, but Murphy had gone too far to stop now. "Yes. He died for keeping his silence. Protecting someone. You like that statue, Mr. Craine? I like the statues of the saints who died for speaking out."

Craine lifted his chin slightly. "And the motto of such foolish men might be *mortui non mordent.*" He lifted his bushy eyebrow. "Dead men carry no tales."

Guests laughed nervously at their host's reply. *Clever, clever man,* thought Murphy. "That is what the pirates say in *Treasure Island,* isn't it? Kill their victims. Steal their gold. Nobody left to talk about it." Murphy gestured toward the silver candlesticks. "And the pirates walk away with the booty." No one laughed. The sound of a fork against a plate sounded loud.

Craine's left cheek twitched angrily, even though the iron-hard smile remained frozen on his face. "Then perhaps you should make your motto, *Cave quid dicis*? Beware what you say, when, to whom."

"That's a tough order for a journalist with ethics, Mr. Craine."

This last insult finally stung the old man beyond his limit of self-control. His flush deepened and his eyes widened with rage. "You take too much liberty! Yes, that's it, too much *liberty*! You! You!" he sputtered, throwing his napkin onto his plate.

Murphy rose from the table. "Liberty," he mused. "Yes, that's what this is all about, isn't it?" He left the room feeling better than he had in quite a while.

There was no doubt in anyone's mind that John Murphy had thrown his job into the toilet and flushed it away.

"This way, Mr. Murphy." The butler looked amused as he led Murphy out toward the waiting limousine. Murphy was still dressed in his dinner jacket and was being hurried away in the dark from San Sebastian without any of the suits hanging in the closet.

Outside the front portals, a gleeful, slightly drunk Clark Gable caught up with Murphy and grabbed him by the arm. "Where ya goin' now, kid?" he asked.

Carole Lombard rushed out the door and joined them, laughing breathlessly. "What a night!" she exclaimed. "That was great! Ought to be in a script! And after you left, Clark stood up and told the old man that what you said went double for him, and besides that—" she giggled helplessly and embraced Murphy—"he told Craine that he loved to go *hunting*! Imagine! Asked Craine if he could go out and shoot a couple of his giraffes tonight!" She was roaring with laughter. Yet another taboo had been broken. No doubt Gable and Lombard would not be asked back to San Sebastian.

Gable was busy scribbling something on the inside cover of a matchbook. "Here." He thrust it into Murphy's hand. "You goin' to Frisco? Stop by and tell 'em that Clark sent ya, kid. Tell 'em what you said. It happened one night, right?" The big man was also laughing as Murphy stood stunned beside the open door of the limousine. They had not even noticed him before now.

"Thanks, Mr. Gable." The two men shook hands warmly.

"I admire a guy with guts," Gable replied. Then he turned to his beautiful companion. "Come on, Carole; let's get out of this joint. I hear there's some *good duck hunting* over near Bakersfield!" He shouted the last comment, hoping that Craine would hear him.

Murphy shoved the matchbook into his pocket as the automobile wound slowly down the long road toward the coast highway. Twenty minutes later, the gate to the Craine property was raised and Murphy asked the driver, "Where are you taking me?"

With a shrug, the driver stopped just outside the gate beside the dark, lonely road that ran along the California coastline. "Right here. Mr. Craine's orders. 'Take him to the road and give him the boot,' he said. Sorry. This is the end of the line."

And so, at twenty after midnight, John Murphy stood outside the gates of the Craine Castle and untied his bow tie. He was leaving a little better off than he came, at any rate. At least he was wearing a dinner jacket now instead of coveralls. It was a long way to Frisco and no traffic was in sight, but at least Murphy was a free man again.

Leah was almost back to the apartment before the image of the empty cupboards and hungry children intruded on her thoughts. If they were forced to remain in hiding, then she would have to buy food enough to survive on for a while.

She mentally calculated her funds. What had been meant for train tickets would have to be stretched to feed them for an uncertain time period. She fingered the bills and few meager coins in her pocket. Stopping on the crowded sidewalk outside a pastry shop, she caught her own small, worried reflection in the glass as dozens of uniformed men walked past her and shouldered their way into the shop.

She turned away and resolutely began the two-mile walk toward the farmers market. There, Austrian farmers brought heaps of fresh vegetables to sell to local housewives and grocers from the central areas of the city. Produce was less expensive when purchased in the open-air square, even if it was more inconvenient. Leah and Shimon had shopped there a thousand times and had come home with bags full of everything from fresh trout to cabbages. Always before, the shopping excursion had been carefree and full of playful bartering. But that had been before.

This afternoon, the trip to the farmers' market was an encounter with terror. Nearly every street had been converted to one-way traffic. This made it easier for the SS men and Gestapo agents who manned the innumerable barricades and roadblocks to stop vehicles and pedestrians for document checks.

Men and women were still being arrested on sight if their papers were not in order. Beyond the barricades leading into the marketplace, Germans bargained with Austrian farmers for food that was being bought up in massive quantities for shipment back to the large cities of Germany. Undisguised resentment stamped the faces of many Viennese as the huge troop transports that had carried soldiers into the city now carried heaping cargos of food away from it.

Leah stopped to stare into the window of a shoe store as she tried to gather her thoughts. Twenty-five yards away was the end of a long line of pedestrians waiting to cross the barricade into the market. How could she pass without being stopped? And if she was stopped, how could she avoid arrest? *How clever are these agents of Hitler,* she thought. *They make it impossible even to purchase food without the stamp of Nazi racial approval.* The terrifying reality of her predicament came crashing down on her once again. She could not go forward into the line, but how could she go back to the apartment without food for the boys?

She closed her eyes for an instant as if to shut out the nightmare that had become Vienna. What was she to do now?

A tap on her shoulder pulled her from her thoughts. "Frau Feldstein?" a man's voice whispered.

Leah opened her eyes with a start and drew her breath in sharply as she faced a small man in a green wool Jäger's jacket. He was in his seventies, Leah guessed. He regarded her kindly, but his eyes darted fearfully from her face to the barricade and SS men, then back to her again. She did not reply but simply stared at him. The fear had become reality. She had been recognized.

The little man tugged on her arm. "Come into my shop, quickly," he said softly. She noticed that he wore a cobbler's leather apron beneath his jacket.

Stunned, Leah followed the man through the glass door of the tiny shop. The smell of leather filled her senses. A bell above the door jingled as he shut out the sounds of the sidewalk behind them.

Leah stood rooted in the center of the shop. The little shoemaker regarded her with undisguised pity. "Leah Feldstein. I have heard you perform many times. The Sunday matinee."

"I . . . I . . . I . . . am not . . . ," she began, but trying to deny her identity was foolish and useless.

The little man simply smiled kindly. He drew down the shade and flipped the *Closed* sign over.

"We feared you had been arrested. Your husband, we heard, was taken the first day."

Leah just stared at him in reply. What could she say? Like the man in the pawnshop who had robbed her of her violoncello by a threat, this man could also call the authorities.

"You have come to the farmers market," he continued. "Not a safe place. They will arrest you here."

"What do you want?" Leah asked hoarsely, wondering why she had not run away when he first said her name on the street. Now she was trapped. The door of the shop was locked. The Gestapo and the police van were half a block away.

"It is not safe for you." The shoemaker shuffled past her. "You. Such a great cellist. You will certainly be recognized, and they will arrest you and throw you into prison, as they have done with every other brilliant and talented Jew in Vienna." His face contracted into an angry mass of wrinkles. "They are thieves, all of them."

"Will you call the Gestapo?" Leah could see the face of the pawnbroker once again. In her mind, the fresh pain of watching the cello pass into the hands of the vile man stung her once again. "What do you want? I can't pay you. I haven't got enough even for . . . "

The shoemaker shook his head vigorously. "Frau Feldstein! It is an honor to have such an artist in my shop!" he exclaimed. "How would I ask *you* for anything? I must ask instead what desperate need has brought you out into such danger! I go to the concerts and you are not there. They fill your place with a cellist who cannot distinguish *forte* from *piano*, and my wife and I worry and worry about the little cellist Leah Feldstein who must surely be in a dungeon someplace, and . . . "

Leah stared at him in disbelief. At last she was faced with someone in this vast city who was concerned! The outpouring of his sympathy caused her facade to crack. She covered her face with her hands and began to cry. "I only came out to buy . . . for food," she said through her tears. "I have not seen . . . I do not know what they have done . . . "

"There, there, Frau Feldstein!" The shoemaker clucked his tongue. "Of course you must eat. You have fed half the souls in Vienna with the beauty of your playing! Wait here! Wait here! I am just an old man of no use to anybody. A shoemaker without a talent these Nazi beasts might envy and destroy! Wait here, Frau Feldstein. I will purchase your food for you, and it will be an honor to do so!"

He quickly dragged a chair over for Leah to sit in, and then, with a timid pat on her back to comfort her, he slipped out the door and stepped into the long line awaiting entrance into the farmers market.

It was dusk when Leah entered the lobby of the apartment building, her arms laden with groceries. Herr Hugel regarded her with a cold sneer from the half-open door of his quarters.

Even before she entered the apartment, Leah knew that something was terribly wrong. Propping the grocery bag against the doorjamb, she stepped cautiously into the dreadful silence of the dark room. Her eyes adjusted to the gloom after a moment. She could see the pencil and paper on the table just as it had been when she left the boys hours ago.

A sickening fear welled up in her. She quickly brought in the sack of food, closed the door, and switched on the light. Where were the boys?

"Louis?" she whispered. "Charles?"

There was no answer. The bathroom door was ajar, the toilet seat up. The place had an unpleasant odor, sour and forbidding.

"Louis?" she called again, opening the bedroom door. Curtains askew. Dresser drawer slightly open.

What had the strange, triumphant look of the fat concierge meant? "Charles?" she called, her voice half choked.

A muffled, sleepy reply came from under the bed. "Aunt Leah?" Two blond heads peeped out from beneath the footboard as the boys squirmed out from a space so small she could not have imagined they could fit!

"Oh!" she cried, suddenly certain that indeed Herr Hugel had been here. "You're safe!" She knelt down and they ran to her, burying their faces against her and weeping silently with relief that she had come home.

"He came here," Louis said quietly through his tears. "He was . . . he came for us, Aunt Leah."

"But he didn't find you!" She stroked their heads and wiped their tears.

"Don't go away again!" Louis cried, while Charles simply laid his head against her shoulder and patted her back.

30
Abduction

"That was Wilhelm on the phone," Anna called to Elisa from the kitchen. "Finished his first solo flight, and he's coming home tonight for dinner!"

Anna had accepted Wilhelm's enrollment in the Cadet Air Corps stoically, Elisa thought, and perhaps even with a touch of pride. Over the weeks she had seldom worried openly, and when she did, Theo had chided her gently. "You married a flyer, remember?" he would say. "Can you expect your sons to stay planted on the ground?"

Such a reminder had always calmed her, and the very nearness of Theo seemed to make the whole world a less fearsome place. Like Theo, Anna believed in the treaties that Czechoslovakia had with the French and British. Even when the riots in the Sudeten territories became more fierce, Anna clung to the belief that it was a civil matter that could not involve the air force, and certainly Prague was far removed from such things. She was, in fact, more concerned about the rickety airplanes Wilhelm flew than she was about the threat of Nazis in Czech-Sudetenland or any possibility that the German army might cross the border and claim that territory for the Reich.

Elisa could see in her father's eyes, however, that he did not hold the same illusions as Anna. When the venomous voice of Hitler crackled over the radio, Theo ordered that it be turned off instantly. But they both knew that refusing to believe the danger did not lessen the reality of the threat.

Tonight the evening meal was a special occasion in the little house in Prague. For the first time in over a year, Theo was to resume his place at the head of the table. And dear Wilhelm would sit proudly beside him in his airman's uniform.

Elisa spread the lace tablecloth as her mother worked in the kitchen. The whole house was scented with the delicious aroma of chicken roasting in an orange-cranberry glaze. It had always been a favorite of Theo's, and Anna had prepared it especially for tonight. *True,* Elisa thought, *it is not the grand table we enjoyed in Berlin, but that does not matter. It is the faces around the table that count. Nothing else.*

Elisa decided that she would not ruin such an event by letting her countenance reflect even a moment of sadness or worry. For the sake of her father and mother, she would smile tonight and laugh as if there were no haunting dreams or terrifying reality shouting from her soul.

"Elisa!" Anna called from the kitchen. "How could I have forgotten!" Elisa laid the last spoon on the gleaming table. There was some satisfaction that the silverware was the same they had used in Berlin. Somehow they had gotten it out, and the thought pleased Elisa. She must find contentment in small things tonight, or she should not be able to act out the charade.

"What, Mama?" she called, poking her head into the kitchen.

"Butter!" Anna was dressed in a beautiful cream-colored silk dress, protected by an apron as she labored over the dishes. "I've used the last of it, and you know how your father loves fresh butter with his kolache! Maybe if you hurry, there might be time to run to market before it closes!" She seemed as young and fresh now as she had a year before in Kitzbühel. The years of care had melted from her with every hour that Theo was home. "Would you, dear?"

"Where is Dieter?" Elisa asked, not wanting to walk the quarter mile to market in such a short time.

"He'll be home in time for dinner. Off at the house of young Marcus Jeleni for some sort of meeting. No phone." She opened the oven and basted the golden skin of the hen.

Elisa glanced at her watch. There was just enough time if she hurried, and yes, Theo did indeed love heaps of butter on his rolls. Tonight everything must be perfect.

The evening air was cool, and the fragrance of spring mingled with aromas from a thousand Prague kitchens. Smoke spiraled up from chimneys and blended into the deepening purple of the sky. Elisa walked hastily down the narrow street that led to Mala Strana Square. It was nearly the dinner hour, and the square was almost deserted except for a few harried pedestrians. All around, the shutters of shopwindows were lowered. No one seemed to notice anyone else as each person hurried on his way.

It was this atmosphere of inattention that first drew Elisa's eyes to the young man waiting by the clock in the square. As the clock struck six and the figures of Christ and the apostles filed out, the young man did not turn to look at them. His gaze was intent on Elisa, fixed on her as she moved toward the arcade.

She looked up at the dancing figures of the clock, then back again, hoping that his frank stare was nothing more than a young man noticing a young woman. But it was not so. The light glinted on the lenses of his glasses. She could not see his eyes, but she could feel them as she quickened her pace. A chill shot through her when she peered back over her shoulder and he was walking toward her. His long legs devoured the distance between them until he was only thirty feet behind her. At that, he matched his own pace to hers and simply trailed after her as the figure of Death emerged from the window of the clock and turned the hourglass when the bells chimed the hour.

Elisa did not look back at him. She could hear his heavy boots on the cobbles of the square just behind her. Her breath came in short, frightened gasps, and in that moment she forgot why she had come out of the house. Ahead of her the shutter of the market slammed down and she remembered. *Butter. Sweet rolls. Chicken roasting for Papa's dinner.* She stopped. The man stopped just beneath the arch of the market arcade. The shadows of darkness filled the place. No light welcomed her from the shops. She looked at the shuttered storefronts of the vast hollow market. Like the stage in her dream, it was empty. She fought the urge to cry out.

Then she turned toward the silhouette of her pursuer. "I came to get butter," she said in a hoarse voice. "But the shops are closed."

A faceless shadow, he did not reply. His hands were in his pockets and he simply stood silent and menacing, blocking her path back out into the square. She looked past him, hoping to see some movement of a pedestrian behind him. But there was no one.

She took a step, hoping to walk around him, but he moved to the side. He took his hands from his pockets and crossed his arms across his chest, his gesture defying her to get by him. He made no attempt to hide his intention from her. They were alone. She would not get past.

"W-why are you following me?" she stammered. "What do you want with me?"

The man tilted his head slightly at her words. "I think you know, Elisa," he said in a low voice heavy with a Polish accent.

He had said her name. This was not a chance encounter. How long had he been watching her? watching the little house on the square? How many times had she left the security of those walls to find some solitude, only to be followed unawares by this frightening apparition?

"What do you want?" She could barely speak. She squinted around him again, judging whether she could run past him and escape. Behind her the vaulted ceiling of the market arcade seemed like a cavern that would swallow her. "I need to go home." Her voice trembled.

The man chuckled and took a step toward her. "Yes. Home. Of course. Home to your mother. To your brothers—" he paused as if to measure the effect of his next words—"and to your father? to Theo Lindheim also, Elisa?"

"Who are you?" she shouted, finding her voice somewhere in the wave of fear that consumed her.

"Is it not enough that I know you?" He was enjoying the game.

"What is it you want? Money? Let me go, and we can pay you."

At her desperate plea, he spread his hands wide and laughed as he walked toward her. "Elisa. Money? No, my dear. Money is not what we need."

She stepped back, and the darkness of the arcade loomed, pulling her back into itself. "Let me go."

"In time."

"I have to go home."

"Not yet." He moved within a dozen feet of her, yet still she could not make out his features.

"Please. Just let me go, and . . . " She tried to run around him, out toward the open square and the last light of evening. He reached out a long arm and clutched her, then whirled her around and clamped his hand over her mouth, stifling the scream that came to her throat too late. Her eyes rolled back in fright and she fought to remain conscious.

"No, no, no, little one. You must not run away. You cannot run away, you see. For days I have been watching. They sent me to fetch you, you see."

Her breath was labored through his fingers. She struggled against him, but he held her even tighter. The coarse wool of his jacket scratched her skin.

"You must not struggle." His voice was insanely patronizing, like a doctor about to give a child an injection. "Come along now. Very quietly, and maybe you will go home."

Elisa could feel the hard steel of a pistol at the man's waist. She forced herself to relax, and as she did, he relaxed his grip over her mouth. "Please," she whispered.

"You will not scream if I let you loose?"

"No."

He took his hand from her face but held tightly to her arm. "Then come with me." He shoved her gently away from the open square, turning her toward the dark bowels of the deserted market arcade. Their footsteps echoed in the vaults above them. From every shuttered shop, Elisa expected to see the grim figure of Death emerge and shake his skull from side to side.

The bookstall of Le Morthomme was crowded this weekend. Herschel worked helping customers with magazines as the German, von Kleistmann, occupied the attention of the old bookseller. Herschel glared unhappily as the two men laughed over something. How he hated this arrogant German! How he resented the fact that a Nazi walked freely on the streets of Paris and talked agreeably with Le Morthomme! If only Thomas von Kleistmann had looked up, he could have seen Herschel's hatred. But the lofty German never condescended to lower his gaze to the little Jew.

Herschel felt a sharp nudge in the ribs, and a German-accented voice spoke softly to him. "That man with your boss is the head of Nazi military intelligence at the German Embassy."

Herschel glanced sideways into the face of a young, dark-haired man who was not much older than he. His clothes were also ragged. He was a refugee as well, no doubt. "So?"

The young man shrugged off his rebuff. "So. You're Jewish, aren't you? Like me?"

Herschel glanced at him again. "What has that got to do with . . . ?"

His young companion smiled. "I just wondered if you hated them as much as I do. I work at the Eiffel Café. Washing dishes. As I wash the slop from the pans, I imagine slinging it into their Aryan faces! Or filling their Aryan pants with it! Then they would not strut so proudly, *ja*?"

Herschel laughed loudly at the image of Thomas von Kleistmann in such condition. He regarded the ragged young man beside him with a new appreciation. "Yes, I hate them too. Especially that one." Herschel was grinning. "He comes here all the time."

"I know. We watch him."

"We?"

"A few of us. Zionists."

"Why do you watch him?"

"We see every move he makes. A vile fellow, this one. Hates Jews. He would have us all deported back to Germany in a cattle car if he had his way!" The young man did not answer Herschel's question. "We watch him for our own reasons."

Herschel bit his lip. He had not taken time to seek out others who were like himself. A stab of loneliness ran through him, and he frowned.

"Are there many of you? I can watch this German when he is here. Do you have meetings?"

The young man nodded. "There are three of us. All from Germany. All here against our wishes now. My family is still in Hamburg. What about yours?"

"In Berlin. Except that I stay with my uncle," he finished lamely. "Where do you meet?"

"A secret," the young man whispered. "But if you would like to come . . . "

Herschel tucked the address of the meeting place into his pocket. His new acquaintance disappeared quickly down the long book rows. He had not purchased anything, and Herschel wondered why he had stopped here. Probably to watch the German officer, he reasoned. Now Herschel would watch him and report on his activities.

As he quietly observed von Kleistmann, the hatred welled up so strongly in him that he thought he might be sick. He was glad the young man had spoken to him. Glad that someone else hated the Aryan persecutors. He would welcome the chance to share his hatred with the others he would soon meet.

31
Hold Tightly to His Hand

The stairway to the cellar was long and unlit. Elisa's captor held tightly to her arm as he rapped three times on the green door at the bottom. A pinpoint of light escaped as the peephole opened, and then the door opened only enough to let them in.

Fingers released her immediately as the door slammed shut behind them. The cellar was a small room about fifteen feet square. Damp, lichen-covered stone formed the walls. Rusty pipes crisscrossed the ceiling, and a single lightbulb glowed from the end of a wire.

An elderly woman had opened the door. She stood regarding Elisa with a toothless smile. Gray hair hung in wisps around her wrinkled face. Her eyes were bright, though the film of cataracts nearly concealed their color.

"Elisa Lindheim?" she chuckled, using Elisa's Jewish surname.

The mention of it caused a wave of fear to course through Elisa. Free from the rough hands of the young man, she backed against the door as the old woman walked close to her. Bony fingers reached up to pat Elisa's cheek. "She is here!" the old woman called, and a door, also covered with green fungus, opened to reveal a larger, brightly lit room beyond. "Well, go on!" croaked the old woman, giving Elisa a nudge.

The young man stood smirking with his arms across his chest. Elisa glared back at him, but his grin only widened in the face of her anger.

"Go on, Elisa," the old woman said again. "They are waiting—waiting for you."

There was movement in the far room. Elisa remained rooted where she stood for a moment longer until a man appeared in the doorway.

Elisa gasped as she recognized him. His gold-capped teeth glinted in a smile. A wreath of gray crowned his bald head. The suit he wore was the same business suit he had worn at the train station. His eyebrows arched in benign impatience. "Come along, Elisa, dear," he said in a soothing voice. "As hard as you have been looking for us, I would think that you would not be so reluctant to come in."

Looking for us! His words penetrated the fog of fear that had nearly choked her. She looked again at the old woman, who at first had seemed like the perfect picture of a witch from *Grimm's Fairy Tales.*

"Waiting, waiting, waiting!" the old woman repeated happily.

Elisa blushed with embarrassment. The old woman was simply an old woman. The sinister young man who had whisked her into the cellar deserved her anger, however. She glared at him as she walked toward the back room, but he simply replied with open laughter.

"You?" Elisa asked as she entered what seemed to be an office with file cabinets, a desk, and even a telephone and a dark-haired matron working hard at a typewriter. The secretary barely glanced at Elisa as the balding man led her to yet another office. Three chairs were placed before an enormous walnut desk piled high with papers and folders, all stamped with the logo of *Prague Commerce Import-Export Company.*

The phone in the outer office rang as the bald man closed the door. "Please sit." He swept his hand toward the row of leather chairs, then sat down behind his desk. "I apologize for Avriel." He shrugged and tapped a pencil on his desk blotter. "He enjoys a sense of the dramatic and sinister, I'm afraid."

Elisa raised her chin slightly in indignation. "And you don't?" she questioned, remembering their first meeting at the train station.

He laughed at her obvious anger. "Well, you are where you have longed to be, are you not? It is best not to question methods. We have our reasons. As you searched for us, there are others who would also like to discover our identity and whereabouts. We would have contacted you sooner, but we were not certain of your identity."

"You called me by name!" Elisa said. "What changed between this moment and yesterday?"

"We had to be sure. A member of our organization told us of your father's enjoyment of *Faust.*"

"Goethe's *Faust*?" Elisa said incredulously, suddenly aware that though the man across from her knew her name, she still did not know his.

"A good book to carry." The bald man nodded. "Didn't I say as much at the station?"

Elisa blinked at him in wonder. Somehow the edition of *Faust* was used as identification for this underground organization. Now she understood why her father had picked that book off the shelf! The only outsider who had spoken of Theo's interest in the work had been the doctor. "All this time . . . " She leaned forward and put her hand on the desktop. "I want to go back!" Her voice became desperate. "Back to Vienna! I have friends who are in need of my help."

"Most of our friends there are beyond our help," he answered coolly. "There is more at stake here than one man or one woman."

Her mind raced ahead. "Shimon and Leah—"

He interrupted with a wave of his hand. "Shimon Feldstein has been arrested by the Gestapo. He has endured well in their hands, our connection tells us." He paused. "Leah we are unsure of."

Elisa closed her eyes and lowered her head in horror at such news. It was the fulfillment of everything she had feared since the first hours of the Anschluss. "Then what is left for me to do? How can I help them?"

"It is not for their sake that we have contacted you." He removed his glasses and polished them carefully as he spoke. "As I said, one life or even two are insignificant now."

"Insignificant!" she protested, remembering how Shimon and Leah had risked their lives for others.

"We speak of millions now, Elisa." He seemed to look through her. "You must not think of your friends at this moment. You must be able to forget even your own life."

"My only thoughts these last few days have been of Shimon and Leah Feldstein! Do you think I had any other reason for looking for you?" She was near tears. "I will pay to get them out! How can you leave them to rot in the Nazi quagmire as other men left my father?"

The bald man sat back and regarded her, unmoved by her emotion. "You are ideal for our purposes. Married to an American. Tenured member of the Vienna Philharmonic. Physically, you fit the Nazi ideal of the perfect Aryan. But if you are unable to control yourself in the face of the everyday brutality that now rules Vienna, then you should save your own life and never again cross the border into Austria." His words were full of warning. "If you are to be of any help to us, you must learn to raise your arm in salute and smile at their jokes even while your insides twist with revulsion at what they are and the evil they serve!" He leaned toward her. "Outwardly you must pretend to be what you most hate!"

Elisa looked away from the intensity of his gaze. "What do you want from me?" she asked miserably.

He exhaled slowly and sat back in his chair. "Go back to Vienna. Go back to the orchestra. Tonight at midnight the frontier between Czechoslovakia and Austria opens again. Before then you will get a telegram from your husband asking you to join him in Vienna."

"From Murphy?" she asked, wondering if he was somehow part of this.

"So it will appear. The good doctor observes that perhaps your mother does not know of your previous activities. Or those of your father. It is best if it remains that way."

They had thought of everything, including a method of getting her out of the house without explanations. "Yes. Thank you."

"When you reach Vienna, you must go immediately to a bookseller. Fiori's Bookstore. Dealer in rare books."

"On the corner of Kartnerstrasse," Elisa said, feeling some excitement. "I know the place well."

Now the man smiled. Gold flashed briefly. "Take him your father's copy of *Faust*. Tell him you have a rare edition to have appraised, and—"

Elisa sat up as if to protest this instruction. "But . . . how can I take it without my father suspecting—"

"He will not question you." There was a knowledge in his eyes now that finally convinced her. Had Theo been part of this plan as well? She did not ask. She would not ask what whispered words had passed between her father and the doctor. Theo had seen her helpless misery and indeed understood why she must return. "The time is right then," she muttered.

The instructions continued. "Tell the bookseller you have a rare edition to have appraised. He will ask if it is Goethe or Marlowe. You must answer Goethe, of course. Then he will tell you what you must do."

"And if I am followed? Or the Gestapo—"

He raised his hand to silence her. "My dear girl!"—his voice was patronizing—"You have done nothing wrong. You are a respected musician. Aryan. Deny everything. Deny anything past or present that might be incriminating. Show them your passport. Call the American Embassy." He was smiling. "Call your maestro and he will call the Nazi minister of propaganda. What harm can come of having your father's volume of *Faust* appraised?"

"And then? Will I be able to help—?"

"You cannot help Leah Feldstein. What you are involved in is not a simple matter of pulling a few Jews from the fire."

Elisa frowned. "A few Jews?"

"We have larger concerns now, Elisa. All of Europe, for instance." He sounded amused. "We are not in the business of rescuing refugees."

"Then why am I here?"

"You have proven yourself on an amateur level of operation. Your name was offered to us as one who would be ideal as a courier."

Elisa sat silently, wondering who might have submitted her name as though it were an application for employment. She did not ask. The man would not have told her, anyway. "And what is it you want from me?"

"Simply carry the volume across the border. You will be given further orders, other things to carry on to Paris. There is an old bookseller there. He is called the Dead Man."

"A strange name."

"He is a strange man. But helpful, nonetheless." The man shrugged and Elisa thought that this Dead Man could not be any more strange than the one who sat across from her now.

"But the children. Leah . . . " She could not let go of the thought of them.

He leaned forward impatiently. "Put those matters out of your thoughts. They are insignificant compared to this operation. We cannot risk it for any individual. If you cannot put that aside, then we have nothing further to talk about."

Elisa lowered her eyes. This was not what she had been hoping for. This man had no connection with the Jewish underground or the rescue of children. He seemed to have no thought whatsoever of those who remained trapped beneath the iron fist of the Nazis. And yet, quite obviously, he was working for the same goal her father had worked for. "All right," she agreed reluctantly, unwilling to give up this tenuous connection with someone who fought Hitler and the Nazi state. "And what if I find Leah?"

"Don't look. If you work with us you are involved in something too important for personal indulgence. You must trust me in this. We cannot risk anything for the sake of one woman. Even your own life will be expendable. You make the choice."

"What choice do I have? I cannot remain here and do nothing."

"You were looking for us before we heard of you. Remember that. You decided long ago which side you belonged on." He smiled at her patronizingly. "Yes. I think it is right that you join us."

The telegram sent to Elisa at the Prague house did indeed look authentic. Now, as Elisa sat beside her father at the dining table, she wondered if he knew the truth. Did he suspect that the summons to Vienna had not been sent by Murphy at all? Only Wilhelm seemed to see right through her deception. She did not dare look at him.

Anna looked unhappily at Theo as she passed a basket heaping with rolls. Elisa had not brought back any butter, but that was not what bothered Anna now. "How can he ask you to return to that terrible place?"

she asked Elisa. "Theo, you must forbid her to go. She cannot go back to Vienna now. Tell her, Theo."

He did not answer for a moment; then he gazed steadily at Anna. "I am only her father, my dear, not her husband." Then he smiled. "And if we had been in similar circumstances when we were young, Anna, would you have let your father dictate to you whether you should join me?"

His point was well taken. Theo and Anna had married against her father's wishes, after all. Anna shook her head grimly. "And now my youth comes back to haunt me."

Theo laughed, then winked at his wife. "Any regrets?"

"You would not have asked me to join you in hell!" she snapped.

Elisa had listened in silence to their discussion of her safety. She was glad that Anna did not suspect the truth. Her marriage to Murphy once again served as a wall of protection even against her mother's disapproval. Now Elisa played out the charade. "Murphy would not ask me to join him if there were any danger, Mother," she said quietly. "We won't be in Vienna long, at any rate."

"One minute within the reach of those vile men is too long." Anna was more frightened than angry. "First Germany. Then Austria. And now the riots in the Sudetenland! Did you hear the broadcast? Did you hear Hitler? They will even have Czechoslovakia if he has his way."

Elisa managed a smile. "Then you might as well let me go to Vienna if they're coming here, too." It was a poor joke and was met by an icy silence.

Theo cleared his throat and dabbed his lips with the linen napkin. He was the only one with an appetite. "Anna," he said, his voice comforting, "tonight the frontier opens again. The situation has calmed enough for that. Elisa has things she must get out of Austria." He looked knowingly at his daughter.

Yes. He knew. It was not for *things* that Elisa must return, but for the sake of much-loved friends who had been left behind.

"Things!" Anna could hardly speak. "Is there anything worth going back for? You can buy her anything she wants. Her American husband can meet her in Paris, and—" Her eyes brimmed with tears. Her protest was in vain.

Elisa wondered what her mother's reaction would have been if it were not for the phony telegram. "Mother, I have an American passport," she reminded Anna. "My husband is a journalist. The Nazis would not dare lay a finger on me. They are still trying to woo the American press into seeing things their way. I will be fine!"

Anna bit her lip and stared down at her plate. The lovely supper was cold. Ruined. Elisa was leaving, and there was no way to stop her. "You must wire us when you arrive," she said weakly. "Or I will not be able to sleep. Or eat."

An hour later, gaunt and gray, Theo leaned heavily against the door of Elisa's bedroom as she packed. They were alone for the moment, and he held out the leather-bound copy of Goethe's *Faust.*

"You will want to carry this?" It was not really a question. The eyes of father and daughter locked in understanding. Elisa was returning, and Theo must let her go now, although he alone understood the danger to her.

Elisa nodded and took the volume; then Theo pulled her close in a final embrace. "Thank you, Papa," she whispered, grateful that he did not make the parting more difficult than it already was. "Don't worry, Papa."

For a moment he did not answer but simply stroked her hair. "So much at stake," he said at last. And in his voice was the yearning for his own child to be safe as well. "I will pray." He released her and she stood before him looking down at the book.

There were a thousand things she wanted to say to him, but there was no time. Perhaps there would never be time. What must be said could only pass silently between their hearts. She had been so young and innocent the night Theo had picked this book from the shelf of his library in Berlin. Now he offered it to her.

He spoke quietly now. "In Dachau I made a covenant with other men and with God. I promised that I would not forget . . . that I would not sit idly by while the innocent perish. You are my own flesh, Elisa. If you have made the same covenant in your heart, I have no right to try to stop you. I will not stand in your way. Know that I offer you all the strength I have in prayers until I can once again join you in the fight."

He lifted her chin with his finger. "I am proud of you because you are my daughter. And I am frightened for the same reason. Be careful, Elisa. Trust no one until you have irrefutable proof of where they stand. You must now pretend to be what you are not, but always remember who and what you are. All the world, it seems, has sold its soul. Hold tightly to the hand of God, Elisa. Hold tightly to His hand."

32

A Song in the Dark

The gun lay on the packing crate beside the flickering candle. The eyes of his companions were now on Herschel. He looked at the revolver and then to each of the young men of this tiny Zionist cell.

"After what is being done to Jews in the Reich, we must show the world, Herschel," said Hans as he touched the pistol grip and nudged it closer to Herschel. "Your name has been drawn to accomplish the deed. Are you man enough to fight for the nation of Israel? to avenge your coreligionists?"

The questions stabbed at Herschel's faltering courage. He was meeting here in this dingy room with three others who called themselves Zionists. They talked together and deplored the acts of the Nazis in Germany, in Austria, and now in the betrayed provinces of Czechoslovakia. What stronger protest could they make before the world than this?

Herschel drew himself up. Light flickered on the faces of the young men around him. Lips parted in smiles of approval as he reached for the gun.

"For the sake of Zion I take up this weapon," he whispered hoarsely. Nods of assent ringed the small circle. "It will be easy to kill him." Hans seemed relieved, Herschel thought. Had he been planning this the first day they had met in the bookstall of Le Morthomme?

"I hate him." Herschel stared at the gun. He clenched the grip in his hand until his knuckles were white. "I have hated him since Berlin." Now Herschel spoke through clenched teeth as he thought of Thomas von Kleistmann.

"Your boss will lose a good customer," laughed Johann, lighting his cigarette on the candle as he spoke.

"There are plenty of Nazis where Thomas von Kleistmann comes from," Herschel said, feeling more confident by the minute. "And I would kill them all if I had the chance."

Uncertainty now showed on the face of Hans. "But only one dead Nazi in the German Embassy will make our point." His voice held a warning. "And the timing must be exact, Comrade Herschel. The day and the date must be fixed to make the strongest impression on the Fascists back in Germany." He paused, as if lost in deep thought. Then, "Yes!" He snapped his fingers as Herschel eyed him expectantly. "May Day!"

Johann and Raphael nodded in instant agreement. "Yes! The day the Nazis will be holding their great celebrations of Hitler's army. Do you remember the parades, Herschel? Remember the torchlight parades in Berlin? The raving speeches by Hitler? Himmler? Göring? Remember how they marched and sang and raged against the Jews?"

Of course Herschel remembered. The thought of it made him tremble with anger. He had listened to the speeches over the radio. He had not dared to venture out onto the streets as the Storm Troopers had roamed through the alleyways in search of a Jew to beat up. This enormous Nazi celebration was one of the most violent of all Aryan gatherings throughout the year. Beads of perspiration popped out on Herschel's darkly handsome young face.

Hans eyed Herschel. "You see, don't you, Herschel? The time of the May rallies is the best time to kill Thomas von Kleistmann. To walk into the German Embassy. To ask for him, and to kill the stinking Nazi right there! If they can do such things to Jews, then we will show them!" The voice of Hans was urgent. He rested his hand on Herschel's. "We will show them, won't we, Herschel? This will give those Jew-baiting swine something to talk about at their great Reich gathering!"

Herschel raised his eyes from the gun to Hans, whose brooding face seemed fixed with the rage and hatred Herschel felt. The object of his hatred was von Kleistmann, but for an instant he imagined a million bodies stacked high on the parade grounds of Germany as the swastika flag waved, bloody and tattered, above them. "I could kill them all and then die easily," Herschel muttered. "It is the vengeance of God that I will show them! I will show them what to expect! Yes! This time I will give the Nazis something more to read. Their papers will scream the headlines! The world will not condemn me for what I do. They will pay me homage that at last someone stands up to their unconcern!"

The three comrades of Herschel Grynspan sighed with relief and sat back. It had been so easy to convince this young Jew what he must do. Hans had spotted him for a crusader the first moment he saw him. Now

Hans offered one final bit of information. "You will not be alone. Herschel. There are others. Others like us, like you, who will strike a blow for the Jewish people. I have heard that there will be others willing to risk their lives to make a statement. To show the world that Jews are not sheep for the slaughter! Through this act the world will see our solidarity, our determination! The Jewish race will not be trampled but will fight!"

No more needed to be said. Herschel held the gun high now. The barrel glinted in the candlelight. The deed would be easy for him. He had lived a miserable existence in the shadows of Paris; now, he would walk the Rue du Cherche-Midi in search of the bold light of noon. He would kill a man in the cold light of day to illuminate the fact that Jews were being murdered in the cover of night. Perhaps, like Dreyfus, Herschel would be taken to the prison of Cherche-Midi! There he would proclaim his cause and his purpose to the nations, and he would find their support!

Herschel rose from his seat. He felt better than he had felt since his arrival in Paris. No longer was he impotent. He held the courage of six bullets in his sweating hand.

As Elisa drove Murphy's Packard toward the Austrian border, she wished she could have waited until daylight to leave Prague. Prague, whose name in the Slavic language meant "Threshold," had felt safe to her, remote from the troubles and riots that had ripped through the outlying provinces. Tonight she had crossed the threshold into the ominous silence of the Sudetenland, where riots had cost the lives of Czechs and Germans alike in the last weeks.

The blackness of the mountainous countryside was illuminated for a moment as the full moon glinted like an angry face from behind the clouds. The forest of treetops bent slightly in the strong spring wind. They seemed to bow toward the tall half-timbered buildings of a small German village perched on the hillside beyond. Here, only the German tongue was spoken. Only two miles back, the Slavic language alone was understood. Tonight, both Slavic and German villages within the Czech frontier spoke of hatred and violence against their neighbors. Men and women trembled in fear of the future, just as the forests trembled before the wind.

The countryside was quiet now. A truce had been called, and the Nazis had withdrawn to lick their wounds while the Czechs did the same. Tomorrow the fighting might begin again, Elisa knew. This might be her only opportunity to cross the border.

It was well after midnight, but she was not tired. The silence, ominous and eerie, seemed filled with ghosts of what had been in the past and foreboding for what might be in the future. In village after village Elisa had seen evidence of the clashes between the two racial groups. Broken windows, paint-smeared buildings, the hulks of burned automobiles were everywhere in these quaint, picturesque places.

The violence had never touched the city of Prague, and Elisa shuddered as the intensity of the conflict suddenly became real to her. The horror stories from Vienna had preoccupied her for so long that the disturbances in the Czech provinces had seemed slight by comparison. The newspapers in Prague had downplayed the conflict, even as Hitler had raged against the vile Untermenschen on behalf of the "downtrodden" German population in the Sudetenland. Only now, as the headlights reflected on the colorless debris of the Czech midnight, did Elisa realize the awful threat that had come even to this place.

Here among the hills the giant Rebezahl was said to dwell. With flowing beard and tangled hair, brandishing his burning staff, he howled with the wind and frightened lonely travelers with his discordant voice. Always Elisa had thought this mystical giant was a mere invention of a local storyteller, but tonight she felt the nearness of evil, the heaviness of the darkness that had settled over the land. A force stronger than Rebezahl now prowled the land. Voices more terrible shrieked for blood. Within the flame of his burning staff, the swastika glowed. Peace was only a momentary illusion. Like the gleam of the moon, it would disappear again behind the clouds of a newly approaching storm.

Elisa downshifted as she rounded a sharp curve on the mountain. From the corner of her eye, she thought she saw a figure in the darkness—a face radiating the flame of hatred. Hair and beard matted with blood, arms thick and shining with the gore of thousands, the creature raised an axe to strike and turned its eyes on her!

"God!" she cried as fear clutched at her throat. "God, help us all!" She slammed her foot hard on the accelerator, careening around the next curve and the next.

The road narrowed into a mountain pass with a steep precipice falling a thousand feet to the valley floor. The beam of the headlights swept the rocky slopes; the car swayed like a tiny boat on stormy waters. The face of Sporer became fresh in her mind as he had leered over her that night in the Judenplatz. The nightmare train filled with the bones of a million children hissed again through her memory as if it were not a dream at all but a vision of some apocalypse! Where could they go? Where in the world could they be safe? It was coming here! Even here, where Theo had imagined his family would be safe.

Beyond the mountain, the tiny lights of Austrian villages sparkled below her. From here the world seemed peaceful and unchanged, but Elisa knew better. With a sigh of weariness, she lifted her foot from the accelerator and slowed the car. She was running from evil back into the very heart of evil. If the creature in the woods had been more than her imagination, it still could not be any worse than the darkness that engulfed the hearts of men. And now the darkness of terror threatened to overtake Elisa.

"Oh, God!" she cried, praying now. "You have to help me, God! I'm frightened. So very afraid."

No hand reached out to comfort her, but Elisa remembered the melody and words of the music of Bach. Softly, as she neared the barricades that marked the end of the Czech frontier, she began to sing:

"Jesu, joy of man's desiring,
Holy wisdom, love most bright;
Drawn by Thee, our souls aspiring
Soar to uncreated light."

The darkness of fear fled before the melody, and Elisa knew that this joy must be her light; this one wisdom must guide her steps. Suddenly she was no longer afraid of the dark.

Throughout the long night little Charles whimpered softly as Leah rocked him.

"It is his ears," Louis explained. "It always used to happen. Mama said it was because of this." Louis pointed to his mouth in childish explanation that the cleft palate caused the excruciating pain Charles endured.

Leah placed her hand against the cheek of the little boy. He was burning with fever. His eyes stared dully at the lamp. Twice he raised his hand as though he held the bow of a cello.

"He wants you to play Vitorio for him," Louis said as he lay down on the sofa and tugged a blanket around his neck.

Leah smoothed back Charles' damp hair and kissed his forehead lightly. "I told you, darling; Vitorio has flown away, far beyond the trees of the Wienerwald."

Charles moaned softly in reply. He missed the music. He missed it almost as much as Leah did.

"Mama used to sing us lullabies," Louis volunteered in a sleepy voice. "Even when Charles was not sick, she would sing to us."

It seemed strange, but Leah could not remember any children's songs. Her own life had been involved in the greatness of the symphony for so long that simple things like lullabies had fled from her memory. "Teach me one," she asked Louis.

It was Charles who tried to sing. A few broken notes croaked from his throat before he dissolved into a racking cough.

Leah imagined the lurking figure of Herr Hugel standing in the hall and listening to everything. She laid her cheek against Charles' head and tried to comfort him. "Shhhh. Hush now, Charles. Don't try. Don't even try."

Louis began to sing softly, his sweet soprano voice reflecting the nearness of his mother. "I am small, my heart is pure. . . . No one shall live in it but Jesus alone. *Ich bin klein, mein Herz ist rein. Soll niemand drin wohnen als Jesus allein.*"

Leah began to hum with him as he repeated the song again and again. Was that all there was to it? Or was that all he could remember? Leah smiled as Louis slowly drifted off to sleep and Charles' labored breathing grew more even until at last he slumped against her in sleep.

Then Leah took up the words and sang them quietly as though they were a shield of protection for the boys . . . her boys. And in her solitude and worry, she almost felt she knew the woman who, like her, had waited lonely hours with her sons as her husband languished in a Nazi prison.

For a brief time Leah closed her eyes. "I am small, my heart is pure." She felt another presence in this little room. "No one shall live in it but Jesus alone." She whispered, "I will watch them for you, Frau Kronenberger. *Ja.* I will take care of these, your little ones. But if you don't mind, will you speak to your God about us? I need a little help, you see. And I have lost Vitorio and forgotten how to pray."

Charles stirred a bit, and Leah resumed the song, singing the words earnestly as she imagined Frau Kronenberger might have done.

33

Miracles

It was before dawn when Leah heard the creak of footsteps on the stairs leading to the apartment. Scarcely breathing, she lay wide-eyed in the darkness, hoping that the soft tread would pass the door. It did not.

Charles and Louis lay sleeping together on the sofa. Quickly, silently, Leah leaped from bed and shook the groggy children awake.

"Quickly!" she whispered. "It is Herr Hugel!"

As sleepy as they were, the children needed no further explanation. They ran for the bedroom and dived beneath the bed as Leah hefted a candlestick and stepped behind the door.

In that instant they clearly heard the rattle of keys and the scratching of the metal as the latch caught and the door popped open with a groan on its hinges. Then there was no sound at all. Leah could hear her own heart and nothing else. Her mouth was dry with fear, and her hands clenched and unclenched around the brass candlestick.

The footsteps entered the front room. There was a faint thud as something heavy was placed on the floor. Leah could just see the side rails of the bed where the boys hid. With the sheets and blankets pulled back, a tiny foot and leg were plainly visible. The sight caused her to draw her breath in sharply. Herr Hugel would see the child also the minute he walked into the room!

The front door closed softly, and Leah heard the lock turn. The intruder did not move for what seemed like long minutes. The slow footsteps moved toward the light switch. A *click* flooded the front room with glaring light. Then there was a gasp, and the voice of a woman called softly, "Who's there?"

It was Elisa!

"Leah? Shimon?"

With a cry of joy, Leah tumbled out from her hiding place. The candlestick crashed to the floor as she rushed into the light.

"Elisa!" Leah wept openly, her arms stretched out as she fell into Elisa's embrace.

Throughout the long, dark hours of early morning, Elisa held Leah's hands and listened to the story of her friend's ordeal.

"After I saw that they had taken Shimon, I wanted only to die. If it had not been for the boys, I think I might have." She wept quietly as she spoke. "Every moment has been a nightmare, Elisa. Herr Hugel—" she shook her head at the thought of the man—"you will smell him coming before you hear him. He wheezes up the steps. He came in here looking for something. For the boys, I think. Little Charles is so bright, Elisa! He hid the papers . . . everything under the bed. Hugel could not bend to look under it. If he fell on his back, he would have to lie there like a beached whale. He seems jolly, like Falstaff in the opera, and yet, so . . . *evil*! He frightens me, Elisa!"

As the story unfolded, Elisa became more convinced that there was no time to lose. Somehow she must help Leah and the children get out of Vienna. No doubt the Gestapo would be searching for the children who had caused such a stir in Germany. Perhaps they could make it to the Tyrol. Then the Wattenbarger family could hide them until they could be smuggled across the border. But how to get them past the fleshy Nazi watchdog, Herr Hugel?

"I'm here now, Leah." Elisa tried to sound confident and comforting, although she was neither.

"Thank God!" Leah said, reaching out to embrace her again as she cried with relief. "Oh, Elisa! Thank God you are here!"

Elisa felt her blouse dampen with Leah's tears. "We'll have to have a plan. Something. We need to be very careful." She frowned and gazed at the violin case that she had brought with her. How many times had she smuggled false papers into the Reich in that case? She could do it again! She would take the photos of the boys with her to Paris when she left for the rendezvous with the bookseller! "Soon I have to go to Paris—"

"You are leaving?" Leah made no attempt to hide her fear and disappointment. "Must you go?"

"Yes." Elisa could clearly remember the stern warning of the men in Prague. She must not get sidetracked, they had said. What she carried in the book was much more important than even the life of one child. That was what they had told her. But now there were two children at stake as well as Leah! How could she ignore them and go on with the assignment as if nothing were wrong?

"When will you come back?" Leah was pleading.

"I'll go there and then come back again. But perhaps I can take the passport photos. Have papers made. There must be a thriving black market in Paris now for false identity papers."

Leah sat back, exhilarated at the thought of getting away. Then she thought about Charles and his terrible deformity. If the Gestapo were looking for him, they would certainly not accept a passport with his picture and another name. "But poor Charles . . . what can we do? His face is . . . " She lowered her voice and glanced furtively toward the bedroom.

It was too late. Charles stood gazing sadly at the two women. His face was flushed with fever. Raising his hand to his mouth, he shook his head in apology. He was the reason they were in danger! He knew it. He had always known it.

Leah groaned as she saw how her thoughtlessness had torn the child. "Oh, Charles!" she began, forgetting her own heartache.

He lowered his eyes and turned away, back to the bedroom.

Elisa swallowed hard at the sight of him. He was so small to carry such a burden. She grasped Leah's hand. "We will find a way," she promised. "There must be a way. I will try to get the right documents in Paris when I am there."

"Paris," Leah said absently. "Yes." Then she looked again toward the dark bedroom. "He wanted to play the cello, and I gave him lessons. Hours every day. I don't know if he meant it for me or for himself. He is . . . he *sees* everything, Elisa. His heart feels the music, and if we ever get out of here . . . someday he will play like an angel."

Elisa nodded, wishing that the child had heard Leah's praise. Leah had told her how she had sold the violoncello for a mere fraction of its value. The instrument had given the child a sense of worth. "One day I will ask him to play for me," Elisa said quietly.

Leah bowed her head and wept again. She had lost everything—Shimon, Vitorio, her papers, and any money that might have helped them. "Thank God you are here, Elisa," she murmured as tears dropped onto Elisa's hand. "This time do not stay away! I beg you!"

At last the sun streamed through the window, and two hungry boys staggered out to the kitchen to gape at Elisa.

"There is nothing left in the apartment to feed them," Leah said in tearful relief. "Nothing at all. It is a miracle that you came when you did."

Elisa was exhausted, but she glanced up at the clock and stood to leave. The farmers' market had already been open for hours. She could purchase everything they needed and still have time to make it to Fiori's Bookstore.

Charles doubled over coughing. He seemed dangerously ill. "I'll go now. I can get everything at the farmers market and then stop at the pharmacy. There must be something we can get to ease that—"

Leah pulled her back. "No!" she cried fearfully. "Oh no, Elisa! You can't go yet! Not while Herr Hugel is still here! He watches every waking minute. It is a miracle that you got in here this morning without him seeing you."

"Another miracle," Elisa commented, glancing at the door, "will be getting out of here if he is that vigilant."

"Already he has had three tenants arrested. All Jewish."

"Besides Herr Haupt?"

Leah nodded. "The Gestapo has given Hugel the title of Apartment Führer now, and he receives a bonus every time he betrays someone."

"But, Leah!" Elisa could scarcely believe what had happened in this once-friendly building. "How have you managed to survive?"

"He thinks that I am you, Fräulein Linder. I have managed to intimidate him. When he prowls by or knocks on the door, I give him the Heil and ask him why he dares to disturb me when I am practicing for a recital for the Nazi Gauleiter of Vienna! He goes away and he avoids the stairs at all costs."

"Because he is so fat," Louis finished. "But he came in here looking for us. Creeping like a bear. We hid under the bed, didn't we, Charles?"

Charles nodded grimly.

"Then how will I get out?" Elisa asked, staring at the door.

"He will leave soon." Leah lowered her voice to a conspiratorial whisper. "He goes to church every Wednesday morning at eight o'clock."

"He goes to church?" Elisa was astonished at this unexpected information.

"To give thanks that he has been made Apartment Führer." Leah sounded angry all over again. "I heard him talking to a Nazi officer in the lobby last week. He says that God has given him this great honor! *God!*"

Elisa smiled quizzically at Leah's rage; then she stood to peek out the window as a garbage wagon rumbled to a stop in front of the building and Hugel emerged lugging a can. Herr Hugel was dressed in soiled leather breeches and a yellowed shirt. His enormous belly threatened to burst the buttons of the shirt, and his eyes bulged with the effort of his exertion. Elisa laughed at the sight of the exalted Apartment Führer in spite of the fact that he was indeed a danger to them all. "Hugel is involving God in his folly, is he?" She glanced back over her shoulder. "I am sure God's partnership in Hugel's success is news to the Almighty, Leah!"

Leah could not bring herself to smile at Elisa's sarcasm. After all, she had been forced to live beneath the threat of this mindless tyrant for weeks. "Then why doesn't the Almighty *do* something if He is so almighty?"

Her disrespect startled both Charles and Louis. They had never heard a grown-up angry at God before. They stood blinking at her, trying to comprehend why she was furious not only at Hugel but also at the heavens!

Elisa put an arm around Leah's shoulders. "But God *has* done something about the Hugels of the world, Leah!" She embraced her friend quickly, feeling the rage dissipate at her touch. "He put people like you here to protect little boys, didn't He?"

Leah wept again in misery at her feeling of impotence. "But I haven't done anything! And I *can't* do anything!"

"What are you saying, Leah?" Elisa held her firmly by the shoulders. "Do you think it was an accident that you were at the Musikverein when the children came? Do you think it was an accident that you brought them here and stood between them and . . . all this?" She gestured toward the window and beyond, to where all of Vienna had become an armed camp of evil. "Think back, dear Leah. Think, and you will see that a gentle, loving hand has guided you this far for the sake of these little ones."

Leah could not find an answer. She rested her head against Elisa's shoulder and let the tears come. Maybe it *was* true . . . *maybe*! "But why have so many others been taken? Shimon—"

"Because there are not enough who are willing to serve as God's hands here in this world. Men like Hugel follow their own evil ambition and then link their deeds to God. Such hypocrisy is slander of the God who created man in His image." She stroked Leah's hair, soothing away the pain of weeks of loneliness and fear. "Don't be angry at God because of what evil men do, Leah. Just do what you know is truly right. And know that love is the only true image of the Christ whom you have feared. Herr Hugel goes to church, but Jesus is not there! No. He is *here*, with *you*, who have put your own life in danger for the sake of love. He has been here with you all along, and He will be wherever there are people like you. The problem is not with God, you see, Leah? There are too many Hugels sitting in church and not enough willing hearts ready to serve and *live* the truth!"

Charles and Louis wrapped their arms around Leah's waist. They understood perfectly what Elisa was saying even if their dear Aunt Leah did not yet fully comprehend it.

Dressed for morning mass, Herr Hugel emerged from the building and stood blinking in the sunlight as if blinded by his own glory. He wore an old army tunic that strained at the seams in agony at the corpulent flesh that threatened to burst out. A red sash dipped below his belly where his waist should have been, and from the sash a saber hung. The tip of the sword clattered against the cobblestones as he marched off to church.

Elisa had already changed into her prettiest blue dress. It would help to look attractive, she thought, in case she needed to talk with any Nazi soldiers. They were less likely to treat a pretty woman harshly. She had learned that much long ago in Berlin.

She waited until Hugel swaggered around the corner; then she hurried to the door. "I'll be back in an hour with breakfast and enough groceries to last awhile if I have to leave for Paris today. Don't forget to hide the passport photos in the violin case so I can take them with me."

"Just an hour, remember," Leah warned. "You'll have to be back here and gone again before Hugel returns."

Elisa grinned confidently and winked at Charles, who blushed at the attention of such a beautiful woman. "A pastry from Demel's for you," she promised and then slipped out the door.

The blue dress did indeed come in handy. Smiling coyly at soldiers and guards assigned to check identity documents at the barricades around the city, it seemed that the men hardly noticed Elisa's papers.

While long lines of women waited to pass into the open-air market, Elisa was escorted through the checkpoint by a short, dumpy captain from Frankfurt who declared that he had spotted her a block before she reached his station. Elisa ignored the angry glares of the women still in the line. She had less than an hour, after all, to load her shopping bag with as much as she could carry. Less than an hour before she had to return to the apartment for the volume of *Faust*. Less than an hour before Herr Hugel returned from his devotions to resume his place as Apartment Führer and Nazi watchdog!

Arms aching, Elisa ascended the steep stairs to her apartment. A box of Demel's pastries was balanced on top of her bag. Leah had watched her coming up the street and threw the door back before Elisa could knock.

She had only four minutes to spare before Hugel would be back.

Elisa grabbed the volume of *Faust,* presented Charles with pastries and a bottle of cough medicine, and hugged Leah farewell.

"I'll be back this afternoon," she assured them. "And if I am to go to Paris, I promise I'll get the papers for you. Don't worry, Leah! Promise me you won't worry anymore." She touched the cheek of her friend. "Everything will be all right."

34

Betrayal

Herr Fiori held the precious volume of *Faust* up to the light of his desk lamp as he thumbed through each page. For nearly an hour he searched for some tiny beam of light in the midst of the script; some message that might identify the woman who had brought *Faust* into the shop.

Twice he rose to peer out the peephole of his office door. The courier was blond and pretty, the sort of woman any man would look at twice. It would be a shame to have such a beautiful face and body fall into the hands of the Gestapo. As she waited, the young woman browsed the bookshelves with interest like any other ordinary customer. But she was not ordinary, Fiori knew that. The volume of *Faust* confirmed it. But what was he to do with her?

Fiori sipped a cup of cold coffee as he examined each page against the light. Line by line, letter by letter, he found nothing until at last he came to the section titled clearly *Trüber Tag.* Dismal Day.

Fiori frowned as the tiniest beam of light gleamed through the first letter of each word in the outraged cry of Faust to the demon Mephistopheles: "In misery! Despairing! Long lost wretchedly on the earth, and now imprisoned!" He read the order regarding this beautiful new courier from Prague, and his heart sank. "As a felon locked up in a dungeon with horrible torments, the fair, ill-fated creature! It's come to that! *Bis dahin, dahin!*"

The thought of what must come to this fair young woman sickened Fiori, and yet here it was. *The order!* For the sake of all, Fiori must obey.

He hesitated and then turned another page until at last he found more small pinpricks of light, illuminating the fate of Elisa Linder Murphy. *"Bis dahin,"* Fiori muttered at last. "It has come to that."

With a twinge of regret, he picked up the telephone and dialed the number of Gestapo headquarters. The line was answered by a curt, heavy German accent, "State police."

"Otto Wattenbarger, *bitte,"* Fiori said coolly.

After a moment the voice of Herr Wattenbarger came on the line. Fiori did not take time for explanation. He simply did what he knew he must do for the good of everyone concerned. "Someone is here whom you may wish to examine."

Otto recognized Fiori. They had spoken before. "Fifteen minutes?" Both were aware that others might be listening.

"I can detain her that long." There was nothing to be said or done. Fiori hung up the telephone, confident that Otto would be waiting when Elisa walked out of the shop with the volume of *Faust* in her hand.

Fiori returned from the back room and cleared his throat as he passed the bookshelf where Elisa browsed. He carried the book of *Faust* in his hand and raised it slightly, then inclined his head toward the front counter.

So this is it, Elisa thought with a rush of excitement as she fumbled to replace a biography about Haydn on the shelf. No doubt Fiori had gotten some message from Prague, or had entered one into the volume. Now Elisa would get the promised instructions: where she might find the one called the Dead Man; when she must leave for Paris. Whatever message Fiori sent to Paris did not matter to her. She did not need to know anything other than the fact that she was a small part in this vast underground resistance. That awareness alone was enough to make her stomach churn with anticipation.

"A very nice volume, Frau Murphy," Fiori said. "Yes. A nicely preserved volume, indeed."

She waited for some word of direction. A time. An address. "Yes." She tried to make some intelligent conversation. "One of my father's finest."

"I am sorry I cannot help you with it today, however," Fiori continued, tapping the red cover absently.

What? What can this mean? "I don't understand," she answered quietly. She wanted to ask him what she should do next. She simply stared.

"The value is difficult to ascertain. Perhaps if you allow me a few days for research. You are leaving for Paris, you say? Perhaps before you leave you may come by here, and I will have had more time to work on the matter."

What it all meant, she could not guess and did not dare to ask. "When would you like me to come back, Herr Fiori?"

"Three days. That will give me enough time to research. You may pay my fee then."

Elisa did not know if she should keep the book or take it with her now. It was all so different from what she had expected. She was to be in Vienna days longer than she thought. This would give her more time to decide how she could help Leah. It seemed like an answer to her prayers!

"Shall I take the book, or do you—"

"I have my notes, Frau Murphy. You take it. By all means."

She nodded, trying to catch some hint of the mystery in his eyes. He betrayed nothing but the mundane expression of a bookseller talking to a customer. Had there been no message to hide in the book? No word to send on to Paris yet? *Three days?* What was the delay?

A brawny Nazi corporal entered the shop, and Fiori turned away to face him with a smile. The visit was at an end. Elisa gathered the precious volume up and brushed past the man in uniform as she left the shop.

Fiori watched through the shopwindow as Elisa walked quickly toward the Packard. He shook his head sadly. Soon, as Faust proclaimed, she would be locked in a dungeon with horrible torments: "Imprisoned! In irreparable misery! Handed over to evil spirits and judging unfeeling mankind!"

Her golden hair caught in the sunlight, and the blue of her dress seemed as fresh and bright as the spring flowers at the Schönbrunn Palace. Fiori wondered how well she would hold up in a Gestapo cell. Would this beautiful woman with the creamy skin crack like porcelain under the stress of fear?

Even as he wondered, Otto Wattenbarger and another larger man with dull, black, sharklike eyes emerged from the alleyway and walked toward her. At the sight of Otto, she stopped; then after a moment, she turned to cross the street. He walked after her, calling her name. Fiori had not realized that Otto knew her. Somehow this made it all much easier.

She did not stop for him when he called but quickened her pace. She walked away from her car. Away from Fiori's Bookstore. She turned a corner and was lost from Fiori's view. Otto pursued and also disappeared, but Fiori knew what the end of this would be. He had smelled the stench of the Gestapo prison. Surely this beautiful young woman would not last long in a place such as that.

When the bell on the counter rang impatiently, Fiori moved away from the window and returned to business.

"Heil Hitler, Elisa?" It was a question, not a statement. Otto Wattenbarger stepped in front of Elisa, blocking her path.

Her blue eyes flashed angrily at the sight of his smirk. She did not reply but tried to simply walk around him. He stepped in her way again and crossed his arms over his chest.

"What do you want, Otto?" she asked wearily.

"I said, 'Heil Hitler!' "

"And I said, what do you want?"

"It is law now, you know. Or have you been away in Prague so long that you haven't heard? The greeting required by law is 'Heil Hitler.' "

"I guess I have been away too long." She turned to go, but he clutched her arm in an iron grip.

"You don't like the new laws of the East Reich, Elisa?" His eyes were steel.

"I don't like you, Otto. And I don't like the company you keep."

"You prefer Jews?"

"I prefer everyone over you. But I am beginning to believe that the only decent people left in Austria, besides your parents—" she saw him flinch slightly—"are indeed Jews."

Rage filled Otto's face. "You refuse, then, to use the required greeting?"

She smiled defiantly. "I choose not to greet the likes of you with any greeting at all."

Otto's eyes narrowed and he glared down at her. He held tightly to her arm and then snapped his fingers. The burly man emerged from the shadows. Elisa gasped with surprise and struggled briefly to free herself.

"You are the most wretched human being!" she hissed.

The two men grabbed her roughly and pulled her toward a waiting car.

"Not half so wretched as you will soon be," Otto replied as they shoved her into the backseat.

35
Trump Card

It was two days before Murphy climbed from the back of a vegetable truck in front of the *San Francisco Union Post.* Unshaven and disheveled, he stepped down from among the heaps of cabbages and thanked his Mexican host in flawless Spanish. He had picked up the language as a correspondent in Spain, and the driver of the truck tipped his straw hat respectfully to the American who spoke better Spanish than just about anyone on the West Coast, regardless of nationality.

Bob Trump. Murphy read the name on the matchbook cover and let his eyes scan the ornate facade of the tall Market Street building. Gargoyles and lions with wings supported the scroll bearing the motto and logo of the venerable publication: *Veritas simplex oratio est.* "The language of truth is simple," Murphy read aloud, hoping that this publication had not forgotten the meaning of the Latin words inscribed on the stone scroll. The date below that read *1876.* A whole lot of simple truth had gotten tangled up since then.

Murphy smoothed his jacket and attempted to straighten his collar. He had seen many a newsman walk into the newsroom in shabby attire, but not many had been hired looking like a skid-row bum . . . in dinner dress, no less.

He had already decided that he would not waste any time in San Francisco. He still had enough cash to get back to Europe and possibly pick up an assignment there, but if he could return on the payroll of the *Union Post,* so much the better. The *Post* syndicate was old and well respected. Publisher Bob Trump was known for his disdain of Arthur

Craine, and he would no doubt jump at the chance to shove in the dagger by hiring Murphy. At least Murphy hoped as much.

He drew a deep breath and walked into the gleaming marble lobby. The familiar sound of typewriters and telephones greeted him. He leaned against the counter of the reception area and waited for a harried-looking blond to notice him.

He flipped open the matchbook. "Bob Trump." He managed his most charming grin as she looked him over disapprovingly.

"You have an appointment?" She did not return his smile but focused her eyes on a spot of beet juice that stained Murphy's once-white shirt-front like cheap red wine.

"Sort of." He brushed his hair back off his forehead. "Clark Gable told me to speak with Mr. Trump."

She rolled her eyes. "That explains it," she mumbled, unimpressed. Picking up the headset, she plugged the cord into the switchboard. "Yeah, Mr. Trump, another one of Mr. Gable's drinking buddies has dropped in." There was a long pause; then her eyes widened and she stared openly at Murphy. "Yes. *A mess*, Mr. Trump! Right." She covered the mouthpiece. "What's your name?" she asked.

"John Murphy."

"Murphy, Mr. Trump." A roaring voice emanated from the headset. "Yessir!" she finally replied; then she pulled the plug and spun around, regarding Murphy with some awe. "He says he's been waiting for you, and where the . . . blank have you been? He figured you must've got killed on Highway 1 or something, so go on up to the third floor before he has apoplexy, will you?"

All of this was spoken in one breath as the woman flung back the half door in the counter and yanked Murphy toward the elevator. "He says he don't *care* if you're a mess! He heard you on CBS after the Anschluss, and then Gable called Thursday from Bakersfield and told him what you said to Craine! Guess you're going to work for the *Union Post*, sir. Sure hope you take a bath once in a while." She smiled, winked, and waved as the elevator doors clanged shut.

"You are quite stubborn." Otto eyed Elisa as she stood in front of his desk.

"You have no right to arrest me!" she spat, staring him down. "Take a good look at my passport. I hold an American passport—"

"With a permit to stay and work within the boundaries of the Reich!" Otto shouted.

"This was still Austria last time I was here! Now I am married to an

American citizen. Call the American Embassy! I demand that you call the American Embassy! They will not stand for this!" Elisa congratulated herself. She was following every instruction with bravado, even though she was shaking inside.

"And what do you suppose they can do about it? You are in the Greater Reich now, Elisa! You must follow the law!"

"Call the embassy."

He ignored her and hefted the book of *Faust*. Then he laid it on his desk and changed his tone until he was almost friendly. "It surprised me that you were married. And to an American, too." He held his hand out. "You'd better leave your ring with me."

She drew back and covered the blue lapis wedding band with her other hand. "I won't."

"Where you are going it will be safer here with me." He was amused.

"I demand that you call the American Embassy!" She stamped her foot defiantly.

"A lovely wedding ring. It suits you. The guards will take it. Or the other inmates in your cell."

Elisa did not reply now. She twisted her band around her finger. It had been like a shield to her since the first terrible night she had put it on. She was not about to turn it over to an animal like Otto now! "My husband is John Murphy of the INS," she began.

"I wouldn't admit that if I were you." He smirked openly. "You are involved in anti-government activities, Elisa. We know about it, and sooner or later you will admit it. It is better if you tell me. An old friend—"

"You were never a friend. Not even to your own family. You have no friends. I don't have anything to tell you! I have done nothing more than try to walk around you on the street. It is no crime against the state for me to hold you in utter contempt! That is no reflection on anyone but you!"

Otto stared down at his stack of files; then he reached over and pushed the button on his intercom. "Yes. You can take her away now." The interrogation was over. Within seconds a guard entered the room.

"Otto?" Elisa questioned as the guard pushed her.

As Elisa was led out of the small office, Otto picked up the telephone. Somehow she felt that what he said was entirely for her benefit.

"If she is involved with any anti-government activities, we have ways of making her talk."

The guard nudged her forward toward the stairs just as a terrifying shriek pierced the long corridor. A rapid succession of screams followed as they descended the steps; then the voice wailed and died away until only the sound of Elisa's feet against the stone was heard. Until that moment, she had not truly known fear of Otto and the Gestapo headquarters.

She turned to her guard. "Where are we going?" she asked, feeling the sudden urge to grasp the iron stair railing and hold tightly to it. Otto's words returned forcefully to her: *"We have ways of making her talk."* The ways of the Gestapo had made some man scream with such pain and terror that Elisa was certain he had been facing his death!

The guard smirked at the frightened expression on her pale face. "Don't worry; I am taking you to Vienna's finest hotel!" He laughed and hustled her faster down the steps.

Outside in the courtyard, he shoved her into a waiting car. Ten minutes later, Elisa stepped beneath the arches of the most terrible of all the prisons in the city. She blinked up at the thick stone walls that had once housed a monastery. Windows were mere slits, set so high above the dark, airless cells that the prisoners knew they would never see the sun once they entered the building.

Elisa walked reluctantly beneath the arches of the building's entrance.

"Your hotel, Frau Murphy." The guard laughed again.

Then he left her with two dour-appearing women guards. They shoved her into a cold little room, slammed the door, and then crossed their arms as they appraised Elisa.

"Strip!" the first guard shouted.

Elisa drew back, clutching the collar of her blue dress. "I won't!" she argued fiercely. "I demand that the American Embassy be called at once!"

"They make no difference here! We have been ordered to strip-search you before we take you to your cell!" the guard screamed with earsplitting force. "You will strip, or we will strip you!"

Both women moved a step nearer to Elisa. They were heavy-boned, thick-jawed peasants. Their hands were rough and calloused and strong from some labor Elisa did not try to guess at.

"My husband will lodge a formal protest with the American—"

Elisa's threat was drowned out by a fierce roar from the second woman. "Do you think we care? You take off your clothes or I will tear them off, and that is the end of discussion!"

Elisa was literally backed to the wall. With the stone blocks behind her and the two women guards blocking any attempt to get away, Elisa timidly began to unbutton her dress.

The two tormenters mocked her, ridiculing her slender body and remarking on the fact that there were men among the guards whom they should perhaps call to witness the search of such an example of femininity.

Shivering in her bra and panties, Elisa stopped, hoping that this indignity would be enough to satisfy these coarse and almost masculine female guards. But it was not enough.

"Strip to the skin!" the first guard shouted again. "We have orders to search you! *Everywhere,*" she sneered, enjoying the torture of stealing the last shreds of Elisa's clothing and composure at the same moment.

Elisa silently vowed that she would not cry in front of these brutes! She would not show them how deeply the abuse and derision cut her.

"All right!" shouted the second guard, giving Elisa a shove away from the wall. "Now we show you how thoroughly we search those criminals who come here, *ja*?" She laughed, relishing the sport. "If you ever get out, you can tell your friends what they have to look forward to!"

A hard slap sent Elisa to her knees. "Put your hands on the floor!" shrieked the first guard.

Mutely, Elisa obeyed. She was powerless now. Her humiliation was nearly complete except for one small detail. She would not weep! She would not show them any weakness, no matter what followed.

Haggard and exhausted, Elisa had been given a thin prison dress to put on before she was photographed holding up a number for the camera.

"Number 377," barked the male guard. "You are number 377, and you will answer to that number or you will be beaten."

Wearily, Elisa nodded. "I am 377," she repeated, wishing only that she could find a place to lie down. How had this happened? What wrong move had she made to end up like this?

"Number 377, you will follow me. Third floor. Women's quarters."

Her feet lost in the loose prison slippers, Elisa followed after the guard. At every cross-corridor armed men stood with bayonets ready. The stink of the place grew more horrible with every step, and Elisa's head began to throb.

The guard stopped in front of a heavy iron door at the farthest end of the corridor. He pulled open a peephole and looked in; then with a huge key, he unlocked the door and shoved Elisa into the cell. The door clanged shut behind her, and she was left standing before the curious but sullen eyes of three other women prisoners. The foul smell inside the cell was a hundred times worse than it had been outside. Elisa noticed a tin bucket full of human waste in the corner of the tiny room. Four iron cots were shoved together so tightly that there was hardly any room to move.

One of the prisoners, a woman with matted gray hair and a gold-capped tooth, perused the newcomer with some amusement. "Welcome to the Savoy, dearie. Our previous roommate was beheaded this morning."

A young woman burst into sobs at the words, and Elisa did not doubt for a moment the truth of the execution story.

The gray-haired woman continued her welcoming speech. "Since she is dead and you are not, you may have her bed. All the beds have fleas, but you will get used to it if you are here long." The gold tooth glinted in the dim light of the single lightbulb. "My name is Marian. This is Suzanne. Here is Karin." She pointed to the young woman who lay so still and silent on her bed that Elisa wondered if the prisoner was dead. "Karin doesn't say much. They killed her husband the first night, you see. We have all been here since the first night. Where have you been? Not here. You are too clean. So what is it like where the sun shines? What is your name? Why are you here?"

Suddenly all of Elisa's determination not to show emotion was shattered. With one wrenching sob, she covered her face with her hands and wept until she could hardly stand up.

Young Suzanne, a sweet-faced girl of eighteen, patted her timidly on the back. "Did they beat you?" she asked sympathetically. "They beat everybody."

Elisa shook her head from side to side. No, they had not beaten her.

"Then why are you crying so?" Suzanne asked.

"It seems so l-long already," Elisa stammered. "So long since I saw the sun."

Suzanne guided her to the edge of the dead woman's bed. Elisa sat down slowly, feeling the nearness of death. She was utterly ashamed. She did not weep because of a beating or the death of a friend. She wept only for herself tonight.

Newspaper publisher Bob Trump looked nothing like his wealthy competitor. His office was spacious but cluttered with dozens of other daily newspapers. It was unadorned except for a number of framed editions of the *Union Post* on a wall with a sign above declaring, *We Were There First!*

Trump himself was a rumpled little man with a face like a welterweight fighter and a swagger like Brutus in the *Popeye* comic strip. Gray hair stuck up on one side, and Murphy suspected that the aging publisher not only took his meals in his office but probably slept on the cracking red-leather sofa behind his desk.

"Well, boy!" Trump extended his hand and snapped a suspender in his pleasure at meeting Murphy. All in all, Murphy thought that he probably could not look much more disheveled than Trump himself. Both of them were in need of a shave. Trump's eyes sparkled. "So you told that old blankity-blank where to stuff it, eh?"

Blankity-blank was a word Trump often used, Murphy discovered. "Let's just say I resigned from the Craine newspaper syndicate," he replied modestly.

"The old blankity-blank Craine won't face facts!" Trump rose on his toes like a revival preacher exhorting his audience to turn from wickedness. "I heard you, boy! Heard you on the CBS broadcast. And I read that piece you wrote about the kids. Far as I'm concerned, if you haven't found another job between here and there, you're hired. What was *he* paying you?"

"Seventy-five a week. Meals and expenses in Europe."

"I'll pay you one hundred, son."

"I have a wife now. In Prague. I need to get back, Mr. Trump."

"Well, shoot ya, boy! Better shave first, though." The old man ran a hand over his own stubble. "Me too, I guess." He frowned. "Want you back over there as soon as you can get going. Quite a crisis developing, you know. German troops too close to the border of Czechoslovakia. We've got to watch London. The Brits will be upside down over this one."

He popped a mint into his mouth and handed one to Murphy. "The truth is good enough for this paper. Write it as you see it, Mr. Murphy. Gable recommended you highly, and—" another series of *blankity-blanks* erupted—"if we close this London radio deal with CBS, you're the man I want on hand." He frowned and stuck out his lower lip. "You need an advance." It was a statement, not a question. He picked up a telephone and ordered someone named Mattie to make Murphy plane reservations to the East Coast and then to book passage back to London on the next dirigible. It was as simple as that.

Murphy had two hours to shower and shave while Bob Trump ordered two off-the-rack suits sent up immediately for his prize. "Stole this young fella right out from under the nose of that old blankity-blank Craine," he said gleefully to the team of tailors who hemmed the cuffs of Murphy's new trousers.

36

In the Hall of the Troll King

There was a hunger among Elisa's cell mates to hear news from the outside world. With an unmerciful determination, they leveled their questions at her one after another without regard to her own unhappiness.

"Are the flowers blooming at the Schönbrunn?"

"What has happened to Chancellor Schuschnigg?"

"We hear that the plebiscite was won by the Nazis. But how many Austrians were allowed to vote?"

"Are they still able to sell pastry at Demel's, or has the Führer had it all shipped back to Germany?"

Most of the questions had no real importance except that they were small things that had been dreamed of or imagined in the stench and filth of this place. It took only a few moments for Elisa to realize that the cleanliness of her own skin and the sweetness of her perfume was like a bouquet of fresh flowers to the women around her. She could smell only the horrible odor of the tin bucket, while all their senses seemed to focus on the fragrance of the outside world that Elisa carried with her. Even poor, dull-eyed Karin brightened and inhaled deeply when the perfumeries of Paris were mentioned.

Paris! The word settled on Elisa like a blow. What if she could not get out of this place? Whom would Fiori send to Paris? Was there some urgent message in the book that now lay on Otto's desk? How would she get word of her predicament to Leah and the others?

In Prague, she had been told to deny everything! She had done that. She had been told to threaten her captor with the American Embassy, with the maestro at the Musikverein. None of that had made the slightest difference to Otto. She was still here, humiliated and deprived of freedom.

"Why didn't they beat you?" asked Suzanne timidly. "They usually beat everyone."

Marian sat down on the cot beside Karin. "They will probably let you go. They don't beat you if they are going to let you go."

There was only momentary comfort in her words. "They let you go for a day or two at first, didn't they, Marian?" said Suzanne with a frown.

"Yes. Here for two days, then out for a day. It is a way of making you crack. You see, once you are here and know this place, you never want to come back. To smell the sweet air of freedom and then to be brought back here—people will tell them anything to get out again. Anything at all." She leaned close to Elisa's neck and breathed in the fragrance once again. For a fleeting moment Elisa felt as if she had been locked into a kennel where humans, left like animals, had acquired the instincts of dogs, sniffing at one another. But she did not pull away. She could not begrudge these poor souls a whiff of perfume.

"But you are still here," Elisa said to Marian.

"I did not tell them anything." She laughed. "Of course, I have nothing at all to tell them. So now they have brought me here and left me. I am forgotten, I think. But they beat me when they arrested me the second time. They beat me, and I knew they would not let me go again."

The world, it seemed, had turned upside down. Elisa had not been harmed, but that was not necessarily a hopeful sign. Even if she was released, these women believed that she would be returned to the cell in due time. That was the way of it. They knew all about the justice that now ruled in Austria.

Marian lifted the back of Suzanne's loose prison blouse. The young woman's bony back was crisscrossed with scars and scabs where the whip had torn away her flesh. Suzanne knew firsthand what it was like to be beaten.

Her eyes were riveted to the ring that still remained on Elisa's finger. It was the only bit of color in the cell of gray-and-black shadows. "They let you keep your ring?" Suzanne pointed to Elisa's hand.

"I would not let them have it," Elisa explained.

"Wouldn't *let* them?" Marian frowned and drew back. Suddenly each of the women, even Karin, eyed her with hostile suspicion.

"What is it?" Elisa asked, genuinely confused.

"Yes, you'll be leaving us," Marian stated. "Look at you. A Nazi to the core. No doubt they put you here to spy on us. To see if poor Helga said anything to us before they executed her. Is that it?"

"Oh no!" Elisa tried to protest, but the women turned from her, determined they would not say even one more word to her. "I didn't let them take it."

"No one keeps a ring," Suzanne told her, confident in her conclusion. "And everyone gets beaten."

Below the apartment, a Nazi watchman strolled from one pool of light to the next as he made his midnight rounds. Leah had not dared to switch on the lamps in the apartment. She watched from the dark window as she had for hours. Something had gone terribly wrong. Elisa had not returned, and now as the bells of St. Stephan's tolled the blackest hour of the night, Leah knew that Elisa would not be back tonight. Perhaps not ever. Still she could not tear her eyes away from the shadows just beyond the streetlights. She could not help but hope that Elisa would emerge and hurry toward the building. *Please, Elisa! Please, God! Do not leave me alone here again! Protect her! I cannot help Louis and Charles alone! Oh, God, if You cannot hear me, then hear the prayers of the children.*

Just then, Herr Hugel lumbered around the corner. He was drunk. Even in the dim light Leah could see the gleeful stupor of his expression as he hailed the night watchman with a cheerful "Heil Hitler!"

"It is nearly past curfew, Herr Hugel!" the watchman retorted, jabbing a finger toward the spires of the cathedral.

At the warning, Hugel leaned forward and attempted to quicken his pace toward the building. The watchman shook his head and rolled his eyes at the sight, then turned to resume his rounds.

Below in the foyer Leah heard the glass panel in the door rattle as Hugel slammed it hard. His laughter drifted up through the stairwell, and he began to sing his own slurred version of the "Horst Wessel" song. Leah covered her ears with her hands and squeezed her eyes tight. *Was this the answer to her prayer? Was God mocking her? Was there no light or hope left in the world for her and Charles and Louis?*

She felt a slight tugging on her sleeve and whirled around to face little Louis.

He blinked sleepily up at her. "Is she coming back?" he asked.

She knelt and embraced him. She needed his comfort now almost more than he needed hers. "I don't know, Louis. I just don't know!"

"Did they arrest her, too?" he said sadly. "She was so pretty. People don't stay pretty anymore when they go to prison."

Leah could not bear to think that Elisa had met the same fate as Shimon. She glanced toward the violin case and the small suitcase Elisa had left beside the door. She would not have left Vienna of her own free will without those things. What other explanation could there be besides arrest! Men and women disappeared for no reason at all. Any hint of transgression against the laws of the state meant arrest.

"I don't know where she is," Leah answered truthfully. "But if she can get back to us, she will."

"Do you want Charles and me to pray for her, too? Like we pray for you, Aunt Leah?"

Leah hugged him closer and nodded. Perhaps the fierce Christian God would not listen to her because she was Jewish. Perhaps He would hear the prayers of these little Christian boys instead. "Yes!" she cried. "Pray for her, Louis! Please do!"

The bulb above her cot burned night and day, and all sense of time was lost to Elisa. Time was kept by the counting of meals. In the morning a crust of bread and a cup of tasteless brown water were served. Elisa managed to choke it down simply because she remembered the words of her father when he had told of those within the camp who had refused to eat. They had died without a fight. She would not begin this ordeal by giving in so easily. If she was to be imprisoned as her father had been, she would eat, even though the food made her feel nauseated!

Her cell mates moved around her as if she were not there. They still believed their first impression. Elisa was a spy. She must be, or else why did she still wear a wedding ring? Why had she not been beaten?

Elisa drew her legs up and sat on her bunk. She closed her eyes and mentally practiced playing a Mozart violin concerto. In her mind she stood before a vast and empty hall. There was a single, bright light above her and beyond that was darkness. For hours she would play, certain that no one but God could hear her. Even without the golden violin she could let her soul sing. Sometimes she would let her thoughts drift back to Murphy in his rented dinner jacket. Row ten, aisle seat. She would play for him and feel his eyes upon her so intensely that she would blush. And then again she would raise bow to strings and look across the stage to see Leah sending silly messages in her smile.

When her concert was finished and the vile crust had been consumed for supper, she would close her eyes and pretend to sleep with the rest of them. Strange wails and moans would fill the corridors of the women's prison during those hours. Cries and sobs would make the night tremble. Then Elisa would open her eyes and gaze at the band on her finger. Behind golden leaves the sky shone bright and pure and blue. She would lie in the shelter of the forest and watch as the leaves moved in the breeze. And always, just before she slept, Murphy would come and bend over her to kiss her good night.

She could not think of Paris then. Or of Leah and the two small boys trapped by Herr Hugel. She could not let herself think of the promised beating or the release and then the next arrest that the women had told her would come. Here, there were only music and prayers and Murphy beneath the blue sky. It did not matter if the others hated her and suspected her. She would eat and dream of better moments, and perhaps she would smell the sweet air of freedom one day again.

Leah was grateful for the radio. The music of *Peer Gynt* covered the sound of Charles as he coughed. Why hadn't she thought to ask Elisa to lay in a supply of the medicine? One bottle was certainly not enough. Of course, if she had known Elisa would disappear, she would not have let her out of the apartment! Not even to purchase an entire shelf of cough medicine!

She sighed and shook her head at the uselessness of her own thoughts. What difference did any of that make now? Elisa had vanished, and little Charles grew sicker by the hour.

Charles followed her every move around the bedroom. His eyes seemed to hold on to her as the music followed some unspoken story that the child could *feel*, even though the substance of it was a mystery to him. He opened his mouth and gave a muffled cry for her attention.

"What is it, Charles?" She knew how his ears ached, how inflamed his throat was. The effort of speech caused his eyes to water.

The boy raised his hand to move an imaginary bow across the strings as the cellos played the prelude to the second act of the play. Louis watched for a moment; then after Charles groaned again in an effort to communicate, Louis said, "He wants you to tell him the story. Is there a story, Aunt Leah? Or only music?"

How could such a young child know that this was more than just music? Could he see the procession of trolls in the Hall of the Mountain King? Could he understand the sorrow of Ingrid's song as she was stolen away? She gazed at Charles in astonishment. Never had she seen a child of such perception.

She smiled and sat beside him, stroking his hair back from his forehead. She had long since ceased to look at the cleft in his lip. The beauty of a clear lake was in his eyes. There was such life and movement just beneath the silent surface. How she had grown to love this little boy!

"The music is from a record," Leah began to explain. "There, do you hear the kettledrums? That is my Shimon playing! He is big and strong like an Indian in an American film, yes?"

Charles nodded, and Louis came to sit beside her. "And you are playing?"

"Yes. That is Vitorio and me. Soon you will hear my friends Elisa and Rudy, too."

"I thought Elisa had gone away." Louis could not understand how Elisa could be gone and yet also be playing the violin on the radio. "And why doesn't your friend Rudy come?"

Charles put a hand on Louis' arm to silence him. He wanted to hear the story. He wanted to feel it in the melody. He could sense the celebration of the music.

"Peer Gynt is a silly fellow. He goes along with the trolls, you see, to a world where cows make the cakes and oxen bring the ale. He wears a tail and swears that a pig is an accomplished musician and cows are as beautiful as women!"

The boys laughed with delight at the vision of it.

Leah continued. "This is the world of the trolls, you see, but they are not funny creatures. No, they are the animal version of man. What a man fears he may become. Can you hear it? Poor Peer joins them, and—"

Again Charles groaned. He raised his finger to trace the Nazi swastika in the air. Louis expressed the thought. "Like Herr Hugel and the Nazis." He giggled. "They think a pig could play the cello, but they will not let you because you are a Jew. Is that right, Aunt Leah?"

Leah did not reply. She frowned and looked away. *Yes. That is true.* She wondered who had taken her place with the orchestra. She wondered who now played her beloved Vitorio. After a moment the music changed to the sad song of Aase's death. Leah heard herself in the melody. She heard the mellow notes of her violoncello, and somehow it made her laugh. "They think they have gotten rid of me," she said to no one. "But there I am. And there is Rudy Dorbransky still playing on the radio. Rudy, whom they killed. Shimon, whom they arrested and . . . *Elisa*!"

Suddenly she could not laugh any more. Indeed the trolls of Peer Gynt had taken over her world. The Troll King had found his kingdom here. Like Peer Gynt, the people of Vienna now wore tails and raised their hands to swear that a cow is a beautiful woman if the Führer declared it so! Was this what little Charles heard in the music? Or had he known it before Leah turned on the radio?

37

Martyr for the Cause

Otto stared at the map in Himmler's Gestapo office in Vienna. Colored pins marked the cities of Paris, Prague, and London.

With a sweep of the hand, the Chief of the Gestapo explained the coming operation to the men he had gathered from the cities of the Reich. Sporer reclined in a chair beside Otto. He seemed at ease and quite confident in the success he was having in the Sudetenland.

"What are a few lives, more or less, when one considers service to our Führer and the Fatherland?" Himmler stood before them now like a meek little schoolmaster teaching his pupils. "What is it that we have learned in Austria and now in Czechoslovakia?" He did not expect an answer from his men. Instead, he answered the question himself. "Every cause needs a martyr! It is, of course, preferable if the man who must die for a cause is better dead than he has been alive. Take, for example our own Horst Wessel, the young fellow who gave us our national anthem. A seedy sort. Son of a prostitute, brawler, drunkard. Yet *loyal*!" Himmler roared the word and rose up on his toes. "Killed in a battle with the leftists, and—" he snapped his fingers—"we had a lovely martyred hero for our own cause!"

The room was blue with smoke. Himmler clasped his hands behind his back and paced the length of the room to-and-fro as though he were lost in deep thought. Sporer nudged Otto slightly and rolled his eyes. He and Otto had already guessed the prearranged conclusion of Himmler's dramatic presentation.

At last Himmler stopped and stared silently above the heads of the two dozen men crowded into the office. "We have heard from our

Führer that perhaps the Reich requires new martyrs to rally the people." He turned to the map. "In these cities such martyrs have already been chosen. They are men in the service of the Fatherland, and yet I assure you, their loyalty is not to the Führer! They care nothing for the Nazi cause! Gestapo surveillance has proven that these men are traitors to us."

A young officer raised his hand slightly. "Then why will we give them the honor of martyrdom, Herr Himmler? Why not simply kill them?"

Himmler smiled slightly and pushed his wire-rimmed glasses up on the bridge of his nose. "The Führer is more clever than that. These traitors are not known as traitors to the German public. Most are from the old Prussian military order. Their deaths will cause a great outcry. Mass riots! Demonstrations! The Führer says this has come to him in a dream! This is our way of getting rid of the Jews who remain in the Reich once and for all! Who in all the world can blame us for hating the Jews if they kill German citizens and political leaders in the capitals of Europe?" He was smiling now at the simplicity of it all.

"But how can the people riot against the Jews for this?" Otto asked.

Himmler laughed at the question. "Here is the beauty of the plan, Herr Wattenbarger!" He gestured for Albert Sporer to take the floor.

Sporer stood erect, his chin high with the honor he felt at being called on. But it could not have been a surprise since he himself had already begun to implement the plan. "In Prague we have recruited a young German Jew to carry out the Führer's plan. Imagine! Using a Jew for our purposes!" Sporer chuckled, and the others in the room also laughed as they tried to guess which of the Führer's unhappy apostates was to be blown up.

"The plan is much the same in London," Sporer continued. "But it is in Paris that we will have our greatest demonstration of the vile Jewish plots! Certain members of our underground there have found a young Jew who wanders the streets of Paris without any sort of papers or work permits whatsoever. He hates those who are of Aryan blood and blames us for all his woes. His family remains in Berlin, but he was sent away to Paris some time ago. The young man carries a deep hatred for a fellow who is associated with the Abwehr at the embassy. It took little effort to convince him that the most sensible demonstration on behalf of the poor, downtrodden Jews of Germany would be for him to walk into the embassy and murder the German officer of military intelligence there!"

A murmur of approval echoed throughout the room. Otto sat in silence with a fixed smile of assent on his face.

"What then?" Sporer smiled. "Simple. The assassination will take place immediately before our usual celebration of May Day. The beer halls will be filled with Storm Troopers. We have only to light the torches for them and open the doors, Otto. Trucks will be waiting to take the men to towns other than their own. For instance, you will take your fellows to Grinsing from Vienna so they will not be recognized." Sporer shrugged. "Once there, they may do as they wish. Stores looted. Synagogues burned to the ground. It is all prearranged. We even have a list of the items to be taken out of the Jewish synagogues before we burn them."

From the back of the room another question was raised. "And the fellow at the German Embassy in Paris? He is *not* one of our own men?"

"A traitor to the core," Sporer assured them. "And yet on the outside, he seems as pure as the snow on Mont Blanc. He will be given a hero's burial, and we will give the people yet another reason to despise the Jews. Another reason to demonstrate their hatred."

Himmler stepped forward now. "Since this Jewish assassin does not have papers of permission to remain in France, we will be able to extradite him easily back to the Reich. Here we will hang him publicly before masses of Hitler Youth. This is the plan and the wish of the Führer. He says that we must initiate the young ones so they will not forget the taste of Jewish blood!"

Himmler looked around the room and smiled briefly. "Heil Hitler."

Throughout the long trip back to Europe, Murphy was torn between his desire to return immediately to Elisa in Prague and the order of his new employer to attend British Prime Minister Chamberlain's press reception in London.

At each stopover across the United States, Murphy had purchased another newspaper reporting that riots by Germans in faraway Czechoslovakia were escalating. Hitler was foaming at the mouth, declaring that the Sudeten Germans must have their right to self-determination. Would England and France honor their treaty commitments if, in fact, Hitler invaded Czech territory? The question remained unanswered. American publications seemed to address the issue out of a detached sense of curiosity. After all, as the latest Craine editorial stated, what did any of this have to do with the United States?

This warm afternoon in London, Murphy sat among the old colleagues in attendance at Chamberlain's press reception. Amanda Taylor smiled and nodded cordially at Murphy as if their midnight encounter had already been forgotten. Murphy grinned and waved his yellow legal pad in reply as the prime minister began to speak.

Chamberlain's owl-like face seemed flushed as he shuffled his papers on the small podium. He looked out over the large group of news correspondents, then down at his prepared statements, then up again, finally clearing his throat nervously. A flurry of questions erupted from the press corps. Chamberlain ignored them all, concentrating on his notes. Tangled sentences about the right of all peoples to determine their own government oozed from his mouth. In the end, Murphy distilled Chamberlain's hour-long rambling into one off-the-record remark: "Personally, in the interest of peace, I favor turning over the Sudetenland to Germany."

"Is that a personal opinion, Mr. Prime Minister?" Amanda Taylor cut in boldly. "Does that mean we will not honor our treaty obligations to the Czechs?"

Good for you, Amanda, Murphy privately cheered as Chamberlain's face reddened.

"In my opinion, neither France nor Russia will honor their treaty commitments to Czechoslovakia if the Germans attack. If that is the case, then Britain will certainly not get herself involved."

Strickland raised his hand but did not wait for acknowledgment before he called out his question. "Does that mean that Czechoslovakia will have to face Germany alone on three sides of her border?"

"It is my contention that this matter can be settled without war. The Germans in the Sudetenland are making certain demands on the government in Prague. Both sides are reasonable, and—"

"Britain will not honor her treaty with the Czechs to protect her territory?"

"Czechoslovakia is a patchwork nation, as you well know. The area of the Sudetenland is populated by two and a half million Germans, and therein lies the problem. Those people are demanding a bit of a say in their own destinies." Chamberlain cleared his throat. "In any case, the Czechs have a well-armed military force of some thirty-five divisions. I doubt that the leader of Germany has forgotten this fact. It seems natural that the German government should express concern for their racial brethren now living across the border in Czech-Sudetenland, however."

Murphy could not decide how much of the question Chamberlain had answered. Did he expect that the Czechs would fight the Germans alone? Did he believe that Hitler would back down in the face of the Czech determination to resist German aggression? If that was the case, then Chamberlain's bottom line was that he didn't really care one way or another as long as Britain was not bloodied in the squabble.

When the press conference ended, more questions had been raised than answered. Chamberlain simply stuffed his notes into a worn attaché case and departed. Reporters were left to draw their own conclusions. The Nazis in Berlin could do likewise. The Czech government had correctly surmised that they were on their own in this matter.

An hour after Chamberlain's comments reached the streets, Hitler summoned his General Staff to a meeting in the war room of his Berlin Chancellery. Triumphantly the Führer explained how the most successful military endeavors began with murder, and then were followed by national chaos. The machinery of a political assassination had already been set in motion in Prague. Soon, Hitler promised, they would all be enjoying their military staff meetings at Hradcany Castle.

Within hours of the disastrous press conference by Chamberlain, Winston Churchill stood before the CBS microphone beside Ed Morrow and drawled his response to British apathy about the situation between the Czechs and the Germans. Churchill's speech had first been delivered at the Free Trade Hall in Manchester before a crowd of several thousand; now, in a lonely studio, he repeated the words with the same drama. Murphy listened to the broadcast in the lobby of the Savoy Hotel.

> *"Here is the practical plan. Britain and France are now united. Together they are an enormous force, moral and physical and one which few would dare to challenge. I should like to see these two countries go to all the smaller states who are menaced, who are going to be devoured one by one by the Nazi tyranny, and say to them bluntly, 'We are not going to help you if you do not help yourselves. Are you prepared to take special service in defense of the Covenant? If you are willing to do so, and prove it by your actions, then we will join together with you and protect each other and the world from another act of aggression.' "*

Murphy applauded loudly, although he was nearly alone in the plush lobby. The midnight desk clerk looked up sharply. "Nobody is listening," he said dourly.

"Oh yes, they are!" Murphy said. "It's suppertime in the States, and everybody in Czechoslovakia has insomnia! They're listening, pal!"

> *"If we could rally even ten well-armed states, all banded together to resist an aggression upon any one of them, then we should be so strong that the immediate danger would be warded off."*

Murphy prayed that such words were indeed having an impact in the right places. He imagined the rage of Hitler at such a plan and hoped that the voice of Winston Churchill pierced even the Chancellery in Berlin.

> *"Is that not far better than being dragged piecemeal into a war when half those who might have been our friends and allies will have been pulled down one by one?"*

The question resounded in Murphy's mind long after the late-hour adjustment to European time dragged him into sleep. Again and again the phrase penetrated his dreams. The hope expressed by Winston Churchill gave Murphy hope, where Chamberlain had offered only the nightmare of appeasement.

"If only they knew, Elisa," he mumbled in his sleep. "They haven't seen Vienna, or they would not throw Prague to the wolves."

Amanda Taylor caught up with Murphy in the plush lobby of London's Savoy Hotel the next afternoon. She patted him cheerfully on the back and linked her arm in his.

"Can I buy you a drink, Johnny?" she asked playfully. "Or have you sworn off the stuff?"

Murphy felt his face redden. He was grateful that Amanda had recovered her dignity enough to speak to him, but her nearness made him uncomfortable. "On the wagon," he replied with a shrug.

"Also canned, I hear." She tugged him toward the bar. "Good for you, I say, getting away from old Craine. Now you can write what you want. A blessing most of us only dream of. And so, my dear boy, I offer you the scoop of the century for your darling American publisher. A trump for old Trump, if you will."

She had barely taken a breath since grabbing his arm, and now with a promise of a story, she had Murphy hooked.

He followed her into the bar, settling in at a quiet corner table in the nearly deserted room. "Okay," he challenged, "what have you got, Amanda?"

She stroked his arm. "First, tell me how you've been. Did you take the wife along to the States, Johnny?" There was a flicker of resentment in her eyes.

Murphy looked down at the starched white tablecloth. She had him there. She wanted to see him squirm, no doubt. "No," he answered quietly. "She's still in Prague."

"With all the nasty riots? Nazis running rampant, and the army mobilizing in the Sudetenland?" She spoke with mock concern. "What sort of place is that to keep a wife?"

"Look, Amanda." Murphy was in no mood for this sort of game. He really was squirming now and the enjoyment on her face was obvious. "We've always been friends, huh? Don't do this."

Her voice hardened. "Do what, Johnny?"

"Play games."

"You're a fine one to talk."

"I was a little smashed," he said by way of apology. "I . . . I'm sorry. The whole thing was my fault. I shouldn't have let it happen."

"Nothing happened." A flash of anger crossed her face. "Absolutely nothing." Now there was a warning in her voice. "Right?"

Dignity was everything to Amanda; Murphy had known that from the first days in Berlin. Now she was telling him that what happened between them did not matter at all as long as he did not discuss it one way or another with the rest of the guys. "Right." Murphy caught her meaning without further need of elaboration. "You know me." He managed a timid smile. "I'm not the type to kiss and tell."

"It wasn't much of a kiss." She relaxed a bit now. "But that's nobody's business either, is it, Johnny? I have a position to maintain here with the other men. It's hard enough, you know."

Murphy felt the same pity for her that he had felt that night in her foyer. "You're a heck of a news reporter, Amanda. You did well in there yesterday with that old owl Chamberlain. Got him while the rest of us were sitting on our hands."

She almost smiled, then brushed her bangs back and resumed her businesslike attitude. The charade was over, and they were simply colleagues once again. "All right then," she said. "I'll pass along a little something from the grapevine." She lowered her voice as a waiter approached and took their orders. Whiskey sour for her and a Coke for Murphy. He had no intention of making himself vulnerable again.

"Why me?" he said a minute later as he sipped his Coke.

"Because you happen to be working for the only sensible syndicate on either side of the Atlantic, Johnny." She frowned and stared into her drink. "Word from the top has come down that we are to take a sharper tone in our reporting of the Czech situation."

"Somebody is telling the London *Times* how to write the news?" Such information seemed terrible but not unbelievable to Murphy.

Amanda nodded. "And not just us. The BBC is getting the same sort of advice."

Murphy raised his eyebrow. *The British Broadcasting Corporation too?*

"Chamberlain doesn't think much of the Czechs," Amanda continued. "He says they're not out of the top drawer. Or even the middle."

That was not news to Murphy. Chamberlain's comments at the conference had made his position clear. "So what's the scoop you lured me in here with?" He was teasing, but for a moment he thought he saw a hint of pain in her eyes. He touched her hand. "So you've scooped us all, and now you can't even use it with the *Times;* is that it?"

His comment seemed to mollify her once again. Dignity restored, she leaned forward and whispered her story in urgent tones. "You remember I told you my husband is a friend of the German foreign minister?"

"Ribbentrop. Yes. They were wine merchants together or something?" Murphy tried to remember the exact details.

Amanda looked over her shoulder and kept her voice low. "Something big is coming in Prague. Something is up; Ribbentrop says it will change everything. He says something is coming that will make even Churchill change his mind about who are the good chaps and who are the bad in this."

"That's it? No details?"

She shrugged. "Sorry, Johnny. That's as far as it goes. But we might try a bit of deduction in the matter."

Murphy frowned. "If there is one thing Nazis are good at, it's turning black into white, and vice versa." He paused, trying to piece it together. He did not have a clue. "What do you think?"

"Another riot, maybe. Then the Nazis can level charges of brutality against the Czechs for squashing it."

"That seems to be working in the Sudetenland."

"Maybe. But that sort of conflict takes time. Hitler is in a hurry, I hear, to get this wrapped up while Chamberlain is dithering on the matter of Czech policy." She stared above Murphy's head as though she could see something written there. "Perhaps an assassination? A political figure. Something to throw the Czech government into chaos."

"I don't know. That didn't work in Austria with Dollfuss."

She smiled, certain that she was onto something. "That's because it was the Nazis who did the killing. If the Communists had killed him, Austria would have fallen much sooner. Maybe Hitler learned something from that little effort."

"Pretty good, Sherlock. But who would be the target?"

"That's not my department. But we should have someone there to report on it if it happens!" She smiled, enjoying the game. Then she waved her hand as if to brush away the nonsense. "It probably isn't anything, Johnny. At least nothing as grim as all that. But here I am, stuck with the

Times and orders from above to take more of a pro-German stance against the Czechs. It's so frustrating. So, there you have it. From the mouth of Ribbentrop to the ears of my ex-husband. One wine merchant to another. The Nazis don't seem very concerned. Quite confident they've got it in the bag. I can't think what it all might mean."

"I guess we'll know when it happens," Murphy replied quietly as he again thought of Elisa. He wished she and her family were out of Czechoslovakia. Out of harm's way, if indeed something was in the wind.

As if reading his mind, Amanda put a hand gently on his arm. "Look," she said, "I know your wife is in Prague. She is a lucky girl to have a man love her like you do. I wonder if she knows." She faltered, then attempted a bright laugh. "Not many men would walk away from me."

"That's for sure," Murphy agreed, but there was a tone in her voice that told him others *had* walked away from her. Her ex-husband, for instance. "A guy would have to be crazy. Like me, huh?"

"Or very much in love." There was no concealing the sadness in her voice now. "I only wish that some nice fellow felt the same about—" she caught herself, suddenly glancing at her watch and pretending that she was in a hurry. "Good heavens! It's almost three o'clock and I haven't even written my story."

"You're one great news reporter, Amanda," Murphy said as she pushed back her chair and gathered her handbag. He knew the words were little comfort to her, even if they were true.

She studied him with curiousity. "And so are you." There was admiration in her voice. "That little piece you published in *Liberty?* You said it all, Johnny. Everything that should have been said about the Nazis and the church, and . . . and you tossed in a good bit more in the bargain."

He shrugged, embarrassed by her praise. After all, they had both covered the war against the church from the beginning. "Well, it was nothing you couldn't say."

She inclined her head slightly. "You're wrong there. A great deal more than I could say." She frowned and looked away. "Like what you told me that night . . . about being *worth* something." She patted him on the shoulder. "Thanks, Johnny." Then she walked quickly from the room—chin high, eyes forward, her dignity intact.

38

Release

Elisa did not realize why she had been brought to the office of Otto Wattenbarger until he pushed a paper across the desk to her.

"Sign it," he said with a patronizing smile.

Through the grime and all the horrid smell of filth that clung to Elisa's body, her blue eyes bore angrily into Otto. He seemed to be enjoying the tattered apparition in front of him. As if he was amused that one so beautiful could be made to suffer simply by placing her in the most miserable of all human conditions.

With some remaining dignity, Elisa picked up the document and glanced over it. It was a release form, stating that she had been well treated, adequately fed, and housed in good conditions. Her needs had been met and she would press no suit nor make any claims otherwise.

"This is all a lie!" she snapped, glaring at Otto.

"Were you beaten?" He raised his eyebrow in surprise at her defiance.

"No."

"Were you fed?"

"Hog swill! The bed had fleas, and there were no toilet facilities."

"Sign it," he commanded, and his smile faded. "Before I lose my patience."

"And what about the poor souls still in that hole? Those women . . . "

Otto crossed his arms. "Would you like to rejoin them?"

Elisa stared at him a moment longer, then averted her eyes to the sunlit window where clouds drifted across the blue sky. She shook her head and her defiance fled. "Why did you have me arrested?"

"I told you," Otto said, tossing a pen onto the paper. "You were suspected."

"Of what? You can't just throw people into jail for nothing."

"Yes, we can. That is the point. Sign, and you may go."

Elisa snatched up the pen and signed the page of lies. "There."

"Good." Otto seemed pleased. "Now, you have plans to travel to Paris?"

"To meet my husband."

"You will not be coming back to Vienna, I assume?"

For a moment, Elisa considered that she would never come to this vile place again. Could she chance that she might be arrested next time for her work as courier? What if a man like Otto found out the truth? Quickly the image of Leah and the two boys came to her mind. "You assume incorrectly, Otto. Just as you have assumed incorrectly about me from the start. Vienna is my home. I have a job with the symphony, in case you have forgotten, and I will be going home within a day or two."

Elisa's clothing was in a paper bag on the wooden chair beside the door. Her copy of *Faust* was still on Otto's desk. Her gaze fell on the red cover of the book. Otto's smile returned. "Ah yes, this is yours; is it not?" He picked it up and began to turn the pages. "Priceless. First edition, isn't it?" He lifted his eyes to hers, then deliberately took the corner of a page and tore it out as she gasped a wordless protest.

"No!" she finally managed to stammer as he wadded up the page and tossed it into the garbage can.

"Now it is no longer priceless," he said. "You may take the volume with you to France, and you will not be arrested for carrying a priceless first-edition copy of *Faust* out of the Reich."

Her eyes narrowed, and for that fleeting second, she thought it might be worth it to fall upon him and scratch his face bloody. "You!" she hissed. "It is hard to believe that you are a son of Karl and Marta!"

The words stung him briefly; then he said stiffly, "I am a true son of my homeland. For homeland, a man will often deny himself many things."

Elisa took the damaged copy of *Faust.* "You sold your soul."

Otto picked up the release form as if he might change his mind and send her back to rot. "It does not pay to be too defiant, Elisa," he warned. "There need not be a reason anymore for men to send others to certain death in some terrible place. No matter how you hate me, you must not show it, or I will send you back there until you learn to nod politely and sign what I say you must sign!" He stepped around the desk and moved close to her. His voice was urgent. "Do you understand me?"

Once again a wave of fear swept through her. She stepped back and nodded.

His jaw was set. He took the book from her and opened it to the torn page. "What you think is truth is sometimes mere illusion. Here I balance on this ledge above the pit of hell, and for the sake of your anger you say things that put yourself in mortal danger!" He grabbed her by the arm. "Tell me then, which of us is the greater fool, Elisa? Is it you? You, who risk everything for the self-gratifying act of defying a Nazi whom you hate? Or is it me? Am I the fool for denying myself? For denying everything I was and am for the sake of some greater good?"

The nearness of Otto and the strong grip of his hand on her arm frightened Elisa. "Let me go," she whispered. "Let me go, Otto."

He held on to her a moment longer, then shoved the book back into her hands. "Be warned. There is no place left in this world for open defiance. They will shoot you for that. Then what good will any of this be?" He ran a hand wearily across his cheek and looked out the window. "Get out of here. Go clean up or you will miss your train to Paris. You must not miss your train to Paris."

Stunned, Elisa picked up the bag and slipped out of the room into the corridor. She stood for a momen, watching as Otto reached into the garbage can and retrieved the torn page from Faust. He opened it and held it to the light of the window; then he struck a match and let the tiny flame devour it. Sensing Elisa's eyes on his back, he turned to face her and smiled strangely as the last corner of the page blackened and curled to ashes.

Elisa could think of nothing now but a clean, hot bath. As Leah fixed her a meager supper of dumplings, Elisa soaked in the tub, drained the dirty water, and filled the tub a second time to scrub until her skin was pink. Only then could she think about food. Only then could she let herself remember Fiori at the bookstore and the fact that she was days later than he had told her to be.

"You should go to bed, Elisa, and rest." Leah's eyes were red-rimmed from grief and concern. Elisa was certain that even after her stay in prison, she did not look as ill as Leah did now. The weeks of unrelenting strain had taken a toll.

Elisa shook her head as she gingerly tasted a spoonful of hot broth. "I can't," she said hoarsely. "I can't stay."

"You are going to Paris?" Leah cried. "Oh, Elisa, you must not come back here! If you go to Paris, don't come back!"

"You're being foolish." Elisa glanced toward the violin case. "I have to get your papers, don't I? Didn't I tell you? I will not abandon you, Leah."

Leah dissolved into tears at the words of assurance.

But despite her outward firmness, Elisa did not feel strong. She remembered clearly the warning of Marian, one of her cell mates, that she would be released soon and then rearrested. To raise hope and then shatter it was the Nazi method of breaking human will.

"But I can't believe that it will be safe for you here," Leah said through her tears.

Charles and Louis peeked around the door of the kitchen. Their eyes betrayed their fear. Aunt Leah was crying. Elisa was going away again. Charles was still not well, and yet they could not fetch a doctor.

Elisa saw them and crooked her finger, inviting them in. She smiled and took Charles by the shoulders. "I am going to Paris to get you travel papers," she said softly. "Would you like to go away from here? Would you like to play in a big grassy field or climb a tree?"

Charles nodded doubtfully.

Louis crowded in. "Can I go too?"

"Yes, you too," Elisa promised. "But first you must be patient just a while longer. You must not be unhappy, but help your Aunt Leah while I am gone."

"And will you get Shimon free too?" Louis asked. He had heard them talking about Shimon.

Elisa glanced at Leah, whose face was a mask of sorrow. "We will do our best. But for now we will think about you two."

Charles tugged Elisa's sleeve and imitated drawing a bow across the strings of a cello. Louis spoke for him. "And will you get Vitorio out of jail also?"

Amazing that the child thought of Leah's cello at a moment like this. It was right somehow. He had no voice for his heart, and neither did Leah since she had sold the cello. *"Yes,"* his eyes seemed to say, *"we must also find some way to rescue Vitorio!"*

It did not matter if Fiori had decided she was too late to be of help. Elisa was going to Paris no matter what. The passport photos were safely concealed beneath the lining of the Guarnerius case. She was familiar with this routine. Enough money in the right places could buy the documents that would free Leah and Charles and Louis!

As she embraced each one in farewell, a wave of fear overwhelmed her. She had been so confident and sure when she had spoken to Leah about the protection of a loving God. But that had been before her arrest, before the stench of the prison cell and the bitterness of her cell mates. That had been before the shrieks of the prison inmates and the shouts of the guards and the warning: *"They will let you go and then arrest you again . . . a way of breaking your will. People will tell them anything to keep from being locked up again."*

The threat echoed hollowly within her. There didn't have to be a reason for arrest any longer in Austria. But there were plenty of reasons why Elisa would be thrown back into the darkest Gestapo hell if they found the passport photos, if they *knew*!

"Hugel just turned the corner," Leah said urgently from the window. "Going to the beer hall. Go *now,* Elisa, and *Grüss Gott*!"

"God bless." Elisa repeated the good-bye and stepped out into the hall. Fear walked beside her, tapping her on the shoulder with each stranger she passed. *Are they watching me? Is he following? Why does he turn and stare at me so?*

Looks that were ordinary to her a week ago now seemed sinister and frightening as she hurried toward Fiori's Bookstore. She wondered if the bookseller would be dismayed to see her, if he would even remember the volume of *Faust* she had carried. What would she tell him about the torn page? How could she explain the fact that she was days late?

The grip of the violin case was wet from perspiration as she walked onto Kartnerstrasse. On this very corner Otto had arrested her. How she wished now that she had greeted him with his silly Heil! Leah had done it with Hugel. Elisa would learn to make the repulsive greeting a natural response. She would play the dreadful game.

The bell above the door jingled as she entered. Two young men in German uniforms looked toward her. Fiori glanced up sharply from his work.

"Heil Hitler," Elisa said pleasantly.

Fiori inclined his head. Was there a smile on his lips? "Heil Hitler," he replied. All very natural, all for the benefit of the soldiers with the swastika armbands.

Fiori focused on his stack of receipts. He seemed genuinely surprised to see Elisa. She saw that much on his face. He caught himself, and the cool look of the merchant greeting a customer returned. "Frau Murphy, isn't it?"

Elisa laid the volume of *Faust* on the desk in front of him. "Three days, you said. I am sorry I am late." There was strain on her face and in her voice.

"Of course." He smiled broadly. "I have the appraisal written up for you. In the back room." He started to rise, but Elisa stopped him with a frown and a shake of her head.

"Since I saw you—" she opened the book to the torn page—"an accident. A page was torn from the book. I don't know how this will affect the value, but . . . "

He did not reply but picked up the volume and hurried into the back room, closing the door behind him.

Elisa felt ill. What if Otto had torn away something of vital importance? She felt somehow that she had failed before she had even begun. She frowned, holding back tears of anger at Otto and at herself for not simply raising her hand in the ridiculous Nazi salute! If some urgent message had been lost because of her stubbornness . . .

Only a minute passed before Fiori emerge again, motioning for her to join him at the counter. He placed the book gently between them. "A volume of great worth," he said slowly. "A pity about the torn page." He took a cigarette paper from his vest pocket and opened it. Printed on the paper was *Le Morthomme #4 Rue de la Villa Paris Friday Evening.*

Elisa tried not to let her eyes betray her emotions as she quickly memorized the address. Fiori tapped tobacco onto the paper and deftly rolled a cigarette. "Do you smoke?" he asked with a half smile.

"No," she answered, barely able to take her eyes off the cigarette as he struck a match and held the flame to it. The address rose up in smoke. Yet it remained vivid in Elisa's mind as she silently rehearsed it again and again. *Friday evening. Only one day, and I must be in Paris. Friday evening. Whatever Otto tore must not have damaged anything. Thank God! Thank God!*

"You might do better to take the book elsewhere. You are going to Paris, you say?"

She replied with a nod as she continued to stare at the glowing tip of the cigarette.

"Good," said Fiori. "With the damage as it is, the value will drop significantly here in Vienna. But perhaps in Paris. In a foreign market you may do well."

She felt as if she were dreaming. This was the moment she had been waiting for since she left Prague! *"Go to Paris,"* Fiori was saying. *"Take the message to Le Morthomme. Leave Vienna tonight."*

"Yes. Then I will take it with me." Her voice was barely visible. "If you think it would be best."

"And will you be coming back to Vienna?" Fiori asked. "Be sure to come by and let me know if it goes well for you, Frau Murphy."

There was no more to be said. She would have to get her ticket. There were things to do for Leah and the children. She managed to smile as Fiori tapped the ashes onto the floor. She wondered if he could see her relief. Perhaps she had not failed after all.

At the Vienna train station, a brass band played a series of military marches as two hundred SS Blackshirts took their places on either side of a long red carpet that stretched across the enormous terminal lobby.

Crowds of excited men and women pushed against the soldiers, jockeying for a clear view.

"What is going on?" Elisa asked a janitor as her stomach contracted with anxiety.

The lean old Austrian rested against his broom and eyed the mob with amusement. "Himmler is leaving today. Came to Vienna to make certain no prison cell is left empty, I hear." He caught himself, aware that what he had just said could land him in one of those cells. He raised his hand laconically. "Heil Hitler," he said, returning to his work.

Elisa had witnessed the madness of Nazi parades in Berlin as Hitler had come and gone from the Chancellery. But she could not comprehend the enthusiasm of the crowd for the head of the Gestapo. Himmler had the manner and bearing of a mild schoolmaster but a heart of ruthless darkness that rivaled that of the Führer himself.

The band began to play the "Horst Wessel" song as a long black limousine pulled to the curb. The soldiers broke into song:

> *"Raise high the flags! Stand rank on rank together.*
> *Storm Troopers march with steady, quiet tread . . ."*

These men were Himmler's own private army. They were the elite among the heartless. Their black garb had made them more than human—or less than human.

The roar of the crowd, the music, and the sight of Himmler striding through his ranks of murderers and thugs made Elisa feel as though she had stumbled onto a scene from the book she carried in her pocket. Demons seemed to circle the building, floating high among the steel rafters on the melody of the Nazi hymn, then swooping low and soaring above the bloodred path where Himmler walked. Could anyone besides Elisa see them?

Did these frantic human souls who shoved and shouted their adoration hear the accusations the fiends shrieked at Elisa? *"Turn now and look at this woman! Tear her violin case to pieces! Rip the pages from her book! She seeks to destroy us! She is one of them! Tear her to pieces! To pieces!"*

Terror returned to her as she saw ten hapless men and women being rounded up by plainclothes policemen and shoved away from the celebration. Of what were they guilty? Were they Jews? Or had they simply failed to raise a hand in salute?

Her heart pounding, Elisa made her way to the nearly deserted ticket counter. The clerk stood on his tiptoes, hoping to catch sight of the man who had established the brutal law of Germany so completely here in Vienna. With trembling hands, Elisa placed her passport and travel documents on the counter as the band began to play *"Deutschland Über Alles."*

The clerk, himself wearing a Nazi armband, clicked his heels and raised his hand high in salute. Elisa did not look. She could not make herself raise her eyes to pay homage to the flag or the monster who stood at attention beneath it. Did the Gestapo watch her? Did they mark her lack of enthusiasm down in a book? And if they asked her why her eyes were lowered, what could she tell them? *I am praying, dear God! Praying for my country! I will tell them I am praying for my homeland!*

The music ended. Himmler raised his voice to speak from the platform beside the train. "And so, already we have made great strides to slash the cancer of Jews and Communists and Socialists from Vienna!"

Great roars of approval echoed in the hall.

"We shall not cease until all the malignancy is cut away and cast into the fire that will purify our race and the Fatherland of all who are sub-human!"

A great wave of applause erupted and then the chant, *"Sieg Heil! Sieg Heil! Sieg Heil!"*

Even the clerk joined the shout.

"And when we are done cleaning our own house, then we shall go on and on! They shall not escape from our grip! The hand of Providence has cast them into our grasp! We shall crush them with the vengeance of all the gods of the German race! It is the mighty goal of this generation to destroy all who are not . . ."

Then the demons hovered close to Elisa. Their voices rasped as one: *"Here is a Jewess—strip her, tear her to pieces! Here is one of the race defilers—she must not live! Kill her, send her head to the Führer! Look! Look here! This one is for your sport!"*

Elisa jumped as a human voice interrupted. "Quite an event, eh, Fräulein? Not every day a man like Himmler comes through! Now, how can I help you, *bitte*?"

Elisa swallowed hard and cleared her throat. "I need a ticket to Paris, please." She extended her American passport. "To Paris."

39

The Goodness of Small Things

It was nearly eight in the evening when Elisa stepped from the train. Inside the vast canopy of the Paris Gare de Lyon station, loudspeakers blared departures and arrivals, and travelers hurried to purchase tickets or catch their trains. Here, unlike Vienna, no uniformed guards or Gestapo agents checked papers. The pleasant, blue-coated Paris police strolled amiably among the noisy confusion, occasionally tipping their hats to pretty women.

A policeman nodded and touched his hand to the brim of his hat as Elisa walked past. She smiled with the sort of relief that could only be felt after comparing the terrified passengers in Vienna to those here in Paris.

The bookstalls along the Seine would be closed now, but Elisa carried in her memory the address of Le Morthomme. Her contacts in Prague had told her that the old bookseller would welcome her no matter what the hour. She had much to tell him since her terrible encounter with Otto Wattenbarger. She could not even be certain that the message she brought with her from Vienna was still intact.

The flat of Le Morthomme was above his tiny, dusty shop in a ragged Left Bank neighborhood filled with artists' studios and coffeehouses. She saw the sign above the shop two blocks before the taxi reached the place. *Rare Books Appraised—Le Morthomme.*

The light in the apartment was still gleaming through a dingy window. Elisa scanned the grimy street and asked the driver to wait. He protested loudly, but she stepped out without paying him, so he had no choice but to obey.

Steps leading to the flat were in a narrow alley that smelled like rotting garbage. From the high windows of the brick building next to the shop, Elisa could clearly hear the sounds of a man and a woman arguing violently over the cost of a new hat for her. Piano music filled the street, competing with the voice of a woman soprano practicing a scale. There was no privacy in the neighborhood of Le Morthomme, and Elisa found herself wondering how many clandestine meetings were held here, which were really a secret to no one. She felt eyes staring down at her.

She climbed the leaning steps, careful not to grasp the railing for fear it would give way. The door opened before she was even halfway up, and a black-and-white cat scampered out, brushing her legs as it ran by.

The door began to close, but Elisa called out, "I am here to see Le Morthomme!"

A heavyset woman with gray hair and a scowling face stepped out on the landing. "You wish to see Le Morthomme, eh?" It was more of a challenge than a question. "Do you not know the time?"

"I have just come from . . . just arrived, and I am leaving again shortly." Elisa paused on the steps and took the volume of *Faust* from her coat pocket. "I have brought this for appraisal."

The woman's cracked lips pressed together as she looked from the book to Elisa's face. "Well?" she asked. "Business is business. Come in, then."

The smells of freshly baked bread, garlic, and cheese permeated the little apartment occupied by Le Morthomme and his stout wife. The furniture was worn but not shabby, a pleasant mix of antiques from several different periods. Dark, shining wood floors were covered with fine Persian carpets of different designs. The dilapidated exterior of the building concealed the pleasant warmth of the small rooms that had housed the couple for over fifty years.

Elisa sat across from the old man as his wife brewed tea and brought a plate of eclairs. Le Morthomme rested his hand on the cover as though he were taking an oath. "I expected you yesterday," he said.

"I was arrested," Elisa admitted with shame in her voice. "I don't know why. It was horrible!" She explained briefly about Otto and their chance meeting on the street as Le Morthomme eyed her with interest. When she finished her story, he gazed down at the book and then back at her face.

"And you say he tore the page from the book and burned it?" He clucked his tongue. "A pity. Such a fine volume here." But his sympathy seemed only to extend to the edition of *Faust,* not to Elisa. "This is your first time as courier, is it not?" he asked.

"Yes, but before that I helped with children, getting them across the border—"

"An amateur effort compared with what you have fallen into, I assure you." He cleared his throat and opened the cover of the book. "And now, let me guess what page it is the Nazi beast tore away." He smiled, showing the gaps in his teeth. "Is the scene called *Trüber Tag?* Dismal Day?"

"Why yes, but how . . . ?"

"A dismal thing it is to be thrown into a prison, as you yourself know." He opened the book to the ragged tear and then, although the page was missing, he began to recite the words that had been written there. "In misery! Despairing! Long lost wretchedly on the earth, and now imprisoned! As a felon locked up in a dungeon with horrible torments, the fair, ill-fated creature!"

"You know the script well," Elisa said, feeling that in his recitation he was telling her something. Trying to tell her . . . what?

"And how did you like prison?" he asked.

"I told you. A ghastly hell!"

"And if you had been there for months or years," he probed, "would you still be so brave as to carry this volume to Le Morthomme?"

"What are you asking me?" Elisa felt cornered.

"I am telling you," Le Morthomme said, "that many will be arrested, tortured for their part in this. Did they beat you?"

"No."

"I wonder why?" He seemed amused now.

"I . . . also wondered." Elisa's voice sounded very small.

"If they had tortured you, would you have told them?"

"Told them what? I don't know anything more than the fact that I was sent here. First to Fiori's—"

"Would you have said the name of Fiori if they had tortured you?" He pressed his hand hard against the open book.

"I don't . . . think so. How can I know?"

"Surely you must have imagined the threat. Did it not cross your mind that you would betray Fiori if they beat you?"

"Why do you ask me this?"

"You must answer in your own heart, Elisa," the old woman said softly.

Le Morthomme sat back and resumed his recitation of the grief of Faust. "'Handed over to evil spirits and judging, unfeeling mankind . . . Hide her growing grief and let her perish helplessly. . . .' "

Elisa drew back, looking from one to the other in confusion. "I don't understand!" she cried. "Please tell me what you are trying to find in me!"

"It is what you must find in yourself," Le Morthomme said quietly.

"You have experienced prison now. You have seen it, and you know for yourself what could happen if you join us."

"If?" She blinked at the volume she had carried so far and with so much fear that first night as she had recrossed the border back into Austria. "But I *have* joined you!"

"Let us say," Le Morthomme replied, "that you have passed a test. You have passed it as other couriers have passed. Although many have failed at their first smell of the stench of a Gestapo jail. Many have cracked before a whip was even mentioned. Others have decided that they do not want to risk their safety and comfort again. Not ever. Not for any reason. There is great terror within those walls; and if you help us, the memory of that terror will never leave you until you are dead, or until you live again in prison without hope of release . . . or until this is finished."

It all became clear to her now. None of it had been real. Otto had challenged her, arrested her, interrogated and bullied her, but for a reason she had never dreamed of. "It was a *test*? All a *game*? And if I had failed?"

He did not answer her question. "You are in France now. You do not have to go back to Vienna. Back to the Reich. If you choose to go—and to help us—then your life may be lost forever in the stink and misery of the hell that has come to earth."

"This means that Otto . . . " She struggled to believe what Le Morthomme told her. "Otto told me that it wasn't as it seemed. He warned me. I thought it was a threat."

"If you take the next step, there will be no changing your mind. To turn back will mean that they will kill you. If you fail us, then we will kill you."

Elisa stared down at her hands. Before her journey into the bowels of the Nazi prison, she had only imagined the danger. Now she was certain of it. Tonight she was being given the choice simply to walk away from it forever. "You will not need to kill me." She nervously worked the wedding band around on her finger. It was no longer a brave game. She, like Otto, would now balance on a ledge over the brink of hell. "Tell me," she said in a choked voice. "Tell me what is required of me?"

"You must join the Nazi Party first. Deny all former associations."

The words were like a slap in the face. "But I . . . "

Le Morthomme raised his hand to silence her. "You *must* turn your back on old friends for the time being. If you survive, one day they may learn the truth. But for now you should expect their hatred."

These words seemed harder to bear than the terrible prison ordeal. The faces of Leah and the two boys rose in her mind. The photos in the violin case almost shouted for her attention. "I have something I must do first," she said. "Please! I need your help. We didn't know who could help us in Vienna. We need papers—identification papers."

Le Morthomme sat back and tugged his ear. "What are you involved in? You are a courier for documents; that is all. What are you talking about?"

Elisa placed the photographs before him on the table. Le Morthomme pressed his lips together in disapproval as he stared at them.

"You were warned not to involve yourself in the smuggling of such items as these."

Elisa was determined. "They are unfinished business. I had to leave them in Vienna the night the Germans marched in."

"Your work as a courier is much more important than individual lives. You were told this in the beginning."

"I cannot leave them there." Elisa closed the violin case and sat down across from the strange little man. "Please. Is there not some way to get them papers? visas? French identification?"

Le Morthomme picked up Leah's photo and then that of Louis. Charles' photo, with his broken face and sad eyes, was left on the table. "Maybe these two. Maybe. But not this one. You cannot do anything for a child such as this."

"Why not?" She leaned forward urgently. "How could they even care about the escape of this little boy?"

"You know the answer to that as well as I do," Le Morthomme challenged her. "Their story was only recently splashed all over the cover of the American magazine *Liberty*. I have a copy down in my shop. You would be amazed how many Americans come in and ask for the new issue each week." Now he smiled and eyed Elisa with interest. "Madame Murphy, it was your husband who wrote the story. It must have been he who smuggled Walter Kronenberger's own words out of Austria. Now you wish to smuggle the children out. Do you think the Nazis will not make the connection sooner or later?"

Elisa blinked at him in astonishment. "Murphy?" she asked in wonder. 'How could he? Where did he . . . ?"

Le Morthomme's mouth twitched in surprise that she did not seem to know this small detail. "John Murphy. Yes. Of the INS, where Kronenberger died. John Murphy is your husband, is he not?"

"My husband." Elisa said the word cautiously. "But he does not know about the children."

"Indeed, he does, madame. And he has reminded the world of them as well. The Nazis will not stand the embarrassment of the survival of these children. I warn you, you cannot help them or we will not be able to use you any further."

"But why?"

"Because you are doomed. As they are. As your friend is. There are other matters now that require everything . . . sacrifice. For the sake of many, some will be lost."

"You are saying you will not help me with the papers?"

"I am saying I cannot. And you must get far away from any situation that might jeopardize what we are doing."

Elisa did not reply. Instead, she took the photos from him and quietly returned them to their hiding place in the violin case. "Then I am afraid that I cannot be a part of this any longer." She looked him squarely in the eyes. "To help many, I must begin with one. One at a time, they must be saved; and in the end, perhaps I will have had a part in the rescue of multitudes. If carrying messages back and forth becomes more important than these children, then I must not be a part of it. A long time ago I had a dream. Children packed onto a train heading to the east, away from freedom. As I watched, it became a train filled with little skeletons."

She looked away at the vividness of the memory before continuing. "I cannot bear the thought that the bones of Charles and Louis and even my dear friend Leah would be among them." She gathered her things. "I will leave you now. Tell whoever you must that I am not strong enough for that. I cannot work for you. Tell whoever is in charge that I failed in this matter."

"You are being very shortsighted, madame." Le Morthomme clucked his tongue in disapproval. "But if you feel so strongly, you are a danger to us. It seems that already you have forgotten the lesson of Otto Wattenbarger. He has denied even his own mother and father. He has pretended since the first to take the side of evil. At times he has even acted the part fully. There is courage in that as well."

Elisa drew her breath in slowly. "I do not have that sort of courage. I cannot pretend to be what I am not."

"If you cannot pretend, then you are among the dead as well. I am sorry. That is the way of life now, Elisa. You must learn to pretend. You must learn to turn your back on small things like love and friendship for the sake of the greater good."

"Without the goodness of small things, there is no greater good, Le Morthomme. That is where we part company."

The Dead Man had told her what duty was required of her, and she could not fulfill it. She had endured arrest and interrogation and terror, but she had failed the test in the end because she could not fail her friend. Love had made her a fool. Love had made her dangerous to the narrow world of espionage.

"You would have been ideal," Le Morthomme said after he sent his wife to fetch the issue of *Liberty* magazine containing Murphy's story. "It is a shame we must part company here."

"I wish you . . . I pray for your success, Le Morthomme, but I cannot forsake my little ones for the sake of your political intrigue. I . . . I am sorry that I so totally misjudged Otto."

Le Morthomme chuckled. "Don't be sorry! It is meant that he be misjudged. This means he is quite good in his role, yes?" The smile faded as quickly as it had come. "And now I wish you well with what you are called to do. If we fail and Hitler succeeds, there will be no hope or light left at all except that which remembers the goodness of small acts of kindness. Already those acts may cost you your life. If you are caught with this"—he took the magazine from his breathless wife as she emerged at the top of the stairs—"then I assure you, you will not survive either. I regret the thought of such beauty being destroyed. I hear the Nazis enjoy their work thoroughly."

Elisa looked at the magazine. The cover had a painting of two small boys in ragged overalls fishing beside a creek. It looked so American. So carefree. So much like she imagined Murphy might have been as a child. The cover art did not seem to match the line at the bottom announcing the horror of Nazi threats against one man and his children.

For an instant she wanted to beg Le Morthomme again to help her with the identity papers. What other hope did she have? But she stopped herself and moved toward the door. Her courage faltered for an instant; she wished Murphy were with her, as he had been with her the night her father had been pulled off the train from Berlin. Murphy would tell her what he thought. He would know what to do.

She held the magazine close to her. "Thank you."

"Get rid of that before you reach the border of the Reich," Le Morthomme warned. "You will be thrown into a concentration camp the minute they see that; I assure you!"

Elisa nodded, then descended the steps into the stench of the alley. She was alone again. She must think what to do. How to get the travel papers. Where to take Leah and the boys.

Her mind was spinning with confusion. Above her, the opera singer continued to practice her off-key aria. The cat screeched and clattered over a heap of garbage as Elisa passed. She clung to the magazine as if it were a letter from Murphy—as if it were Murphy himself. If only he were here; he would know what to do!

40

Rendezvous

The taxi driver was as surly from the long wait as Elisa was depressed from disappointment. She had carried the passport photos all the way to Paris for no reason, it seemed.

The Eiffel Tower, awash with light, pointed like a finger toward the sky. *What am I to do now, God?* she silently prayed. *Whom can I turn to?*

Clearly the thought seemed to come to her. She remembered the voice of Thomas! Paris! *"The café! Call me there. Ask for Thomas. Do not use my last name. The owner is a friend of mine."*

Ahead of the taxi was the ornate facade of the Gare de Lyon station. Elisa glimpsed the huge face of the clock. There was still nearly an hour and a half before her train was to leave for Vienna. Surely that was time enough!

She paid the driver and hurried into the packed building. Clutching the copy of *Liberty Magazine* in one hand and the violin case containing the photos in the other, she made her way toward the glass telephone booths near the Train Bleu Restaurant. There were half a dozen callers in front of her. The wait seemed interminable as one by one, men and women entered the booth and placed their calls through the slow and inept Paris exchange.

Elisa closed her eyes and prayed. Prayed that Thomas would be there. Prayed that he would be willing to help her!

Loudspeakers echoed departures and arrivals. Couples hurried out of the elegant Train Bleu. The line moved forward too slowly. But after twenty minutes Elisa finally stepped into the booth and looked up the number of the café. *Let him be there! Oh, God, please let him be there,* she prayed as the phone on the other end rang harshly.

"Café de Triumph." The man's voice sounded gruff and impatient.

Elisa could hear the noisy buzz of customers behind him. "I am calling for Thomas!" Elisa was shouting over the din that threatened to drown out her words.

There was a long pause. "Thomas, you say?"

"Yes. Thomas—" She almost said his last name but then remembered the warning he had given her. "You are a friend of his?"

"Yes, madame." The words grew more gentle. "But he is not here tonight."

"But I must talk with him! I must see him."

"See him, madame . . . " He paused and turned to shush the laughter of a woman behind him. "Who is this?"

"Tell him Elisa."

An angry man tapped impatiently on the glass of the booth.

"Elisa!" The café owner knew her name.

"Yes! Tell him I am leaving on the express for Vienna, that I will meet him in the Train Bleu Restaurant. Tell him please that I must see him!"

"*Oui,* mademoiselle, I will send Henri for him this instant! Do not leave! Train Bleu at Gare de Lyon!"

As she hung up, the angry man behind Elisa banged his fist against the glass once again. She did not move for a moment but stood holding the receiver even as the line clicked dead. Thomas was coming; he could help her! He would not let her down this time as he had when her father had been arrested. Didn't he say he loved her still? Hadn't he promised to give up everything for her?

"Get out of the booth! I have an urgent call to make and my train is leaving in moments! You think you are the only one who needs to use the telephone? Get out of there!"

Elisa opened the door, barely feeling the shove as the man pushed past her.

She stood blinking at the huge hall, half expecting Thomas to enter through the main doors at that very instant.

Elisa adjusted the grip of the violin case and then walked slowly toward the women's lavatory. In an empty stall, she opened the case and carefully extracted the envelope containing the photos from beneath the hiding place in the lining. *Thomas will come! I will give him the photographs, and somehow he will buy the forged documents!*

Leaving the lavatory, she walked against the flow of hurried passengers and made her way toward the crowded restaurant. The maitre d' smiled with appreciation and bowed slightly as the beautiful young woman entered.

"I am waiting for someone,"Elisa said distractedly. "Could you seat me near the front?"

"Mademoiselle!" He bowed again and led her to a small table near the pastry carts. She did not look at him as he placed a menu in front of her. Her eyes remained riveted to the entrance of the restaurant. *Thomas will come! He will help us!*

Throughout the long night, Le Morthomme labored to decipher the code locked within the pages of the book Elisa had brought. The bright light of the desk lamp strained his eyes as he found one letter at a time and wrote the German word to be translated first to French and then into English.

There was danger here for young von Kleistmann. The Dead Man had gotten that far. For weeks he had suspected as much, watching the tall German officer as he strode away from the bookstall. Yes, Thomas von Kleistmann's life was worth little tonight. Le Morthomme's suspicions had been right. Thomas had been followed. He had been marked for assassination.

But there was also much more here. Thomas was a small, almost insignificant piece of the puzzle. Something . . . *something!*

He wiped his eyes with the back of his hand and sipped the tea his wife brought him. No doubt he would be at this process all night. Thomas was not to be the only victim, and the end of all of it was to be the end of nations and peoples.

The Dead Man felt justified in having sent the lovely young courier away without forged papers. As each new word was revealed to him, he felt certain that the fate of two small boys was a matter of little importance compared to what he now extracted from the pages letter by letter.

Traffic slowed to a crawl as the clock tower of the Gare de Lyon came into view.

Thomas leaned forward, straining to see beneath the arch where travelers passed in and out of the station. *Is that Elisa there among them? waiting for me?*

"Do you know," he asked the driver, "when the Orient Express leaves?"

The driver cleared his throat and stuck out his lower lip as he peered out the window at the face of the clock. "If you wish to catch the Express, monsieur, you will not make it in time. Not with traffic as it is."

Thomas did not answer. Already he had his wallet in his hands. He tore a handful of bills out and threw them onto the front seat. He didn't know how much—it did not matter. He jumped from the taxi as the astonished driver shouted his thanks. Horns blared as Thomas dodged through the creeping automobiles.

"Crazy man! You want to be killed?"

The sidewalk cafés on both sides of the street leading to the station were packed with after-theatre crowds. Thomas did not take his eyes from the clock face as he ran through the throngs of people. Women gaped and men shouted angrily as he slammed through them. *Elisa is in the Gare de Lyon. Elisa, in Paris!* Nothing else mattered. He did not see the startled faces or hear the shouts. The hands of the giant clock above the station moved, and Thomas ran harder. She was there, somewhere beneath the gilded dome of the vast station.

The lights of a thousand cars threatened him as he stepped from the curb. Was he being followed? At this moment it did not matter. Elisa's train was leaving. He must stop her, keep her here in Paris. The rest did not matter. The world did not matter. Canaris and Oster. England. The Reich might tumble into hell, but Elisa was here in Paris looking for *him!*

The hands of the clock clicked forward. . . .

Elisa stood on tiptoes on the platform beside the waiting train. She searched the teeming throngs in the great echoing hall and beyond. Thomas was not coming.

"All aboard! Last call!" the conductor shouted. The other passengers were in place in their compartments. The Express would not wait. The conductor touched her elbow. "He is not coming, madame," he said sympathetically. The French were always sympathetic in matters of the heart. "Stopped by the theatre traffic, no doubt." He guided her to the open door of the compartment. She stepped up and took a seat among four other travelers.

Through the window Elisa scanned the heads of the crowd in the lobby. She would spot Thomas easily; if he was there, she would see him. The conductor was right, although he had mistaken her anxiety for love.

The envelope with the photographs of the children had grown damp from the perspiration of her hands. Thomas was not coming. He could not help her. He *would* have, she believed, if only she could have seen him and looked into his eyes. He would have helped her for the sake of love.

She closed her eyes, feeling very much alone. She had promised the children: *"If only you will be patient a little while longer . . ."* Now she must return to Vienna without travel documents for them.

Thomas slammed into a porter, knocking luggage everywhere. Angry curses followed him as he passed beneath the arches of the station.

Across the enormous hall, the whistle of the Express shrieked its warning.

"Elisa!" Thomas shouted, but his voice was lost to the shrill cry of the train whistle. All along the crowded platform friends and lovers stepped back as the compartment doors slammed shut in obedience to the authority of the timetable. Conversations continued through open windows. Words of farewell and final embraces took on a tearful urgency.

Thomas ran harder across the marble floors, dodging around the mob that blocked him from her. He searched the open windows of the compartments. "Elisa!"

She was there; he saw her profile, eyes cast downward. "Look up! I am here!" Still only halfway across the hall, he shouted her name again as the shrill whistle sounded one last time. *Why does she not look up?*

The conductor signaled. Passengers leaned out the windows for one last touch, and fingertips reached up from the platform. Once more the whistle sounded as Thomas reached the edge of the platform a dozen cars behind Elisa's. "Elisa!" he cried again. But the train slowly glided away to slip into the night.

Herschel Grynspan took a certain pride in his work for Le Morthomme. The old man at first had allowed him to work only as a porter for customers too weak or weary to carry away their purchases. But now the bookseller was teaching Herschel something about the books he carried. Occasionally he was given the duty of tending the tables where the less valuable books were stacked. After a short time listening to the banter of Le Morthomme, Herschel was able to talk a bit about bindings and value himself.

"You are just a parrot." The Dead Man laughed, but Herschel could sense a certain pride in the old man's voice.

Every morning Herschel stacked a few francs beside his uncle's breakfast plate before he slipped out into the still-dark streets of Paris. He wrote his parents of his work and saved his extra cash for them, hoping to find a way to help them as they struggled to survive the boycotts against Jews in Berlin.

Twice Le Morthomme had saved Herschel from deportation when he had been asked to show his work permit. "He works for me," the Dead Man had explained. "I permit him to work for me." A few francs had exchanged hands, and perhaps a valuable volume had been tucked into the pocket of the French inspector. "You are a strong boy," the Dead Man explained to Herschel. "My customers like you. Even the Nazis like you."

"They don't know that I am Jewish."

"And are you fool enough to tell them?" The Dead Man smiled.

Customers might have liked Herschel, but there were some for whom he had no affection. Germans came in every size and variety. Many were refugees like he was, but many others were German officials who were stationed in Paris, or perhaps passing through the city just long enough to visit the cabarets and pick up illegal books at the famous book market.

The regular customers seemed preoccupied and often arrogant, Herschel thought. There was one in particular who seemed never to notice Herschel, although Herschel recognized him almost immediately.

Even in Berlin, when he had worked with his father at Lindheim's Department Store, Herschel had hated the self-assured young Wehrmacht officer who had stolen Elisa's heart so completely. Theo Lindheim had brought the man into the alterations department and had introduced him as "a member of the family." Thomas von Kleistmann had stood in stony silence during his fittings. It was quite obvious that the man felt himself above all Jews, whether they were only tailors or men like Herr Lindheim himself. In the end this proud, strutting Aryan had even placed himself above Elisa. Everyone knew it. Everyone but Elisa had known that von Kleistmann was a spiritual son of Hitler.

Often von Kleistmann came into the bookstall of Le Morthomme, and when he came, Herschel turned away and silently hated him for what he was and what he had been in Berlin. He was head and shoulders taller than Herschel, handsome and strong and everything that reminded Herschel of the terror of Germany. Sometimes he wondered if the German officer could sense the hatred that radiated from Herschel's body. But von Kleistmann seemed oblivious to everything but the books Le Morthomme chose for him to purchase and read. Had he ever seen Herschel in Berlin? Or had he always looked over the top of the young man's head as he did now?

Only Le Morthomme noticed the seething flush on Herschel's cheeks time after time. At last he asked the young man, "What has this German ever done to you?"

"He is an anti-Semite." Herschel did not look up from the stacks.

"So? Are you advertising that you're a Jew today? Has he kicked your teeth in?"

"Not him—men like him. They attacked my father in Berlin last year. Beasts like this man let the Gestapo drag away innocent—"

"He is a good, paying customer."

"He doesn't pay enough. I would like to make him pay!"

"He has never even spoken to you."

"Nor would he if he noticed me."

Le Morthomme smiled. "I have a package for him. You must carry it to the German Embassy for me."

"The embassy?"

"He works there."

"I cannot go to that place! I am a Jew!"

"You are in France. Here you work for the Dead Man. Everyone who knows me—and that is everyone—leaves my help alone. So, take this package to the German Embassy. Ask for Thomas von Kleistmann. You speak good German. My other boys speak only French and English. You must go quickly for me, Herschel, or I will lose a customer."

Like a bell, the alarm sounded inside Herschel's mind at the words of Le Morthomme. *Yes! The old man will still lose a customer,* he thought as he ran quickly to his garret room. Had there been some divine instruction in the way Le Morthomme had expressed himself?

Herschel charged up the leaning stairs and flung open the door of the hot, stuffy room. He pulled back the mattress, revealing the precious gun he had kept just for this moment. Here was his opportunity! What did it matter if he was a few days early? The German would die just the same! The statement of Herschel's grief and frustration would be made!

He held the weapon gently in his hand. "For the sake of Zion I will kill those who kill my people." He was practicing the statement he would give when the bulbs of press cameras popped and reporters shouted their questions: "Why? Why did you kill Thomas von Kleistmann? Tell us your political motivation for such a deed!"

Herschel slipped the gun into his pocket. He would answer them all. His shot would be a reply to every Nazi boot that had smashed the face of a German Jew!

"They will hear me," he vowed as he retraced his steps, descending to the subway that would take him to the front entrance of the German Embassy. Only when he stood before the wrought-iron arch, stammering that he was a delivery boy for Le Morthomme, did he notice that he was trembling. Fear gripped him. The power of the swastika seemed to tear through him like a saw blade, slicing into his courage. He looked at the checkerboard tiles on the floor of the foyer and slipped his hand into his coat. The gun he felt there was now his only hope.

41

Vitorio's Revenge

Le Morthomme had meant for his gift of *Liberty Magazine* to frighten Elisa with the certain knowledge that little Charles and Louis Kronenberger would never be allowed to pass alive beyond the borders of the Reich.

As the train moved slowly up the mountain passes toward the border of Austria, Elisa reread the story Murphy had written. She was proud of his words; his final statement of truth found its way deeply into her heart. Far from making her afraid, the story renewed her determination that something must be done. She was returning to Vienna without the precious papers she had counted on; there should have been no glimmer of hope left in her. But then she read Murphy's words once again:

> *It began as only a crack in the fortress of Right. Men looked away as other men decided who was worthy of bearing children. They looked away as the state decided first which child was worthy of life, and then who among the elderly was still fit to live and consume the food of the nation. From there it was merely a small step to deciding that those with a deformity must not live. Those who were mentally ill were raked into the ash heap as well. Then the small crack widened into a great chasm as the state declared that those of a certain racial heritage, religion, political persuasion, skin color, eye color, and on and on, were not worthy to live among the great Germanic "Christian" race.*
>
> *In the end, even the One who said, "Suffer the little children to come unto Me" has been driven from the great churches of Germany.*

Jesus Christ, Himself a Jew, has been hounded from His rightful place. Cathedrals have torn the cross from their altars. The Bible now is openly burned in bonfires that celebrate the return of the German pantheon of pagan gods. Mein Kampf is declared the holiest book of all generations.

Christ, who healed the sick and embraced the weak of His society is crucified daily because of His command to love. In Germany today, the strong are praised and extolled, and the weak are despised and rejected.

The Nazi Reich, which began as one small crack in the fortress, is now a yawning gulf into which the innocent, like Jesus Christ before them, are being flung. The back of the true Church has been broken. It is not enough any longer for one man or even a dozen to protest the wholesale slaughter of the infants yet in the womb. Their voices are lost forever in the prisons that now hold more true believers than the empty churches.

It is too late for them. Too late for Walter Kronenberger and his wife and sons. As a reporter who has watched the walls between right and wrong crumble more every day, I am certain that those who cried out a warning did so too timidly, and too late.

As I return to my homeland, I see the same horrible signs beginning here. I tremble for my own country. For the children. For the church. For the simple men and women who wish only to live in freedom.

Permitting the state to decide who is "worthy" of life opens the floodgates of destruction. A government that permits, encourages, and ultimately requires the death of those deemed "unfit" will find it easier to eliminate other "undesirables" as well. And who is to say what physical, racial, mental, or religious attributes may one day determine "worthiness"?

God alone has the right to decide the worth of human life. I pray that it is not too late for us already!

Again and again Elisa read over the words until their meaning in English became clear in her mind. All this time she had not thought that John Murphy was anything more than a newsman! She had never guessed that beyond his easygoing exterior he had the depth to grasp the entire tragedy so completely.

Elisa looked out over the snowcapped peaks of the mountains where the warmth of the winds had begun to thaw the ice. She smiled as she considered how her own icy perceptions about Murphy had begun to thaw. She certainly had not known what she was doing, but somehow she had married a man who prayed with his pen, just as she prayed with her violin!

If ever she saw him again, she decided now, she would look him in the eye and tell him that she had read his heart in his words, that his words had given her courage.

Yes, it was too late for Walter Kronenberger, she thought. But maybe there was still hope for his sons!

Murphy had a story to write. A deadline to meet. But it wasn't getting done. One line followed another, stopping midway through as the typewriter carriage clanged. Then the image of Elisa came to him so strong that he had to close his eyes and catch his breath before he tried again.

He could not understand why her face and the gentleness of her voice became so clear at that moment. It irritated him that the thought of her smile and the sweetness of her skin intruded on his concentration. He had important stuff to do. The whole world was teetering on the edge of disaster, and all Murphy could think about was a woman!

He tore the page out of the carriage and inserted another clean sheet to try once more.

This morning Prime Minister Neville Chamberlain publicly denied British responsibility in the matter of . . . Murphy stopped again, his index fingers poised over the keys of the typewriter. He closed his eyes to shut out Elisa, but she was still there before him, more vivid than ever. Murphy ripped the page out and crumpled it into an untidy ball, then flung it angrily to the floor.

There was something else he had to write first or he would never make his deadline.

Dearest Elisa,

I am supposed to be writing a story about the situation in Czechoslovakia, but all I can think about is a certain woman in Prague. Yesterday in the lobby of the Savoy I heard a recording of Vivaldi's "Four Seasons." You see how much I have learned from you, darling? I can even spell Vivaldi now and recognize a violin!

Murphy paused and smiled, feeling instantly better. He had wanted to write her for weeks. Wanted to talk to her, to tell her . . . everything. This was going to be a long letter, he knew. Maybe he would miss his deadline anyway. But this was long overdue. If he had not dared to tell her his feelings in person a year ago, he should at least have written her.

Maybe she had not seen his heart shining through his eyes when he looked at her. But there was more to love than tender looks. Suddenly Murphy wanted her to *know* him! He wanted her to hear his heart the way he had heard hers when she played the violin.

> *When I heard the music of spring, I found that I had closed my eyes so I could imagine you there. Three other newsmen were sitting with me, and they thought I had dozed off. But I was wide awake and dreaming of you.*

There was more to loving than sweet words, too, Murphy knew. He longed to share with her all he was feeling at this instant of counterpoint when the world was torn between rage and apathy. Both lines of the melody lead to destruction . . . the annihilation of men like Walter Kronenberger and the end of millions of children like his sons. He wanted to tell Elisa what he had come to believe—that hatred was the bludgeon that beat innocence to a bloody death, but apathy was its partner in crime! Apathy allowed evil to overpower goodness!

Yes. Murphy wanted to tell her that, although he was certain she already knew. She was someone who really cared. Perhaps that was why he had come to love her so fiercely. There was nothing about her that he could ignore—not a hint of apathy in his passion to know her mind, or his longing to lose himself in the sweetness of her embrace.

> *I should be working, but all I can think about is you. Like the music of Vivaldi, you fill all the seasons of my thoughts. There is no moment when you are not with me. There has not been an hour since I saw you last that I have not turned around in a crowd and somehow hoped that you were there.*

An hour passed, and then two. The deadline slipped away and still Murphy sat at the typewriter filling page after page with his hopes and fears. For the world. For himself. For Elisa—and for the children she might someday bear.

At least twenty messages had been sent to Thomas through the bookstall of Le Morthomme. But this was the first time that the Dead Man had ever sent a courier to the German Embassy.

Thomas buttoned his tunic as he descended the steps to the lobby, where the surly boy waited with a paper-wrapped volume clutched in his sweating hands. Something in the look of this small, dark-eyed youth made Thomas uneasy. He had seen him countless times at the bookstall, but now, in the foyer of the embassy, his face seemed almost distorted with a silent hatred. For an instant the memory of another face, much younger, came to mind. *Berlin?* Thomas had always assumed that Le Morthomme's helper was French.

"I am von Kleistmann," Thomas said curtly. "You have a package for me?"

The boy nodded, only once. "From Le Morthomme," he said in French. His brooding eyes did not leave von Kleistmann's face.

"You speak German, don't you?" Thomas snapped.

The boy nodded, again only once, in reply.

Thomas glared at him, certain now that he had seen him in Berlin. "You are not French," Thomas said. The words were an accusation.

"No. Not French," the boy responded, now in the hard accent of a Berliner.

For a long moment, Thomas appraised him, trying to remember *where* in Berlin. . . . "I thought not. I have seen you before."

"I am always at the bookstall of Le Morthomme," the boy answered with an edge to his voice. Then he extended his hand in expectation of a tip. "I have come far, Herr von Kleistmann. It is customary . . . "

It didn't matter who the young man was, Thomas decided. If Le Morthomme felt that information was urgent enough to deliver to the German Embassy itself, then Thomas would waste no more time in conversation with this sullen youth. He flipped him a coin, then turned sharply on his heels and quickly climbed the stairway toward his quarters.

As Elisa stepped from the train beneath the immense red banner of the Reich, the great hall of the Vienna Bahnhof was subdued and nearly deserted. Perhaps everyone going anywhere had already left. A few uniformed soldiers sat around on the long polished wooden benches, but there were no bands to bid them farewell from Vienna. There was no red carpet. No screaming mobs. Only somber silence and the weary hissing of the train behind her as she made her way toward the arched portal that led to the sunlight.

Elisa had failed to bring the papers that would have allowed two small boys and Leah to leave this place. She felt the failure of her promise now as she made her way to the streetcar. What would she say to Louis and Charles? How could she explain that all their weeks of waiting had brought them no nearer to escape even as the danger to them grew? She regretted her promise now. She embraced the violin case where their passport photos were still hidden. Perhaps she could take them to

Czechoslovakia and have documents made, although now papers from Prague were receiving intense scrutiny by the Gestapo.

She frowned as the green-and-white streetcar clicked toward her. It was nearly vacant. A few intrepid passengers who had followed her from the building now climbed on behind her.

Wordlessly she paid her fare and took a seat on the shady side of the car. She laid her violin case on the seat as protection from anyone who might wish to sit beside her. She had to think what she must do now. She could not count on any help from anyone.

Leaning her hand against the glass, she watched as her beloved Vienna slipped past. Never had she imagined that she would long to leave this place filled with so many happy memories. But all that was over now, just as Murphy had warned her it would be. There was nothing left to stay for. If it had not been for her friends and now the children, she would never have come back. The Vienna of her joy was dead. The Vienna of bright music and carefree times had vanished in one night. The melody was locked away.

Elisa looked down at her violin case. Suddenly she remembered another promise she had made, one much simpler to fulfill. *Yes! I will get Vitorio out of jail,* she thought as the streetcar chugged to a stop near the little shop of the pawnbroker who had cheated Leah.

Perhaps Elisa would not have to return to the flat in total defeat! The thought of it made her almost happy as she hurried toward the shop Leah had told her about. Sunlight glinted on the window, and through the glass Elisa saw a jumbled mix of every sort of musical instrument on display. Violins, cornets, oboes, trumpets, a bassoon, and two violas—and there, in the corner of the display, stood the dusty cello! Vitorio, the fine Pedronelli violoncello that had been so lovingly cared for by Leah, was now baking in the sunlight behind the glass of a pawnshop! Inwardly Elisa cringed; then she exulted in the fact that it had not been sold. That, at least, was something!

Pushing open the shop door, she entered a small room that was more cluttered and dusty than the display window. The shopkeeper looked exactly as Leah had described him. From bald pate to tiny Hitler mustache, the man seemed every inch the arrogant Nazi. Today he wore the armband. He looked up and smiled at the sight of the lovely blond Aryan woman who had entered his shop.

Elisa smiled pleasantly and raised her hand. "Heil Hitler."

"Heil Hitler!" His greeting made his smile even wider. She had not attempted to soften the hardness of her old Berlin accent. He took her as a true woman of the Fatherland. He bowed curtly and rubbed his bald head nervously. "How may I help you this morning?"

"I am looking," Elisa said, glancing toward the shopwindow, "for some sort of instrument to bring to my nephew as a gift. I am a musician myself. I came here to play for Himmler's visit and . . . well, I wish to bring back an instrument from Vienna, where all the greatest musicians have lived!"

"A delightful idea! Delightful!" He hurried out from behind his counter. Brushing his hands on his apron, he shuffled toward the window where a green velvet curtain served as the backdrop for his display. "I have all kinds—everything! All the Jews in Vienna have been trying to sell their junk in here, but I only buy the best! Just the best!"

Steal the best, you mean. Elisa tried to curb her thoughts and continued to smile, nodding her head. "Well, I'm not interested in anything of great quality! I could buy a fine instrument easily. I know the difference. But this is for a child. He is quite clumsy, and no doubt whatever I get him will simply be a curiosity."

The shopkeeper climbed on a box and leaned into the window to pull out a violin and a flute. "Something small, like this, perhaps?"

"Not a flute. I am a string player myself." She let her eyes linger on the violin he held up. It was indeed a fine old instrument, and Elisa could not help but wonder how many others besides Leah had been cheated. "A lovely example!" She reached for the violin. "Truly a beautiful instrument!" she cried, setting down her own case and getting out her bow.

"I purchased it from a little Jewish fellow! He pretended to be German, but I can spot them! I know a Jew when I see one! Sneaky eyes." He pointed to his eyes and nodded. "I paid dearly for that little gem; indeed, I did!"

"No doubt." Elisa raised the instrument and tuned it; then she began to play as if she stood on the stage of the concert hall. The music of Beethoven's spring violin sonata filled the shop as she closed her eyes and swayed with the melody. *How the seller must have grieved to part with such an instrument!* Elisa thought. She stopped midway through and looked up to see an expression of glee on the shopkeeper's face. Whatever he had paid for it, he was now convinced that he had acquired a priceless treasure.

"Beautiful tone!" He clapped his hands together. "And you play very well, Fräulein," he added.

Elisa could see that he was mentally calculating how much he could charge her for such an instrument. "Indeed," she said with awe, "you have a treasure in this instrument! Whatever you paid for it, I am certain that you are the one who got the bargain." She placed it respectfully on the counter. "How much?"

He raised his chin slightly and gazed soulfully at the violin. "I myself paid one thousand shillings for it."

"A bargain," Elisa whispered. "You have something here of such value!" Then she added, "Do you have a case?"

"A case? Why, certainly. A case."

"You should leave it in its case. Out of the sun and dust, or it may warp. It will certainly be ruined."

"Yes, yes, yes!" He appeared instantly worried. "Of course." He did not want to lose the thread of the conversation. "You were asking how much?"

"Yes, I was." She nodded. "But if you paid one thousand, I am certain that your price is beyond what I can afford. I am only a poor musician myself."

He frowned and stuck out his lower lip, judging that he had started too high in the negotiations. "Well, then, perhaps another violin?"

"That would be nice."

He placed the second instrument in her hands. It had a high table like a Stradivarius but was an obvious copy. "Beautiful!" Elisa said with mock astonishment. "You truly have the finest instruments anywhere. That is what I was told: *The best for less!*" She read the words off a placard above the door.

"My motto, Fräulein," he agreed proudly.

As Elisa tuned the instrument, she mentally remarked that the "best for less" was always at someone else's expense. She raised the instrument and began to play from the Dvorák American composition. This violin was not nearly as fine as the first, but Elisa was certain that the little man could not tell the difference. When she was finished, she cradled the instrument gently and said with admiration, "Better even than the first, don't you think?"

"Never have I heard such a tone!" he agreed. "Such beauty!" He pursed his lips. "I only paid eight hundred for this one. I could let you have it for—"

"You only paid eight hundred!" she gasped. "Dear sir, if I did not already own a violin and if I had the money, I would buy this for two thousand for myself! What an instrument! What glory!"

He seemed pleased but puzzled. "Really?" he mumbled. "This I purchased from a student, who—" He caught himself, not willing to reveal that he had lied.

"You must not let this one go for less than that," she advised. "You would be cheating yourself. What an instrument!" Then she plucked a string and leaned close to confide, "But you must not leave it in the sun in a shopwindow. It will warp and be of no use to anyone except to carry home as a souvenir!"

"Indeed! Well, I have never dealt with instruments much before this sudden rush of Jews to sell everything." He had not even heard himself reveal his fraud—he was not really an expert on instruments, after all.

"Well, I never could afford something this fine. I would not dare to give such an instrument to a child like Gus. Perhaps something more sturdy. Like a viola?"

The shopkeeper, overwhelmed by his good fortune, pulled out both violas on display. Elisa played them easily, careful to choose music that was uncomplicated but beautiful. Each instrument sounded little more than adequate, but by the time she finished, the shopkeeper was certain that he was in possession of two of the lost Stradivarius violas! "I am fortunate indeed! I am blessed by the heavens! You will not believe what I paid for these!"

"Oh, yes, I would believe it. But you must not sell them for anything less than three thousand each, or you will be cheating yourself!"

"Indeed! Three thousand!" The man was ecstatic. "I won't; I promise. Perhaps I should take them to the Musikverein. Someone there might wish to purchase such instruments."

"Without a doubt," Elisa replied. "But you must take them out of the window as well. They will be of no value to anyone at all except as a child's toy!"

He laid them reverently on the counter beside the others. He was thrilled with the discovery of this hidden treasure, not to mention the free appraisal. "I will see to it, Fräulein."

"Now what is left? Violins? Violas?"

"A guitar, Fräulein."

She shook her head in disapproval. "Never touch the things. Instruments of sluggards and . . . Spaniards!"

He drew back in revulsion at the word *Spaniard.* Had Hitler also declared them inferior? "Of course not. Certainly not. Not anything that is even remotely German about a guitar."

"He is just a child. A rather large and clumsy child, at that. I need something that will convey the mood of Vienna but is not really of much value. It is just a memento, you see."

He frowned. He was pleased that he had such an inventory of great value, but now what could he sell her? "Are you interested in . . . might you like . . . is a cello anything you might be interested in?"

She glanced toward the window. "Like that old beat-up thing?" She nodded toward Vitorio and silently breathed an apology. "I don't know." She hesitated, plucking the strings of a violin. "It is rather large."

"Cellos are sturdy, Fräulein." He was already wrestling it out of its corner in the window. "Just the thing for a small boy. Or a large boy." He presented it to her proudly.

Elisa raised her eyebrows in disdain. "Really? Who told you that?"

His brow furrowed in a frown. "Why, the woman who sold it to me said—"

Elisa plucked the string coolly. It was out of tune, and she winced at the sound of the sour note. "Hmmmm? What did she say?"

"That it was very . . . valuable."

"What did you pay for it?" Elisa already had heard the ridiculous number from Leah. Thirty-five shillings for an instrument that would sell at an auction for no less than three thousand. The violoncello had not been purchased. It had been stolen.

"Not too much," replied the embarrassed shopkeeper. Now he searched his mind for an amount that did not sound too high for such a monstrosity. Such a piece of junk.

"How much?" Elisa raised her eyebrows as if to say anything was too much.

"Two hundred," lied the shopkeeper.

"*Two* hundred! *Two!*" Everything in her tone told him that only a complete fool would pay that for such a thing. She plucked the string again. The wobbly note bounced around the room.

"Maybe it wasn't. Maybe. Let me think. Good heavens! No, I could not have made such an error as that. It was . . . thirty-five, I think. Two hundred for the other one that I sold yesterday." He was lying again, but at least Elisa had gotten him to admit the actual price he had given Leah.

"Thirty-five, eh? Well, then, you shouldn't take too much of a loss on the thing."

"Loss?" the man squeaked. "But she told me—"

"You know how easy it is for people to cheat." Elisa clucked her tongue and plucked the out-of-tune instrument again.

"Cheated!" He wrung his hands and looked hatefully at the cello. "I have been cheated!"

"This is one you may as well leave in the window. It doesn't matter if it warps anymore!"

"I have been cheated! She told me it was of such value! She said I had not paid her a fraction of its worth!"

Elisa spun the instrument around. "Of course, if you do leave it in your window, the musicians of Vienna will see it and recognize it for what it is—"

"A piece of worthless junk!"

"And then they will laugh, and word will get around that you are trying to sell—"

"Worthless trash!"

"You would not want anyone to get the idea that you might be trying to cheat a young student!" Elisa frowned. "No doubt it would make them doubt the quality of your other instruments!"

"Certainly! Yes! Thank you for the advice! Of course you are right!" For a moment he looked as if he might kick the Pedronelli. Elisa pulled it back as if to replace it in the window. "No! No! Don't put it in there, Fräulein!"

"Well what should I do with it?"

"How much will you give me for it?"

She shook her head as if he must be joking. "*Give* you? For this?"

"For your nephew. A clumsy boy, you said! A child's toy! Just a little memento of Vienna, you said! Wouldn't you like to take it off my hands, Fräulein?"

"Certainly not for what you paid for it. Thirty-five shillings? A ridiculous price!"

"Then I will give it to you for half that," he said eagerly.

She still looked doubtful.

"Will you give me ten for it?" he begged.

Elisa stared hard at the cello. She was softening. The shopkeeper could see that he might have a sale. "It is so big. Very hard to carry."

"It has a case!"

"And bows? I wouldn't want to bring it home without bows!"

"Yes!" He clapped his hands together. "Two bows in the case! What do you say?"

She sniffed reluctantly and strummed it again louder. Now the shopkeeper winced. "Ten shillings? For a souvenir?" She hesitated.

"With case and bows. You can throw it into the luggage car and not have to carry it yourself." He bit his lip. "All right, then. Eight shillings and not a penny less."

"I'll give you five."

"Done!" The little man ran back to fetch the case. He returned with the old, familiar, beat-up case that had protected the instrument of the finest cellist in Vienna

Elisa counted out the five shillings, placed them on the counter, and prepared to leave.

"You bargain like a Jew!" The shopkeeper laughed.

Elisa smiled and hefted Vitorio carefully. "And you deal like a Nazi."

He took her remark as a compliment, opened the door for her, then mopped his brow with relief that the entire incident had cost him a loss of only thirty shillings.

42

Message to Nineveh

Violin in one hand, cello in the other, Elisa maneuvered her way through the front door of the apartment building. She did not remember Herr Hugel until it was too late.

The door to his downstairs flat opened and he emerged, eyeing her with a curious disdain as if to tell her he was on guard against all intruders in the building.

His mouth twitched slightly, and his eyes shifted from the instrument to Elisa's flushed face and then back again. "Heil Hitler," he said with a challenge.

"Heil . . . " Elisa replied. "You can see my hands are too full to give the proper salute." She tried to sound lighthearted. Still, he did not smile. Where was that ubiquitous chuckle Leah had told her about? Perhaps he had a hangover. He certainly looked as if that were the case. He did not offer to help her with her burden; she was grateful for that.

"What do you want?" He continued to stare at the instruments.

Elisa did not answer for a moment. "Apartment 2-B."

He nodded. "Ah yes. Elisa Linder. She is ill, I think. I hear her coughing sometimes." He was becoming more animated. He wanted to demonstrate his knowledge of the tenants in the building. "Is that her cello?"

"Why, yes." Elisa started to walk toward the steps. "Since she has not been able to come to rehearsal, I thought I should bring it to her."

"You are a musician, too?" he called after her.

"Yes." Elisa climbed the stairs as she spoke. He was acting as if he might want to chat after all. She wanted only to get away, to hide with Leah behind the door.

"You play for the Führer too?"

"As often as I can." She reached the landing. Now his eyes opened with awe; he was Apartment Führer of a building that contained musicians for the *real* Führer himself! Hugel chuckled with pleasure—not at Elisa or her occupation, but at himself and the pinnacle of society that he had reached.

"That's good!" he shouted up after her. "I saw Himmler, you know! Just yesterday at the rail station, Himmler shook my hand!" He gurgled his pride and waved the Himmler-blessed hand as Elisa knocked softly on the door.

A moment of silence was broken by Leah's trembling voice. "Who?"

"Me," Elisa answered.

"Well," Hugel shouted, "nice to meet you! Heil Hitler!"

"Heil Hitler," Elisa replied as she slipped through the door.

Thomas turned the pages of the book one by one in front of the lamp. He did not dare keep the message the Dead Man had deciphered from within the volume, but the meaning of each tiny pinprick of light bored into his consciousness.

> *The life of the senior officer Abwehr German Embassy Paris is in extreme danger. Murder set to coincide with the uprising in Czech Sudeten. High Command to Brit government date for invasion end of May. Stand firm with Covenant. Hitler will not survive military resist by many world powers.*

The fact that his own life was in immediate jeopardy did not surprise Thomas. He had felt the nearness of harm a thousand times over the last weeks. He had accepted the possibility when he had agreed to stand beside those in the High Command who opposed Hitler. If his treason was discovered, he was marked for a slow death. The idea of a quick assassination was almost a relief to his troubled thoughts.

This brief message from Vienna was more important than a mere warning of peril, however. The British must know! They must be told in person of the impending invasion of the Czech frontiers! And if Thomas was to be murdered by Nazi sympathizers, then the foreign secretary must be told!

Thomas had two days of leave coming. He would take them. It was only a short train ride to the coast of France. Once there he could find a thousand fishermen who would be willing to take him fishing.

"I have failed," Herschel said miserably to his companions. "I was right there. In the foyer of the embassy. Le Morthomme had sent me there, and I took my gun, but I could not . . . I was afraid! It was as if fear held my hand from the gun. I simply handed him his package and let him walk away." Herschel cradled his head in his hands as the little group looked on.

"No matter, Herschel," Hans soothed. "It is not yet time. I will give you the signal, remember?" He thumped him on the back. "May. That is when it must be accomplished! When the Nazis are all drunk in their beer halls, *ja*? I will tell you when you must shoot, and then, believe me, you will find your courage!"

Johann and Raphael nodded in good-natured agreement. Herschel looked somewhat relieved that he had not been branded a coward by his only friends.

Johann patted his arm and spoke comfortingly. "It was not fear, Herschel, which kept you from shooting him. Not fear, but the hand of Providence. There is a proper day planned. There will be many demonstrations by us Jews against the world powers! Wait until the signal is sent; until then, do not attempt to find courage when it is not yet required."

Their consolation gave Herschel a new determination. "Yes! I will wait and pray for the moment when the deed will be done," he said in a shaking voice. Even as he spoke, he knew the chance would come again. Thomas would stand before him, and Herschel would pull the trigger without remorse.

"For Zion!" Hans proclaimed as he downed a glass of bitter red wine.

"For Zion!" the others repeated, drinking their toast to the death of another Nazi.

Laughter and joy rang in the little apartment. While Leah played the cheerful Bach Suites, Charles sat up in bed and clapped his hands as Louis danced around her in delight.

Elisa had kept her promise; Vitorio was out of jail at last. The beautiful singer had been redeemed from the terrible prison of the dishonest shopkeeper.

Leah could soar again with the music. She could close her eyes and make even the angels dance as she played.

When Elisa told them the story of how the shopkeeper had practically begged her to take the precious instrument off his hands, Leah doubled over with laughter and hooted until tears streamed down her cheeks and her stomach ached.

Little Charles smiled with his eyes as he gazed on the rich glowing wood of his old friend. Everything was going to be all right now; the violoncello was back. Some stories still had happy endings.

Louis tugged on Elisa's skirt as she took out her violin to play with Leah. "And did you get a passport for Vitorio too?" he asked.

The question made Elisa freeze where she stood. Leah's laughter died away as she saw that perhaps not everything had gone well. Elisa had not been able to keep every promise.

Elisa looked at Leah. "I couldn't get them," she said quietly. "I tried. I even tried contacting Thomas, but . . . "

Leah raised a hand to silence her. There was no need to say more. "There never was a friend so faithful," she told her. And then she began to play as though it did not matter anymore what happened. She could believe in small miracles now, and for the moment, at least, she could forget her fears and let her soul soar to freedom on the music.

The cold winds of the English Channel seemed to penetrate Thomas' heavy overcoat. He pulled his collar up against the chill. The bow of the little fishing boat struck the white-capped waves, dividing the waters as it pushed onward toward England.

Thomas wondered why the British prime minister could not see that Hitler's dream of the future did not stop at the conquest of Austria and Czech-Sudetenland. The eye of the Dragon looked much farther than that! From his nest in faraway Berchtesgaden, the Führer could plainly see the cliffs of Dover and the crumbling Houses of Parliament.

Seagulls cried out as they trailed after the fishing boat. These birds had come from the coast of France. Tonight they would rest in England. Thomas looked up at them and shuddered. Did the English prime minister not realize how very short the distance was by air? Had he not heard the devastating verdict by the American hero Charles Lindbergh, who declared that the Nazi air force was now the most powerful in the world? In Paris, the French government trembled at the verdict Lindbergh had brought away with him from Germany. Why, then, did Chamberlain think that Hitler would stop with the Sudetenland? It was indeed only a short flight for German bombers from the Reich to London. If this handful of scruffy seagulls could cross the choppy waters at will, so would Hitler unless he was stopped soon.

This was the message that Canaris and the others were sending through von Kleistmann to the leaders of the British government. There was no time to waste for codes to be translated and messages to be sent to this or that secretary. The message of such urgency was fixed in Thomas' memory. Any day a climax was coming in Czechoslovakia. An assassination of someone in a high post of the government, then chaos and rioting, followed by the march of German divisions across the Czech border to restore order as the nation was absorbed into the Greater Reich!

There were no more specific details than these. It was not known which of the Czech leaders was to be killed or how. Thomas hoped that the English would not need such minute facts in order to rally behind the government in Prague. It was enough to know that the massive plan was about to be achieved by one small bullet in the head of . . . someone in Prague. No doubt Himmler and his Gestapo were well informed about the intended victim and his assassin. But because Himmler hated Canaris and the Abwehr, he would never share such information. Like the prophet Jonah, Thomas was being sent to warn this modern-day Nineveh. If they did not believe him, then before the week was out there would be the certain end of one more little nation, and one more irrevocable step would have been taken toward an apocalypse that would sweep across these waters onto the shores of Britain!

Thomas was no longer cold. The prickly sweat of fear crept down his spine. *And if they do not listen?*

Myriad gulls shrieked and banked off in clean formation as the vessel neared the shores of England. Effortlessly they flew with the wind at their tails. They would reach land long before the boat slipped into its mooring. Perhaps Hitler had watched the gulls too. Perhaps he had seen from the first how easy it would be to cross the Channel!

43

Otto's Role

The idea was hopeless, Elisa knew, and yet there was no other hope. Waiting until Hugel stumbled off to church, she slipped out of the building and hurried to the terrible place Otto had taken her.

She smiled as she entered the Gestapo headquarters, even though she was trembling inside. She entered the building as a free woman, knowing full well that she might not leave again at all. The lobby was filled with young and old women at their typewriters. Desks were cluttered with stacks of report folders; every folder represented a human life locked away in the hideous prison system. The folders were handled with more care than their human counterparts.

Elisa leaned against the counter and gazed upward along the marble façades of the vast open lobby. This had been some sort of government building in the days before the Anschluss, she remembered. Social welfare or housing, maybe. A far more grim purpose now used the space.

On a long wooden pew against the far wall, ten women sat waiting. Some held babies. Others had brought packages bound for the prison cell of a husband or brother or father. They all awaited word about their loved ones. The word was never happy. Leah would have been sitting on the long bench if she hadn't been very certain that she was also wanted by the Gestapo.

Elisa tried not to look like another one of the hopeful women who had come to ask, "Where have they taken him? Has he been sentenced? Will he ever come home again?"

A husky, blond young clerk looked up at Elisa, surprised at the smile on her lips. "I'm here to see someone," Elisa said. She felt the hostile stares of the women at her back. "Heil Hitler," she added.

"So is everyone else." The clerk jerked her head toward the bench. The woman's accent was clearly German, not Austrian.

"This is a social call," Elisa managed to say lightly. "The man I wish to visit is in an office, not a cell."

"That's a switch." The clerk laughed. It was clear she felt no pity for the anxious little band in the lobby. They were a nuisance. They were always there even if their faces and the names they sought were different.

"Otto Wattenbarger. Is he in?" Elisa's voice cracked with the strain of this charade she was playing. Just as she had told Le Morthomme she could never do. She had raised her hand in the Heil! She was paying a social call to the office of the Vienna Gestapo.

"Otto? Sure. Does he know you're coming?"

"I don't think so."

"Let me warn him. Third-floor interrogations and investigations, you know. We must not interrupt." She winked. The implication of the wink was almost obscene. What must they not interrupt? A strip search? A beating? How could Otto exist in the center of this evil?

"Of course. Tell him Elisa is here, will you?"

The clerk dialed and waited. "Busy? Somebody named Elisa. Yes." She glanced toward Elisa and grinned. "He says come on up. You know your way?"

Elisa nodded, remembering the shrieks she had heard in the corridor the day Otto had arrested her. She had walked these halls over and over again in her nightmares. Yes. She would never forget the way.

She waved cheerfully and marched past the long bench, pretending not to see the women who were as much prisoners in their hearts as the men they longed for. Leah's heart was there among them all. Elisa knew that and felt it; still, she pretended.

This time she took the elevator up to the third-floor corridor. The hall was silent, as if the shrieks of victims had driven away all sounds for a time. The floors were highly polished marble. Elisa imagined that she could see traces of blood in the swirling pattern of the stone.

Ahead of her, Otto stepped from his office and stood watching her with his arms crossed as she approached. She tried to smile even now, but his expression was anything but pleased at the sight of her. He stepped back and let her pass into the small cluttered cubicle. He shut the door behind her but did not move to sit or offer her a chair.

"I thought you were through with us," he said in a hushed voice.

"You heard?"

"Enough. You're better off out of it. It was a bad idea, anyway." He looked away and then back at her face as though he wanted to say something else. As if he wanted to ask her if she understood what it had all been about.

"Your idea, Otto?"

He nodded. "You said you were going to Prague. The night of the Anschluss, at the border. Your American passport! All of it. It seemed like a good idea at the time."

"And you wanted me to know, didn't you?" She suddenly understood. He had not given her name and description to the men in Prague only because he thought she would make a good courier. He wanted her to know what he had sacrificed. What he was really doing in the thick of it.

"Maybe that was part of it," he agreed. For a moment great sorrow reflected in his eyes.

How lonely he must be in this outpost of darkness, Elisa thought. *How difficult it must be to live a lie that causes your own family to reject you*!

"You perform well, Otto. I cannot play the role. I know that much about myself. That is why I have come to you for help."

Before she could say more, he put a hand to his head and groaned. He brushed past her and sat down. "Don't." He could barely speak. "Don't ask me, Elisa. I know what you want, and I can't help you. Not today."

Elisa waited for a long moment, then quietly asked, "Why, Otto?"

He turned to her, his face tortured. Maybe it was easier to pretend when no one else knew. "Not now. There is something . . . today . . . I can't say. But I dare not jeopardize myself now. If you understood!"

"I don't understand, Otto. How can anything be more important than . . . "

"Those boys," he finished lamely.

Elisa stared hard at him. How could he know what she wanted to ask him? "Boys?"

"Kronenberger. I saw them the night of the Anschluss. It was after curfew, and they were with your friend. I had gone to your apartment; I was thinking about what you had said. I had been working to stop all this." He waved his hand toward the stacks of files. "Passing along what I heard. Hoping it would make some difference. Maybe stop the worst from coming to Austria. Then it all happened so fast. I don't know why I walked to your place that night—just *feeling* what you said, and feeling my own failure. I made no difference at all. It happened. I couldn't do anything to stop it. I gave up my life. My family. And in the end it made no difference."

"Then help us! Help them, Otto!"

"I can't. Not now. Not now," he finished lamely as the crisp clacking of heels sounded in the corridor outside. Elisa and Otto looked at one another; then, as if to fix the proper expression on his face, Otto rubbed his hand over his mouth, and when he pulled it away he was smiling.

"Otto!" a voice shouted from behind the heavy door. "Helga says you've got a woman in there! Can I have a little bit of her too? You don't share with your friend Sporer? Come on, Priest, open up!"

Elisa went pale and turned quickly away, wishing there was a place to hide. Otto straightened his tie and managed a hearty laugh. "Come in, you great clown," he called. The act was perfect. Everything was once again under control.

The door was flung back wide and Albert Sporer strutted in. His eyes immediately traced the lines of Elisa's body. He did not attempt to disguise his appreciation. "And who are you? Has our priest been keeping you satisfied, darling?" He walked behind her and peered over her shoulder, ogling her throat as if he wanted to bite her.

Elisa raised her hand instinctively and managed a nervous laugh as she stepped back almost against the window. "Who is this, Otto? You should have warned me; I would have worn my nun's habit." The words sounded playful enough. She congratulated herself on the performance as Sporer laughed with appreciation.

"A nun's habit, eh? I find nuns particularly tasty!"

"That has seldom stopped Albert, Elisa," Otto said flippantly, but Elisa was almost sure he was not joking.

"That's right. I am a man who gets what he wants." His eyes ran down the buttons of Elisa's blouse. "Every time."

This time she found it impossible to laugh. A chill coursed through her. She looked pleadingly at Otto. "I have to go now."

"What's your hurry?" Sporer grabbed her hand. He did not seem to notice her uneasiness. "Ask her to have lunch with us, Otto. Tell her I promise not to pinch or bite." Then he held up her hand and touched the wedding ring.

"I'm already taken, anyway," Elisa said, grateful for the ring, grateful for Murphy, wherever he was.

"A married woman." Otto shrugged.

"Well, that never stopped me, either." Sporer kissed her hand and Elisa felt ill. She remembered his hideous grin that night he accosted her in the Judenplatz. She imagined him issuing the orders that had ended Rudy Dorbransky's life. She could see him clearly at the border between Austria and Czechoslovakia as he had stripped the Jewish woman and beaten her husband. "There are plenty of beautiful Aryan women who have joined the Lebensborn program to provide the Führer with a baby

. . . with or without the help of their husbands." Sporer laughed suggestively and raised an eyebrow in Otto's direction. "Perhaps that is what you two are doing? I hear that two Jewish obstetrics clinics near Vienna have been taken over. Already the beds are full of candidates."

Otto frowned in disapproval. Everyone knew about the establishment of these SS stud farms for the sake of production of the master race. "Elisa is not—" He was not allowed to finish.

Sporer interrupted as he gazed at Elisa with renewed interest. "When you tire of Otto, Frau Elisa, please remember that there are other men who would enjoy fulfilling your desire to provide a racially pure child for the Fatherland." Sporer moved a step nearer to her. "I myself have always longed for fatherhood."

"Thank you, anyway," she managed to say. "You'll have to get permission from Otto, however." She smiled and winked at Otto, then slipped out the door as a startled Sporer teased Otto.

"Well, there's one I would not have guessed from you, Priest!" Sporer's voice followed her down the corridor as the shrieks of the Nazi prisoner had done. Elisa did not wait for the elevator. She ran down the narrow curving steps, then past the long bench in the lobby and out into the sunlight.

Otto had told her the truth. He was much too near to the ultimate evil to find a way to help her now. He had known about the boys and Leah all along. His gift to them had been silence. He could do no more. There was something *terrible* at stake here, and he could not say what it was.

Jubilation lit Albert Sporer's face as he sat across the table from Otto at a little village café outside Vienna. He had already consumed half a bottle of wine, which was unusual for Sporer, but today he had cause to celebrate.

He leaned forward and said in a low voice, "You see how easy it was, Otto? And you missed it all! A few dead Germans in Czechoslovakia for the sake of propaganda, some very nice news photos of the Czech police beating *innocent* civilians over the head, and now the British prime minister is declaring that Prague should give up her military positions in the Sudeten territory and hand it over to the Führer! Our mission is a success."

Otto raised his glass in a toast. "Congratulations, Sporer. No doubt you will be awarded . . . something. . . . " He took a cheerful swig of the wine. "Remember me when you are a field marshal, will you?"

Sporer laughed, causing heads in the tiny restaurant to turn and stare. "Remember you? My fine fellow, if you would be more willing, I would drag you to the top with me!" He downed his wine and poured another round. "And when I am the Gauleiter of Sudetenland"—he lowered his voice again—"trundling all those filthy little Slavs off to summer camp, and their Jews with them, we will have our choice of women! Of good wine and food and maybe even art, like Göring? *Ja?* Have you ever seen Göring's cigars?" He laughed drunkenly now.

Otto put a finger to his lips. "We aren't in Czechoslovakia yet, Albert," he chided.

Albert Sporer sat straight and widened his eyes in mock indignation. "As good as done, and you know it! You read what Chamberlain said. France and Russia won't raise a finger to help, so neither will Britain. The Czech army won't even get out of bed without them." Now his face became serious and he dropped his voice to a whisper. "I tell you, Otto, look out your window in two days. You will not see an SS soldier or Wehrmacht man anywhere on the street. In two days we march into the Sudetenland, and no one will be there to stop us! Just like the Rhineland. Just like Austria. And if they knew!" He peered through his wine as if it were a crystal ball. "If the idiots knew how the generals grumble . . . and how the Führer trembles at the thought of the resistance of the Czech divisions! Thirty-five divisions, and they could put up a fight on the high ground, too. But they won't. Frankly, if they had the courage, we wouldn't march."

"We could beat them easily," Otto scoffed.

Sporer shook his head. "I have seen their fortifications. They are better equipped than the French. I tell you, Otto, the issue would be in doubt if courage entered in. But the little Czech pygmies have no courage without the British and the French to back them up." He laughed again, satisfied that the Czech territories were as good as in Nazi hands. "So, in two days, my friend, when everyone asks where the soldiers from Vienna have gone, don't tell them!" He snorted and spilled a drop of wine on the tablecloth. "Military secret." He put a finger to his lips. "Nobody's supposed to know until after. I'll lose my promotion, see. If I tell anybody . . . " Sporer was plainly drunk.

Otto looked nervously around the room, but no one seemed to notice. "Shut up, or you'll get us both hanged."

Sporer winked broadly. "The fools don't know. They didn't know in Austria, did they? Panzer units broken down all over the place. At least we're bringing mechanics into the Sudetenland! But we're not any better prepared." He stuck out his lower lip thoughtfully. "In six months we could crush them. But the Führer was right. He's always right. Always right about such things. We're moving in like lions, but we're really just little foxes, you know."

Otto rose and took his companion by the arm, pulling him out into the fresh air. "I know one little fox who has had too many grapes from the vineyard." He laughed, giving Sporer a playful shove into the car. "And if all this is going to happen as soon as you say—"

"Two days."

"Then you'd better sleep this off. Such a jovial mood does not suit you, Albert." He slammed the door. "Sober with a splitting headache is the way you must be to shed the blood of the Czechs, I think."

Albert Sporer talked on in detail as Otto drove slowly back to Vienna. The coming takeover of Czechoslovakia by the Nazis was to be predictably ruthless. Now, as Sporer's head lolled drunkenly from side to side, he revealed the exact elements of the plan.

"Everybody in Prague knows that President Beneš has ordered a performance of the opera *Die Judin*. Jewish drivel!" He shouted the last sentence as they passed a housewife hanging her wash on the line.

Otto looked in the rearview mirror as the woman stared after the car. "So what, Albert? Let the little monkey have his Jewish composers and Jewish operas. What are you talking about?"

Sporer laughed and plucked his glasses off his face. He closed his eyes in contented relaxation. "The opening performance is tomorrow night. The little Slavic pygmy will attend it! He will mingle with every Jew in Prague! They have bought out the whole auditorium, the Jews have! And we," he declared, thumping his chest, "have recruited *one* Jew in particular to perform a little job for us! Only he doesn't know it is for us! He thinks he is acting on behalf of the Communists!"

Otto was now certain of the plan, but still he pressed for details. "And this Jew will murder the president of Czechoslovakia? Correct? Am I right, Sporer?"

Sporer nodded sleepily. "Like the American president Lincoln. Rather poetic, I thought. I myself came up with the plan after Beneš expressed that he was an admirer of the American president Lincoln." He opened one eye and peered at Otto. "Did you hear that speech?"

"Sorry."

"Beneš was going on about the Civil War. American Civil War. Holding the country together. Hoping to hold Czechoslovakia together like Lincoln. Not wanting to give up the Sudetenland." Sporer closed his eyes again. "So I dreamed up this fitting end for Beneš. He gets shot on the opening night of the performance. The Jew-lover dies like the slave lover Lincoln!" Sporer languidly put his finger to his head and pulled the imaginary trigger.

"So what? It will be like the murder of Dollfuss in Vienna. A great funeral, and the Czechs will choose another idiot for chancellor. What's the point?"

"This time nothing will go wrong!" Sporer did not like the challenge. He sat upright and grasped the dashboard. "It is a Jew and a Communist who will kill the ape! Don't you see? We have it all arranged. Riots. Fighting for the sake of our cause against the Reds! And then the army marches in to restore order and rescue the three million Germans who live within the Czech borders!"

Sporer's face flushed with excitement. "You see, Otto? You see what you have missed all stuffed away here in Vienna? Within two days we will have it all, and the British idiot Chamberlain has handed it to us! The British will not move to stop us! The French will not! And as for the Czechs themselves, they will have a dead president on their hands! Riots to quell! They will be crushed before they hear the first tramp of German boots over their border!"

With all of this said, Sporer relaxed once again. He leaned back in his seat and yawned. "Well?"

"Inspired," Otto replied with admiration. "And to think I might have played a part in it." He sounded genuinely disappointed now, but Sporer had already drifted off to sleep and could not comfort him with promises of more action to come.

44
Honorable Treason

Here in the study of Winston Churchill's estate, Thomas von Kleistmann searched his meager English vocabulary for words that might convey the urgency of his message to the great man.

Churchill glared at him from the settee. His lower lip extended angrily as he drawled, "You mean they would not see you? The prime minister? The foreign secretary? You have come here at the peril of your very life to warn them, to warn Britain of the plans drawn up in the war room of the German Chancellery by Hitler, and they refuse to admit you?" His eyes blazed.

"I could not get past the secretary." Thomas shook his head. "And yet I come here to Chartwell. You must be the only sensible man left in England, Herr Churchill."

"Sensible, perhaps. But I am powerless in the face of such negligence. The speech by the PM to the press was deplorable. I have already spoken to the Czech ambassador. He is naturally distressed by the perceived abandonment of his nation. As distressed as Herr Hitler is pleased."

"You cannot be powerless, Herr Churchill. Or if that is so, then I have come here for nothing. There are men in the German High Command who advise this madman at the helm of our country. These men advise him that our army is in no way ready to meet any challenge with force. They tell him that the Wehrmacht cannot fight now. He says that they will not have to fight, that the English and the French and the Czechs are cowards. I spoke with the French minister of defense before I came here. The French look to England; what will the English do? And the English look to France to see what the French will do!"

Churchill cleared his throat. "And all the while the world slumbers."

Thomas saw his own reflection in the silver teapot on the tray before them. For an instant it flashed through his mind that any man could have been sitting here, but for some reason he had been chosen for this honorable treason. Perhaps some world destruction would be stopped because he and Churchill now sipped tea together overlooking an English country garden.

"Yes. The world sleeps, and I will tell you just how vain are the British dreams of peace!" The figures were clear in Thomas' mind. "Day and night for four years Germany has been rearming. There has been no year in which less than 800 million pounds of sterling have been spent on war preparation. The whole manhood of the country is harnessed to war. The children are taken from church schools and forced into the Hitler Youth. Every six weeks a new army corps is added to our active forces. Every thought is turned to the assertion of race, Herr Churchill." Thomas paused and looked out at the peaceful garden. "I come here in the hopes that you will cry from the housetops. The little nation of Czechoslovakia will perish within the week, unless . . . "

Churchill's lower lip protruded farther as his bulldog features locked into a scowl. "We have made certain covenants with the small nations of the world. And now I fear that the League of Nations has become no more than a lovely, whitewashed sepulcher. There must be a vision here, or indeed Hitler will rule the world; and piece by piece he will work his way across the Channel. Together the nations of the world might face down such a terrible force as you have described. We must arm ourselves and stand by our Covenant!" He leaned forward, his gaze fierce with determination. "Tell your generals that this I promise: I will cry it from the housetops. Never before has the choice of such blessings or curses been so plainly, vividly, even brutally offered to mankind. The choice is open, and the dreadful balance trembles!"

The cab had pulled into the estate of Winston Churchill just as the tall, handsome young German stepped from the front door. Murphy recognized him instantly—it was the same man who had emerged from the hotel room of Churchill and Anthony Eden in Cannes just before Eden had been forced to resign from his post of foreign minister.

Today, as then, the dark-haired young man tugged his hat brim low on his brow and averted his face from Murphy's view. He walked briskly down the drive to where another taxi waited, its driver fast asleep, his head lolled back against the seat. Suddenly he sat upright as the German quickly opened the door and slipped into the backseat.

The same chilling sense of foreboding that Murphy had felt in Cannes now filled him again. In France, the man had carried himself with a distinct military bearing. Although apprehension had been evident in his manner, he had seemed almost defiant as he had passed Murphy in the hall. Today, his every move communicated fear. Murphy continued to sit in the taxi as the first cab sputtered reluctantly to life. For a moment, Murphy considered following him until he saw the bulldog scowl of Winston Churchill as he waited at the front step.

Churchill carried a small paper bag of bread crumbs to feed his ducks. His estate was covered with ponds and waterfalls that Churchill himself had constructed stone by stone.

Cigar smoke rose over his head as the two men walked the expansive grounds. Murphy could not help but compare the statesman to a chugging locomotive.

"Quite an excellent broadcast," Murphy said, noticing that they never were out of sight of an extremely large bald man who resembled a wrestler.

"Just the sort of thing that might make someone angry." Churchill followed Murphy's gaze to the large fellow. "He is my bodyguard, Mr. Murphy. You might have noticed with a study of history that wars and international incidents usually begin with the assassination of someone who is the opponent of an aggressor. I am an opponent of Herr Hitler; however, I would regret it if my untimely demise might spark an incident."

"You are worried that you might be a target?"

Churchill chewed his cigar stub thoughtfully. "A rather large target." He smiled, then strolled onto a wooden footbridge that creaked beneath his weight.

Murphy followed him and watched silently as at least twenty ducks quacked at the sight of Churchill and swam excitedly toward him as he opened the bag of crumbs and tossed a handful over the rail. "Who was the man that left just ahead of me?" Murphy ventured.

Churchill looked up sharply. "A dead man, if his presence here is ever found out," he warned.

"He was with you and Mr. Eden at Cannes. A German—"

"A brave man," Churchill interjected. "And there are many among the German people. Such men have conscience, and by the risk of their own lives they become the conscience of others who are not so noble or brave. Here is a fellow who understands the difference between right and wrong, between aggressor and victim."

"Between his own country and the Czechs?"

Churchill gave a brief nod. "I'm afraid that those of us who are true believers are like these few ducks here. We quack and bob on stormy waters. And no one pays attention." He offered the bag to Murphy, who took a handful of bread crumbs and tossed them into the feathered mob.

"I have to believe that someone is listening. The speech you made to Parliament—"

"No doubt there are a few other frightened ducks out there. A few." He pointed to a large black-and-brown duck that chased the others away from their feast. "That is an interesting creature, Mr. Murphy. You will notice that it does not matter how much he gobbles; he always wants what every other duck on the pond has. He often gets what he wants too. That is why the others are not quite as big as this one. Why, they swim away when they see him coming. They squawk and make quite a racket while Herr Big Duck steals their food. But you see?" He tossed in another handful of crumbs. "While he steals, they do nothing more to defend themselves. He takes from one, and another grabs what he can and swims away." There was bitter amusement in Churchill's eyes. "Together, they could keep him out of their center. A covenant of fowls against the bully." He sighed and leaned against the rail. "Our prime minister would do well to stock his own pond with ducks. He might learn something about Herr Hitler."

Murphy nodded and frowned as the large duck attacked a very small mallard with only one crumb in its beak. "Maybe you should send Chamberlain a few of yours."

Churchill turned away from the scene. "The German High Command has sent warning after warning. I'm afraid this last one was turned away by a ministry secretary. I intend to send the PM a cooked goose when the time is right, but this feathered bully—" he jerked his head toward the big duck—"I intend to carve up on my own table."

"You have gained some reputation as a prophet, Mr. Churchill. When do you see the next step against the Czechs taking place?"

Churchill grunted and snatched his cigar from his mouth. "I am no prophet, and the British government knows when and why Hitler will move as well as I do." He paused. "The German population in the Sudetenland are having their elections this coming weekend. If there is trouble—and Hitler is expert at manufacturing trouble—then we may well see the German army march against the Czechs within the week."

Murphy followed Churchill from the footbridge to a stone bench beside a smaller pond. "That soon?"

With a level gaze, Churchill replied, "I am aware that you have acquired a wife, who is now in Prague. Young man, if I were you—if I were a young journalist—I would not be talking to the Jeremiah who is warning of invasion of Czechoslovakia. The story will not be here by the end of the week. The fate of the nation of Czechoslovakia is squarely in Prague now. That is where you will find your story. We have abandoned her, I am afraid. We have forsaken our part in the covenant of nations and forgotten that right is right and there truly is a difference between victim and aggressor, no matter how Herr Hitler and his propaganda machine may portray the situation."

The great man's cigar was cold now. He searched his pockets for a match but found none. Murphy was already wondering if he could catch a plane to Prague tonight. Beyond that, he must find a way to get Elisa and her family to safety.

"Yes, young man," Churchill drawled, "if I were you, I would catch the next flight to Prague."

45

The Prague Plan

Herschel now carried the gun with him everywhere. When the call to his duty came from Hans, he did not want to waste even one second running after his weapon. Again and again he rehearsed the scene in his mind. He would call the name of von Kleistmann. He would pull out his gun, and as the bullets tore through the German's body, he would shout his purpose for all to hear.

The sun was hot today in the bookseller's stalls. Still Herschel wore a bulky sweater to conceal his gun. Customers discussed the news from London. Chamberlain had offered no hope. Churchill had offered brave words to a world of cowards! Only the muzzle of a loaded gun would speak to these Nazi butchers, Herschel was convinced. And the cowardice of the world did not matter. He would show them; he would show them all!

He stacked a box full of used books that would be carted back to the small, dreary shop of Le Morthomme tonight. His thoughts were far from business. He prayed for Hans to come with *the word*!

He did not notice anyone until he felt a light tap on his back. He turned to face the radiant gaze of Hans. A smile curled up one corner of his mouth.

"When?" Herschel asked.

"Tomorrow," Hans replied softly. "Be ready at noon."

"Bis dahin," said Otto quietly as the sound of Sporer's footsteps receded down the corridor. "It has come to *that*!"

Indeed, the plans of the Führer were faultless in their conception. Tomorrow night, as the president of Czechoslovakia showed his support for the Jewish population of his nation, he would be assassinated by a Jew. Albert Sporer would be waiting in the dark shadows of the streets of Prague. He would be watching for the moment when he could sound the cry and gather his young Nazi sympathizers to attack the dismayed playgoers and riot in the square.

And more than one man, certainly, would die tomorrow night. The life of President Beneš was not the only life that would end in the planned slaughter. The violence that had shaken the Sudetenland would infect the rest of the county, giving Hitler the perfect excuse to march his divisions across the border to "restore order" in Czechoslovakia. Indeed, the Führer had planned his strategy well. Hitler had used the tool of propaganda to conceal the fact that *he* was the evil force behind the uprisings. He had stupefied the leaders of Britain and France into believing that appeasement and apathy were the road to peace.

Otto slammed his fist hard on the desktop. The frustration he felt was mixed with anger that Hitler's plan was guaranteed success now that Chamberlain had stated his position. There was nothing to stop it now. Otto had sent his warming that the upheaval would culminate soon. Elisa had carried the book to Paris, and from there it had gone to London. Why had the British government not heeded the warning? Men and women had risked their lives to stop the momentum that Hitler gained with every success.

Why would the English not hear the words? *Stand firm against this evil! Do not give an inch to threats and broken promises!* No one had listened to the warning, it seemed. No one but Winston Churchill and a handful of men who were out of favor.

Otto cradled his aching head in his hands. There was no time to send another courier to Paris and then on to London. What good would that do, anyway? It was obviously of little concern to Chamberlain if the president of Czechoslovakia dropped dead from the bullet of a Jewish gun or a Nazi gun. No matter that the idea was conceived in the mind of the madman who led Europe relentlessly on toward destruction!

"God," he whispered, feeling cut off from all hope, "what am I to do? What can I do now to stop this?" Up until this time, Otto had been only a whisper, sending warnings and information on to those in power who might be able to do something with the information! Now Sporer was ready to drive back toward the border to tap the first domino in a chain that would end the freedom of millions of Czechs. Otto knew that a whisper of warning was not enough to stop it. If President Beneš was assassinated, the abduction of Czechoslovakia into Hitler's Reich was a certainty.

There was no time left; only a few grains of sand remained in the hourglass. Word must be sent to Prague immediately, to President Beneš himself.

Otto calculated his chance of making it through Czech territory and then into the presence of Beneš. He spoke Czech only haltingly. His German appearance and accent would stop him at the first barricade.

"Who, then? Whom can I send?" He rose and stood before the window. Beyond the wide square, the dome of the Vienna State Opera House was clearly visible. The Musikverein was not far from there. Beneš would die during the performance of *Die Judin* at the National Theatre. Otto mentally rehearsed the details as he watched the swastika flag flap above the dome of the opera house. Soon it would also fly above the National Theatre in Prague . . . *soon!*

The letter from John Murphy in London lay on the closed top of Anna's grand piano.

Her hands folded in her lap, Anna gazed at the return address. *Savoy Hotel, London, England.* Since its arrival in the morning post, Anna could think of nothing else. The terrifying question returned to her again and again. *Why had Murphy sent Elisa a letter here in Prague? Wasn't she supposed to be with him now, safely at the side of her husband?*

Anna leaned forward on the piano bench and touched the corner of the letter. Was Elisa coming home? Had Murphy sent her back to Prague for some reason? Or—Anna closed her eyes at the frightening thought—was it possible that Elisa had never reached him in the first place?

No doubt the answer lay within the envelope. If Elisa did not come home by morning, Anna decided, she would open it. In the meantime dread hung heavy over her.

She glimpsed her own reflection in the mirror above the china hutch. A thousand times when Theo had been in prison, Anna had seen that same look on her face. There was something, *something* in the wind! Something sinister walked the narrow lanes of Old City Prague, and like the fog that rose from the river, it drifted just beyond the threshold of explanation.

Anna shuddered as she felt the cold breath of evil brush by.

Murphy threw his clothes into his bag and called the front desk of the Savoy.

"I'm checking out," he said. "Could you tally my account and grab me a cab?"

He was feeling good. Better than he had a right to, he figured, since it looked as if the sky was definitely falling on Europe. But all he could think about was Elisa; before the night was over, he would be sitting in the same room with her again. Whatever else happened, they could see it through as long as they were together. He wanted to *tell* her everything he had written. He wanted to see the expression in her eyes. He wanted to find out once and for all if he had a chance with her.

This afternoon he had filed his story and wired Trump that he was heading for Prague. Trump had sent a reply that nothing at all was happening in Prague. Paris was the place, and London. The order had been given: *STAY PUT!* Maybe Trump had figured out that Murphy had other reasons for going; hadn't Murphy mentioned a wife in Prague?

It didn't matter, Murphy decided. He wadded up the telegram and pitched it into the garbage, then made his plane reservations. Amanda had said it: Somebody ought to be there *in case* something happened. Murphy was convinced that even if nothing happened on the political scene, he was going to *make* something happen with Elisa. He was going home. Going to Prague. Going to be with her again.

"Maybe if I go back to Prague." Elisa and Leah had discussed the possibilities for hours.

"Papers from Czechoslovakia aren't worth anything now, Elisa. Listen to the radio. Every day Hitler blasts the Czechs. They are only one step higher than Jews in his book," Leah said. "That would be an improvement for me, but I would not want to add that burden to the boys."

"French passports," Elisa commented. "That was my first inclination, and I still think it is the best. I shouldn't have left Paris without them." She looked toward the violin case. "If Otto can't help, then I'll try Thomas again." She smiled sadly. "If I knew where Murphy was, maybe . . ."

Leah snapped her fingers. "What about the fellow at the American Embassy? The one who married you and Murphy?"

"I was already there. Scotch was the man's name. Got transferred to Argentina last month. Seems the Nazis didn't think much of his traffic in American documents. He's lucky he didn't end up . . ."

"Like Shimon," Leah finished. She rose wearily. It was a habit now to look out the window, to peek out at the busy street below and long for freedom. "Well, then—" she sighed—"I suppose a Czech nationality is better than being Jewish. And for the boys, it's better than having no country at all." She touched the edge of the curtain slightly. "There goes Hugel." She shook her head. "Pride of the Reich. Guardian of my freedom. We closed our eyes and woke up to the world of the Troll King. And everyone—*everyone*—who has lived by the laws of humanity is in some sort of prison. It is a crime to say, 'To thine own self be true.' They have made truth a crime. Now we live the law of trolls. Like Hugel, 'To thine own self be enough! To thine own self be everything!' "

She fell silent and watched as Hugel ambled down the street. "So, here I am. I cannot even be true to myself." Leah turned around and spread her hands in a playful gesture. "Not only will I deny that I'm a Jew, I will dress in a nun's habit if it gets me out of here! And I would happily make my Shimon a priest to buy him freedom."

"There are plenty of nuns and priests in prison to keep him company," Elisa said. "The collar of a cleric is no guarantee of safety—unless the fellow is willing to trot along behind Hitler."

"Well, then, it looks as if we have run out of options. I'll learn to speak Czech. I have always been an admirer of Dvorák! Music sounds the same in Prague as it does here. And then . . . maybe somehow . . . Shimon . . . " The brave facade began to crack as she realized that she would be leaving Austria without him—if she was lucky enough to get out at all.

"Leah . . . " Elisa tried to think what she might say to comfort her friend. There were no words left. They had all been spent, and yet all the politicians and all the words in Europe had not managed to purchase even one life. Not even the life of the gentle tympani player. Their words could not rescue Leah or Charles or Louis. Words had not saved Walter Kronenberger or his wife. They had not softened the heart of a society that murdered honorable men and deformed children and the aged and the weak.

Stubbornly Leah brushed back a tear that had managed to escape. "You are going back then." It was not a question. "Don't drive through the Sudetenland. The Nazis . . . "

She was interrupted by a sharp rapping on the door. Hugel must have come back! She blanched and stood rooted before Elisa.

Elisa touched her elbow, wondering how she could leave Leah even for a short time! Her sweet friend had reached the end of her control. "I'll get it," she said. "What can he do to us?"

The knock sounded more insistently. Elisa trembled inside in spite of her brave words. Both of them knew full well what Herr Hugel could do.

"Coming!" Elisa called. She touched the knob, then turned to make certain that the boys were still in the back room. Leah put a finger to her lips to warn them of the need for silence; then she closed the bedroom door and nodded at Elisa. "Who is there?" Elisa asked sweetly.

A low voice replied. "Otto." There was a long silence. "Please, let me in."

"It is arranged. The murder of a prominent Nazi official in Paris tomorrow, just to set the stage. And then another murder tomorrow night in Prague. The events will seem unrelated, but . . ."

Evening invaded the little apartment, but they did not turn on the light. Leah brewed tea. Otto stirred it absently as it grew cold. "Already the troops are beginning to move toward the frontier. By the back roads. Farm roads. Military exercises, they have told the newsmen. Does anyone believe it?" He looked painfully from one face to another. "I am certain Chamberlain received the message, and now you have heard his reply: 'The problem of the Czechs is not Britain's problem!' " He bit his lip and stared into the cup as if he could see the future there. Indeed, he had seen the future clearly. "And so, tomorrow night at the National Theatre in Prague they will assassinate President Beneš. Sporer will be there, waiting with a thousand of his men to begin the demolition of that society also."

Elisa cleared her throat, feeling that Otto had some reason for telling them this. "Why have you come here, Otto? Not to unburden your heart, surely."

"My heart is of little importance in this." He drew a breath and plunged in. "Sporer must be stopped. You have seen him. You can recognize him. President Beneš must be warned somehow, and then—"

"You want me to go to Prague?"

"That's it."

"I have failed your test. I will not turn my back on Leah. I will not leave her here. Or the boys."

"I thought of that." He looked down at his hands as if to say they were tied. Then he said, "Where are they? The boys?"

"You will frighten them." Leah pointed to the swastika band on Otto's sleeve.

He tore it away. "I want to see them." He stood, and without asking permission, he opened the bedroom door and switched on the light. Charles and Louis lay sleeping on the bed. Charles' breath rattled fiercely. Otto gazed gently at the child's pale skin and frail body. He switched off the light and quietly closed the door. "They will kill him," he said with a certainty that sent a chill through Elisa. "There is a reward for the sons of Kronenberger. They will find him soon enough, and they will not—cannot—let him live. To take him out of the country could cost the life of President Beneš if you are caught."

"I did not say I would go."

Otto's eyes burned fiercely through the dim light of the room. "You *must* go."

"Not without Leah and the children."

"You cannot take Leah. And the two boys seen together will mean certain capture." Now his voice took on excitement. "But little Charles cannot stay here in Austria. Not another day."

"I won't leave Leah!" Elisa put her arm defiantly around Leah.

"You must leave me," Leah answered quietly. "Can't you see, Elisa? If you're planning to bring me a Czech passport, that will not do any good at all if there is no Czechoslovakia to go to!" She was smiling now at the irony of it all.

Otto nodded in curt agreement. At last someone was talking sense. "Good. You see the reason of it."

"But, Leah . . . "

Otto turned on the lamp beside the sofa. "I'll have the travel documents made up tonight. I know a man . . . I can do this."

"But . . . for whom?" Elisa was stunned by Otto's change of heart.

"For Charles, of course. They cannot stay together. I will take Louis and Leah—"

"But where?"

"To my parents' home. In the Tyrol. Franz can help them across the Swiss border from there." He said it as if it were already accomplished. "Elisa, *you* must take Charles. He is too ill to hike out over the passes. And his appearance has marked him here." He shook his head. "There is even a poster up on the wall of the Gestapo office. A photo of the child. His lip makes him unmistakable, even though the picture is old." Otto had taken control now. "Do you have the passport pictures?"

"Yes!" Relief flooded through both Elisa and Leah. They embraced and then scrambled to retrieve the violin case where the photos still remained hidden.

"We will have to destroy this." Otto held up the picture of the child with the sad eyes and broken face. He tore it in two. "Burn it," he commanded. "From the nose up he looks just like Louis. We will use the same picture on both of their documents. You can conceal his mouth. I have seen the way you did it. A scarf maybe. Or a bandage." He frowned in thought. "No. They have taken to stripping off bandages as a routine now."

"What can we do?" Elisa asked as the momentary exhilaration was replaced by an ominous sense of what lay ahead. The memory of other searches was fresh in her mind. Yes, the Nazis would tear away a bandage from the face of a child.

Otto glanced at his wristwatch. "I'll think of something," he said irritably. Time was precious, and he had much to do. "I'll do my part. Documents and . . . "

Leah sat forward in her chair. Her expression was tense and hopeful. "Herr Wattenbarger." She hesitated. He looked up at her; the gentleness she had glimpsed had vanished. "My husband is in prison. Somewhere. Maybe here in Vienna. His name is Shimon Feldstein. I . . . I cannot bear to leave without him." Her voice became pleading, but Otto's expression did not soften. He was doing all he could do. At some point his heart had to harden. Leah had brought him to that point.

"You will *have* to bear it, Frau Feldstein." He shoved the photos into his pocket. "We all must bear our share of that which is unholy and unjust." He looked toward the door. "I cannot do more than this."

"Otto!" Elisa wanted to shout against his fresh display of hardness. Had he become so calloused that even here, in secret, he could not show compassion?

"No, Elisa." Leah read her friend's outrage. "He is right. He is hard, but he is right."

Otto did not address the issue as he moved toward the door. "Be ready to leave by midnight. I want no delays." He slipped out of the apartment. Neither woman spoke as the sound of his heels receded down the stairs.

46

Death Warrant

The two women did not wake the boys but switched off the lamp and sat quietly talking in the darkness of the front room. Elisa could not make out Leah's features, but the sound of her friend's voice etched a memory on her heart that would remain there always. This was the moment of their good-bye. Elisa felt it. The bittersweet sense of ending surrounded them both. And yet, they did not speak of *farewell* or *forever.*

As they remembered together, Leah laughed—the clear, sweet laughter of a bell. Behind the laughter, Elisa could hear the chimes of St. Stephan's ringing the hour. From now on when she heard the bells, she would remember this moment, this wordless farewell.

They talked about Shimon and Rudy, about the time Murphy had brought ham to the Zionist party. They recalled conductors and professors at the Mozarteum in Salzburg, and sneaking by the dorm mothers after hours. What memories they had! Why had they not recognized then that it had been nearly heaven in its rightness? How had they missed the fact that those had been the final fleeting moments of their innocence and joy?

"Remember during Mendelssohn's *Reformation Symphony*?" Elisa asked. She hummed a bar from the symphony. "'A mighty fortress is our God' . . . and *crash!* The music stand fell down!"

Leah's bell-like laughter rang out. "And later Rudy said it was the ghost of Martin Luther because Mendelssohn was Jewish and never should have been plagiarizing a Lutheran hymn. Remember?"

The room filled with peals of laughter and then silence. The unspoken thought came to both of them that now Mendelssohn's music was not allowed to be played here anymore. But they did not speak that thought, or the one that followed: *Maybe someday the music of the Jewish composers and musicians would be heard again in Germany. In Vienna. Maybe someday the voice of God would be recognized in their creations.* But never again would these two play it together. This was good-bye. They knew it. This was forever.

Elisa reached out and took Leah's hands—strong hands, able to play for hours without ever tiring. Beautiful hands. Trimmed nails and calloused fingertips that danced over the strings. Elisa wanted to raise those fingers to her lips and kiss them good-bye. But she did not.

"Whenever I hear the *Reformation* I will think of you," Leah said. "'A mighty fortress is our God' . . . I didn't know the words to it before."

Elisa could not find a voice to answer for a long time. "God bless your hands," she murmured at last. And then those strong hands reached for her; gentle arms embraced her.

"I will not forget," Leah whispered. "Never will I forget."

The cellar beer hall was filled with smoke and the clamor of the boisterous men who gathered there. Barmaids with trays balanced high above their heads wriggled through the press of bodies. Foam spilled from steins and clung to drooping mustaches and stained vests of the patrons who sang and toasted and discussed the events of the day.

It was here that Herr Hugel found his only true moments of peace, here among men like himself who had no real roots, who had only recently found their true purpose in the service of the Greater Reich. Hugel leaned over the table, listening to the accountant from the porcelain factory tell his story.

"Not a word to anybody! That's what the Gestapo fellow told me! 'We'll get back to you on the matter;' that's what he said." He looked around at his enthralled audience. "But he never did! As far as I know, the Gestapo caught the brats and that officer got all the reward! I gave him all the information. About how I took them to the Musikverein. Looking for their Aunt Lena, the one said. I left them there with that woman cellist. The only person there, she was, and she didn't want them either! But I left them all the same, and if she knew, she might have collected the reward on them."

"Ah well, what can you do with five hundred Reichsmarks?" someone teased.

"I could buy us a night of beer, that's what!"

Hugel raised his stein, sloshing his beer on the man next to him. "Then here's to the reward! Finding the two brats and the lady from the—" he paused with the stein to his lips—"what was this woman you left them with?"

"A cellist. A case as big as a coffin! You couldn't miss it. But she didn't want them. Probably took them right to this Lena person and dumped them off. That's what I told the Gestapo fellow. Find this cellist, and you're going to find Lena and those brats. That's what I told him, and I suppose he's already done all that and never mind my reward!" The group around him were all nodding in sympathy. It didn't matter that the Nazis were in power. Government was corrupt no matter what. Officials made sure the common man never got what he deserved.

"What do you say, Hugel? Are you buying tonight?"

The question went unheard and unanswered. Where the enormous bulk of Hugel had been sitting, only his beer stein remained. The froth still oozed from it onto the table.

"Well, where is the fat man going in such a hurry?" They watched Hugel shove his way through the crowd on his way to the exit. In his haste he nearly knocked over a barmaid and sent her tray of steins toppling on the floor. "Twenty years he's been getting drunk here, and I never saw him leave a full stein on the table. Never saw him pass by a barmaid without giving her a little squeeze, either."

The men in the beer hall laughed and shrugged and split Hugel's beer among themselves. That was all the reward they could expect.

Otto waited in stony silence as the engraver labored over the passports and travel documents. It appeared as though the papers were only for one child. Otto would give Charles the passport, then handwrite a note on Gestapo stationery giving travel permission. Louis would carry the authentic travel documents and Leah would travel as Otto's sister.

"A foolish thing," he explained. "Left their papers on the train."

The engraver needed no further explanation. He was being well paid. Otto had an impeccably ruthless reputation. Such a man was certainly not a smuggler or a forger of false documents. "It will be a while longer." The rotund little man bent close to the document.

"We'll miss our train!" Otto snapped.

The man shrugged. It was not his fault that papers had been lost. Was he responsible for a missed train? "These things take time."

Time! That was one thing Otto did not have. Now he regretted telling Elisa that he would provide the papers tonight. He could have sent her on with the promise that he would see to Leah and the children! Precious minutes were ticking away, and here he sat in an ink-stained office with a printer who seemed not fully awake! He had broken the first rule;

he had softened for just a moment, and now the outcome might be decided by the ability of the engraver to work a bit faster!

"If our glorious Führer can command a building be built in three months, and it is up in three months when the architect said a year—" Otto straightened his back and peered arrogantly at the man—"then why can you not reproduce documents, simple ink and paper, in an hour?"

"You have asked for French passports, Herr Wattenbarger. French travel visas! This is the Reich! Why did you not awaken someone at the French Embassy for this?"

"How do you think they would feel if a Gestapo agent pulled them out of bed, eh? Be sensible. I do not want trouble for my sister and her son!"

The printer continued his slow, laborious task. "There are a hundred of our agents in France now carrying French documents that I forged! Even the French cannot tell the difference. Therefore, if you want quality, you have come to the right place. If you want speed, go someplace else."

"Do you know who you are speaking to?" Otto was arrogant. It made little difference. The engraver was an artist, unimpressed with the workings of the Gestapo.

"You are just another customer to me," he said curtly. "These things take time."

Charles watched mutely as Leah packed their things in separate bags. Elisa had kept some children's clothes in store for the little ones she had smuggled through to safe refuge in her work in the underground. Now the few items left would be used for these boys since their own clothes had been lost in the square. As Charles continued to watch Leah, he remembered how his father used to pack for them. Always two sets of little trousers and nightshirts had been packed together. Always together.

Louis sat half asleep on the edge of the bed. "But where are we going?"

Leah did not look at Charles. "A nice man is going to take us high up in the mountains. To visit a farm. Would you like that?"

Elisa had spoken of climbing trees and running in meadows. Charles was too ill to do either. Did Leah mean that he was going to this place, too? Why would she not look at him? Charles wondered. And why were his trousers not folded next to those of Louis?

"Did you hear that, Charles?" Louis awakened now at the thought of visiting the mountains, trees, and meadows. "We are going to a farm, Charles!"

Charles opened his mouth and groaned a reply as he shook his head *no* and patted his chest. Leah looked at him, then turned away quickly. He saw it in her eyes. He was not going with them.

"Of course you are going," Louis argued. "We are all going, aren't we, Aunt Leah?"

Leah frowned. Were those tears in her eyes? "Charles is going with Elisa. To Prague," she said stiffly.

"No!" Louis stood and stamped his foot. "I am going where my brother goes! And he is going where I go!"

"Please, Louis," Leah began. She looked at Charles, who slipped his fingers to his mouth. Charles understood it all. Everything. They could not stay together. It seemed too much for a child to comprehend, that men pursued him because of the cleft in his lip. The look in his eyes made Leah's heart ache. She sank onto the bed and brushed his hair back from his forehead. "You understand, don't you, Charles?"

He nodded.

"No!" Louis cried. "I cannot go anywhere without him. I want Father! I want my mother!"

Charles gazed solemnly at Louis and raised a finger, commanding him to be silent. Louis obeyed but dissolved into racking sobs as he dropped to the floor at Leah's feet.

"You will be together again." Leah stroked the boy's head.

"That is what Father said!" Louis said through his tears. "But we will not be with him again. Not *ever*!" Now he sobbed harder. "They killed him. Like they killed Mommy! And now they want to kill Charles, too!"

"Charles will be safe." Leah was helpless before his grief. Her reassurance meant nothing. How *could* it mean anything, after all?

Charles climbed out of bed. He swayed a moment and grimaced with the pain in his ears again. He knelt beside his weeping brother and wrapped his arms around him, as his father might have done—or his mother if she had been there. Gently, Charles rocked him back and forth. *It will be all right, Louis,* Charles' eyes said. He tried to hum the melody, "I am small, my heart is pure, no one shall live in it but Jesus alone."

The ragged attempt soothed Louis. He looked up at Charles. He did not see the mark on his brother's face, only the love in his eyes. "I will pray for you every day and night, Charles," he promised. "That someday we will be together again. With Mama and Father, too."

Charles nodded and stroked his brother's head in a gesture so tender and so hopeful that Leah had to turn her eyes away to hide her own tears. *Good-bye. I love you. Forever. Good-bye.*

Hugel's sausagelike fingers were trembling with excitement as he opened the top bureau drawer and pawed through his shorts for the gun. Suddenly it had all become clear to him. The sound of the cello music. Giggles that sounded like children. Why had he not seen it before? *Ah! It is the hand of Providence guiding me once again to victory! All along they have been in my building, and now I will capture them! Five hundred Reichsmarks!* The accountant would be so jealous. The Gestapo had not brought them in. No, Augustus Hugel would aim his gun in the name of the Führer and the Reich!

Hugel checked to see that the bullets were still in place. Just as they had been in place when he had last checked. He held the gun high over his head in exultation.

He would go slowly, quietly, up the stairs. There was no use in alerting them. He did not want to give them a chance to hide. Small children could hide in all sorts of inconvenient places. Hugel did not want that. He did not want the woman jumping from the window to kill herself as so many criminals had already done in Vienna. He did not want the mess of blood on the sidewalk. A simple arrest would do.

He took the key ring off the hook beside his door. Tucking the gun beneath his arm, he sifted through the keys until he found the one that opened the door to 2-B. He held it poised and ready to insert into the lock. He would turn it and spring on them, and . . .

Hugel frowned and glanced at the phone. Perhaps he should call the Gestapo. Little children had a way of dodging through the legs of a citizen and escaping. Perhaps he would need help. He lowered his chin and stuck out his lower lip in thought. If they dodged him, he would simply shoot them. He cocked the gun and steeled his will. Capturing human monsters and putting this matter to rest would earn him a lot of adulation. Five hundred Reichsmarks would buy a lot of beer.

Hugel cursed the steepness of the stairs. When he was promoted for the capture of these criminals, he would ask to be given a building with an elevator. He was out of breath, panting, by the time he reached the landing. Gripping the banister, he stood swaying in the dark hall. He would wait a moment before he burst in on them. He would wait. And listen. And catch his breath. Just a minute longer.

He wiped away the sweat with the back of his hand. Keys rattled together. He moved toward the door and pressed his face against the wood to listen.

Yes. There were voices. Two women. The voice of a child with them. Hugel drew in his breath. He must not give them warning of his presence. Must not give them time to hide or leap through the window. He would bring them in alive!

"But, Aunt Leah, where is this place? How far from the place where Charles is going?"

Charles! The name was that of the monster child whose photograph was on the bulletin board. Hugel had seen it; he had commented how contrary to nature it was that such a freak should live and consume the food of good German children. *Charles!* Yes, that was the name of the little beast.

The woman's voice answered softly, "Not so far away. In a place where there are no Nazis."

The voice of the other woman spoke now, worried. "Where could he be? He told us to be ready at midnight, and it is already two hours past! He should be here by now!"

He? Herr Hugel frowned and pressed his damp face harder against the door but could not hear the soft reply.

So someone else was in on this! Perhaps he had stumbled on to an entire nest of anti-government criminals. He frowned even deeper and glanced back down the stairs. Perhaps he *should* go back and call the Gestapo. Perhaps he would need help if he was up against more than just two women and two boys.

Then he imagined struggling up the stairs again. It was late. *He,* whoever *he* was, was late already. Supposed *he* came while Hugel was on the phone?

Hugel cocked the gun and stepped back to aim the key at the lock. The gun had bullets enough. Hugel had managed to bring in a few Jews before this. This was nothing he could not handle. He would shoot them if they tried anything. That was easy enough. He would shoot them.

At the sound of the rattle of the doorknob, Leah's eyes met Elisa's. A sigh of relief passed between them. They were indeed ready. Small suitcases. The cello and the violin. They would not be coming back here. They were ready.

The knob turned as Elisa reached to open the door. "Otto?"

Leah gasped as the door swung open to reveal Herr Hugel. She moved between the children and the barrel of the gun. Elisa stepped back as Hugel waved the weapon around the room. It was cocked and loaded. His fat finger was curled around the trigger.

"So!" he shouted in triumph as he kicked the door closed. "So! You thought you could get by me, did you? You thought I was not watching, eh? Well, I will tell you I have been alert to everything! *Ja!* I have been watching for these children! That freak you are hiding behind you, woman! I noticed! I heard everything! The sound of the cello!" He pointed the gun at the cello case as though it, too, were the enemy.

"What do you want?" Elisa tried to control the shaking of her voice. They had been through too much for it to come to this. "Money? We can pay you—"

He was insulted. "Money? *Ha!* I am incorruptible. My honor as a son of the Fatherland is without dispute. However, I shall tell the police that you offered me money, that you have money to offer, but that I refused to take it. You will not bribe me." Now he was chuckling. His honor pleased him. Only a very good man would refuse a bribe.

"Let us go. We will make certain—"

Now he raged. "*You*? You will make certain of *nothing*! I arrest you in the name of the Reich! Heil Hitler! I arrest you and this little mutant." He pointed the gun at Charles, who covered his mouth with his hand. "Don't try and run around me. I will shoot you as easily as a rat. I *know* who you are! I read it all! Because of *you*—"

"Shut up!" Leah took a step forward.

"Don't come closer!" Sweat poured from Hugel. "We will wait here for *him*! For your partner! And then I will take you all in. I have bullets enough to go around. Do not doubt!" His watery blue eyes bulged with stress. He looked wildly from one to another and then back again. "All of you! Hands against the wall!" He had seen the Gestapo method of arrest. Against the wall was the first order of business. If they did not obey, then . . .

Charles was the first to step to the wall. Elisa followed, glancing angrily at Hugel and then to Leah as if to ask what choice they had. Otto was coming, but Hugel knew that, too, somehow. Leah put her hands against the wall as Hugel jabbed the gun barrel behind Elisa's ear. "And I thought you were such a pretty lady! I thought you were one of us!"

The medicine had worn off, and Charles began to cough again.

"Let him lie down," Elisa said, her own arms aching from the hour Hugel had forced them to stand facing the wall.

Hugel was relaxed, enjoying his power now as he sat back on the sofa and stared at his captives. "Shut up," he menaced. "And *you*!" he barked at Charles. "You can stop that noise if you want! Shut up!"

Helpless, Charles continued to cough, finally leaning against the wall in exhaustion.

"Stand up there! You will not trick me with such an act, you little monster! Troll! Stand up there, I tell you!"

Charles could not find the strength to obey.

"*You* are the monster!" Leah cried, kneeling to hold the little boy.

"Get back up there—hands against the wall," Hugel commanded, struggling to his feet.

Leah did not move away from Charles, who now rested his head wearily against her shoulder. Hugel lunged forward, grabbing Charles by the back of his shirt and swinging him around as he kicked Leah hard in the back.

She cried out and toppled over as Hugel pressed the barrel between Charles' eyes. "Little monster. Who would notice if I put another hole in your face? Something to match this one, eh?" He moved the barrel to the child's mouth. Louis began to weep bitterly.

Elisa cried, "He is just a baby!"

Hugel held him off the floor. He put the gun barrel in the boy's mouth where the tissue was painfully tender and inflamed. Tears came to Charles' eyes, but he did not cry out.

"A baby! A baby what! I have shot cats that are not so ugly as this!"

"Isn't it enough?" Leah cried as she struggled to her knees. "Isn't it enough that you hold us here? Must you also be so cruel?"

Hugel laughed at her accusation. "He doesn't understand what I am saying! He has no mind! A brainless idiot! I read all about it! A drain on society, he is! Better off if he had died at birth. Or been put out of his misery!"

Terror that Hugel might be the one to end the boy's life filled Elisa and Leah. They dared not speak another word. How could they argue with this? What was left to say in the face of such abysmal self-righteous cruelty? Any moment Otto would walk through the door, and then it would all be at an end.

Hugel threw Charles to the floor and let him lie there gasping for breath. "Don't try anything," Hugel growled. "I am at the end of my patience." He came near each of his prisoners in turn, pressing the muzzle of the gun to each neck. He let them feel his power, the nearness of death. He was fully sober now, and with the sobriety his viciousness had deepened.

Elisa closed her eyes and prayed for Otto. Perhaps he had listened at the door and had heard Hugel. Perhaps Otto had turned away and left them there in the hands of this man. The minutes dragged by, and with their passage, the hope that Otto might somehow help them vanished.

When the job was finished, Otto scrutinized the documents under the strong light of the engraver's lamp. "A good job," Otto said with satisfaction.

"Good? No one can tell the difference between these and the real thing!" The engraver was proud of his handiwork.

Otto flipped a few bills out onto the desk. "That is enough." It was half of what the man had demanded.

"Enough? I told you—," the engraver began to protest.

"And now I am telling you—" Otto stopped him with a steely look—"one word of this to anyone, and there is a dark cell waiting for you."

Otto had a reputation of ruthlessness to maintain. The engraver nodded and gathered up the money. He had done his job. No one would hear about it—at least, not from him.

It was well past midnight when Otto reached the Gestapo building. This was the hour when the halls were crowded with terrified men with nightshirts tucked into trousers and handcuffs on their wrists. This was the hour when the tormented howls of victims echoed in the halls like the baying of dying wolves.

Otto lowered his head and ran quickly up the steps past a guard who shoved a weeping man to the floor. This was the hour when Otto most hated himself and this place, when the madness of his mission threatened to overcome his sanity and send him screaming into the night.

He slammed the door of his dark office, trying to shut out the screams of the inferno. Still the sound penetrated the wood and bored into his senses. He took out a sheet of stationery and began to write:

> *To whom it may concern:*
>
> *Charles Murphy, aged five, bearer of French passport and in the company of Elisa Murphy, is a sufferer of tuberculosis. By order of Gestapo, he is to be allowed to pass through the Austrian frontier. Destination: Heldorf Tuberculosis Sanitorium; Marienbad, Czechoslovakia. Any delay or harassment will result in inquiry by Vienna Gestapo HQ.*
>
> *Signed Otto Wattenbarger*

It was done. He had put his name to the document that would smuggle out of the reach of the Reich a child who represented a threat to all Hitler stood for. There could be no explaining this act away if he was discovered. This threat of Gestapo investigation was empty. Even as Otto stamped the paper with the official Gestapo seal, he knew that this was also the seal used to verify death warrants and notices of execution. Perhaps he had just sealed his own death warrant as well as those of Elisa and the boy. Whatever it meant, it was done, and Otto would not undo it.

He waited long enough for the ink to dry, then slipped the notices into an envelope bearing the seal of the Gestapo. He stamped each side with his personal officer's seal, then clicked out the light. As the shrieks of a woman resounded in the halls, he hurried out into the darkness that was Vienna.

47

Flight From Darkness

Murphy sat disconsolately in the empty waiting room at Heathrow. Like Sandburg's poem, the cursed fog had come in on little cat feet and had trapped every available bird in its claws. Nothing was flying to England and nothing was flying out either.

Murphy paced for a while, pausing every few steps to glare at the gray wall in front of the window. The thought that he was this close to seeing Elisa again and yet unable to reach her made him not only worried about her, but irritable. He told the ticket clerk just what he thought of this ridiculous air-travel nonsense, and then he turned down a ride back to the Savoy. Now there were no taxis either. Only a crazy person would drive in this stuff. Or fly. Murphy was the only man crazy enough to want to.

He wished now that he had gone back to the Savoy. Wadding up his coat, he stretched out on a bench and pretended to sleep. It was night, after all. A man was supposed to sleep at night. And if he couldn't, he at least ought to look as if he were trying.

An hour later he realized that there was no one at all in the building to see him trying to sleep. Absolutely everyone else in the world had gone to bed. Murphy sat up and scanned the walls for the light switch, then, with a sigh, turned out the lights at Heathrow.

Hugel sat up straight as footsteps sounded outside on the stairs.

"You!" he snapped to Elisa. "Go to the door."

Elisa hesitated until Hugel shook the gun at her.

The rapping was barely audible. Otto was back.

"Ask who it is," Hugel demanded in a whisper.

"Who . . . ?" Elisa's voice faltered.

"Otto. Hurry up!"

Hugel stood beside the door, his gun trained at eye level. "Open it," he told Elisa, and his lips curved in a slight smile.

Crestfallen, Elisa obeyed. The door groaned on its hinges.

Otto raised his eyes to the barrel of Hugel's gun but showed no emotion. Elisa watched him, but he did not gasp. He did not frown. He stepped over the threshold as Hugel motioned for him to enter, but even then he did not display surprise or anger or fear.

"Who is this fat cow?" he asked Leah.

"I am Herr Augustus Hugel! Apartment Führer! I arrest you in the name of the Reich. Heil Hitler!"

"I should have such dedicated men on my staff at the Gestapo." Otto raised his hands as Hugel brandished his weapon menacingly.

"Gestapo!" Hugel appeared surprised. "A traitor? A traitor to the heart! Stand against the wall!" he shouted.

"Apartment Führer? You have missed your calling, Herr Hugel. You would do better in a job like mine." Otto obeyed.

"Perhaps I *will* have your job! I know all about everything—these children, the little beast. You are going to take them . . . somewhere."

"A true Nazi. Listening at keyholes. Congratulations, Hugel. Such diligence will be rewarded." Otto's hands were high above his head. He continued to talk calmly. He was looking at the still little figure of Charles as he slept on the floor. "So tell me, now that you have captured our desperate little band, what do you do next?"

"*Now* I call the Gestapo!" Hugel picked up the telephone in triumph. The phone was dead.

"It has been out of use since the Anschluss," Leah said.

Hugel threw the receiver onto the floor. "Fine! Mine works perfectly. Come on, come on, all of you. Keep your hands high!" He nudged Charles with his toe, a gesture that brought the first glimmer of anger to Otto's eyes.

"Leave the boy alone," Otto warned.

"And what will you do if I don't?" Hugel chuckled. After all, he was the man with the weapon.

"I will kill you," Otto said calmly. There was no hint of doubt in his voice.

Hugel chuckled again, this time nervously. He stepped back and opened the door. "Get him!" he said to Otto. "Pick up the freak if you care so much." With his arms full of the child, Otto would not be quite so ready to kill anyone.

Otto bent down to scoop up Charles. He propped the drowsy child against himself, then pulled a handkerchief from his pocket and covered the boy's mouth and nose with it. The ragged breath pulled the cloth and then released it as Otto tied it loosely to conceal the cleft.

"Come on!" Hugel spat impatiently. "It is too late to hide the creature's face!"

Otto raised his eyes to silence the fat man with one deadly, menacing look.

"Pick him up!" Hugel shouted. "And the other one too!"

Louis was asleep where he stood leaning against the wall. Otto gathered him into his arms as well. He held the brothers gently, and for a moment, Elisa looked at the tall, strong man and imagined him as he might have first been. *If only . . .*

"You first!" Hugel's face reddened as he screamed at Otto. Moving his prisoners was a bit more complicated than simply standing them against the wall. "Single file!" he commanded, backing toward the door. "One false move, and I mingle the monster's brains with your own." He placed the gun to Charles' head. The child slept in Otto's arms. Merciful sleep.

Elisa found herself focusing on the tiny fingers draped over Otto's shoulders. Perfect hands. Hands that one day might have played the violoncello as beautifully as Leah. *If only . . .*

"Keep your hands above your head!" Hugel stepped all the way back to the banister as they filed out into the corridor.

Otto could not raise his hands with Charles and Louis cradled in his arms. The sight made Hugel feel safe. A gun at the head of a five-year-old in the arms of a man who cared! No one would dare challenge him. Providence had arranged it all. He would go to mass and thank God for this moment. He would give 10 percent of the reward to the offering box.

Leah had not spoken. This was the culmination of all her nightmares. The worst had come to pass, and there were no words to stop it. Nothing to change it. The gun was poised, cocked, and ready at the back of Charles' head. And yet the child slept peacefully, as if nothing whatever was wrong. He would not live to see the next morning dawn. None of them would. Still he slept in Otto's arms.

Hugel backed to the stairs. "I will go down first." He gripped the banister. "No funny business. It is a simple matter of my finger and the trigger."

They did not argue but shuffled silently after him. He stood facing them. For Hugel, going *down* stairs had always been easier than going up. But he had never done it backward with prisoners in line before. "No tricks," he warned again as he jabbed the gun.

Charles stirred.

Then Otto asked the question—a simple question that had no place in this moment. His voice was quiet, as if he was trying not to wake the children. It was gentle, as though Hugel, standing before him at the top of the stairway, were an old and dear friend. "How long has it been since you have been to confession?"

Hugel snorted, furious at the tone of voice, enraged that Otto still did not take the loaded gun seriously. "Confession!"

Otto smiled, and with the ease of taking another step, he drew back his boot and slammed it hard into Hugel's groin.

Hugel screamed with pain as the force of the blow hurtled his bulk backward. The gun, still in his hand, dangled crazily from his trigger finger and fired, sending a burst of flame into the floor at Hugel's feet.

Otto whirled and shoved the children into Elisa's arms as Hugel fought to regain his balance. The rest was simple. One more well-placed kick sent the fat man to his back. Like a log in a shoot, he hurtled down the stairs, screaming all the way. The gun discharged four more times in rapid succession as Hugel's head slammed against each step. His body gained momentum; his weight propelled him with a velocity that swept him to the bottom of the stairs. He slid across the marble floor, smashing his head into the wall on the far side of the lobby.

Otto stood at the top of the stairs and narrowed his eyes as Hugel twitched for an instant and then lay still. Hugel's head was cocked to one side and lay against his shoulder. His eyes stared vacantly up toward Otto. The mouth was open in a bizarre grin. Otto was sure that the immense weight of Hugel's body had snapped his neck.

Doors from other apartments began to open. Shouts and questions filled the hall.

"Herr Hugel has fallen down the stairs!" Otto answered. As voices cried out for an ambulance and others for the police, Otto turned to Leah and Elisa. Each of them held a child. "There is no time. Get what you need."

He herded them back into the apartment and sorted the documents. "Elisa, you must hand the soldiers this." He held up the letter. "They will not touch Charles after they read it. Tuberculosis. He's on his way to a sanitorium. Remember that!"

The halls of the building buzzed with excitement. Every tenant peered over the banister at the body in the lobby.

"What is happening?" Louis raised his head and looked around.

"We are leaving." Otto took him from Leah's arms.

Charles woke up then and stretched his arms out to Leah in a final embrace. She hugged him and then picked up the violoncello. He embraced the well-worn case with his eyes. Such beautiful eyes. They asked silently, *"Will I ever see you again?"*

There was no time to reply now. Otto shook his head at Leah. "You cannot take that." He opened the door. "We will drive only as far as Kitzbühel. You cannot carry it over the mountains."

Elisa raised her chin in defiance of this order. "I will take it for her, rather than have her leave it in Austria."

Now Charles could relax. The question left his face. Vitorio would go with them, and so he *must* see Leah again! He *would* find Louis again! One day they would be together. . . .

The little group made their way out through the crowd of gawkers who now surrounded the body in the lobby.

"A foul man . . . "

"No doubt drunk again."

"Not surprising he would clatter down the stairs."

Around the corner the sirens wailed the approach of Gestapo cars and an ambulance. Hugel still held the gun in his lifeless hand. There would be questions about the death of the Apartment Führer despite the reek of beer on the man.

Elisa could not embrace Leah. No time. No time. They had already shared their moment of farewell. Charles clung to the violin as Elisa carried the cello to her car. Leah, Otto, and Louis slipped around the corner to where Otto's car waited.

Three Gestapo cars, lights whirling and wailing, screamed past Elisa as she helped Charles into the front seat of the Packard. When she placed Vitorio in the back, the cello seemed to take on the appearance of another person.

Charles peeked over the back of the seat at the uniformed Nazi officials shoving their way into the lobby. It would take a lot of men to lift Herr Hugel, he thought.

Elisa turned the key in the ignition; it coughed and died. She prayed out loud. "Please, God!" The engine coughed and caught with a roar. She ground the gears as the car lurched away from the curb. Yet another police car passed them.

Charles strained his eyes to look past all that to where the taillights of another car receded up the street. He raised his fingers slightly in a wave and watched the lights until they rounded a corner and disappeared from sight.

Otto's car had not even passed beyond the fringes of Vienna before the notice came over his shortwave radio:

> *"All officers are asked to take special diligence in this matter. Two women, a man, and two boys are sought for questioning by the Gestapo in the matter of the death of a loyal Nazi Party member early this morning. They were seen together right after the—"*

Otto switched off the radio.

A now wide-awake Louis leaned forward eagerly to listen to the news. "Were they talking about us, Herr Otto?"

"No," Otto answered truthfully. "They are talking about two women, a man, and two children. We are only one man, a woman, and one boy who should be sleeping now, *bitte*."

Leah glanced at Otto with a strange mix of admiration and confusion. What sort of man might he have been if his life had not become so tied up in all this? And what sort of man was he really now? *A good man,* she thought. *A good man who has chosen a hard way to make some difference in this madness.*

The immense buildings of Vienna were shrouded in darkness, colorless hulks in the sleeping city. The headlights of Elisa's car reflected on the shiny cobblestones of the empty Ringstrasse. For a fleeting moment she could remember the peace and beauty of what had been her home. A twinge of sadness passed through her and then was instantly replaced by the urgency of their escape.

The windows of buildings no longer seemed to be eyes closed in dream-filled sleep. Behind every shade and shutter were watchers now—those, who, like Hugel, had traded the mundane hours of a simple life for the rush of excitement flowing from the voice of their new Führer. They had come to believe that *they* were the superior race he longed for. Fat and thin, young and old fell into line with the endless marching columns. Crooked teeth, balding heads, pockmarked skin . . . still they were the beautiful ones, the *purity* of the Aryan race! Shopkeepers and thieves, farmers and headwaiters now raised their arms in automatic salute. Heil Hitler! Gone from Vienna was the gentle expression, *Grüss Gott*—"God Bless!"

Even the buildings now seemed like colossal tombstones to Elisa. She was not leaving the home of her greatest happiness; she was fleeing a cemetery. Here the living dead sought to destroy the lives of those who resisted the disease that had claimed their souls! Elisa shuddered as she turned onto the highway that led from the City of the Dead! Regrets vanished. She would not come back here. It did not matter anymore.

Elisa caught a glimpse of the dim reflection in the side window. Little

Charles sat erect, pressed against her side, his eyes consuming the gloomy sights of the passing of Vienna. Did he sense Elisa's thoughts? His brow furrowed in a frown. She did not ask him what he was thinking. He could not reply with words, but she saw it clearly in his expression. Charles was more than just a child. He was a million children, innocent and bright, herded onto that terrible train Elisa had witnessed in her nightmare. He was the purity and trust that Evil could not tolerate! He was the gentleness and innocence that Evil must pursue and destroy or be put to shame.

This one child embodied those millions of children whom Evil had marked for destruction. An end in an unmarked grave, flesh consumed by fire! Charles, whose imperfection inspired such hatred in the mindless evil of the Reich, was the child on the lap of Christ, the one whose heart and faith were promised the Kingdom of Righteousness. Without uttering one word, this little boy had torn at the conscience of a dying nation and a dying church!

Men had, indeed, turned from the evil doctrines of Hitler because of Charles. Hugel had been right about that. Men had seen the truth in Charles' clear blue eyes. Could any government have a right before God to end the life of a child? Only if the state also publicly ended the life of God. The very soul of the nation was weighed in the balance of eternity and found wanting. The state had sought to end the life of one child in the name of "mercy." That one tiny tear in the fabric of morality led to the deaths of thousand of others judged "unworthy." How many more yet to come would be executed by a government that claimed the right that only a merciful God had held before?

Without a spoken word, Charles was the voice of an unnumbered multitude. Elisa was once again the courier of that message: *Stand firm against Evil, or it will consume you as well! Stand against those who steal the minds of your children and replace their prayers with platitudes! Guard the rights of the helpless, or one day you will be helpless and there will be no one there to save you!*

Elisa glanced up again and saw the reflection of her own face beside that of the little boy. One image fleeing the darkness. One image pursued by the angry eyes of Evil.

48

Border Crossing

Less than three miles beyond Vienna, as the eastern sky began to lighten, Elisa spotted the first taillights of the army convoys on the road ahead. To either side of the main highway, she could hear the rumble of a thousand other vehicles that had driven around the city and now were converging into one crawling line before her.

She downshifted and braked, matching her pace with the crawl of the army vehicles. She turned on the radio, hoping for some word of a detour for civilian traffic, but the music of military marches was all she could find.

So this was it—the army of the Reich, trucks and transports of sleeping young men who still did not know why they had traveled east all through the night. Elisa bit her lip. She could tell them all about it. A murder would take place in Paris today at noon. And tonight, unless she found some way to get through all this, there would be a second murder in Prague, followed by riots and slaughter in the streets.

Charles' face grew ashen at the sight of so many soldiers. It was the same sight he and Louis had watched the morning their father had left them in Vienna. It had been a terrifying adventure then. Now he trembled at the thought that these soldiers might be going where Elisa was going. Was there no end to them? Was there no safe place? No place to get away from the bloody banners and trembling earth beneath the wheels of field artillery and tanks?

Elisa spoke for the first time since they had left. "They will turn off. They cannot go all the way to the Czech border!"

But the guns and tanks and lorries did not turn off. Occasionally a vehicle broke down, and the entire column would grind to a halt. Hours passed, and Elisa felt no nearer to the safety of the border than she had at dawn.

Her stomach growled with hunger. They should have been across the border by now, eating breakfast at a small Czech café she knew of. A glance told her Charles was also hungry. He clutched his stomach and peered out the window at a group of Wehrmacht soldiers eatomg bread and cheese by the side of the road. He knew as well as Elisa that he could not eat, however. Even if there was a place to stop, Charles could not dare to remove the kerchief over his mouth.

"Not much longer," Elisa said gently, but the words held little meaning. The car lurched forward and stopped again. As the column rounded a long curve, Elisa could see a dozen other civilian cars sandwiched in between the huge vehicles of the Wehrmacht. And one at a time, a soldier on a motorcycle would drive to those civilian cars and demand identity papers.

Elisa's mouth grew dry. She worked her fingers nervously on the steering wheel and looked down at the Gestapo seal on Otto's letter. She prayed silently for herself and for Charles, for the president of Czechoslovakia and for the man who was to die at noon. She prayed for the millions beyond the borders of the Reich who would be affected by all that must take place today!

The fog at Heathrow lifted midmorning, and with the sunlight a flock of taxis arrived from London. Cab after cab disgorged reporters who jammed in through the entrance of the building and vied for places in line at the ticket counter.

"A ticket to Prague."

"When's the plane to Prague leave?"

"What? You mean we can't get out of here until this afternoon?"

Murphy greeted every one of his three dozen colleagues as they wandered past the bench where he was comfortably stretched out waiting for his two o'clock flight to Prague. He watched with amused interest as a fistfight broke out between Cedric Wells of the *Edinburgh Examiner* and Keith Walpole of the dignified *London Morning Post.* It seemed that Cedric had crowded into line and managed to purchase the last ticket to Prague.

Amanda Taylor spotted Murphy after Walpole bloodied the nose of Wells, winning the fight but losing the seat to Prague anyway. She waved cheerily and brought steaming cups of coffee to share.

"I thought you would already be in Prague, Johnny!" She sat beside him.

"Me too. Fog." He held up his ticket. "Let's just say I was the first in line. I thought you weren't supposed to go to Prague."

"That's what I thought. Seems Editorial has come to its senses." She gazed somberly at him. There was no hint of amusement left in her voice. "Every last Wehrmacht soldier in the Reich is being moved east. The Germans are not attempting to hide the fact, other than giving the explanation that they are simply staging dress rehearsal in case the Czechs attack. Something is up. More is up than anyone is admitting, but too much for even the conservative *Times* to ignore. Looks as if you may have a chance to introduce me to your wife, Johnny."

He frowned at the scruffy, anxious crowd of reporters. "War. I've learned to see it coming by the buzzards who fly in for the pickings."

"You're a fairly prominent buzzard yourself, Johnny." Amanda was smiling again. "We don't make the news, you know. We just write it."

It was not yet noon when Thomas von Kleistmann strolled into the stall of the Dead Man, looking haggard and worn. *Vulnerable,* Herschel thought with surprise as his hand moved instinctively toward his hidden weapon.

Herschel tried not to gawk. How had Hans known so precisely that von Kleistmann would come here today? Throughout the morning, Herschel had assumed that he would have to find the Nazi at the German Embassy and shoot him there. Somehow, it had all been made easy. Here, beneath the canvas awning of the Dead Man, there were no swastika flags or glaring SS guards to intimidate him.

Herschel shielded his eyes against the brightness of the sun and looked toward the sky. Perhaps it was the guiding of Providence that had delivered his enemy into his hands. "Rue du Cherche-Midi," Herschel muttered, remembering the street and the prison that had held the French Jew Dreyfus. "The Search for Noon." Somehow that memory stirred Herschel's courage once again. Other Jews had suffered. No doubt he would be arrested for the killing of this Nazi, but he would recall the others who had languished behind bars and thick walls. He would be brave as he followed such footsteps.

"Did you enjoy your trip to the countryside, Major von Kleistmann?" asked Le Morthomme pleasantly.

"I tasted some excellent wines. . . ."

"And did you have a woman to share your wine with?" The old bookseller grinned.

Herschel remembered Thomas with his arm around Elisa back in Vienna. How small she had seemed beside him, and how easily he had crushed her heart!

"Women in the country? There are enough to go around in Paris. And what can compare with a woman from Paris, Le Morthomme?"

"Well, then, did you find any good books to read?"

Thomas spread his empty hands wide. "I have come home empty-handed, I'm afraid. Have you any new volumes just arrived that I might buy?"

The old bookseller laughed apologetically. "There is nothing new under the sun, as they say! Nothing you might care about. Nothing at all, I'm afraid."

Thomas frowned and stood silently over a table that sagged beneath the weight of hundreds of books. He absently thumbed through one and then another, finally sighing heavily and looking up at the Dead Man. "Well, then."

He was going to leave! Herschel knew it! He could tell by the way the tall German gazed beyond the bookstall. Herschel searched frantically for a way to keep him here. He must not leave until the appointed hour. He must die at noon, along with all the others who were destined to perish today in this statement against Nazi brutality!

Herschel touched his gun; then, almost panicked at the thought of losing his quarry, he called, "Nothing new? There are several new volumes since you were last here! And many old among the new that you have not read!"

Herschel's words and bravado seemed to surprise Thomas. He turned and with a curious smile he said, "So the Dead Man is making a bookseller out of you."

Herschel nodded and licked his lips nervously. Sweat poured from him. It was still so long before the hour! Hans had said that every target must fall at the same moment.

"Yes, he may sell books, but he still has something to learn about the reading preferences of my customers." The old bookseller seemed to dismiss Herschel with those words, but still the young man persisted.

"Have you looked at this table?" Herschel stepped aside, but Thomas had already returned his attention to the old man.

"There is nothing to be done. Nothing but to wait," Thomas said in a low voice.

The Dead Man put a leathery hand on Thomas' arm. "You must be careful, then."

Herschel stared at the old man with amazement. Of what was he warning the German? Had Le Morthomme guessed Herschel's purpose? Had he seen the gun or heard the whispered words?

Thomas nodded. "Thank you," he said, as though he were leaving.

The sun was high. The bells of Notre Dame had not yet chimed the hour of noon, but Herschel could not wait for the other unnamed assassins across the Continent to take their aim on some inhuman Nazi target.

He opened his mouth and cried, "Wait!"

But Thomas did not wait. He turned to leave, passing between overloaded tables.

Herschel fumbled to pull the weapon from his waistband. "Von Kleistmann!" he screamed. "Do you not remember Elisa?"

Thomas stopped midstride. He turned as Herschel cocked the gun and held it up with trembling arms. "How do you know—?" Thomas began. He froze as his eyes caught the glint of the sun on the metal of the barrel.

"Cherche-Midi!" Herschel shouted the name of the prison; then his finger slowly squeezed the trigger.

Le Morthomme raised his hands in dismay. "No!" His cry was stopped by the first bullet from Herschel's gun as the old man threw himself forward in front of the barrel.

Herschel's eyes widened with horror as the Dead Man's mouth opened and closed in angry surprise as blood oozed from behind his gaping teeth.

Thomas rushed forward, snatching the smoking gun from Herschel's hand at the same instant he caught the crumbling body of the Dead Man.

As shouts echoed from all corners of the book market, Herschel backed away. His hand was like a claw, as if he still held the weapon. Cries of anguish pierced the air around him. On the ground, the Nazi, von Kleistmann, worked to stop the flow of blood as he shouted for someone to find a doctor.

"Le Morthomme! Someone has shot Le Morthomme!" Several took up the cry, and the bells of Notre Dame joined in tolling the terrible hour!

Herschel shook his head, then turned to push past the frantic crowd that rushed in. When he reached the banks of the Seine, he began to run. He ran all the way to Rue du Cherche-Midi, past the thick stone walls of the prison where the persecuted hero Dreyfus had languished. The boy did not stop running until he collapsed in the dark attic room, where dreams of glory had illuminated his soul like the noon sun.

"To the side! Pull to the side of the road, *bitte*!" The inspecting officer in the sidecar of the army motorcycle shouted to Elisa over the droning of the engines ahead and behind her.

Elisa obeyed and turned the wheel sharply, rolling to the shoulder of the road. Immediately a transport lunged forward to take her place. Her hands were shaking as she gathered the papers. The officer sauntered slowly up to the car door. He peered in at Charles, who sat quietly beside Elisa with his hands folded in his lap.

"*Guten Tag,* Officer! What is all this?" Elisa tried to sound pleasantly curious.

"Military exercise. To see how ready we might be in case of attack." He answered as he must have answered every inquiry through the long and difficult morning. "You will step out of the car, please."

Elisa continued to maintain a look of pleasant compliance. "As you wish."

"Him too," said the officer, jerking a thumb toward Charles.

The child started to move. "Just a minute, darling." Elisa stopped Charles as he began to cough.

"I said, *he* will step out of the vehicle also." The officer would tolerate no argument.

Elisa handed him the envelope with the official seal of the Gestapo. Let him argue with Otto. With the state police. Not with her.

His eyes widened slightly as he removed the letter from the envelope and began to read. "Tuberculosis?" He stepped back involuntarily. "Quite. He may remain where he is seated, Frau . . . Murphy?" He pronounced the name with difficulty.

Elisa gained courage. "Is there any way we can get around this? As you can see—" the exhaust caused Charles to cough harder—"the boy needs attention. I would not have brought him out in this if I had realized."

The officer read over the document again, then glanced up at the passing vehicles. "Perhaps, Frau Murphy . . . " He rubbed his cheek in thought.

Another motorcycle rattled up beside his, and a young Nazi messenger in a coat and dirty goggles called out to him, "Word from Vienna!"

"One moment, Frau Murphy." The officer walked to the messenger. "What is it?"

"They want you to be on the lookout for two boys. Two women and a man. Something to do with those Kronenberger twins we've been watching for."

Elisa's heart was thumping as the officer nodded. The expression of boredom on the face of Charles did not change. Surely the child had heard his name mentioned, yet he did not react.

"I haven't seen them." The officer gestured toward where Elisa stood by the open door of her automobile. "But I've got a problem here. Sick child. Tuberculosis. Going to the sanitorium at Marienbad." He waved the Gestapo stationery. "All the truck fumes can't be good for him. Let him follow you up to the front of the line, will you, Schmidt? Sixteen miles, eh?"

The messenger nodded and lifted his goggles for a second look at the beautiful blond beside the American car. He grinned at her. "Sure! A pleasant duty, compared to this."

The officer looked relieved. He waved the paper toward Elisa. "Schmidt will have you to the border in no time!"

"Danke schön!" Elisa waved.

"Heil Hitler!" said the officer with relief as he handed her the papers.

She returned his salute, praying that he would not see her fingers shaking as she took the documents from him. "And good luck," she added, revving the engine and pulling out behind the sputtering motorcycle on the far side of the creeping convoy.

Three miles from the border of Czechoslovakia, the convoy disappeared, peeling off to the right and left along the dusty farm roads.

There, they would wait for word. *Prague in shambles. Wehrmacht called upon to restore order.* Then they would march across the border. They would follow the same road along which Elisa now fled. They would cross the Sudetenland and continue on to Prague, where Albert Sporer prepared a place for them. They would rumble into the streets of Prague and drape their banners on the Hradcany Castle and the National Theatre! They would break down the doors of everyone who resisted. They would find Theo again. They would find Charles and all of this . . . all of this . . . would have been for nothing.

Who could stand against an army like this? Who could resist such force? The British and the French were quaking at the thought of it. President Beneš, who vowed his nation would fight alone if they must, would be dead by tonight if the plan of Sporer was accomplished. Unless . . . unless . . .

The Nazi messenger on the motorcycle pulled to the side of the road as the Czech border station came into view. Elisa slowed long enough to thank him.

"My pleasure." He waved. "Maybe I'll look you up in Marienbad tomorrow."

"But that's Czech territory," Elisa teased.

"Today it is." He laughed, but he was not joking. "Who knows about tomorrow?"

Elisa felt little relief as she approached the barricade and stopped.

Czech customs officials walked somberly out to greet her. The road behind her was deserted, but they could see the clouds of dust. They knew what lay beneath the cloud.

Even crossing the border she did not feel safe. Otto had warned her. There were Nazis everywhere inside the Czech border now. Like worms in an apple, they had eaten away the core of the nation. Even Elisa could feel no safety.

It would be hours before she reached Prague. If she arrived too late for President Beneš and the Czech nation, then it would be too late for Theo. For Charles. For a million others . . .

49

Die Judin

The oncoming traffic of troop lorries and armored divisions moving eastward seemed endless. Wehrmacht troops, stationed in the passes of the Alps near the Wattenbarger farm, were being transferred to the frontier surrounding the country of Czechoslovakia.

A hundred times that day Otto was forced to pull to the side of the road to let German officers pass the long procession at a quicker pace. The head of the Nazi serpent was already in place to strike through the heart of the Sudetenland. Now the tail writhed toward that same destination.

It was dusk before Otto looked upon the high peaks of his native Tyrol. They finally passed the end of the troop movement. A few broken-down transports were stalled at various locations beside the road, but that was all. The sight of the endless army had frightened Leah. It also confirmed that every word Otto had spoken was true.

Otto said little throughout the long journey from Vienna. The strain of exhaustion showed on his face. He turned on the radio and fiddled with the dial in hopes of hearing some news from Paris.

German polkas and folk music faded in and out as they drove between the craggy peaks. Lights of tiny villages winked on. Otto listened, but there was no news from Paris. The raging voice of Hitler did not shriek about the death of an honored Nazi at the hands of some young Jew. Hess and Goebbels did not interrupt the music with the latest report of the rage of the nation over the act of the Jewish beast! Music played on insanely. Something had gone wonderfully wrong in Paris. The military attaché was not dead. There was no unemployed Jew to be captured and extradited to receive justice in the Reich!

Otto was almost smiling now as the last rays of sunlight faded over the Alps. Was it the fresh, clean air? his nearness to home? Or the uninterrupted music, the lack of news?

After an hour of pleasant silence, he looked at Leah. "They have nothing to report. No crime against the Reich. Something went wrong in Paris today. Thank God. Thank God."

Something *had* gone wrong in Paris. Albert Sporer turned off the radio and faced the dozen men who would lead the bands of demonstrators tonight.

Sporer shrugged. "It doesn't matter. Nothing will go wrong for us. Even if the Jew should miss, we have a backup gunman in the box just opposite Beneš' box." He was smiling now. Beneš would indeed die like his hero Lincoln—only his death would not mark the end of war but the beginning. "It seems fitting he should perish during a performance of *Die Judin*, does it not? When the tympani sounds and the flames rise to devour the young Jewish bride."

The image sparked his imagination as he mentally rehearsed the scene. "The Jew will fire first. He is a young fool, quaking in his shoes at what he is about to do." Sporer removed his black dinner ket from the closet of the cramped room as he spoke. "But if he misses, someone else will not miss. When the flames devour the Jewess, when the tympani rolls, then Beneš will die."

Still ninety miles from Prague, the tire on the Packard blew, sending Elisa to a swerving halt beside the narrow road. It was almost six o'clock in the evening. In two hours *Die Judin* would be starting at the National Theatre! Two hours, and it might all be over for Beneš—and all over for the Czech nation as well!

Exhausted, almost hopeless, Elisa laid her head against the steering wheel. *What now? What next?*

There was no time for despair. Charles patted her demandingly on the back. He shook his head. There was not time to rest!

"I have never changed a tire," Elisa said, as though this explained her slowness to move.

He shook his head again. That did not matter. He moved over to the door and climbed out. So thin and frail, and yet he opened his mouth and sounded an impatient, almost angry cry. He beat his fist against the flat tire. She would *have* to change the tire and would have to do it *now*!

President Beneš was a small man, a man of gentleness and reason who faced a pack of reporters as fearlessly as he faced the crises in his country. "We have just this hour received assurances from the German ambassador that troop movements are a drill—"

"Do you believe this?" called a Frenchman. Murphy did not recognize him among the newsmen who were packed into the gilded anteroom of Prague's Hradcany Castle.

"We hope that their word is good."

"And if it is not? Will Czechoslovakia fight alone? Do you still say that you will fight alone, even if France and Britain do not honor their treaty commitments?"

Beneš frowned. He was a man of patience. He believed that ultimately his nation would survive the pressure from Nazi Germany without and the racial Germans within the Sudetenland who threatened to tear this vital area from the control of Prague. "We are negotiating with the leaders of Sudetenland. Those of racial German heritage, and—"

"Negotiate!" a German reporter interrupted rudely. "Blowing off their heads, you mean!"

Beneš would not be trapped. He ignored the comment, aware that the reporter who shouted at him was in the employ of Adolf Hitler. "We hope . . . that negotiation and reason will prevail in this matter that divides people who are citizens of the same land, although of different heritage."

"President Beneš, it is widely discussed that tonight's performance of *Die Judin* was ordered by you and will, in fact, further inflame the racial sensibilities of the Germans in your country."

Murphy sat up to see who had asked that question. It was a good one. The entire issue at stake here was a racial one. Civil war in Czechoslovakia would last only long enough for Hitler to invade.

"There is nothing sensible about racial sensibilities, sir," Beneš answered carefully in English. "Our nation, like America, is a mix of races. It is stated in our constitution that all men are free to worship as they please. That means men and women of all races, be they Jews, Czechs, or Germans. Racial hysteria has no place here. *Die Judin,* an opera about a young Jewess who falls in love with a Christian and is then executed by the church, is a play that seems very appropriate for our time. I asked that it be performed not to arouse conflict but to show that conflict is mindless in this matter."

"Some of your German citizens have threatened to march against this obvious display of Jewish propaganda," said the German. "Will you have troops on hand to brutalize them as you have done in the Sudetenland?"

"There will be no need of troops at the National Theatre tonight." He smiled grimly. "For those unfamiliar with the play, I will state simply that the young Jewess burned by the cardinal turns out to be the daughter of the cardinal. There is a lesson there that our more racist German citizens might learn."

"The tickets were all sold to Jews," scoffed the reporter. "No Germans will be able to attend."

"Were there any Germans in the ticket lines?" He pointed past the Nazi reporter to Amanda. "Yes? A question?"

"Plays are all very nice, but the German Wehrmacht now performs a dress rehearsal on your frontier. The question remains: Is your country strong enough to withstand an attack, should they invade?"

Beneš nodded. "They would not get past our frontier or our military fortifications. Our line of defense surpasses that of France. But again, I must stress that this deterrent is only a part of our policy. We seek, as men of goodwill, to discuss the future of our state with the citizens of our state. Herr Hitler is not a citizen of Czechoslovakia, and his policies have no place within the structure of our democracy. We stand firm on that point! The German Führer has overstepped his bounds. We will not tolerate the foot of one SS soldier upon the soil of free Czechoslovakia!"

Beneš was full of brave words, considering that the wolf was skulking at his door. As for Beneš continuing his policy of support for the Jewish population of his country, Murphy had to admit that the little guy had guts. A performance of the opera *Die Judin* in the Czech National Theatre was just one more way for Beneš to tell Hitler what he thought about his new German racial theory. Of course, everybody, including Beneš, knew what Hitler thought of the Slavic race. "Just above Jewish vermin," Hitler said yesterday on the radio. Right up there with monkeys.

A real swell guy, Hitler. Beneš should have sent him an engraved invitation to the opera tonight.

Murphy's letter still lay unopened on Anna's piano. Theo had forbidden Anna to open it. There was some knowledge in his eyes that he did not express verbally. His prohibition had angered Anna, but she did not touch the letter all the same.

There were other matters to think about now. Wilhelm stood before them proudly in his airman's uniform. He was being called up with hundreds of thousands of reserve troops. With a touch of humor, he repeated the claims that Hitler was making. "It's just a drill, Mother." He kissed her on the cheek. "Like the German divisions are drilling. We are going to see which army can drill the best, I suppose. Funny thing. They can see our positions and we can see theirs. I went up with the spotter and they've put just about everything on the line out there." He laughed. "You know, the Swiss Red Cross Corp could waltz into the Reich and take over right now. There's nobody left at home. They're all craning their necks for a peek into Czechoslovakia!"

Theo embraced his son. "You just stay on this side of things," he said. A thousand times he had thought about the fact that Wilhelm might someday be fighting against old schoolmates and friends, the Hitler Youth who had learned to hate him. "But I don't believe that it will come to blows. Beneš is a reasonable man. This is not Austria; it is . . . " It was the place where he had put his hopes. Had he been foolish? Would he wake up to the sound of hobnailed boots on the sidewalks tomorrow morning? "God keep you," Theo said softly.

Anna held tightly to her son. Tears dampened the front of his uniform. "What good is a uniform unless a woman cries over it?" She tried to laugh as she brushed at the spot.

"Then leave your tears, Mother. I will be back in a day or so." He kissed her cheek and slipped out the door, running down the steps and looking back just before he rounded the corner. He raised his hand in farewell.

Theo put his arm around Anna, and she sagged against him. "Is there no place we can go, Theo? No place where our son might have been spared this?"

Theo did not answer. The news on the radio had been grim and frightening. The denial of France and Britain was chilling in its implication. Only boys like Wilhelm stood between Hitler and Prague now.

The headlights of the oncoming Czech army vehicles blinded Elisa. The trucks were not so many or so new as those of the German Wehrmacht, but they traveled relentlessly back along the road she and Charles had just passed over. They would meet the Wehrmacht somewhere in the middle. They would face the German Nazi troops and Panzer divisions, and they would hold them at the command of President Beneš! The voice of Beneš had come clearly over the radio. The voice of reason. The voice of his nation. Would that voice be silenced tonight at the whim of Hitler?

The thought made her press her foot down hard on the accelerator. Charles, wide-eyed at the speed of the car through the darkness, leaned forward and clutched the dashboard as if to will the automobile to move even faster.

Murphy hurried from the press conference, not stopping to discuss the points President Beneš had made. They were clear enough to any man of reason who had ears. Beneš and his belief in democracy had saved the nation from chaos and disaster on a daily basis since the Sudeten trouble began. He was a man of honor and of hope.

It was no wonder that Theo had chosen Prague as the second home for his family, Murphy thought as he hailed a cab. "Old City," he directed the driver in Czech. Then, in English, he added, "And step on it, will ya, Joe? I'm going to see my girl!"

The dinner on the table of the Lindheim house was untouched. Murphy paced the length of the small dining room and back again. Elisa had gone to Vienna? Back to Vienna? And she had told them that she was going to be with him. What was there to do about it now, tonight? The frontier was closed already in anticipation of confrontation.

Anna stared at Murphy, following him with her eyes. Theo simply looked at the floor.

"I'll see if I can get a flight to Vienna tonight," Murphy said. "She had friends there, see . . . " He looked at Theo. Did Theo remember the night they had escaped from Vienna? Did he remember Elisa's grief at leaving Leah and Shimon? "I am certain that is what this is all about."

Anna simply could not comprehend it. They had not heard from her since she had left them weeks ago. Now to find that she had never even seen Murphy, that it had all been a charade, a deadly game she had played for the sake of *friends*! "You have not been with her," she repeated dully as the reality settled in on her. "She was not going to be with you."

Murphy grimaced. He had seen Vienna. He knew what she had gone back into. "I'll get a car and leave tonight if there are no planes!" he said, pulling back the curtain and staring at the empty street.

Sporer checked the cylinder of his revolver. He ran his thumb over the bullets, confident that at least one of them would find its mark. *Tympani, and the song of a dying Jewess!* The audience would hardly notice the pop of the gun. They would not see anything until the little Jew stood up to run—after Beneš fell forward in his seat. *Shrieks and wails!* Sporer would pump in another bullet for good measure. The failure in Paris didn't matter. Chaos was guaranteed in Wenceslas Square tonight! Chaos, and then the triumphant slap of boots against the cobblestones!

He tucked the gun into the waistband of his trousers and leaned close to the mirror to straighten the black bow tie. Tugging on the lapels of his dinner jacket, he thought he looked handsome. He would be one of the few Aryans in attendance tonight. He alone was the Nazi answer to the Jewish opera! Beneš would pay for his sentimentality with his own blood. The Czech army would flee before the face of the Wehrmacht. They would fall without Beneš to give them courage. By tomorrow night the proud sign of the swastika would fly from the spires of Hradcany Castle!

From the shadowed alleyways, groups of angry men watched as the rich Jews of Prague drove to the National Theatre. Women adorned with furs and diamonds were helped from long, sleek automobiles. Such baubles had been gained at the expense of German men and women.

The watchers readied their clubs and scythes. Soon these arrogant, elite Jews would run screaming and sobbing from the theatre! They would tear their hair and clutch at their jewels in dismay! Beneš would lie still in his own blood, and then the slaughter of the Jewish swine would begin in earnest!

50

Coming Home

The lights in the great theatre had not yet gone down. Jewels glittered; dark hair shone, and satin gowns gleamed. The scent of many perfumes mingled in the opulent auditorium of the Czech National Theatre. The constant hum of expectant conversation hovered in the air. This was a night of unity, a demonstration of support. "Many races under one flag," Beneš had proclaimed. Tonight he showed his dedication to that ideal of tolerance. Troops were at the fortification; Hitler would not dare to confront a man like Beneš! Not now. Not yet.

As the houselights dimmed, a fanfare burst from the orchestra pit, and all the humming of voices fell silent. The audience stood as the national anthem began to play. The spotlight fell on the presidential box high and to the right of the stage as President Beneš emerged and stood with his hand over his heart.

The footlights came up, illuminating the stage, and the curtain began to rise.

Eight o'clock. The tall spires of Hradcany were glowing like golden fingers pointing into the clouds. Searchlights swept the night sky of the city. They came from the square in front of the National Theatre.

Elisa recognized their location easily. "I have to take you to my mother, Charles," she explained. If there was bloodshed, she did not want Charles trapped in it. "I can stay a few seconds only, but I will come back. You must stay with my mother." Elisa disregarded traffic lights, swerving around corners on her way to the Old City house. "You must not be afraid, Charles. Just pray! Pray for me, Charles!"

The boy placed a hand gently on her shoulder as she drove wildly toward her destination. Eight o'clock. Beneš must be in place! Everyone must be, including Sporer and his men!

Elisa prayed that she would not be too late. She prayed that she could find Beneš easily, and that he would believe her!

A mousy little man, Sporer thought as he eyed President Beneš through the opera glasses. He made a ridiculously easy target. Sporer could have killed him then and with scarcely any effort. But he would wait for the flames and the rumble of the tympani, for the clamor of the final act.

He directed the binoculars to the center of the first balcony, where the little Jewish Communist sat sweating and rolling his program as he stared mournfully toward his victim. Sporer was not certain that the Jew would go through with it, even for the sake of his cause. It made little difference. After Sporer killed Beneš, he would simply lean forward and point at the Jew. He would shout that there was the man who had pulled the trigger. They would find the gun on the Jew. No doubt the Czech police would kill their prisoner before they reached the jail.

Sporer sat back against the plush chair. Visions of chaos and blood-soaked satin filled his thoughts. He was a patient man, and this virtue had always assured him success.

Murphy grabbed his hat and had his hand on the doorknob. "I'm going to see if I can get a call through to Vienna. I have friends there. No doubt she checked in at the Musikverein."

"Please—" Theo swayed a bit with the strain. Why had he let her go? If something had happened, how could he forgive himself? He could not even look at Anna's face.

Anna had aged visibly in moments. "You will not leave again without letting us know," she begged Murphy. "If your friends can tell us anything . . . find out about her."

Murphy frowned and exhaled slowly, searching for some way he might ease their worry. "We have to remember that she has an American passport. That still counts for plenty." He shook Theo's hand. "I'll go by the American Embassy as soon as I put the call through." He opened the door as the headlights of a car swung around the corner, falling on the trio like a spotlight.

Theo raised his hand to shield his eyes as the car screeched to a halt in front of the house.

"Papa!" Elisa shouted as she leaped from the still-running car. "Murphy! Dear God, *hurry*! They're going to kill President Beneš!"

Sporer! Murphy remembered his face well. He remembered clearly the evil of the man who had tortured and murdered Rudy Dorbransky. And now he was here, Elisa said! Here somewhere among the thousands who had come to the National Theatre!

There was no place to park, no way to get close to the front of the building. Cars were parked everywhere, blocking the road. Searchlights scanned the sky above the theatre.

"Hurry, Murphy!" Elisa cried. They were so very late already. "Otto said there would be men waiting in the side streets, waiting for the word that Beneš is dead!"

Murphy rejected the idea of parking on a dark side street next to the theatre. He turned the corner, then revved the engine and bumped up the curb onto the broad sidewalk. Chauffeurs scattered as he careened towards the steps leading into the vast lobby. The car scraped the stone as Murphy urged the machine up the steps to where ushers, replete with red uniforms and gold braid, gaped in astonishment at the sight of the green Packard struggling toward them.

"Get out!" Murphy shouted when the wheels caught and spun against a step.

Elisa obeyed and Murphy followed, letting the car roll backward into a limousine parked at the curb.

Ushers and soldiers shouted and ran toward Elisa and Murphy. *We got their attention, at any rate,* Murphy thought as a man grabbed him in a hammerlock and wrestled him to the ground.

"Tell them, Elisa!" Murphy shouted.

"They're trying to kill President Beneš!" she shouted as two guards dragged her into the lobby. "Please! You've got to stop them!" She suddenly realized that she was shouting in German. When she repeated the words in Czech, the guards held her tighter still, and slammed her against the wall, knocking the breath out of her. She could see Murphy was receiving even rougher treatment.

"Who?" A guard shook her by the front of her blouse, tearing buttons. "Who is trying to kill—"

"Nazis!" Elisa was crying. This was not what she had expected. She thought she could simply tell them, and—

"What Nazis?" The guard shook her again as if to jar the information out of her.

"They're . . . please! Go warn Beneš! Go now!" She could hear the music of the final act beginning.

"He is in his private box! He is surrounded by guards!"

"Don't you see—?" She was pleading. "They are going to *kill* him. There are men waiting. In the streets . . . they will kill you too. Dear God! I have come from Vienna! To warn you . . . the Gestapo!"

The voice of the huge guard was lost to her now as beyond the golden staircase music kindled the flames that would soon devour both the young heroine and the president of the nation!

"Get an officer!" Murphy demanded. "Can't you understand? They are going to kill Beneš! *Now!*"

A frantic-looking group of six white-gloved officers descended the grand staircase to witness the mad couple pinned against the wall of the lobby. They whispered among themselves as they strode toward Elisa. Outside the doors of the theatre, there were other whispers. Angry voices. Hostile eyes glaring across the square at the smashed Packard.

It was all true! Just as Otto had said! Tonight the president would be killed. By morning Prague would disappear into the Nazi inferno, just as now the flames leaped high around the Jewish bride onstage. The ending had been written in Berlin, tacitly approved in London! Now it was being performed here in Prague tonight!

"Please!" she cried again. "I must see President Beneš at once! I have to tell him."

The officers exchanged nervous glances. "How do we know that *you* do not intend to harm President Beneš?"

The staircase sweeping up to the second tier of private boxes was adorned with the proud Czech flag. President Beneš had walked up that staircase only a short time ago. They would carry him down, unless . . .

"Let me go! You are hurting me!" Elisa cried breathlessly.

"Let her go," commanded the officer in charge. "Now, what is this all about?"

"You don't understand!" Elisa tried to push past the man who blocked her way. "There is an assassin in there!"

"I suppose you are trying to tell me that Hitler will kill the president in retaliation of the performance tonight?" He laughed and glanced at Murphy, who struggled to get up.

In that instant of inattention, Elisa found her courage. She bolted around the stiffly dressed middle-aged men, scrambling across the slick marble floor toward the staircase. Shouts pursued her as she bounded up the stairs two at a time.

The doors to the private boxes were numbered along the corridor. Elisa dashed down the red carpet toward the far end, where the entrance to the presidential box was. Ahead of her stood yet another small coterie of officers. Behind her came the cry, "Stop her! She's trying to get to the president!"

At his warning soldiers drew revolvers and sabers in alarm and moved toward her. On the stage the flames leaped high, reaching toward the young, beautiful heroine. Her song rose and fell in grief.

The weight of a body slammed into Elisa, knocking her to the floor. Her own cry was lost in the wails of the earthly hell now depicted on the stage below them.

Elisa's cheek smashed hard on the door of the presidential box. Hands reached out to grasp her. So *close*! She could hear the music swell. In an instant would come the roll of the tympani.

Sporer held the gun inside his jacket. The Communist Jew had also drawn his weapon. Flames soared higher onstage. Beneš leaned forward, conveniently engrossed in the play. He was a perfect target. Perfect.

Sporer pulled back the hammer, aiming through the fabric of his coat. The Jewish Communist looked up—an obvious gesture. Too obvious. He sat on the edge of his seat and stared at Beneš.

The tympani player raised his arms, and the mournful song of the dying heroine grew louder. A moment more—

In the back of the theatre the doors to the lobby burst open. A grisly apparition staggered forward. His suit was torn, his nose dripping blood. He waved his arms wildly and shouted. His dialect was imperfect, foreign, but his meaning was clear.

"They're going to kill Beneš!" Murphy screamed above the music! "Beneš!"

The president stared down at Murphy as the Jewish assassin stood and fired wildly. Beneš ducked as an officer to his right was felled with a bullet to the arm.

The shrieks of the audience drowned out every other sound. Sporer stood, knocking over his chair. There had been no chance. He waited a moment longer, hoping that Beneš would raise his head. The door to the presidential box opened for an instant, and in that instant Sporer saw her! *Elisa!* The woman who had been in Otto's office! On impulse he aimed and fired, sending a bullet crashing into the wall an inch from the woman's head. Fresh screams erupted, and the door slammed tight.

"There!" Someone pointed up at Sporer. "He has a gun! That man up there!"

Men and women fell to the floor, covering their heads as Sporer fired again into the crowd. He jumped onto the edge of the box and grabbed at the curtain, swinging downward as the fabric tore from his weight.

As he fell heavily onto the stage, Murphy ran down the aisle, jumping over prostrate bodies, clambering toward the steps as Sporer fought to regain his wind.

The heat of the flames burned on, although the actors had fled and were crouched in terror backstage. Murphy took the stairs in one leap and fell upon Sporer before he could pull himself erect. Sporer lifted the gun, firing again. The flame burned Murphy's cheek.

With the shout of a madman, Murphy grabbed Sporer's hair and lifted his head, smashing it against the stage. Sporer kicked and screamed. The gun flew from his hand into the flames that had been ignited to end a Jewish life. Again and again Murphy bashed Sporer's head against the boards until at last Sporer lay still beneath him.

It was nearly midnight as Otto's car began the final ascent up the steep and narrow road toward the Wattenbarger farmhouse. Over the radio, the Mendelssohn Symphony No. 5 played. *The Reformation Symphony,* Leah thought as Elisa came to mind. "A mighty fortress," she said aloud.

Otto looked at her curiously. "I guess that station is from Geneva. That is one advantage to living here. We were always closer to the Swiss than the Germans. It helps if you want to hear the truth over the radio."

"Do you think she made it?" Leah asked.

"I think that President Beneš still lives," Otto answered. "Somehow. He still lives. He will call Führer's bluff, and by morning Hitler will be declaring that this is all much ado about nothing! He will say that he has been slandered! He never intended to invade anyone!"

"You think so?" Leah was suddenly full of hope. The fresh mountain air filled her lungs. She looked out the window and toward the great canopy of glistening stars that swept from peak to peak.

"By now we would have heard otherwise if the Wehrmacht had invaded. If Beneš were dead, we would have known it hours ago."

"Good." She draped her coat over Louis, who snored loudly in the backseat. "And now what will you do?"

The ruts in the road deepened. For a moment Otto did not answer. Then he pointed to the lights of a large farmhouse perched on a rise that sloped down to a broad meadow. Panes of glass made golden squares, illuminating the hillside with a brilliance that blended in with the stars. "There is my home," he said simply. The statement was his answer.

The front door opened and the plump figure of a farmwife emerged and was joined by a tall, lean man with a drooping mustache. They stood silhouetted in the doorframe. The woman placed her hands on her hips as she rose on her toes to see whose car might be coming up their road. "Your mother and father?" Leah asked.

Otto nodded. He seemed unable to speak. "I'm coming home," he whispered. *"Home!"*

Murphy's love letter lay open on the pillow. *Clean sheets. Quilts turned back.*

Elisa's eyes held Murphy in a tender embrace until he felt a little drunk with the nearness of her. "I didn't know you knew how to spell *Vivaldi,*" she whispered.

He reached up to touch her cheek. "There are a lot of things you don't know about me."

"Yet." She pressed her lips willingly to his, savoring his touch. She kept her lips against his cheek as she repeated the words that he had written to her, " 'All I can think about is you. Like the music of Vivaldi, you fill all the seasons of my thoughts.' "

He pulled her closer and kissed her again. "' There has not been an hour since I saw you last that I have not turned around, hoping somehow you would be there.'"

She smiled and laid her cheek against his broad shoulder. "I'm here now, Murphy." She sighed. "For all seasons. If you want me, I'm here."

The cello case stood propped in the corner of the bedroom like a tall sentry on guard. Anna had tucked Charles into the warm, soft bed hours before. It was a nice bed. It belonged to Anna's little boy who was now grown-up and off somewhere flying an airplane to stop the Nazis. Anna had told Charles all of this so he would not worry. "Everything will be all right," she had said. Hitler would not come here to Prague like he had come to Vienna.

A warm spring wind had come up, and now it ruffled the curtains, bringing in the scent of flowers and newly budded trees. Charles lay very still and wondered if he would be able to run in a meadow, like Leah had said. Or maybe climb a tree.

This thought made him miss Louis very much. And then he missed his father and his mother too. He closed his eyes and tried to imagine them in a meadow of tall green grass. Silently he prayed that God would watch over them, that angels would play music for them just as Aunt Leah had played Vitorio when he had been sad.

He opened his eyes again and was glad that Vitorio was with him. For a while he lay beneath the downy coverlet and just looked at the case. As he climbed out of bed and tiptoed to Vitorio's case, he could hear the muffled laughter of Elisa through the wall.

He unlatched the catches and swung back the lid; then carefully he pulled back the silk scarf that covered the glowing red wood of the precious instrument. He would leave the case open just for tonight; whenever he felt lonely he would open his eyes, and there would be his old friend Vitorio watching him from the corner.

This thought made him feel better, even happy now. He tucked the blanket up under his chin and settled into the deep feather bed. He closed his eyes, and his heart smiled. There was the melody. Yes. He heard it clearly now as the gentle fingers of the wind strummed the strings of Vitorio.

Charles sighed with contentment and thought of green meadows as the angels played his lullaby and a soft, sweet voice sang him to sleep.

Digging Deeper into Prague Counterpoint

What would it be like if the country you live in changed radically in *one day*? March 12, 1938, was indeed a dark day for Austria. In one day the face of the nation was stripped away and discarded as though it had never been. And all because of the strategic planning of Adolf Hitler, the man without a soul, and the people who chose to go along with, or avert their eyes from, his devious, satanic schemes.

Men and women who had been Austrians the previous day stared at the new red-and-black swastika flags unfurled from every window and at the devastation all around them. Jewish shops were destroyed, priceless statues were defaced, and neighbors' houses stood empty. The Jews of Austria, and those who tried to defend them, had been thrust overnight into a living hell. Only a few would escape to safety; most would lose their lives. Yet a few brave souls, such as Leah Feldstein and Elisa Murphy, chose to risk everything to rescue orphans from the evil clutches of the Third Reich. In that courageous choice, they became part of a miracle.

And that takes us to you, dear reader. We prayed for you as we wrote this book and continue to pray as we receive your letters and hear your soul cries. No doubt you, like Leah and Elisa, have gone through times when everything around you seems dark. No doubt you have myriad life questions of your own. But are there ways in which you have been—or can be—part of a miracle too? Following are some questions designed to take you deeper into the answers to these questions. You may wish to delve into them on your own or share them with a friend or a discussion group.

We hope *Prague Counterpoint* will encourage you in your search for answers to your daily dilemmas and life situations. But most of all, we pray that you will "discover the Truth through fiction." For we are convinced that if you seek diligently, you will find the One who holds all the answers to the universe (1 Chronicles 28:9).

Bodie & Brock Thoene

SEEK . . .

Prologue

1. Imagine *you* are being driven from your home—the same home where your parents and grandparents have lived. It's likely you'll never return in your lifetime. What are you thinking? What emotions are you experiencing?

____

____

2. What items remind you of joyful times (as the violoncello reminds Yacov)? Why?

____

____

Chapters 1–3

3. If today was the last day of your life, what would you do? What plans would you make? How would you rearrange your day?

____

____

4. "Charles had grown wise through his pain—wise and tender" (p. 2). Would others say this of you? Why or why not?

____

____

5. "Those too young to remember Germany in war needed to be reminded" (p. 17). Do you think it's a good idea to teach the present generation of children about past wars? Why or why not? (Translated into English, a sign at Dachau concentration camp today reads, "What we don't remember will happen again." Do you agree? Why or why not?)

____

____

Chapters 4–6

6. *It would be kinder to let this life end before it begins"* (p. 23). Have you ever wondered if it would be more merciful to let someone—whether a child or an adult—die? In what situation?

____

____

7. "One night I went to a hill outside Dachau. I stood for a long time and thought of the stories Papa had told me about this place. Men killed for no reason other than the fact that they thought differently than someone else. Maybe that's why Papa chose to buy a house so near . . . so near to where the old stories happened" (Elisa, p. 32). What stories from history or your past have helped shape who you are today?

____

____

8. "Some truly courageous men . . . live and breathe and hope and pray in the valley of this terrible shadow of death. You must believe that those men exist" (Theo, p. 34). What examples do you see of courageous men and women today who stand strong in the midst of evil?

____

____

Chapters 7–10

9. "If Louis forgot this moment, Charles would remember for both of them. His young eyes were filled with the sorrow of understanding that was far beyond his years" (p. 51). Have you experienced this kind of understanding at a young age (whether through the death of a loved one, betrayal, abandonment, abuse, etc.)? Describe the situation and what changed in your thinking . . . your world.

____

____

10. Do you think we should care about political events in another country today?

____

____

11. Imagine you are one of the refugees walking toward the Czech border (see p. 57). You carry a few meager possessions. As you approach this potential gate to freedom, what are your thoughts? your emotions? If you had one minute of worldwide television time to ask for help for yourself and your fellow travelers, what would you say?

____

____

Chapters 11–13

12. "She wanted to cry out loud with the worry she felt, but circumstances made it impossible for her to act out her own emotions. Against her will, she now had the feelings of these two children to consider. She was forced to remain strong when it would have been the height of self-indulgence to cry and rage against what was happening" (Leah, p. 81). In what situation(s)—past or present—have you needed to consider others' feelings and circumstances above your own? Why? Did you "remain strong"? If so, how?

____

____

13. "Elisa studied [her father] thoughtfully, as if she were meeting a true hero for the first time" (p. 85). Whom do you consider to be a "true hero"? Why?

____

____

14. Do you agree with Theo (see p. 86, and also pages 108-109, 161-163) that there is a connection between a person's views of sterilization, abortion, and religion? Why or why not?

____

____

15. "There was nothing she could do. No way to help. Her personal life was out of her control. The events of the world were beyond her comprehension. 'What use am I here?' she cried softly. 'God, I am so *useless*!' " (p. 92). But yet Elisa's father called her "an instrument in the hands of God." All of us feel useless at times. In what situation(s) have you felt this way? How did you respond?

____

____

Chapters 14–16

16. Have you, like Charles, ever been "despised for something you had no control over" (p. 111)? When?

    ____

    ____

17. "We would have arrested Hitler for endangering the peace of Germany if only someone had stood up to him" (Canaris, p. 115). One person *can* change history in the making. Think of a few examples of men and women who have changed history—for the better. How did they stand up and make a difference? How did they bring "the ways of justice and morality" (p. 116) back to their home, their community, or their nation?

    Remember Admiral Canaris' encouragement: "We have much to do, and you must be a part of it" (p. 116)!

    ____

    ____

18. Would you be willing to commit treason against your country (as Canaris asked Thomas to do) for a higher goal? Especially if you knew you could "lose your life in a most horrible way" (pp. 118-119)? Why or why not?

    ____

    ____

19. "Why, why, why?" Hershel asks as he runs from a family who doesn't want him (p. 127). Have you felt that way—unwanted? like a prisoner (see p. 128)? When?

    ____

    ____

Chapters 17–19

20. When Murphy received orders to go to California (see pp. 135-136), he was caught between his duty to his job and his promises to Elisa. When you are caught between work and family, what do you do? Explain.

    ____

    ____

21. Imagine that you've just arrived in Vienna during this tumultuous time. You see the word *JUDE* smeared across shopwindows, piles of broken furniture from houses and synagogues, and buildings marked either by a six-pointed star or the broken cross of the Nazi regime. Would you agree with Skies when he says, "God left Austria when Hitler marched in" (p. 147)? Why or why not?

____

____

22. *"What did those prayers gain them?"* Leah wonders. *"I have no faith in miracles!"* (pp. 155-156). Do you believe that prayer accomplishes anything? Do you have faith in miracles? Why or why not?

____

____

Chapters 20–24

23. "There was no middle ground left. It was one side of the fence or the other" (p. 163). What choice(s) have you made that have put you on "one side of the fence or the other"?

____

____

24. "If [the Jews who escaped the Reich] had not understood the meaning of the phrase before, tonight they embraced their freedom like drowning men who had been pulled to safety from a riptide" (p. 177). What does "freedom" mean to you?

____

____

25. *"If we had covered Hitler's war against the church and thousands of families like the Kronenbergers with more enthusiasm, then Paris would not be full of refugees, and Vienna would not be full of Wehrmacht troops!"* (p. 179). Do you agree with Murphy that the media is this powerful? Why or why not?

____

____

Chapters 25–29

26. "Murphy remembered Strickland's advice clearly: *'The Chief loves animals. Talk about animals. Avoid politics!'* " (p. 195). Have you ever been told not to "rock the boat"? In what situation(s)? How did you respond?

____

____

27. "Little Charles, symbol of the last fight of many good men in Germany" (p. 218). How is Charles a symbol? What symbols of goodness and truth do you see around you today?

____

____

28. "Liberty . . . Yes, that's what this is all about, isn't it?" (p. 225). If you were talking to a powerful person, and he or she said something you don't believe in, would you defend your beliefs publicly, as Murphy did, or take a different route? Explain.

____

____

Chapters 30–32

29. "Refusing to believe the danger did not lessen the reality of the threat" (p. 231). Have you ever pretended that something dangerous doesn't exist? When and why?

____

____

30. "One life or even two are insignificant. . . . You must not think of your friends at this moment. You must be able to forget even your own life" (the bald man, p. 239). Do you believe that one life is insignificant and should be sacrificed for "the greater good"? Why or why not? (See also pp. 299-300.)

____

____

31. "All the world, it seems, has sold its soul. Hold tightly to the hand of God" (Theo, p. 243). What evidences do you see today of a world that has "sold its soul"? How can you "hold tightly to the hand of God" and spread hope in the darkness? What "covenant" can you make in your heart?

Chapters 33–36

32. "Don't be angry at God because of what evil men do, Leah. Just do what you know is truly right. . . . Jesus . . . is *here,* with *you,* who have put your own life in danger for the sake of love. He has been here with you all along, and He will be wherever there are people like you . . . willing hearts ready to serve and *live* the truth!" (Elisa, p. 255). If you truly believed Elisa's words and adopted them as your life philosophy, how would your life change?

---

33. If you were suddenly taken off the street, interrogated, strip-searched, told you were now merely a number, and then thrust into a filthy cell, as Elisa was (pp. 261-268), how would you respond? Especially if the others in the cell thought you were a spy (see pp. 272-273), which meant you would be friendless?

Chapters 37–39

34. Do you believe we should "protect each other and the world from another act of aggression" (p. 281), as Winston Churchill stated in 1938? Why or why not? And if so, how far should we go in that mission?

---

35. When have you, like Amanda, felt "*worth* something" (p. 285)? What person or situation contributed to your feeling of worth?

---

36. "What you think is truth is sometimes mere illusion" (Otto, p. 289). Have you found Otto's statement to be true in your own life? If so, how?

______

______

Chapters 40–42

37. Hershel, a Jew, judged Thomas von Kleistmann as "a spiritual son of Hitler" (p. 308) when he had no idea who Thomas really was. A boy in the Hitler Youth called Leah and Shimon "Stinking Jewish scum!"(p. 3). Have you ever judged one person just because he or she was part of a "category" you disliked? When?

______

______

38. "[Evil] began as only a crack in the fortress of Right" (Murphy, p. 311). Do you agree that evil starts as a small crack, and then widens into a chasm? Explain.

______

______

39. Do you think the state should have the right to decide who is worthy of life (see p. 312)? Why or why not?

______

______

Chapters 43–50

40. When Elisa realizes the role Otto is really playing and glimpses the great sorrow in his eyes for all he has given up for the greater good, she suddenly sees him in a different light (see p. 331). Have you ever changed your mind about someone because you saw his or her true heart? Why?

______

______

41. Churchill declares, "Never before has the choice of such blessings or curses been so plainly, vividly, even brutally offered to mankind. The choice is open, and the dreadful balance trembles!" (p. 338). Although this statement was made in 1938, do you think it is also true today? If so, how? If not, why not?

____

____

42. "*Stand firm against this evil! Do not give an inch!*" (p. 344). How can you, even in a small way, stand firm against evil *today*? How can you "*guard the rights of the helpless*" (p. 367) and become part of God's miracles?

____

____

About the Authors

BODIE AND BROCK THOENE (pronounced *Tay-nee*) have written over 70 works of historical fiction. Over 35 million of these bestselling novels are in print in 30 languages. Eight ECPA Gold Medallion Awards affirm what millions of readers have already discovered—the Thoenes are not only master stylists but experts at capturing readers' minds and hearts.

In their timeless classic series about Israel (The Zion Chronicles, The Zion Covenant, and The Zion Legacy), the Thoenes' love for both story and research shines.

With The Shiloh Legacy and *Shiloh Autumn* (poignant portrayals of the American Depression), The Galway Chronicles (dramatic stories of the 1840s famine in Ireland), and the Legends of the West (gripping tales of adventure and danger in a land without law), the Thoenes have made their mark in modern history.

In the A.D. Chronicles they step seamlessly into the world of Jerusalem and Rome, in the days when Yeshua walked the earth and transformed lives with His touch.

Bodie began her writing career as a teen journalist for her local newspaper. Eventually her byline appeared in prestigious periodicals such as *U.S. News and World Report, The American West,* and *The Saturday Evening Post.* She also worked for John Wayne's Batjac Productions (she's best known as author of *The Fall Guy*) and ABC Circle Films as a writer and researcher. John Wayne described her as "a writer with talent that captures the people and the times!" She has degrees in journalism and communications.

Brock has often been described by Bodie as "an essential half of this writing team." With degrees in both history and education, Brock has, in his role as researcher and story-line consultant, added the vital dimension of historical accuracy. Due to such careful research, the Zion Covenant and Zion Chronicles series are recognized by the American Library Association, as well as Zionist libraries around the world, as classic historical novels and are used to teach history in college classrooms.

Bodie and Brock have four grown children—Rachel, Jake, Luke, and Ellie—and nine grandchildren. Their children are carrying on the Thoene family talent as the next generation of writers, and Luke produces the Thoene audiobooks. Bodie and Brock divide their time between London and Nevada.

For more information visit:
thoenebooks.com

THOENE FAMILY CLASSICS™

✪ ✪ ✪

THOENE FAMILY CLASSIC HISTORICALS

by Bodie and Brock Thoene

*Gold Medallion Winners**

THE ZION COVENANT

*Vienna Prelude**
Prague Counterpoint
Munich Signature
Jerusalem Interlude
Danzig Passage
*Warsaw Requiem**
London Refrain
Paris Encore
Dunkirk Crescendo

THE ZION CHRONICLES

*The Gates of Zion**
A Daughter of Zion
The Return to Zion
A Light in Zion
*The Key to Zion**

THE ZION DIARIES

The Gathering Storm

THE SHILOH LEGACY

*In My Father's House**
A Thousand Shall Fall
Say to This Mountain

SHILOH AUTUMN

THE GALWAY CHRONICLES

*Only the River Runs Free**
Of Men and of Angels
*Ashes of Remembrance**
All Rivers to the Sea

THE ZION LEGACY

Jerusalem Vigil
Thunder from Jerusalem
Jerusalem's Heart
Jerusalem Scrolls
Stones of Jerusalem
Jerusalem's Hope

A.D. CHRONICLES

First Light
Second Touch
Third Watch
Fourth Dawn
Fifth Seal
Sixth Covenant
Seventh Day
Eighth Shepherd
Ninth Witness
Tenth Stone
Eleventh Guest
Twelfth Prophecy

CP0064

THOENE FAMILY CLASSICS™

✪ ✪ ✪

THOENE FAMILY CLASSIC AMERICAN LEGENDS

LEGENDS OF THE WEST

by Bodie and Brock Thoene

Legends of the West, Volume One
- *Sequoia Scout*
- *The Year of the Grizzly*
- *Shooting Star*

Legends of the West, Volume Two
- *Gold Rush Prodigal*
- *Delta Passage*
- *Hangtown Lawman*

Legends of the West, Volume Three
- *Hope Valley War*
- *The Legend of Storey County*
- *Cumberland Crossing*

Legends of the West, Volume Four
- *The Man from Shadow Ridge*
- *Cannons of the Comstock*
- *Riders of the Silver Rim*

✪ ✪ ✪

THOENE FAMILY CLASSIC SUSPENSE

by Jake Thoene

CHAPTER 16 SERIES

Shaiton's Fire

Firefly Blue

Fuel the Fire

THOENE FAMILY CLASSICS FOR KIDS

LAST CHANCE DETECTIVES

by Jake and Luke Thoene

Mystery Lights of Navajo Mesa

Legend of the Desert Bigfoot

THE VASE OF MANY COLORS

by Rachel Thoene (Illustrations by Christian Cinder)

✪ ✪ ✪

THOENE FAMILY CLASSIC AUDIOBOOKS

Available from
www.thoenebooks.com

CP0064